The Spiral

ALSO AVAILABLE BY ROSANNE LIMONCELLI

The Four Queens of Crime Mysteries

Death at King's Cross

The Four Queens of Crime

THE SPIRAL

A THRILLER

ROSANNE LIMONCELLI

CROOKED LANE

NEW YORK

Books should be disposed of and recycled according to local requirements. All paper materials used are FSC compliant.

This is a work of fiction. All of the names, characters, organizations, places, and events portrayed in this novel are either products of the author's imagination or are used fictitiously. Any resemblance to real or actual events, locales, or persons, living or dead, is entirely coincidental.

Published in the United States by Crooked Lane Books, an imprint of The Quick Brown Fox & Company LLC.

Crooked Lane Books and its logo are trademarks of The Quick Brown Fox & Company LLC.

Library of Congress Catalog-in-Publication data available upon request.

ISBN (hardcover): 979-8-89242-786-9
ISBN (paperback): 979-8-89242-787-6
ISBN (ebook): 979-8-89242-788-3

Cover design by Nebojsa Zoric

Printed in the United States.

www.crookedlanebooks.com

Crooked Lane Books
34 West 27th St., 10th Floor
New York, NY 10001

First Edition: October 2026

The authorized representative in the EU for product safety and compliance is eucomply OÜPärnu mnt 139b-14, 11317 Tallinn, Estonia, hello@eucompliancepartner.com, +33757690241

10 9 8 7 6 5 4 3 2 1

To John and Valentino

Chapter 1

Growing up in Brooklyn, I became an expert at mixing cocktails the way other kids mastered math formulas or piano scales. The summer I turned fifteen, I could sling drinks as fast as any bartender at my grandfather's Italian restaurant. The restaurant was my whole world back then; from the revolving cast of troubled employees to the inebriated customers, it was one big chaotic drama. Life was full of simmering anticipation broken up by regular whacks from fate. Every day I felt like I was clutching an overfilled water balloon with the faucet still on, waiting for it to burst. And just when I'd start to think I was home free, something bad would happen.

August of '79 I was bartending at The Realm, an Italian restaurant on the edge of Midtown, my latest job in a string of restaurant jobs since I'd left Brooklyn and moved to Manhattan. The day before the chaos began was almost ordinary. There was no way I could've guessed that the next day, that summer Sunday morning, the balloon would finally burst.

Saturday had no real lunch rush to pull the day forward. The time just meandered in an uneven ebb and flow, and I was content to float on the waves. Days like this I might play different characters as new customers came in or fantasize about my brilliant future. Big surprise, I'm a bartender *and* an actress.

"Hey, barmaid! Gimme a Scotch on the rocks."

I walked toward the noise, a paunchy man with comb-over hair, stopped in front of him, checked out the little alligator on his tennis shirt, and looked at his pasty face.

"I think you meant to say bar*tender*, since I don't *make* the bar, I *tend* it." I leaned toward him to drop a tiny white napkin on the bar.

"But the customer's always right? Huh, babe?" His bleary eyes dipped below the neckline of my bargain-basement T-shirt dress and I took a step back, a familiar feeling of revulsion in my gut.

"Or you can just call me Nina." Service with a forced smile. Suffering fools was in my job description. I lived to serve. Literally. So I packed a glass with ice, poured the exact amount of Scotch in an amber arc, and placed the drink in front of him. Then I took his money. Because that's what it's all about.

As I rang up his cocktail and dropped the bills in the proper slots in the cash register, I let my eyes drift to the mirror behind the rows of liquor bottles. My nineteen-year-old face stared back at me accusingly, my delicate jaw, pointy nose, and prominent eyebrows. I smoothed my long, coarse dark hair. As many hours as I'd been imprisoned behind a bar, I sometimes wondered if I was born to be a bartender. But that was only when I was having a bad day. This was not the plan. When I felt down about my employment status, I'd tell myself, *Nina, don't sweat it, everything is temporary.*

I turned up the volume on the house music. The mellow voice of Vic Damone singing *I'm Nobody's Baby* was the perfect background music for The Realm, stuck in the past as it was. I'd had the dubious pleasure of pouring drinks in Midtown Manhattan since March. The Realm was a pretentious name for a restaurant, I thought. The owners had to have pretty big egos to call it that. Not that I'd actually met them in the six months they'd been paying my under-the-table wages—they were far too above it all to fraternize with the employees. The Realm served authentic Italian cuisine in a dining room separate from the long, dark-wood bar, behind which I was sequestered four days a week. The restaurant passed as upscale but not fancy. Jacket and tie not required. They took anybody's money.

On Saturdays the quality of the customers was unpredictable. Exhibit A: Mr. Comb-Over Scotch Drinker. Most weekends brought the brunch crowd in their loafers or deck shoes. Next came the sports enthusiasts watching The Game, whichever game that was. Last but not least (or weren't they?) came those lonely humans pulled from their weekday routine who couldn't figure out what to do on a day off, so they drank it. Some days I hardly blamed them.

Nick the smarmy manager approached. He didn't bother me too much considering he was after half the women who walked in the door, all while engaged to be married. He was paying two alimonies and looking for number three. He stood at the service bar and ogled my décolletage.

"Nina, honey?"

"Yes, Nick, honey?" I said with as little sarcasm as possible. I kept my eyes on the lime I was carving into wedges.

"My cousin Bobby is stopping by later today." Nick hiked up the shoulders of his gray suit and stretched his arms to expose his gold cuff links. I wasn't impressed.

"Yeah?" I waited for the punch line.

"You should come out for a drink with us after work."

Um, no, I thought. *Nope, nuh-uh, no way.* But I kept my thoughts to myself.

"Gee, that's sounds like fun, Nick." I looked him straight in the eye. "But I already have plans for tonight." I added a disappointed pout.

"Too bad. I think you'd like him, and he really likes actresses." Nick stretched his thin lips across his crooked-tombstone teeth. "He'll probably show up before the end of your shift, so you'll get a chance to meet him."

"Can't wait." I gave my own imitation of a smile and then almost cut my finger instead of the lime. The last thing I needed was to get involved with a cousin of Nick's. Especially one who "really likes actresses." Whatever I was doing tonight, I wouldn't be doing it with Cousin Bobby.

The Realm started to fill up with people who were hungry and thirsty. I was ready for them, and so was my tip cup. I usually made enough to survive plus a little extra to put away, but bartending wasn't the most secure of careers. No insurance, medical or unemployment; no pay for sick days; no recourse or severance if I got fired for no good reason. Bartending kept me firmly on the edge, just what I was used to. Acting wasn't so steady either, and it was even harder to get a paying job, but they were the only two things I knew how to do.

Acting is pretending, and I'd been perfecting that skill my whole life. And when I'm in a bar I know what's what even if it's my first time walking in the door. I know who's the boss, who's the joker, who's the scapegoat. It's the one place I know who I'm supposed to be.

The customers packed the bar, and I hustled back and forth to keep their glasses full, their cigarettes lit, and their taste buds tempted. Some of the tourists needed advice on their social plans, some of the neighborhood regulars hadn't heard my latest jokes, and a few lonely souls just needed a smile and a comforting word. That was my job: cruise director, comedian, priest. It was good training, I kept telling myself, for wherever else my life was going to take me, whenever the hell it decided to take me out from behind the bar.

I finished serving the last of the late-lunch customers and started stocking up for the night shift. I couldn't stop my perpetual motion—it's harder to hit a moving target. I filled the refrigerators with bottles of beer and house wine and cut up enough wedges of lemons and limes and slices of orange to fill the trays. My favorite prep job I saved for last: lemon twists. I cut both ends off the yellow fruit, then separated the pulpy inside from the peel by inserting a spoon into the white pith and wedging it around in a circle until the fruit and peel spun free of each other. I popped out the pale citrus, the tart juice dripping to my elbows, and sliced the fragrant peel. The bright aroma never failed to raise my spirits.

A new customer entered The Realm and sat at the bar closest to the dining room. His deep-brown eyes were languid under long lashes, and the hints of gray at the temples of his dark curly hair suggested experience more than age. I approached him as I wiped the acidic juice from my hands with a bar towel. His smile invited more fear than encouragement.

"What can I get for you?"

Nick popped out of nowhere, making me jump.

"Bobby, you made it." He grabbed him in a hug.

"Hey, Nicky, you look great." Bobby held Nick at arm's length by his shoulders, making a show of appreciating Nick's suit selection. I waited for instructions or introductions, whichever came first.

"Nina, this is Bobby."

"What're you drinking, Bobby?"

Bobby peered down the bar at the bottles of booze, glanced at his gold watch, then aimed his chocolate-drop eyes at my waist and slowly tilted them up to my face.

"I'll have a Cutty Sark on the rocks." His tongue wetted his bottom lip before he smiled. Just as I thought, a smile to be feared. Cutty was what the local connected men drank. The men connected to organized crime. They liked to mark their membership to the club via that brand of Scotch.

Bobby turned to Nick to say something quietly, and his suit jacket opened. That's when I saw a dark shadow at his waist shaped like a handgun. I reached for a clean glass, almost knocking it over, and poured his Scotch over ice. Nick was "buying."

"I told Bobby all about you, Nina." Nick almost panted with excitement. "He was dying to meet you."

"Really?" Perspiration broke out on my scalp. "What did you tell him?"

"Everything," Nick said. "How smart and pretty you are, how you're going to be a famous actress someday."

"Yup," I agreed without visible irony. "That's absolutely everything about me. But so far, I'm just studying at The Studio in the Village."

"The Studio? I know plenty of actresses who go there." Bobby drained his glass with his second sip. "Good dancers. I meet them at the downtown clubs. I know a lot of people in the movie business. You want to be in movies? I can introduce you around."

"So far I'm focusing on theater." The lie was automatic. The movie people he knew probably produced the X-rated type. He wasn't my first rodeo clown. Better to change the subject. "But Nick didn't tell me anything about you, Bobby."

I gave him my best twenty-percent-tip smile while I poured Nick a soda. Bobby's lips smiled back at me. He was a prowler, all right; it was written all over his face. I was off duty in twenty minutes, and it couldn't come soon enough. The more he talked, the more I felt sweat trickle down the middle of my back. He told me he liked to go out dancing in clubs, drink expensive champagne, and eat in fancy restaurants, just what he thought I wanted to hear. I gave him a rehearsed expression of interest and glanced under the bar at my shoulder bag and my daily transportation: roller skates. Eggshell-white sneaker skates with three blue racing stripes on each side. The wheels were gray from the grime of the city streets. I'd rather be on roller skates than anything. Skating, on the street or at the roller disco, was the closest thing to flying.

Mike the night bartender arrived late, bringing buckets of fresh ice to the bar. Nothing left to do but close out my register while he picked up the new customers. Bobby got up and moved out of sight, I assumed to powder his nose. Maybe I could escape before he got back. I dumped out my tip cup, traded in the change and singles for big bills, and counted out my register. Right on the money. Mike checked the change in his register drawer and pushed it closed. The shift had turned over.

In the back-bar mirror I saw Bobby return to his seat. Nick appeared at his elbow. I was trapped.

"Nina, honey?"

"Yes?" I stowed my tips in my bag under the bar and handed Nick the bank pouch with the receipts for the day. He handed me my cash pay for my four-shift week.

"Come and have a drink with me and Bobby. We're going to sit at table one." They looked at me with vile anticipation. My stomach seized.

"I really can't, Nick. I'll be late for my date if I don't head out right away." I hoped my eyes didn't give away my panic. My foot nudged my skates under the bar, rolling them closer to my purse for quick access. "Too bad I didn't know in advance. But I'm pretty much always booked on Saturday nights."

This was so very not true that I thought the opposite in my head to make it sound real, a simple acting trick. Or lying trick. Same difference. Bobby took my hand that I had carelessly left resting on the bar. He held it as tight as if he wanted to save me from falling off a cliff. Or stop me from escaping.

"You'll have a much better time with us. Saturday night is party night." That sexy-yet-scary smile. "Cancel your date."

"I couldn't possibly do that." A little breathless from his mesmerizing stare, I dove deeper into the role, smiled and raised one eyebrow as if to say *The man I'm meeting is just as dangerous as you are; that's the way I like my men.* I was taking it too far. But once the drama took over, I couldn't help myself. I liberated my hand from his grasp. "It was nice meeting you, Bobby."

Grabbing my purse strap and the loop of my skate laces, I scooted out from behind the bar and headed straight for the door. "See you Wednesday, Nicky!"

I passed from the cool air-conditioned dimness of The Realm into the fading brightness of Thirty-Second Street, the hot air smacking me in the face like steamed cotton batting. I hugged my tip-filled purse close as I squinted at the low-hanging sun glaring from across Sixth Avenue. I stopped at the corner to lace up my skates, and then I raced the taxis and trucks toward the west side as the fading summer heat drifted up around me in waves. What a Saturday! Crazy busy, great tips, nutty Nick and his cousin Bobby. Who knew what the story was with Bobby, really? Maybe I was letting my imagination spin out of control; nothing had really been out of the ordinary, had it? It was Saturday night, and I was off work for three days. No regrets about not having a real date. I was on sabbatical. A thick novel filled with adventure waited for me at home, and tomorrow I had brunch with my friend Benny Banlon.

Sunday morning light filled my loft apartment, tricking me into thinking I might have a nice day. I showered, pulled on a denim skirt, a robin's-egg-blue tank top, and my worn strappy sandals.

I padded down the cement stairs of the old factory building that housed my loft and let the industrial metal door bang shut behind me. Outside the clouds were thick and low, making it seem more like dusk than day. The air felt still and close, as if I was locked in a sauna instead of out on the street.

I walked south, taking my usual Ninth Avenue route downtown toward Hudson Street, picking up the Sunday

Times at the corner newsstand. The street felt eerily deserted, although empty streets were normal for a Sunday morning, since the Village celebrated Saturday nights till dawn. Only a few places even bothered to open for Sunday brunch, and none of the antique stores or boutiques would be open till the afternoon. Corner garbage cans overflowed with empty take-out containers and beer bottles, confirmation of a raucous night. The hot stink of it filled my nose.

Just past Horatio Street near the opening of an alleyway, I saw it—a red leather platform sandal. The style wasn't too chunky, and the leather was soft and rich, the skinny strap around the ankle reminding me of strawberry licorice. I picked it up. How could someone lose just one shoe? *Some Saturday night she had.*

Looking to my right into the dim brick-lined alley, I saw a speck of red halfway down. The other shoe. These were expensive, and they looked like they might be my size. *What a score.* I walked halfway down the dim alley and leaned over to pick up the other shoe. Just as my hand touched it, my eye caught something sticking out from behind a dumpster. It was a foot at the end of a naked leg—connected to what, I couldn't see.

My grip on the second shoe went limp. I dropped the first one. My newspaper scattered as it hit the pavement. I stumbled backward up against the brick wall. The foot, with its red polished toenails, had probably worn the red platform sandal I had been holding, the one that seemed to be just my size. I turned toward the open end of the alley. It seemed far away. My back felt stuck to the rough brick wall; my knees buckled under me. I stared at that leg. The shoeless foot and the naked leg were most likely attached to a dead body, and my imagination started to produce images of how it got that way.

I pulled myself up, scraping my back, and began to stumble toward the street. My feet moved faster and faster until I felt like I had when I was a kid, trying to get away from some monster in my nightmares, imagining something evil slithering up behind me. I tripped forward, running almost faster than my feet could manage, struggling to stay upright, the monster surely catching up to me as I ran. It wanted to grab me and rip my shoes off and do whatever it had done to that other woman. Tears stung my eyes. My throat was swollen. But I couldn't run to my mother like I used to when I was a kid. Those days were far behind me. I was on my own.

CHAPTER 2

My grandfather owned a small neighborhood restaurant in Brooklyn, and I started helping out there at a young age. His place was named The Corner for an utterly unromantic reason: The previous business was called The Corner Store and had a three-part blue neon sign in the window. He thought it was a waste of money to buy a new sign when the old one was in perfectly good working condition, so he just took down the STORE part, and The Corner was born. But a rose by any other name still stinks. The drab stucco walls were dotted with cheap framed prints of the Amalfi Coast. It was a casual place with homemade Italian food for a reasonable price. It never tried to be anything more.

My mother worked there during the day while I was in school. She kept the books and helped with the cooking when it was busy, but she rarely brought me there. *A bar is not the place for a child,* she used to tell me. She forgot to impress that philosophy on my grandparents. After I turned eight, I spent more time there, helping my grandmother in the kitchen peeling garlic and onions and learning how to make the sauces. When I was older, I waited tables, carrying plates loaded with spaghetti pomodoro and veal Parmigiana. By the time I was thirteen, it was just me and my grandfather at home. It was easier to be around the bustle of the restaurant than our empty apartment upstairs. When I left Brooklyn and moved to Manhattan, I was hoping to leave the drama behind. Or transfer it to the Broadway stage.

But hopes are like fears: You never know if or when they're going to turn into reality.

I stumbled out of the alley. The silence was very un–New York City: no people, no traffic, no sirens. All I could hear was my hammering heart. To my right was a phone booth. I ran into it, pulled the folding door closed, and dialed zero.

"Give me the police. Please." My voice sounded strange to me, pleading and insignificant, like a child's. After I hung up, I clung to the receiver inside the booth, waiting. Someone in an apartment above me turned on a radio, got nothing but static, turned it off again. A gang of pigeons overhead flew eastward; halfway across the sky they changed their minds and flew west. A few blocks away, a truck rumbled over a series of potholes, its roll-down back door making a bang on the last bump as loud as a gunshot, and I flinched. Everything echoed in my head.

This was one of my most familiar streets. My acting school, The Studio, was a few blocks away. The bar where my friend Benny worked, the Sazerac House, was just down the street. Benny tended bar during the brunch shift on Sundays, and I always looked forward to seeing him, seasoned Greenwich Village character that he was. We'd known each other only a few months, so there was no history to weigh us down. Hanging out with Benny let me step away from my boring daily routine, put aside my fears and responsibilities, and have some fun in the moment. Between working at the restaurant, going to auditions and acting classes, and rehearsing my scenes with my new best friend, Marissa, I didn't usually spend that much time with Benny. But since the calendar had flipped to August, I'd been seeing more of him. I'd been choosing to have fun for a change instead of working so hard. Benny was my summer vacation. Sometimes I wondered if the escape could be as dangerous as drugs or alcohol, easy to get lost in. But like they say, I had it under control. I could quit anytime.

My eyes kept drifting to the alley entrance, just to make sure nothing was coming out to get me. I walked that route ten times a week at least. How would I ever be able to walk down that block again?

Two hours later, or probably just ten minutes, a police car pulled up. A summer-blond cop in the passenger seat gestured through the open window. I stepped out of the phone booth.

"You Nina Esposito?"

I nodded. The cops in uniform got out of the car. I pointed toward the alley. The blond cop went in to check it out. The taller, darker one waited with me—or guarded me like I was a suspect; I wasn't sure which. I wanted to sit down, but there was nothing available but the cruiser. I considered leaning on it but wasn't sure if it was polite or even legal.

"I'd really like to sit down." My voice sounded wispy to me, as if I didn't have enough air in my lungs to push out the words. The officer opened the back door and offered me a seat. I looked into the airless dark of the police car.

"Um, never mind." Sitting in the back of a cop car would make me feel like I'd been arrested. I was already nervous that they'd think I had something to do with the body. Wasn't that what always happened on TV? The person who found the body was an instant suspect? "I'll be all right. I guess I'm just a little in shock or something."

"Suit yourself."

Thanks for the sympathy.

I tried to distract myself by looking in the gutter at the discarded pull top from a soda can and an empty Marlboro pack, a soft pack with the outer cellophane still in place. The silver paper at the top had been precisely ripped away to open the pack, and three flattened cigarette butts lay on the ground next to it. It struck me as odd that such a precise person would litter. My mind kept drifting to that naked leg sticking out from behind the dumpster: the pale color of dead flesh, dirt on one side of the foot, the chipped red toenail polish. I gripped my shoulder bag with one hand, my other hand shredding the worn hem of my denim skirt.

The blond cop stalked out of the alley, muttering into his walkie-talkie. He nodded to the other cop, who took a pad of paper and a pencil out of his pocket and turned toward me.

"Can you tell me what happened, Miss Esposito?" He adjusted his face into a serious-cop expression. I tried to regain some of my composure.

"Sure." I told him everything, except the part where the shoes looked like my size.

"Did you go anywhere after you called?" He glanced toward the phone booth.

"No, I waited inside the booth until you drove up." *Where was I going to go, out for a cup of coffee?*

"Okay, wait till the detective shows up. He's going to want to talk to you."

"Look." I shifted my feet. "I'm supposed to be at the Sazerac House just down the road. Can't I wait there for your detective? I'm not going anywhere else, I promise."

I wanted to sit down somewhere and have a cup or three of strong tea. I felt the need for some sort of normalcy, and quick. The two cops conferred and agreed to my request, as long as the tall officer came along.

When we got to the Sazerac House, cop number two held the door open for me like a gentleman, then waited outside. The familiar smell of the Saz on a Sunday—cigarette smoke, beer, and lemony eggs Benedict—helped immediately. As the front door closed behind me, I stood inside the entrance for a moment. I could see Benny behind the bar at the back of the dining room, one hip against the beer cooler, his top half obscured by an open *New York Times.* The air conditioner put out a hum that sounded like someone playing a low D flat on a baritone sax. Benny shifted the sports section, revealing his expressionless face and his tall, powerful body. I watched him turn the page. It seemed like the newspaper should just crumple in those big hands of his.

The first time I saw Benny, the cherry trees on Hudson Street were just showing pink; the air was fresh and clear. When I stepped into the Saz, Benny was whistling and polishing highball glasses. I heard him before I saw him. He had a whistle you'd never forget, tuneful and slippery. My eyes adjusted to the gloom and my nose to the smoky smell of sour mash whiskey. As I stepped up to the bar, he turned and blinked at me through thick, black-framed glasses, his gray eyes magnified as if from the back end of cartoon binoculars.

I had already been to a few bars in the West Village, evaluating the atmospheres, sipping club sodas, looking for a place near The Studio, where I had just started studying acting. I needed a hangout joint for between class sessions. Restaurant bars were my homes away from home, so I was looking for the best spot. I knew that one would feel right when I found it.

The places I'd tried so far had fallen into two categories: Either the bartender was annoyed because I wasn't drinking fifty-dollar cognac, or the male-only clientele gave me the cold shoulder. As a young woman in New York City, I felt safer in gay men's bars, but I wanted a place that would choose me as much as I was going to choose it. It had to be the right mix. Some of the places were like those boys-only clubs that every neighborhood had when I was a kid. No matter how much of a tomboy I was, I wasn't allowed to join. That had been one of my first introductions to life's disappointments. That and when I found out I'd never be able to play baseball in the major leagues just because I was a girl.

Even before I sat at the bar in the Sazerac House that first day, I knew there was something I liked about the place. It felt comfortable, more than usual for a restaurant, even familiar. I took the barstool near the service station, noted the upbeat rhythm of the Neville Brothers singing *Yellow Moon* coming from the speakers, and ordered a seltzer. Benny Banlon squeezed the trigger on the soda gun, arcing the stream high without spilling a drop, impressive considering he had both eyes trained on me the whole time.

Benny's real last name wasn't Banlon, he explained, but he'd been dubbed that since he always wore those synthetic Banlon short-sleeved shirts, usually brown. He was born and bred there in the Village, never thought about going anywhere else. He admitted to me (one night after a few Hennessey cognacs) that he'd only been north of Times Square once. Benny and me, we just clicked. We had the restaurant life in common, we both loved movies, and his sense of humor helped make life bearable.

Hanging out with Benny was like a break from reality, a night off from being a responsible adult, a foray back into childhood—a childhood I never really had. The Sazerac House, with Benny behind the bar, made sense to me.

"Hey, Nina." Benny's face launched a smile as I moved toward him from the front door. "I didn't hear you come in. What happened, did you sleep in this morning?"

I climbed onto the padded barstool, remembering I'd dropped my newspaper in that alley.

"It's a long story, Benny." Feigning calm. But my voice shook, and my hands gripped my shoulder bag too tightly as I placed it on the bar between us. I couldn't help imagining that it could've just as easily been me in that alley. My neighborhood, my usual paths, my world—was I too cavalier about walking around the Village at all hours?

"Hey." His eyes looked from my hands up to my face. "How about I get you a nice cup of tea?"

"Yes, please, nice and hot, and—"

"Lots of honey," he finished, and disappeared into the kitchen.

Cop number two slipped in the front door without a sound and stood just inside, far enough away from the bar to blend into the background, out of earshot, but able to take advantage of the air conditioning. Suddenly I felt my body start to shake. On familiar ground, my defenses began to crumble. I was afraid I was going to start blubbering. Benny was a good friend, but I didn't want to be crying all over him. Especially not with a uniformed officer standing watch.

Benny returned with my tea and a ceramic pot of honey that reminded me of Winnie-the-Pooh. He watched me make a mess before he took over and made the tea as sweet as I needed. I got it to my lips and down my throat just in time to stem the storm of tears that threatened. The heat loosened the tightness in my throat, and the honey flooded my brain with something close to sunlight.

Benny was already bringing me another cup as I finished the last drops of the first one. His kind attention almost made my eyes fill up again. I fixed the second cup more calmly and peeked up at his concerned face. His smile stretched all the way up to those gray eyeballs behind his thick glasses. Older by a good twenty years, he was an unlikely friend. How had I ended up with this guy as a buddy?

"Thanks, Benny."

"What're friends for?" He took the empty first cup, turned, and dropped it in the bus tray.

I glanced toward the front of the Saz. The cop was discreetly looking out through the large plate glass window facing Hudson Street. I was beginning to feel comforted: Benny doting on me, my own personal bodyguard at the door.

"Want to tell me about it?" Benny leaned toward me, his elbows on the bar, a hint of Old Spice drifting toward my nose.

"You're not going to believe it." I shook my head.

"Try me."

I leaned back, took a deep breath, and thought about where to start. "I saw this red shoe on the sidewalk." I should've minded my own business. *Why did I even pick it up?*

"A red shoe?" Benny asked.

"Yeah, a red leather platform shoe." I told him my short, weird story. Saying it out loud made it seem even more surreal. I felt slightly sick to my stomach. Benny stood there staring at me.

"An alley near Horatio?" His usually gruff voice went soft.

"Yeah."

"A dead body?" Benny looked a little pale.

"Well, technically I didn't see the whole body, just a leg." I gulped my second cup of tea. It had just the right amount of honey, and the temperature was so perfect I almost drank it straight down.

"That's awful." Benny shook his head and tried to straighten a pile of newspapers on the bar, but he just made a bigger mess. I looked toward the entrance.

"They asked me to wait for the detective, but I told them I'd wait in here. He's going to come by and talk to me."

"What?" Benny looked at me hard.

"A police detective is going to come in here and ask me what I saw."

"Who?" Benny's voice got louder.

"I don't know, Benny, some police detective." I raised my voice to match his. "They've got a uniform waiting with me now. In case I decide to take off, I guess." I waved vaguely toward the cop by the door. "Like I'm a suspect or something." Benny saw him for the first time.

"Oh, that's got to be good for business." Benny's sarcasm wasn't subtle.

I looked around. I was the only customer. The waiter was sitting at a back table playing solitaire.

"What business?"

"Wiseass kid." Benny picked up a section of the newspaper and opened it to a middle page. He was finished hearing about my morning. Nothing to do now but wait for the detective.

I shuffled through the newspapers on the bar. *New York Times*, the *Post* and the *Daily News*. Maybe the funnies would take my mind off things. I opened the *Daily News*. The lights over the worn mahogany bar were barely bright enough for reading, making me squint.

"Hey, how about some breakfast?" Benny peeked around the edge of the newspaper with a sheepish smile. Nausea and hunger battled for control over my stomach, but at his suggestion, hunger won.

"Okay. Eggs Sardou?"

Benny ambled off to the kitchen to put in my order and came back with silverware and a napkin. He plunked it down, less than gently, in front of me.

"What?" He put me on the defensive.

"I'm worried about you, Nina. You gotta be more careful. Wandering down dark alleys. Picking up old shoes. Rooting around garbage dumpsters." He was ranting. "Who do you think you are, Alice in Wonderland?"

"Hey, I've been wandering around this city all my life, and that's the first time I ever found a body, okay?" I was unnerved enough.

"Well, just something to think about is all." Benny rustled the sports section open.

"Yeah, I got a lot to think about. Okay?"

"Okay."

"Fine."

"Fine."

I grabbed a section of the *Times* and spread it out in front of me, not even seeing it. Feeling a bit pissed off brought back some of my strength. My mind started to focus. Who had killed that woman? And who was she? A murder, right here in this neighborhood? I looked up at Benny. He peeked at me over the top of the newspaper.

"Want a club soda with bitters, Nina?"

"Sure, thanks." *What a goofball.*

"What do you think about those Mets?" He squeezed the trigger on the soda gun and shot a stream of bubbles and water into my glass. Then he shook in the reddish-brown liquid from the bottle of Angostura bitters. The Mets had lost to Montreal the day before.

"Well, if they don't get any better, they're bound to get worse." The newspaper pages rustled in agreement as I turned them.

"Yeah, I'm with ya."

I skimmed through the paper with my usual fascination for whatever tragedies had descended upon the country and the world. *Four people killed in thunderstorms*, the paper reported, *two of them Boy Scouts.* Even the weather was deadly. Benny put my eggs down in front of me. The lemony smell of the Hollandaise sauce made my mouth water. I downed half the plate before the front door of the Saz opened. In came Gorgeous Charlie, and there went the peace and quiet.

Chapter 3

Charlie was about thirty with soft, curly blond hair that you couldn't help but want to reach out and touch. Hair, I imagined, that an angel might have if such a thing existed. His eyes were soft brown and his clothes rich and perfectly tailored to his fit physique. But then he opened his mouth. Gorgeous Charlie was the type who couldn't stand the silence. He always had to be filling it up, usually with the sound of his own voice. Benny and me, we preferred to savor the Sunday morning quiet.

Charlie sat a few stools away from me, toward the curve of the bar.

"Plenty of cops up the street." Charlie expected us to be interested. We disappointed him. His hair glistened with scattered raindrops, making him look even more angelic. My eyes followed the wet splatters on his fitted pale-blue linen shirt down his flat stomach, where it was tucked into his tight designer jeans. I heard some distant thunder.

"Beer, Charlie?" Benny put down his paper.

"Yeah, and a ham-and-cheese." Charlie leaned in my direction. "Did you hear what they found?"

"One ham-and-cheese!" Ben bellowed toward the kitchen, making me jump. The cook could probably hear Charlie from his seat; the kitchen window was only ten feet away and the Saz was empty.

"We know about it, Charlie." I picked up my drink.

"They found a body in the alley." Charlie was almost bouncing in his chair. "They've got the whole area roped off, looking for clues." He made it sound like a game. "This cop I know over there told me it was the body of a girl, or should I say, young woman." He gave me a look that made my flesh crawl. "About your age, Nina, and about your size."

Charlie's comment shattered my attempt at calm, but Benny fired back, "That puts her somewhere between puberty and womanhood."

I leaned back in my barstool, hoping my pretense of calm was convincing. Benny's comment was obviously a crack at my age and my height, or lack thereof. I was no giant, but I could still make a standing shot from the foul line nine times out of ten, the result of many hours spent tossing basketballs at the hoop by myself in the playground when I was a teenager. But so much for trying to forget I'd found a dead body. I certainly wasn't going to tell Charlie I was the one who found it. I would just pretend it hadn't happened.

"So I'm only five foot tall. So what?" I gripped the bar to still my hands. "It's been fairly beneficial so far. People let me stand in front of them at parades, and I always get some tall oaf to reach the stuff that's too high." I picked up my fork and poked at what was left of my eggs. "That's why I hang out with you, Benny. If you weren't so tall, I would've split a long time ago."

Benny grabbed a few maraschino cherries from the fruit bin and plopped them in my seltzer.

"Well, that and the free cherries."

Charlie was miffed at our detour.

"The cop told me she was bashed on the back of her head, her neck was twisted, and all her clothes were ripped off." He leaned closer to me. Pierre Cardin cologne mixed with the smell of beer on his breath and soured my belly.

"Benny, I guess I'm done here." I pushed my plate toward him.

"It was murder, maybe a sex crime." Charlie took another gulp of his beer, half the mug's worth.

"Charlie, nobody cares. Be quiet and eat your sandwich." Benny put the plate down in front of Charlie with a plunk. "You know something? You watch too much TV."

"Sex crime." I tried to keep a sudden chill from making me shiver. "Hmm, you know, I've never really understood that term." I shook my head to get the picture of her rigid leg out of my brain. "I mean, does it really have anything to do with sex? As far as I can tell, it only gives sex a bad name." I calmed my hovering hysteria by focusing on winning this argument with Charlie. I looked at him as innocently as I could. "In fact, if you ask me, I think they should call it an anti-sex crime. Yeah, that would make more sense. Anti-sex crime." I nodded convincingly.

"They call it a sex crime, Nina"—Charlie spoke to me like I was five years old—"because the guy who killed her had sex with her."

"Really, Charlie? You call that having sex?" I tried to look casual instead of sick to my stomach as I returned to my newspaper. "You would."

Charlie opened his mouth to speak, his face turning red.

"That's enough." Benny leaned on the bar between us. "Change the subject."

A bartender is always part referee. Benny was right; there was no getting through to Charlie. Sometimes I found myself just staring at Charlie when he talked. What a waste.

I returned to the paper. *Ten-second earthquake in California registers 5.9 on the Richter scale, strongest earthquake in sixty-eight years.* Great. *The Hooker Chemical Company violated pollution laws in at least three other states in addition to New York.* Lovely. That was one mean paper full of bad news. I turned the page gently, so it wouldn't hurt me. I was just an innocent bystander, for Pete's sake. Reading the paper was a poor distraction.

I rubbed my midsection to soothe a familiar stabbing pain just below my left ribs. It felt like a thin-bladed knife, and I had to watch what I ate, drank, and thought, or that thin blade could turn into a chainsaw.

I flipped the page. If you were a petite young woman with long dark hair like me, according to the Metro section, there was an excess of similar bodies floating around the neighborhood.

Body Found in Greenwich Village Last Week Identified

I pulled the paper closer. The woman's name was Teresa Torres. They'd found her two weeks earlier in the stairwell of her apartment building two blocks from the Saz, naked, raped, broken neck, wound to the back of her head. The article was a public interest follow-up. *How did I miss the first story?* There were gut-wrenching reactions from her family, etc., etc.; she was such a talented aspiring actress, etc., etc. No suspects.

"Hey, Benny, there might an epidemic around here." I showed the article to him.

Benny picked up the paper from where I'd left it open on the bar.

"Five foot two, long dark hair, twenty years old. Police still have no suspects." As Benny read the details out loud, they gave me an image of myself lying at the bottom of a stairwell or behind a dumpster—my head twisted, my long dark hair fanned out on the ground, my eyes open but strangely blank. Benny put the paper down on the bar. His eyes rested on me. He leaned against the back bar and crossed his arms.

"Why are you looking at me like that, Benny?" I nervously pushed my hair behind my ears. His lids hadn't budged since he put down the paper.

"Well, you're pretty easy on the eyes, you know; where should I look?" He blinked and stuck a toothpick in his mouth.

Talk like that from Benny made me blush. I sure didn't feel the way about him that I suspected he felt about me, but he never tried anything, which I appreciated. Even at nineteen, I'd had enough wrestling experience to be in the WWF.

When I first met Benny, I had just moved out of the apartment above the restaurant in the old brownstone where I'd lived with my grandparents since my mother died. Losing my mother had been unreal, one of those freak accidents you hear about on the news that make you shake your head. It happened exactly three weeks after my eighth birthday. On August 29, 1968, she was hit on the head by falling debris from an old building in Manhattan. They got her to the hospital fast, but she was already in a coma. She lasted three days. They only let me visit twice. My grandmother was the only one with her when she took her last breath. The sadness and anger can still surprise me, surfacing when I least expect it, as fresh and vivid as it was that day.

She was everything to me, my whole family. She was my filter on the world. I saw everything through her eyes, and she explained it all to me. Without her, the world suddenly seemed full of sharp corners and bitter smells. It felt overly real and distorted at the same time. When she died, I lost all perspective.

Maybe it would have been different if I had known my father. But she would never tell me anything about him. I didn't know if he was dead or alive. *I'll tell you all about it when you're older,* she used to say to me. Good plan, Mom. It was a lie. Intentional or not, I'll never know.

Benny would probably hate it if he thought I considered him a father figure, yet I couldn't deny my obvious psychological condition. Just before meeting Benny, I'd begun to recognize my older-man attachment syndrome (OMAS). I seemed to get into these situations where I thought an older guy was my friend and he thought something else. So far, Benny and I were platonic, and I was working hard to keep it that way. I was just tripping along from one learning experience to the next, trying to keep out of trouble, hoping that when I was thirty, I wouldn't be attracting eighty-year-olds.

"Esposito!" Benny yelled.

"What?" I jumped. "Why are you shouting?"

"Just trying to contact you from Earth." Benny snapped the bar towel at me. "Gimme the funnies."

"Gimme the sports section."

"Even trade." He smiled at me with those curly lips and contradictory sad gray eyes. Was it my fault the guy had it in for me? I couldn't help how I felt. I wouldn't hurt Benny for all the beer in Germany, and I wouldn't want to lose him as a friend either. He helped me keep things in balance. But how does anyone keep that balance and not teeter over and fall into a hole? I had too great a learning curve when it came to men.

I'd been born into a female world: no father, no brothers, no uncles, just one grouchy grandfather. I liked men; I just didn't understand them.

Observation and contemplation—that's what my acting school taught. I hid behind the sports section. Watch and think, that's how you learn, and I was still learning about men. I just hoped I wouldn't come across the guy who liked his women a little too dead.

Murdered. Did I have to worry about getting murdered now? I had enough to worry about.

There was an unnecessarily dramatic crack of thunder, and the rain slapped the sidewalk like it had a reason. Those cops in that alley were going to get wet.

The front door of the Saz flew open as a man pushed into the restaurant. He was medium everything—height, weight, and age. Even his male-pattern baldness was medium sized. He stood just inside the door and shook off the rain, not unlike a Labrador retriever. His dull beige short-sleeved shirt looked like it had never seen an iron, and the front of his brown trousers showed shadows of his fast-food lunches. He stood there for a moment until his eyes found me, then his posture changed and he sauntered toward me. This was my mystery date. Through the glass front window of the restaurant, I watched the uniformed officer make his escape in the rain.

"Are you Nina Esposito?"

"Yes." I placed the newspaper on the bar.

"Detective Tom Barry." He flashed his badge. "Can we sit over at a table and talk for a few minutes?" He tried a smile, but he just showed me how long it'd been since he'd visited his dentist. If he even had one.

I felt my body stiffen. On a normal day, cops weren't my favorite species. Most of the cops who'd frequented my grandfather's bar had been from the same "club" as the rest of the drinkers. My opinion of them didn't include any sort of trust or respect. This guy was already acting like he owned all the air in the room and he thought I'd used up my money's worth.

"How about if we talk right here at the bar?" I felt comfortable where I was.

"Can I get you a drink?" Benny was looking for that tip, always nice and polite. I wanted to tell him this cop was the deadbeat type. People tip well because they either care about people or care about appearances. This guy with his cheap clothes, old shoes, and puffy face didn't care about anything. Not even himself.

Detective Tom Barry looked from me to Benny. He took a seat. "Got any Heineken?"

Benny pulled a bottle from the cooler, popped it open, and put it in front of him with a glass. Tom the Cop threw down a five, grabbed the bottle by the neck, and took a long slug in a demonstration of pure class. I thought cops weren't supposed to drink on duty. I guess that's only on TV.

"Ah, that hits the spot. I got up way too early this morning."

Apparently, he was used to sleeping late on Sundays. Not exactly a regular churchgoer. He looked at me with that easily readable look that I can't stand in a guy. Why can't they look at your face instead of groping your body with their eyes? This cop respected women about as much as that murderer did. The carousel in my stomach started up again.

Benny rang up his beer, left the change on the bar, and moved a few steps away toward Charlie. They lit fresh

Marlboros and did a pathetic job of pretending they were absorbed in their newspapers.

"I need you to tell me everything that happened this morning when you got on that block." Tom the Cop sounded bored as he took a notepad and pen from his jacket pocket and looked at me with annoyance. "Can you do that?"

"Yes, I can do that." I probably sounded a little snotty, but what a jerk. Pen poised, he waited. I told him everything. There wasn't much to tell. He wrote it all down.

"So you moved the first shoe?" He scribbled in his notepad.

"Yes, it was on the sidewalk, and I brought it into the alley with me. But I never picked up the second shoe." I was embarrassed by my shoe lust.

"Are you in this neighborhood often?"

"I take classes at The Studio three nights a week. On Bank Street." I fidgeted on my barstool. "And I come in here a couple of times a week." I looked at Benny. His expression was between a smile and a frown, wary and protective.

"What's your height?" Tom the Cop took another swig of his beer.

"What?" That surprised me.

"How tall are you?" Tom the Cop measured me with his eyes. "I'm gonna guess five feet."

"Almost five one." I adjusted my posture. "Why do you need to know that?"

"Can I take a look at some ID?" He extended one hand toward me impatiently, palm up.

I fumbled in my purse for my wallet and gave him my recently renewed driver's license, which had my new Manhattan address. He wrote a few things down in his notebook.

The front door opened, and a black umbrella came through with a man behind it. He closed the umbrella, set it next to the doorframe, and looked toward us. He stood tall, with a confident but relaxed stance, and held up one hand in a motionless wave. Tom the Cop gestured to him, then turned to me and handed me back my license.

"I have to speak to my partner a minute. We're not done yet."

They walked toward each other, met halfway in the dining room, and spoke quietly. Tom the Cop wrote something down in his notebook. The partner's appearance was such a contrast to Detective Barry's that I couldn't help staring. He was younger. Taller, too, probably six foot two, with a full head of dark curly hair and a sharp jawline outlining his handsome face. Nothing medium about this one.

They approached the bar.

"This is my partner, Detective Lopez." He pointed at me. "Nina Esposito."

As Detective Lopez leaned toward me and held out his hand, the clean scent of Ivory soap followed. He gave my hand a quick shake, firm and gentle.

"Nice to meet you, Ms. Esposito." He had a warm smile and looked straight at me like I was an actual person, no shyness in his dark eyes. "I'm so sorry you had this experience. We're only going to take up as much of your time as is absolutely necessary."

I mustered a nod. I wanted to thank him, but his kindness produced a lump in my throat that made me incapable of any verbal response. Tom the Cop sat back down next to me with a hard glance at Detective Lopez, who hovered between us.

"A purse was found near the body with some identification in it," Detective Barry continued. "I just need to check if you recognize the name. We haven't had time to contact her family yet, so I'm going to ask you to keep this information confidential." Tom glanced down the end of the bar at Benny and Charlie, who quickly looked away to prove they weren't listening.

"Why would you think I know her?"

"It's possible you traveled the same route—you frequent this neighborhood." Detective Barry sounded like he was talking himself into a good reason. "Anything we might find out could help."

I nodded. I just wanted to get this interview over with and forget the whole episode. He slid his notebook toward me on the bar. His handwriting was as disheveled as he was. The scrawl read *Jessica Roman*. I felt a sting in my lungs.

"Yes, I know her." It suddenly felt difficult to breathe. "She's in my class at The Studio."

"She *was* in your class." Detective Tom Barry stowed his notebook in his pocket. "Anything you can tell me about her?"

"No, I barely knew her." I reached for my club soda, wishing for something stronger. "Are you sure it's her?"

Tom the Cop and I both looked at Detective Lopez.

"We can't be one hundred percent sure yet." Detective Lopez spoke softly. "But the items we found, clothes and purse, all seemed connected to the scene as much as the shoes."

If only I hadn't seen that shoe. I looked at the newspaper on the bar, still open to the story about the other girl. I reached for it and pulled it closer.

"This story, in the paper, this other girl who was murdered two weeks ago." I looked at Detective Barry, then at Detective Lopez. "Is there any connection?"

Detective Barry flashed an annoyed look at Detective Lopez, who shrugged in defense. I'd touched a sore spot.

"Why do you ask that?" Detective Barry wasn't happy with my question.

"Something about them seems similar." My answer sounded lame, but I couldn't explain it.

"The only thing they have in common is that they're both women. But then, the killer had a fifty-fifty chance at that," Detective Barry said dismissively.

"We're not ruling anything out." Detective Lopez didn't seem bothered by me the way Tom the Cop did. "Do you know anything about the other girl?"

"No. I just read about it. Just now." I closed the newspaper and pushed it away. "It's just that . . . two girls found murdered in the same neighborhood . . . it's . . . unsettling."

"All murders have that in common." Detective Barry looked at his watch. He seemed overly casual about the situation. Certainly not as concerned as I was.

"What are you going to do about it?" I knew that sounded disrespectful, but I couldn't help it. I was angry. And scared. Two aspiring actresses murdered near The Studio where I studied? Who would be next? Me?

"I'll be doing my job, as usual." Detective Tom Barry stood up. "I'll put it right next to the other cases on my desk. The seven shootings, five stabbings, two guys that got pushed off apartment buildings, and oh, that guy that was bludgeoned to death. Not to mention the two dozen bank holdups, the countless bodega robberies, purse snatchers, and everyday muggings. And that's just in the last two weeks." He turned to Detective Lopez. "Did I miss anything?"

Detective Lopez shook his head and looked sheepishly toward the door. Tom the Cop took a card out of his wallet and tossed it on the bar next to me. I looked at it as if it would burn my fingers.

"You can call me if you think of anything useful," he said. "I already have your information in case we need to get in touch with you."

"She probably had friends around The Studio, but I wasn't one."

"Well, okay then, *Nina*." Tom Barry gave me another grimace-smile. "Thanks for all your cooperation."

Was that sarcasm? It wasn't my fault I found her body and knew nothing about how it got there or had anything to help his case. And I hated it when people who didn't know me called me by my first name, like we were old buddies. Who gave him permission? I wanted to say *It's Ms. Esposito to you.* But I didn't always say what I wanted to.

Detective Tom Barry drank the last of his beer, picked up his change, didn't leave a tip, and slumped toward the exit.

"Thank you." Detective Lopez started to go, then turned toward me, lifted one eyebrow, tilted his head toward Tom as he exited, and half rolled his eyes. I smiled in appreciation. He gave me back a smile that significantly brightened the dim barroom of the Saz. "And sorry to take up so much of your time."

I nodded and returned his smile. *He can take up as much of my time as he wants,* I thought. He practically redeemed the entire species of law enforcement in that moment. My eyes followed his confident exit as he walked to the door and retrieved his umbrella. He tossed me one last smile just before he dove back into the rain. *Adios, Detective Lopez.*

Chapter 4

Benny made his way closer to me as my eyes followed Detective Lopez through the window as he walked down Hudson Street. I felt like Dorothy in *The Wizard of Oz* looking out at the world spinning while sitting in the center of a twister. Two dead aspiring actresses, one I knew by name, both of them enough like me to be my sisters. It was a lot to take in on a Sunday morning.

"She went to The Studio, Benny." I reached a shaky hand for my club soda. "And that girl in the paper, the paper said she was an aspiring actress. Don't you think that's kind of weird?"

"Nope. It don't mean a thing. How many girls in that school?" The words rushed out. "Hundreds, I bet, maybe thousands. And The Studio isn't the only acting school in New York City, that's for damn sure. Besides, half the women under thirty in this city are actresses. At least ninety percent of the waitresses are."

Yeah, sure, Benny was right; there were thousands of aspiring actresses in New York City. I was just a face in the crowd. I buried that face in the sports page. How many girls fit that profile? Too many. But did that fact lower my risk? Jessica Roman went to the studio. Jessica was small and dark like me, and the other one, Teresa Torres, was an actress and had a similar appearance. Both strangled and raped? It was only three blocks to The Studio from here. Teresa's apartment building was just two blocks away. It was a lot to process.

I took classes at The Studio three times a week, so I was always around the neighborhood. My scene study and improvisation classes, with the handsome Tony Award-winning Ron Meyers, on Mondays, Tuesdays, and Thursdays, didn't get out until nine, and we always hung around after class. Nine at night felt early in the Village, especially in the summer. Most shops didn't even open until noon, and they stayed open till midnight, even pet food stores. Midnight never really felt late in the Village.

Did I now have to worry for my safety when I got out of class? Had a serial killer made himself at home in the West Village? Just a couple of summers ago, that Son of Sam guy had practically piled up dead bodies uptown. Maybe he had a cousin who liked my type. Or disliked my type, as it were.

"You've got to admit, it's kind of freaky." My voice sounded loud to me. The more I thought about it, the more unwound I felt.

"It's the same crime-ridden city you grew up in, nothing new." Benny tossed a glance at the big front window to illustrate his point. "I wouldn't waste time worrying."

"Yeah, it is what it is," Gorgeous Charlie agreed.

"Nobody asked you, Charlie." Benny shot him a dirty look over his shoulder.

I watched Benny clear Charlie's empty plate and refill his beer, then settle back into his newspaper. He was right: There were hundreds of young women who answered to my description in this city, to which I bore witness every time I went on an audition. What made me stand out from the crowd?

"Okay, okay." I drained my club soda. "Thanks for putting it into perspective."

Move on, forget about dead bodies, typecast like me or not. It was just that simple. I flipped to the international pages, better to keep away from the New York news. But I couldn't focus on the print. Not with the image of Jessica's bare leg in my head. Maybe I should stick to the comics. Or maybe I was just done reading. For that matter, done sitting there too.

I scooped up my change, minus tip, off the bar. "See you all later."

"What?" I'd taken Benny by surprise. I usually hung out with him most of the day on Sundays.

"For all I know, one of those detectives is going to make his way back in here and bother me again. I don't feel like talking about that any more today." I tossed a meaningful look at Gorgeous Charlie.

"I wasn't going to bring it up again." Innocence emanated from him.

I grabbed my shoulder bag, hopped off the barstool, and turned to look at Benny. He stared back at me with his hands on his hips. He hated it when I took off suddenly. If he didn't pin me down about when I'd be around next, he knew he might not see me for days. I shrugged at him and wiggled my fingers in a Three Stooges wave.

I slid out the door and then stopped a moment to pull my compact umbrella from my bag, always prepared for variable weather conditions. According to last night's TV news, the local experts didn't think the rain was going to stop till the wee hours of the morning. Unfortunately, the rain didn't make it feel any cooler, just steamier.

I walked south on Hudson and turned left onto Christopher Street, walking the length of it to Seventh Avenue South. Every door was familiar to me—the antique stores, a bakery that made cakes in the shape of breasts, the men's clothing stores with plenty of leather on display in the windows, and a couple of bars that had been around for more than a hundred years. Very historical street, that Christopher.

I ducked down the stairs of the subway station at Sheridan Square. What a creep Detective Barry was. I shook the rain off my umbrella and tried to shake the feeling of him out of my head. *Cops.* Detective Lopez was pretty nice, though. My interaction with him had been short, but it had been . . . refreshing. I felt my smile return.

As a child, I'd been brought up to respect cops. They were The Law, Pillars of Good, put on earth to Protect us from Bad. When I was little, my mother would often stop a police officer on the street and introduce me. They were always polite about it. I think she did it so I wouldn't be afraid of them. At that age I thought of them as neighbors, as friends.

But as I got older, life exposed me to a different kind of cop that came into my grandfather's place when they were off duty. They told dirty and racist jokes, never tipped, and expected a lot of free "samples." Worst of all, when I was as young as fifteen, they hit on me. Perhaps the regulars I knew from that time were a minority of the force. But I couldn't stop the memory of them from filling my head, or forget the feeling of authority they wielded that I didn't know how to oppose.

There was another group that frequented The Corner that I associated with those particular cops. My grandfather used to call them landlords, but I could hear the quotation marks when he said the word. They came around every week to pick up the "rent" from the restaurant. The legal term is *extortion*. It was the protection fee my grandfather had to pay to run an establishment in that Brooklyn neighborhood. It didn't matter that it was a hole-in-the-wall, didn't matter if a certain week was so slow he hardly made a profit. Rent was rent. My grandfather never spoke to me about it, but I would hear the bartenders talking. I understood what it was.

A man named Tommy Ryan would pick up the money every week. It was no big drama. He'd have a free drink at the bar, take his little package, and leave a big tip. When I was older, I noticed he also handled the gambling action for the neighborhood. He'd have score sheets for sports and took regular bets for basketball and football, college and pro, not to mention horse races. Toward the end of my grandfather's life, when he had a penchant for such things, he treated Tommy with a lot more camaraderie.

Last time I saw Tommy Ryan, I was eighteen and it was at my grandfather's wake. There were a lot of people paying their respects, and Tommy came in with a few men I had never seen. They knelt at the open coffin, made the sign of the cross, and then, one by one, shook my hand. Tommy's hand was cold and clammy, his eyes bleary with alcohol, as he mumbled his condolences. I thanked them all without meeting their eyes. I suppose if they hadn't been around, my grandfather would have found someone else to give his money to. But to me they were just slime that had done nothing for my grandfather except contribute to his misery and death.

Sometimes I see Tommy's face in my dreams, that blue-white skin and those black bottomless eyes. Looking at him was like looking into the face of hell. I guess I made him the icon for everything in my life that was bad at the time. The Corner had started out as a neighborhood place where you could get homemade Italian food. At the end it was little more than a bar full of sad people who drank too much, just like my grandfather.

Detective Tom Barry reminded me of Tommy Ryan from Brooklyn. There was something similar in the way they talked to me, and they had the same first name. They looked nothing alike, though; Brooklyn Tommy was as thin as death, and Tom the Cop had more than a couple dozen doughnuts hanging over his belt. I hoped that was the last time I saw him.

What a weekend: Get hit on by creepy Cousin Bobby, find a corpse in an alley, and then get bullied by Tom the Cop. The tiny bright spot was meeting Detective Lopez. It was amazing how much one truly nice person could stand out from the crowd. It proved how rare they were. Maybe he was even a good cop, if there was such a thing.

I didn't believe Detective Tom Barry cared enough about either of the murdered women to put much into the case. He'd sure let me know his caseload was full. And I'd felt no respect in how his eyes wandered up and down my body. Was Detective Lopez any better? He hadn't seemed like a jerk, but he was NYPD. Hard to know.

Maybe I'd start asking around The Studio to see if I could find out anything. But it was Sunday, and any private investigation I might launch at The Studio would have to wait until class tomorrow.

I needed a distraction. I reached into my shoulder bag and took out the movie times I had ripped from *The Village Voice* earlier in the week. A girl never knows when she's going to have time to slip into a movie. The rain wasn't going to stop anytime soon, so I might as well take refuge.

Movies were my usual way to fill up extra time, and what else can one do on a rainy summer Sunday afternoon? Especially when I needed to replace visions of death with anything else.

I checked to see what was playing in Midtown. I'd watch anything at the Ziegfeld Theater, a big, old-fashioned mammoth of a movie house. Almost any movie looked and sounded convincing in its cavernous space and on its giant screen framed by two towers of scarlet velvet curtains. Anything I saw there would take me away from reality.

Sweat dripped down my neck as I stood on the grimy platform for the local number one train waiting to head uptown. I counted the gray flattened discs of discarded chewing gum on the cement floor to pass the time. When I leaned over the garbage-strewn tracks to see if the train was coming, I could see rats running between the puddles. Why are subway trains always delayed when it rains? They're underground, for Pete's sake.

I felt the wind of the oncoming train just before it pulled the newspaper clipping from my hand. I chased the scurrying paper and was reaching down to scoop it up just before it could fly onto the tracks when I felt the train whiz past. I stood up, realizing how close I was to the edge. I inched back as the train came to a stop, my heart racing.

When the graffiti-covered doors opened, I entered and grabbed the pole next to a tiny, ancient Asian lady with too much lipstick, applied rather crookedly. She smiled at me politely. If I ever made it to her age, I'd wear as much lipstick as I damn pleased too.

As was my habit, I looked around the train. To the left of the lady with the bright-red lipstick was a boy who looked too young to be on the train alone, yet he didn't seem to be with anyone. He looked about eight years old, but maybe he was ten or eleven. I hadn't been allowed to take the train without an adult when I was a kid. My grandmother was a bit protective. *I guess some parents are less paranoid.*

I turned to my right. Closer than I realized was a man in his late twenties looking me up and down. His dark curly hair surrounded his pudgy face, his gray sweatpants were too tight, and his black net T-shirt did nothing to hide his beer belly. He must have gotten on right behind me. I turned away.

"Hey," he said, "does this train stop at Thirty-Fourth Street?"

"Um, yeah." I didn't turn toward him. "It does."

"Thanks." In my peripheral vision, I watched him measure the short length of my body with his eyes. My stomach churned. He moved closer to me. "Where are you getting off?"

"Next stop." In hopes that he'd leave me alone, I plugged my earphones into my ears and slipped a mix tape into my portable tape player. Music was always a good way to distract my mind from too many spiraling thoughts or annoying people. The tape was halfway through its playlist, and when I flipped it on, Chic singing "Le Freak" flooded my ears with its disco rhythm and rhyme. I turned toward the door just as the train pulled into the Fourteenth Street station.

I jumped off as soon as the doors opened, walked quickly to the next car, and got back on. *Creep. Who tries to pick someone up on a subway?* And that black net shirt, yikes.

The train picked up speed right away. I turned around at the wrenching sound of metal as someone opened the door between cars. Clinging to the pole with both hands, I watched Black Net Shirt Guy enter my car.

Had he followed me from the street? I turned and edged my way toward the other end of the car. I watched him out of the corner of my eye. He moved closer.

At Eighteenth Street I got out of that car and flew to the next one ahead. If he followed me again, it was no coincidence. I took shallow breaths on the hot train. The windows were open, but the humid air from the subway tunnel didn't do much to make the ride more comfortable. In what century would they finally put air conditioning on the NYC subways? It was worse when it rained; it just trapped the hot, humid air belowground, making it even hotter. I dripped sweat from all my creases. I tried to look casual as I took one step every few seconds, making my way toward the far end of the train. Sure enough, Black Net Shirt Guy came through the door from the other car again, following me forward. He wasn't looking at me, but why else would he keep switching cars whenever I did?

Had he followed me from the alley? Was he the murderer choosing his next victim? I looked at my sandaled feet, solidly on the subway car floor. Surely I was just being paranoid. He was just a normal subway rider making his way closer to the end of the train that would be nearest his exit at the station. Didn't I always do the same, ride the car closest to the station exit to wherever I was going? As if that made the ride any shorter.

The train stopped at the Twenty-Third Street station and I kept my place, the disco rhythm of Chic singing about how chic it was to "le freak" on the dance floor still pounding in my ears. I almost hugged the shiny pole next to me. Black Net Shirt Guy didn't move, and we started up again. The train barreled down the track, and then the lights blinked off, plunging us into darkness. *Breathe, Nina, breathe in and out. Nothing to be afraid of; it's only darkness, hot, airless darkness. Everything is the same as when it's light. Dark doesn't mean there's anything different than in the light.* I pushed away my childhood fear, which hadn't completely left me. The lights flickered back on as we rolled into the Twenty-Eighth Street station. He still didn't move.

The ride was taking forever. Of course the train had to be a local. Had he moved closer? I couldn't tell if he was watching me. Thirty-Fourth Street coming up. If he didn't get off, what should I do? I made a move to the door leading to the next car. I hated walking between trains, but I had to get away from him.

The door felt heavy as I tried to pull it sideways, and it opened with a jerk. The noise of the train going over the tracks was deafening. I stepped over the gap. I watched the track hurtling below. I stared at the rushing metal. If I fell right now, if one foot slipped through the gap, I'd be mangled beyond recognition. My life would be over. They might not even be able to identify my body. I'd disappear off the face of the earth as if I never existed. Who would miss me? No one. I obsessed on that for a moment, unable to move, picturing my demise.

I forced myself to go forward as I shook my head to stimulate some sense back into my brain. The door into the next car was even heavier; it seemed stuck. I tugged on it with both hands, trying to slide it on its sideways track while still keeping my balance. It didn't budge. My palms started to sweat, the handle got slippery, and I gave it another big yank. It opened. I flung my body inside and slid the door closed. I stood there, still clinging to the door handle, trying to quiet my loud panting so everyone wouldn't stare at me.

The train pulled into the Thirty-Fourth Street station. I looked back into the car behind me to see if he would exit. He was getting off. I breathed a sigh of relief.

"Watch the closing doors. Forty-Second Street next," the conductor announced. The doors started to close. But someone wedged their body into the car at the last minute, forcing them to reopen. Black Net Shirt Guy. He was following me for sure. Now what? If I waited until Fiftieth Street, he might follow me right to the theater, and then I'd be stuck with him. I should get off at Forty-Second Street and walk the rest of the way, try to lose him on the street. In all my dealings with drunk customers and weird strangers in the city, I'd never had anyone follow me on the subway before. Was it because he knew I'd found Jessica's body? Or was he just some pervert? I didn't know which was worse—if he was really following me or if I was losing it. My mind was on overdrive, spiraling into darkness at the possible danger.

The train pulled into the Forty-Second Street station. Black Net Shirt Guy was in the middle of the train car, holding the handle hanging above a seat. He was turned my direction, even though he didn't seem to be looking at me. But he would be able to see me out of the corner of his eye. I held on to my pole. The train stopped and the doors opened. I waited, barely breathing. People got off. People got on. The conductor made his announcement.

"Watch the closing doors. Fiftieth Street is next." *Bing-bong.* The doors chimed as they started to close. I jumped from my spot and slid out onto the platform just before the doors came together. They closed behind me, and I tried to catch the breath I'd been holding. I looked back into the train as it pulled away. Black Net Shirt Guy looked at me through the window. I smiled and waved. He looked surprised and a little confused. Was he surprised to see me because he thought I'd gotten off on Fourteenth Street and hadn't even noticed me since then? Or was he amazed because he'd lost the chance to keep following me?

I guess I'll never know.

CHAPTER 5

I made it to the theater, rain still coming steadily down, twenty minutes to spare. I had to clear my mind of my twisted reality, plunge my brain into fantasy. No one was following me. My life had nothing to do with Jessica's death. Or that other girl, Teresa. It was all just a passing coincidence. I had enough time to buy my ticket, grab some munchies, and pick a good seat in the front third of the theater. I walked down the aisle and waited until the screen filled my peripheral vision, all the way from side to side, and then I picked my chair in the middle of that row. My eyes so filled with the screen it would put me as close to the movie as if I were inside it, where there were no naked legs sticking out from behind any dumpsters or Black Net Shirt Guys.

There weren't many people who wanted to see *Dracula*, starring Frank Langella, on a Sunday afternoon at the end of its run, so there were plenty of prime seats. I sidewinded into the middle of the tenth row and settled in, taking in the warm salty smell of my popcorn as I lifted the red-and-white-striped cardboard container close to my face. I figured this movie wasn't going to be a masterpiece, but, from an actor's point of view, there was something to learn from almost every movie. The Ziegfeld was dark, cool, and otherworldly. On a day like this, when life was worth evading, any movie'll do.

The lights went down. I slumped in my seat and folded my legs yoga-style. I crunched my popcorn ever so softly as the music started and the titles came on the screen. Laurence Olivier was in it; it couldn't be all bad. The velvet seats smelled musty and earthy, like the attic of a haunted house, and I began to sink into the darkness of my imagination.

The setting was classic Gothic: rain, fog, and horse-drawn carriages at night. I loved plastic horror movies, especially when the acting was overboard. That's the only way to do it. If a horror movie took itself too seriously, it didn't work for me. I'd rather laugh at scary things than be frightened—enough of that going on in real life. I had to work on not taking life too seriously. Even finding a dead body wasn't the end of the world. At least not the end of my world. Was it?

There was a lot of lust in the movie: bloodlust, sexual lust, food lust, lust for the sake of being good. But it was the theme of punishment for sexual promiscuity that made me uncomfortable, the misery of my Catholic upbringing rearing its ugly head. Sex equaled death or damnation or both, which simply wasn't fair. The movie probably wouldn't go over big with the free love crowd, but my grandfather would have liked it. He was purely puritan when it came to sex. He constantly gave me grief. Mostly he ignored me; I wasn't worth the effort, but when he felt like ragging on someone, I was an easy target.

One memorable night, I was setting up the bar at the start of happy hour at The Corner. Even though I wasn't eighteen, family was allowed to work behind the bar and serve alcohol, just not drink—or at least not get caught drinking. A crowd of construction workers had just come in, hungry and thirsty after their hard day finishing the new Twin Towers in downtown Manhattan. They took up all the seats. I was relieving Donna, our daytime bartender, who had been working for us since I was in elementary school. She was the closest thing I had to a big sister. She'd teach me new drinks, Spanish words, and life lessons, and she did her best to deflect my grandfather's mood away from me.

She went downstairs to fill the ice buckets, and I set up the customers with beers, shots, and cocktails while taking orders for steamed clams, fried calamari, and hot antipasto. Construction workers were good eaters and great tippers.

My grandfather sat at the end of the bar, crowding the service bar and the walk-through opening. Donna came back with buckets of ice but couldn't squeeze through. My grandfather was already half in a funk and wouldn't move out of her way, so she left the buckets at the opening for me. I walked toward my grandfather as he shook his empty glass at me, banging a tempo on the bar with the thick highball glass as I got closer. I made it a point never to pour him a drink. He could help himself and he knew it. What was he going to do, fire me? Who would pour him into bed at night or pay the bills or make the bank drops? He usually didn't test our little treaty. I gave him a withering look. His eyes didn't meet mine. Instead, they searched my clothes. As I bent down to grab the handles of the ice buckets, I had to lean closer to him.

"Puttana."

His hoarse voice cut straight through the buzz of customer conversations that surrounded us. Italian for whore. My lungs froze, and my face felt hot as I straightened up, lifting the heavy buckets, feeling the weight of the ice in my shoulders and the echo of his voice in the pit of my stomach. Sure, it was okay for his other bartenders to wear low-cut blouses behind the bar, but my scoop-necked peasant blouse was too much. I looked at his face straight on, his sunken cheeks, his pallor, his expression of blank meanness. He reminded me of Dracula that day. *How much longer can he last?* I tried to reassure myself. *He already looks dead.*

He got up and pushed past me to make his drink. I swallowed hard and turned to face my audience of customers. *No time for self-pity; got to smile to get those tips.* Money was my ticket out of there.

In the cool, conditioned air of the Ziegfeld Theater, my shirt was suddenly damp with cold sweat. A wave of nausea hit me as the credits rolled. The humiliation and shame were as fresh as if my grandfather was sitting next to me. *Puttana.* It was like I was watching the memory on the screen instead of the movie *Dracula.* I waited for my head to stop throbbing. At least that part of my life was over. I didn't know why I'd felt so responsible for my grandfather. Why hadn't I just run away? I guess once you've been abandoned, you can't consciously do it to someone else, no matter the circumstances.

Usually movies helped me forget. Right after my grandfather died and I sold The Corner, I spent all my free time in movie theaters. I went almost every day that fall, winter, early spring. There were many times I saw more than one movie in a day, and that's not even counting the ones on late-night TV. Since then, I'd cut back considerably. I allowed myself only two movies a week in the theater. I figured that was almost normal. Of course, sometimes I cheated.

I stood in the lobby of the theater and gazed out the tall glass windows that looked out onto the shiny rain-soaked streets. My mind slowly returned to the present. I lived alone, not with my grandfather. He couldn't hurt me anymore. My life was my own, however pathetic.

As I turned to leave, I saw a poster for *Apocalypse Now* announcing the opening for Wednesday night. It would be my second movie, filling my quota by midweek, but who could resist Francis Ford Coppola's new movie? I bought myself a single seat at the nine o'clock evening show on opening day.

I stuck my headphones in my ears and flipped the switch on my cassette player to listen to the radio as I walked to the subway. Herb Alpert's mellow trumpet playing "Rise" lifted my spirits a bit, giving me an escape from vampires, grandfathers, and dead actresses. Time to go home, cook supper, and work on some homework. My newish best friend Marissa and I were partners for a scene from Lillian Hellman's *Little Foxes*, and I had to finish memorizing my lines. Other people's words, other people's lives to disappear into—better than being me, if only temporarily. It's what I was good at.

I got up early Monday morning, pulled on shorts and a tank top, and trotted down the stairs in my socks, my skates slung over my shoulder. Sitting on the bottom step, I tied on my wheels and pushed out the door before I allowed my brain to come into focus about Jessica's murder. But the image of her leg surfaced and gave me a cold shiver even in the hot August sun. I pulled the door of my building closed, and the metal panel gave a sympathetic shuddering clang that reminded me of a church bell at a funeral service. Jessica was dead and I was alive. Who was making those decisions?

I skated slowly down my block, toward Union Square Park, my chest tight. The grimy streets, the exhaust-spewing trucks, the garbage bags piled on the curb waiting to be picked up, the puddles of slime in the gutter clogged with litter—all looked the same as usual. But it felt different. Broad daylight normally felt like protection; it was always easier to feel safe from dawn to dusk. Nighttime brought what it did. I accepted that. Now even daylight felt threatening. I crossed the avenue and passed the bodega I frequented for supplies. The orange tabby cat that guarded the door looked up at me, ears back, tail whipping back and forth, abnormally wary. Normally I'd scratch her behind the ears until she purred, but I didn't dare. What was she sore about?

I felt the sun soak into my skin, beginning to warm the chill out of me. I'd witnessed enough death in my own family to know every day was a crapshoot. Whoever was calling the shots was deciding in my favor so far. I'd take it for as long as I could get it. I pushed the image of Jessica's leg in that alley out of my mind for the millionth time.

Monday mornings in the park weren't too crowded. I'd get in a pretty good skating workout and a tan at the same time. Skating was about the only exercise I liked, although I loved sports. I'd watched almost every local team on TV with my mom when I was young, and she'd taken me to plenty of Mets, Knicks, and Rangers games. In elementary school I could spout baseball stats without thinking and knew every basketball player by sight. I'd skated around pretending I was a hockey player since I first put on roller skates at age four.

In real life I was a disaster at playing sports. In third grade our gym teacher had a sadistic streak for making us play kick-ball every day. He almost always picked the same two boys to be captains, and they'd call out names, one by one, until two teams were formed. If I wasn't last, I was second to last, leaving only Billy Forman, who was overweight and slow. I was weak and scrawny. I had good aim, but when I kicked the ball, it would barely roll a few feet. If Billy got his weight behind it, it carried a wallop, but usually it went right to the pitcher or fouled off to the side. Some days they couldn't decide which one of us was the bigger liability and didn't call either of our names. We would just drift to the closest team, try to be invis-ible, and pretend we weren't devastated. I didn't know which was worse: being chosen last or feeling like I didn't exist.

I skated faster around the north end of Union Square and wondered what happened to Billy. I hoped he was less trau-matized by the phys ed experience than I was, but I doubted it. Perhaps he was getting even with the world by being a murderer. I took the west corner of the park fast, almost too fast, but fast was good, especially if I had to escape a serial killer looking for actresses.

The usual number of suspicious-looking characters held court on park benches as I skated past. Drug dealers, pick-pockets, con men with three-card monte games. Normally I ignored them—the Village was the Village, and I had as much right to be here as they did. But today felt different. Every person I saw was a possible suspect. I didn't see Black Net Shirt Guy, but hey, the murderer could be anyone. How would anyone go about finding a murderer? New York had seven million residents, and New Jersey was just across the river with another seven and a half. How did you narrow it down to actual possibilities? This was no country manor house mystery with a finite cast of characters. There were too many people to consider. I skated around a curve, dodging the overflowing garbage can, and tried to apply logic.

Both Teresa and Jessica had been found dead in Greenwich Village. They were both actresses, or trying to be. They were both of petite build with dark hair and eyes. Were these deaths a pattern or coincidence? Jessica had gone to The Studio and I'd been in class with her; could the killer be someone from The Studio? And what was I going to do about it? If I asked around and I asked the wrong person, would that make me a target? My skates hit a pebble and I almost crashed. I steadied myself. If I tried to find out who the murderer was, it might be dangerous. But if I didn't and the cops didn't care enough to find him, I could be in danger anyway.

I turned up the volume on my cassette player as I speed-danced around the park to *Making Movies* by Dire Straits, the music pushing the bad thoughts from my head. Every song on the album fit cosmically into my life this summer. I was wearing the music right off the tape, playing it every day while I skated. Somehow it made me feel more like me than I felt in silence. Especially the song "Skateaway"; it felt like they'd written the lyrics after seeing me on the street. I was a real-life roller girl, and that song was perfect for moving.

The first time I ever put on skates, I was four. It was early spring and an unusually warm week. My mother and I took a walk, and she led me to a toy store. The skates were in her hand and she was paying for them before I knew what was happening. They were heavy and metal and they strapped onto my shoes. I remember putting them on and feeling taller and more substantial somehow. I felt like I was meant to be in them. I still felt like that every time I put on skates.

I scoured the crowd at Union Square Park to make sure there was no sign of Black Net Shirt Guy and convinced myself no one was especially interested in me. I was invisible and thankful for it. I kept to myself, letting any thoughts about the murders rest in my subconscious. I practiced a new move, skating backward into a jump turn. I almost had it down.

As I spun until I was dizzy, my eye caught sight of my scene partner Marissa's boyfriend on the east side of the park headed toward the subway station. Dave Kapour was one of my favorite people, another actor working as a bartender. Even from that distance, I couldn't mistake his dark wavy hair, tanned skin, and bright smile that never quit. It cheered me up just to see him. I speed-skated toward him so I could catch him before he disappeared underground into the subway station. Just as I got close, he turned right and I almost ran into him. He didn't even see me coming.

"Whoa." I pulled up fast, waving my arms so I didn't fall over.

"Hey!" Dave grabbed on to me so neither of us would fall.

"Sorry, you all right?" I laughed as I steadied myself on my skates. "I was trying to get your attention."

"I guess you got it." Dave laughed and shifted his gym bag on his shoulder. His tight gray T-shirt proclaimed *West-Side Gym* and showed off his substantial muscles.

"What's up with you guys?" I asked. Had they heard about the murder yet?

"Marissa's temping and I'm off today." He pushed his dark hair out of his eyes.

Most bartenders had Mondays off, restaurants taking that slow post-weekend day to close. I knew Marissa earned her rent as an office temp most weekdays.

"Want to grab some lunch?" I was closer to eye level with six-foot-two Dave on my skates. Somewhat closer.

"Can't today." Dave glanced toward the subway station entrance. "I've got to get uptown for my workout."

Dave had gotten into kung fu when he started watching Bruce Lee movies in middle school. He was a bit obsessive about it and skilled too. I'd seen him flip a guy twice his size and toss him halfway across the gym. That thought made me consider the possibility that he was also strong enough to grab a young woman and twist her neck. And he certainly knew plenty of actresses at The Studio, since he took classes there too. I felt my smile freeze on my face. What was happening to me? Was I going to try to fit everyone into the killer's profile? I pushed the thought out of my head. "Maybe we can hang out later this week, you, me, and Marissa."

"I'm working almost every night and Marissa's temping every day; we hardly have any overlapping free time together lately." Dave tapped the front of my skate with his sneakered toe. "But maybe I'll stop by The Realm for one of your shifts."

"Sure. Wednesday through Saturday," I reminded him. "I'll be there slinging pasta and pouring Chianti." Dave started to move toward the subway entrance, and I rolled slowly with him. I felt the pressure release from my head like a valve had just opened up. *Chill out, Esposito. Return to normalcy.* I certainly knew Dave well enough to know he wasn't a killer. Didn't I?

"Hey, did you see the paper today?" Dave shifted his gym bag from one shoulder to the other. "There's some story about a girl we knew from the studio who got murdered."

My heart lost its beat.

Chapter 6

So much for normalcy.

I almost stumbled as my left skate rolled over a bit of gravel. The police must've confirmed it was Jessica and contacted her family, if the murder was in the paper and they had released her name.

"Marissa pointed it out to me." Dave continued toward the subway station. "I think she recognized her name; she said she was in your class. Name sounded familiar."

"Uh-huh."

"What was it?" Dave stopped and looked up, as if the Wicked Witch of the West might be writing the name across the sky in smoke to prompt him. "I forget, but she was definitely murdered, definitely found in an alley, and definitely went to The Studio."

"Yeah. I definitely got it." I rubbed my damp palms on the sides of my shorts. We were standing on an incline, and I started to roll away from him. I turned one skate sideways to brake. "It was Jessica Roman; remember her?" I watched his face. "She was in that spring showcase." Was he pretending not to know her, or was his memory really that bad?

"Jessica Roman?" Dave's smile was tense and rushed. "Oh, right. Now that you mention the showcase, I remember. I didn't put that together. Look, I gotta run or I'll be late."

"See ya." I watched Dave disappear down the subway stairs as I slowly skated backward. How well did I know Dave, really? Dave and Marissa had met in Chicago at college. After graduating with theater degrees, they moved to the East Village. They'd been living together for almost a year, doing the struggling-actor thing. They both took classes at The Studio, but with different teachers. I was pretty close with Marissa considering she was someone I had met less than a year ago. Dave was on the perimeter. He was an adjacent friend.

I skated across the park toward the newsstand. I had to find the article Dave was talking about and see if there was any new information. I was surprised at my suspicion of Dave, but it was just occurring to me that maybe my positive opinion of him was based on the fact that he was attractive. Okay, he was hot. And since when was a hot guy only good at heart? Maybe loneliness was fogging my thinking. Or my hormones. They sure could build up when you'd been celibate for a while. That was one of the problems of being in the New York theater world: All the men who weren't gay or cads had been snapped up. Purely a pool for friends, not dates. Not that I was really in the market.

I skated faster to the corner of the park and picked up the *New York Daily News*. I usually read at least two newspapers a day, sometimes three or four. I was a junky for current events. I wanted to know what was going on in the world at all times, partly because I'd never been out of New York. Newspapers were my travel ticket. Working in bars, I scavenged other people's papers and ate them up. I was a fast reader and loved to fill my free time with print, newspapers, books, magazines. It was the only higher education I could afford.

I plopped down on a bench and flipped right to the Metro section, where I found the article Dave mentioned. They'd released Jessica's name, although they hadn't made the connection to The Studio or the other murder. But they did say she had been raped and smashed on the back of her head (like the first murder) and that her flowered summer dress, white bra, and underwear were behind the dumpster, folded neatly. Creepy. They didn't mention the red platform shoes.

Probably everyone at The Studio knew by now. What was class going to be like? People would be whispering about it. I'd just as soon save the drama for the stage, but I was more than curious. It wasn't gossip to me. If these two murders were connected and the killer was out there targeting short dark actresses, where did that put me? I wondered if our teacher, the talented Tony Award–winning Ron Meyers, would say anything about Jessica in class. I hoped we wouldn't discuss it like group therapy. That picture of her bare leg was still in my head, and after reading the article, I couldn't help imagining someone's strong hands around Jessica's neck. But whose hands? Did they belong to someone I knew? Someone at The Studio? It was all spiraling around in my head. I couldn't get rid of it.

"Are you done with that newspaper?"

Dirty fingernails at the end of long, bony fingers reached toward me, grasping at the section of the paper I'd left next to me on the bench. I leaned away involuntarily, the hair on the back of my neck doing a levitation trick. The hands belonged to a skinny old man in a worn gray suit. Old bony hands with dirty, ragged fingernails that reminded me of my grandfather's hands.

"Here you go." I pushed a few sections toward him. He was getting a little too close for comfort, and my ultrasensitive nose was on high alert. His hair smelled like car grease, and his old suit of clothes was neat but hadn't been cleaned in a while. The material had that shiny look. There was another smell too, one that reminded me of my grandfather in his last months. The scent of a human at the end of his life. It was an odor that made my stomach turn. I hadn't even seen this guy approach. He'd slipped next to me as quiet as a ghost. Time to be somewhere else.

I skated to the south end and turned onto Fourteenth Street. One block later I waited for the light to change at Fifth Avenue, trying to feel normal, like the days of my life before I'd found a dead body. A middle-aged couple walked up next to me. Normal people. Happy people. She had her arm tucked into his. I caught myself staring.

"Excuse us." The woman's short kinky black hair had just started to turn gray at the temples in an attractive way. "Is this way uptown, or is it that way?"

Always glad to have the chance to disprove the myth that New Yorkers were rude, I pointed down Fifth Avenue.

"See those two tall towers?" I smiled as nice as could be. "That's the World Trade Center; that's south, downtown." Then I turned and pointed again. "See that tall pointy building? That's the Empire State Building; that's north, uptown." More smiling. "You can always tell which way is north or south by looking for those buildings, at least when you're below Thirty-Fourth Street. Have a nice day!" The light changed and I skated away. I imagined that the tourists were impressed and grateful, that I was their hero of the moment. I envisioned a red cape flapping behind me as I rolled on my way.

That night Marissa and I weren't scheduled to run our scene in class, but it was going to be just as interesting to watch the others try to figure it all out. The Tony Award–winning Ron Meyers wasn't in class yet, but about half of the students had already drifted in and were chatting with each other or studying scripts. I took a chair near the back, saving a seat for Marissa. Where was she? I looked at the other women. A handful were ethnic like me; some were darker skinned, some blond. The male actor palette was about the same. A few of the girls got all dressed up and wore full makeup every week. That's what Jessica had been like. But sometimes Ron threw an exercise at us that required rolling on the floor or crying our eyes out, so I liked to wear something comfortable and skip the makeup. Tonight, that meant faded cutoff denim shorts and a rainbow tie-dyed T-shirt.

How many students knew about Jessica? She didn't have many friends that I'd noticed; she seemed to think more of herself than most of the other actors. Was there a motive, or was the killer just picking random dark-haired actresses? None of the chatter seemed to be about Jessica. I didn't see her scene partner. Everyone was there except those two and Marissa.

Ron stalked into the classroom exactly on time, wearing his energetic stage presence like a wizard's cloak. The class was magically silent as if he had waved a wand.

"Okay, everyone, I'm sure most of you have heard about the untimely passing of one of our students, Jessica Roman. We are all saddened by the news. You will all experience tragedies in your life. That is unavoidable. You must learn to use it."

There was a flare of whispering and muttering as those who had heard the news caught up those who hadn't. Ron quieted us down just as Marissa slid into the chair next to me. She was yet another dark-haired actress but stood at a towering five foot three. Ron continued.

"Acting is not pretending; it is remembering and feeling, it is being. But it is having control of those feelings at all times." He paced grandly back and forth in front of us. "Tonight, we will practice this control. Let us begin."

Class started with two of our classmates doing a scene from the play *Bus Stop* by William Inge. Janette was a tall, buxom copper-skinned beauty, and Larry was so white and skinny I imagined she could pick him up and floss her teeth with him. Larry was new to The Studio, but Janette and I had been in class together since early spring. I admired her confidence. They did a solid job of portraying the lonely cowboy and the emotionally lost female country bumpkin. Ron had some comments, and he asked them to do a section over again. He asked them some questions, and I could tell he was leading up to something. He paused and looked at the whole class.

"Let's say you're asking your mother or father or grandmother or grandfather, whoever cared for you as a child, for permission to go on a trip, or to visit another relative or a friend, we'll say. But in the back of your mind, you know that your life is in danger, that this very person you are asking so politely to excuse you is someone who wants to kill you, in the most Shakespearean way. Maybe not that very night but someday soon, and getting their permission to leave at that moment just might save your life." He looked around the room at all of us. "You are asking for permission in the most innocent of terms, but all you can think about is that you must leave, at this very moment, or it will be the death of you. Your mind is full of it, but you can't say it in your words. Do it."

Janette and Larry each did the improvisation with him and fared pretty well. Ron called each of us up to the front, one at a time, and gave us the same task, as he played the antagonist. Then it was my turn, last but not least, and my head was reeling. My grandfather was the obvious choice; I'd felt threatened in his presence many times, no imagination needed. And with everything running through my mind about Jessica and the other murder, the feeling that my life was in danger was an easy one to summon for this exercise. The trick was going to be, as Ron had said, keeping it under control. I walked to the front of the room, a bit shaky, and looked at Ron. I'd never thought of him as threatening, only intimidating, but he gave me such an evil smile that it jump-started the exercise. I was easily transported to my fourteen-year-old self.

I started the scene. "Grandpa, it's time for me to leave for Maria's house for the sleepover party. I cleaned my room and scrubbed the bathroom. I washed the dishes, and I even took out the trash."

"You're not going to any sleepover." Ron sat in a chair across the room.

"You said if I did my chores, I could go." I sounded whiny.

"I changed my mind." Ron mimed reading a newspaper.

I switched to false confidence. "But I'm . . . expected."

"I don't care what other people expect." He stood.

The more I spoke, the closer I felt to the edge, and Ron tried to push me over it with every reply. I reminded myself that the exercise was about control.

"Okay, I won't sleep over, I'll just go over there for pizza, and then I'll come right home." I mimed zipping up my backpack. My tone was light, but the speed of my words betrayed my fear.

"And what am I going to eat for dinner if you're not here to cook it?"

"I made your dinner already. It's on the table with a plate on top to keep it warm. You should eat it before it gets cold." In real life I would have run out the door as soon as he looked away.

"I'm not hungry now. It's too early, and I don't like cold dinner. You can cook it over again when I'm ready."

Ron was doing a pretty damn good impression of my grandfather. I was beginning to wonder if they'd met.

"How about I just go over and give her the present I bought her? Then I'll come back in time to make dinner."

"You. Are. Not. Leaving. This. House." Ron took a step closer with each word. I focused on miming physical business with my imaginary backpack. My technique was to be casual instead of confrontational.

"I'll tell her that I have to miss the party because you need me. I'll just go, real quick, and be right back. Just to drop off the birthday present."

Slowly, Ron hovered even closer to me as he spoke. Suddenly he even looked like my grandfather.

"Over. My. Dead. Body."

I stood still and waited until he stopped in front of me. I wanted to do something I'd never done with my real grandfather—turn the tables, push his buttons like he'd always pushed mine, go on the attack, yell in his face, punch him in the chest until he fell against the wall. My life was at stake; this man was going to kill me if I didn't escape. Didn't I know exactly what that was like? Hadn't it always felt fatal with my grandfather? I didn't need to act; all I needed to do was remember. So I let it all take me like a rushing river swollen from a storm.

I never knew when my grandfather's habit of ignoring me would flip and suddenly I'd be the center of his attention. He rarely yelled at me at The Corner. He seemed out of control when he'd come at me at home, but he somehow managed to keep a lid on it at The Corner. At home I kept my bedroom door locked in case he came home in a rage, but it wasn't always that simple.

One night I came home late at night—or rather, early in the morning, after two AM. I walked into the house, trepidatious as usual. But it was quiet, no blaring TV or crashing kitchenware. I thanked my lucky stars, entered, and quickly moved toward my bedroom. Suddenly my grandfather came out of the kitchen, faster than I'd ever seen him move, stalking straight toward me.

"Where the fuck have you been!" he roared. Like he ever cared about that. "I'm sick of your whoring and all your bullshit!"

I backed up to the nearest wall, but there was no shelter. He grabbed me by both arms, lifted me off the ground, and threw me across the room. I don't know how his emaciated body had the strength, but it was as if I weighed less than a feather. So much for luck. The only luck I had was that by throwing me, he had gotten me closer to my bedroom door, so I scrambled to my feet, ran inside, and slammed it shut, my heart imploding in my chest. He didn't spend much time banging on my door; he had already gotten his jollies. But the noise in my head didn't stop till dawn.

He'd won, as usual. He'd exerted his dominance over me and reminded me I was powerless. My only victory, I told myself, my only control, was that I didn't cry and I didn't fight back. I didn't give him what he wanted. He wanted a fight, the sport of it, and I wasn't playing. I simply disappeared into submission and into my room.

In class with Ron, it all came back to me: the fear, the powerlessness, the breath-sucking tension. I disappeared. It was as if a loud freight train went screeching by, obstructing all sound, obliterating the existence of my voice, of myself. I didn't even know what was happening. I took him on like a verbal Golden Gloves champion. Then suddenly it was over, and we were standing in front of the class listening to applause. I didn't remember exactly what I'd said, but I'd held in the tears.

"This is exactly what I was talking about. Nina showed control, yet we could all feel the emotional depth beneath her words." Ron addressed the class. Then he turned to look at me, and his satisfied smile changed into something familiar and it made me uncomfortable. The look in his eye, it was . . . voracious. I had been planning to ask him what he knew about Jessica after class, but in that moment I lost my nerve.

The other students were a bit surprised at my performance, but I had an advantage. For them, the task was to use their imagination to guess what it might be like. For me, it was to wrangle a hurricane of emotions I was trying to forget. My chest still felt stormy. I was as surprised as they were. I was used to spending most of my energy suppressing ugly memories. During the exercise, something took over, outside of my power. So much for control.

I was the first to walk out of the room after Ron, but he made a quick exit, so I lost my chance to ask him what he knew about Jessica even if I could've worked up the courage. A blond, bubbly type that I slightly recognized came out of another classroom and stopped a few feet in front of me. She stared, her face turned white, then she wavered and felt for the wall to steady herself.

"What?" I stared back at her and put my hands on my hips.

"Oh. Oh! I thought you were someone else for a minute." She let out a relieved laugh. "I thought I was seeing a ghost." She passed me and disappeared into the ladies' room. I was already wrecked from that exercise. I didn't need more drama. It wasn't the first time someone had mistaken me for Jessica. But this time was different.

Marissa came out of the classroom, pulled me over near the empty coatrack, and lowered her voice.

"Are you okay?" She gave my arm a gentle squeeze. She knew a few details of my past.

"Yeah, I'm fine." My heart was still dancing faster than normal, but I played it cool. "Just acting, you know." Janette and Larry stopped next to us.

"Some scene, Nina," Skinny Larry said. "I'd like to do an improv with you sometime." He winked and gave me a kind of hungry look. *Jerk.* But then, anyone that skinny must always be hungry.

"Um, thanks, Larry." I moved away from him and looked at Janette. "You guys did a great job with the *Bus Stop* scene."

"It was a good night for all of us." Janette gave my shoulder a squeeze and moved Larry down the hall.

"Let's split, Marissa."

"Wait a minute, listen, I've been dying to talk to you. Did you hear what happened?" Her voice dropped to a whisper. "To Jessica Roman?"

"Yes, Ron announced it in class before you came in."

"I read in the paper she was found right near here." Marissa was speaking softly, overenunciating each word. Her expression was one of interest and excitement, but my stomach was simmering. I couldn't find a way to tell her I had found the body.

"Do we have to discuss this right now?" I whispered back and glanced over at Skinny Larry, who was now hovering over a petite actress with long dark curls. He sure liked to lord it over short women. The poorly lit grimness of the actors' lounge was enveloping me like a shroud.

"Lighten up, class is over." Marissa poked me. "Let's go have a cup of coffee or something."

We emerged into the balmy summer night. The air smelled fresh, and I felt my lungs begin to loosen up as we walked east.

We settled onto metal chairs at a tiny table in a grungy corner coffee shop called, coincidentally, The Bus Stop. Coffee for Marissa, tea for me, a crispy plate of french fries on the table between us. The salty, greasy smell filled my nose with the hope of salvation. The radio behind the counter played cheerful salsa music. It almost succeeded in pushing the murders from my mind. Almost.

"What have you heard about all this with Jessica?" Marissa dribbled a few drops of milk in her coffee as was her habit, barely lightening the color. I couldn't see the point; she might as well drink it black.

"What have *you* heard?" I focusing on the swirling liquid in my cup as I stirred.

"Just what I told you—that body I read about in the paper was her."

I nibbled a french fry. "Right." The image of the naked leg floated into my head.

"And I heard Ron talking to one of the other acting teachers about her after class."

"What did he say?" I squeezed the spent tea bag and parked it on the saucer.

"Not much." Marissa scooped up a blob of ketchup with a long skinny fry. "He didn't seem to care." A bright-red drop of condiment dripped on her white T-shirt, right over her heart. "And I thought Ron and Jessica had a little something going on the side." She licked her salty fingers.

"Did they?" I handed her a napkin. She dabbed at the ketchup on her shirt but just ended up making it into a bigger slash.

"I saw them cooing and giggling in the hallway after class."

"You mean she was cooing and giggling at *him*," I scoffed.

"It looked pretty mutual to me. At least the cooing part. Like *you* wouldn't jump if he aimed his big brown eyes at you."

"Jump? I'd jump, skip, *and* hop." We laughed, but mine was forced. Come to think of it, I had also seen Ron and

Jessica together in the hallways. Had there been some sort of relationship?

"People say they saw them together outside of The Studio." Marissa nabbed the last french fry.

"He played it pretty cool in class tonight." I watched as she rubbed the potato strip in the salt at the bottom of the dish.

"Well, he would, wouldn't he?"

"Oh, what does it matter anyway?" I was tired. I wanted to go home.

"What does it matter?!" Marissa looked at me like I was the village idiot. "Well, I guess that depends on if Ron Meyers killed her or not."

Chapter 7

My mouth hung open while a response tried to form in my head. Not a single coherent thought congealed. I'd been suspicious of every other guy I passed on the street, but I hadn't been thinking that Ron could be the killer. He was too real, too close to home. But if they had been in a relationship, was it possible? He had been so effectively threatening in our scene just moments before. That smile he gave me—like the cat who was just about to eat the canary. But I didn't want it to be possible.

"Don't be ridiculous, Marissa." I straightened my teacup in its saucer. If I denied this, maybe the possibility would evaporate. But I wondered if the cops had questioned Ron, and if not, maybe I should give them the idea. Or maybe I could talk to Ron myself. But this was my gruesome adventure; I didn't want to involve Marissa. I changed the subject. "Have you taken a look at that scene from *The Little Foxes* that Ron wants us to do?"

"Yeah, I read it." Marissa pushed the empty plate away from her. "It's a great scene for you as Birdie. It's practically a monologue."

"It is her best scene in the play. She doesn't have much else." I looked at the check and put down some singles. "Alexandra is so much of a better character. The next scene has great lines for you."

"But Birdie is so complex and dramatic. It's a great part." Marissa counted out her portion of the bill.

"Dramatic and pathetic. It's been depressing studying her." Why had Ron chosen me to play the alcoholic target of abuse? Did he recognize some sort of victim status in me? Her backstory was full of issues I was trying to forget.

"Well, it's good practice not to get too attached to your character." Marissa gave me a wry smile. "How are you ever going to play Juliet or Desdemona? You don't have to actually die at the end of either of those plays. It's called acting."

"Thanks for the tutorial, sensei." I stood and gave her a little bow. Sometimes Marissa felt the need to remind me that she had a full college degree in theater compared to my paltry few months at The Studio. We walked outside. "Are you coming with me to that cattle call tomorrow morning?"

"I told my temp agency I was unavailable for typing due to impending stardom." She winked at me. "They didn't laugh. God save us from corporate types. I'll meet you in line, ten AM–ish."

"We say *on line* here in New York, you Midwesterner." I gave Marissa a quick hug. She walked east toward the tenement apartment she shared with Dave. I walked north toward the loft I shared with no one since I moved from Brooklyn. Sometimes I wondered what it would be like to go home to someone. Someone nice. Someone I cared about. Someone who cared about me.

Just as I passed the entrance to the IND subway line at Fourteenth Street, a man came stumbling up from the staircase and almost bumped into me. I pulled back instinctively. He looked like a regular businessman, white shirt, gray suit, black shoes. But his dark tie was loose, his shirt wrinkled. Then I saw that his face and hands were covered in blood.

"Help me!" He sputtered blood in my direction. I took another step backward and almost fell off the curb into the street. I caught myself and moved sideways on the sidewalk, unable to look away from him.

The bloody businessman stumbled and held on to the wrought iron railing next to the entrance of the subway. Blood dribbled from his nose as he wiped his hands on his shirt. I was finally able to catch my breath and speak.

"Are you okay? Did you get mugged? Should I call the police?"

"No police! No."

He wavered, then slumped down and sat on the ground. He looked up at me through watery eyes and leaned his head back on the railing. My breath forgot how to expand my chest. *Don't panic. Keep focused.* I looked at him more closely. His eyes were bleary, and he couldn't keep his head upright. He was drunk. He'd probably tripped up the stairs and fallen on his face, ergo the bloody nose. My fear and concern turned to disgust. My empathy for alcoholics was permanently damaged. Too much exposure to the wreckage.

People exited the subway, gave him quick glances, and kept moving toward their own destinations. I was the only one who had stopped. I took some tissues out of my bag and give them to him. He took them and rubbed his hands.

"Do you want me to call a cab?"

"No. No cab. No." He slumped slightly, seeming calmer. "I live over there." He waved vaguely in the direction of a large apartment building down the street.

"Okay." I moved away from him, walking backward. "Okay."

He didn't look at me. He seemed embarrassed or just zoned out. My heart was still recovering from the scare he'd given me. I turned and walked away, looking back at him as I put some distance between us.

There's always something to catch you off balance in this city, especially at night.

In bed, I found myself thinking too much. How did Jessica and Teresa feel about being dead? Did they know they were dead? Or were they just gone? Their families must be devastated. Would anyone be devastated about me if I disappeared? I rolled over and closed my eyes. Sometimes I got so tired I felt I could sleep like the dead. Sometimes I felt so dead tired I was afraid I might not wake up. That thought popped my lids open. Sleep wasn't a comfortable place for me. Too many nightmares and bad memories. Sometimes sleep felt terminal, like a massive coronary.

I had to turn my thoughts around. But how could I feel safe unless the killer was caught? I wouldn't. I couldn't. If I didn't trust the NYPD to do the job, well, as my mother used to say, if you want something done right, you've got to do it yourself. What could I do? But now I had to sleep. If I could ever get to sleep. I flipped over on my stomach and turned on the radio.

That Patti Smith piece "Wave" was on. You couldn't really call it a song; it was more a monologue with music, or half of a dialogue, anyway. She was talking to someone on the beach. You could hear the waves breaking on the shore and the wind blowing. The music sounded sort of Middle Eastern and mysterious.

That piece always grabbed me somewhere in my gut. Her voice sounded so small and vulnerable that it made me think of me when I was eight, right after I'd lost my mother.

The radio station often played it in the middle of the night, which was probably most effective for the listening audience. I gathered that the idea of the song was that she was talking to Jesus or some other prophet, but it made me think of my mother. Like running into her angel on the beach and getting to speak with her, just for a moment. It had a peaceful feeling to it. The sound of the waves, the soft rolling music—it all made me feel sleepy and nice. Maybe it was a way of being close to my mother; maybe she was still with me in moments like that. Just by listening to that song and thinking about her, I could almost feel her. Maybe some of her spirit was in the room when that song came on. Like the girl in the song, thinking about waving to a loved one now gone, it made me feel happy.

Waking up in the morning was often disconcerting. I would have a moment of flashback, or something like that, just as I came awake. Sometimes I thought I was home with my mother; sometimes I heard my grandmother call me to breakfast. Other times I'd relive the early mornings when I'd wake to hear my grandfather crashing his way into the house after he'd been out drinking all night. That one sure got my heart pumping.

That Tuesday I came awake quickly and reminded myself that I was on my own. This usually brought me relief, although on the mornings when I thought I heard my mother moving about the room, it filled me with sadness. People talked about communicating with their dearly departed and feeling like they were right there with them. It didn't work that way for me. I tried to talk to my mother, but I never felt like she heard me. Not as if she wasn't there at all; more like I had just missed her, like she'd already turned the corner or she was just out of earshot. Those mornings when I thought she was in the room as I woke, she'd disappear as I opened my eyes and I'd want to call out *Wait!* But it was always too late.

Maybe she just figured I didn't need her. She'd been big on letting me do things for myself when I was little. I'd ask for help, my head stuck in my turtleneck, but her response was always *No, honey, you can do it all by yourself, I know you can.* I guess it was good for me, probably helped me grow up into my current resourceful self. But sometimes it felt lonely. Little did I know that I would find out what lonely really felt like right after I turned eight.

The only antidote to my flashback sadness was speed. I showered, pulled on a red T-shirt dress, and was at the corner newsstand in less than twenty minutes. My long damp hair kept me cool in the already roasting morning sun.

I picked up my usual stack of news and, because it was baseball season, the *New York Post.* After class that night I'd also get *The Village Voice.* It didn't come out officially until Wednesday, but they usually delivered it to newsstands just before midnight on Tuesdays. This was very useful if you were apartment hunting: You got a head start over the other schlubs. But mostly I bought it for the movie times. It listed every theater in the city, all the revival houses, special screenings at museums, every movie in town. It was my bible for the week. I would almost memorize it and then, just in case, cut the listings out and keep them in my bag. Never knew when I might want to hit a movie, especially in the steamy hot days of a New York City August or on a rainy Sunday.

But today I had an audition. Well, really a cattle call. In an audition you perform a monologue, read some lines, or sing or dance in front of a director or casting agent. A cattle call is when hundreds or maybe thousands of beginners like me, with no agent or union card, parade in front of casting agents in the hopes of being picked for an audition. This one was for a big Hollywood film, and it would be crowded. I'd been to a lot of cattle calls and never been chosen. But I kept showing up. Truculence or determination, who's to say?

Newspapers acquired, I scrambled some eggs and buttered some toast and sat at my big old wooden table, the only piece of furniture left over from my grandparents' house. I spread out my newspapers—more than a ritual. I had to have my papers open in front of me while I ate breakfast.

I was reluctant to read anything but the sports section after the last few days, so I skimmed the back of the *Daily News* while I ate my eggs and toast. My mother had always read the sports page first. Fan that she was, she'd read out all the scores to me from the day before. She even read me the horse race results. I loved to hear the names of the horses: Barb's Delight, Lightning Orphan, Ask the Fare. I always wondered what the names meant—they made wild stories come to mind.

The Mets had been off the day before, and the Yankees had won. Light sports news day. Lou Brock had made his three-thousandth hit. I wondered if I'd drawn three thousand beers from the tap. No time to do that useless math; I had to get to that cattle call. Hurry up and wait, as they say. Save the *Times* for the line; I'd have the opportunity to read every word. The call was in Midtown and it didn't start until one, but the line would be around the block by eleven. I had to put on some makeup too. Not my favorite thing but it was all part of the circus.

In front of the mirror, I paused at the full view of my morning visage. I poked at my pointy nose and smoothed my full eyebrows. If Brooke Shields could get away with it, why not me? At lease my heritage gave me a great tan in the summer. I would need extra foundation to cover the dark circles under my eyes. I knew I hadn't been sleeping well, but I hadn't realized I looked so ghastly. I flipped on the radio to distract myself while I painted my face. That hit song by Rickie Lee Jones, about Chuck E. being in love, was just ending. It was a happy song, but it made me depressed. I sure hadn't had any luck with love . . . or any positive experiences with men, come to think of it.

My grandmother had tried to teach me about men when I was young. God knows I wasn't interested at that age, but she felt it was her job to teach me all things womanly after my mother died. In her mind that meant cooking, cleaning, and men. She used to say to me, *Nina, don't be too picky about men. No one is perfect. As long as he doesn't drink, gamble, or fool around.* Real romantic. I guess she followed her own advice. As far as I know, while she was alive, my grandfather never gambled, fooled around, or drank to excess. But he sure made up for it after she died.

My main experience with members of the opposite sex was falling for the type who didn't know I was alive. I'd worship them silently for a while, but once I was interested, I couldn't let go. I'd trail behind them like a lost puppy whether they noticed me or not. It was almost better if they completely ignored me; I'd eventually give up. But when they gave me a little bit to go on, they had me hook, line, and sinker. Then they'd drag me around until I was bruised and bloody. Sometimes they seemed to make a game of how much I'd take before they'd walk.

Why did I stick around when they gave me such a hard time? I couldn't figure myself out. In the rest of my life, I was cool, collected, unflappable. Give me a full bar at happy hour, fifty feet long and three deep with thirsty customers, and they'd have full drinks in one hand and be tossing me tips with the other in no time, no wait, no sweat. Walk me into an audition in front of the most famous director and ask me to sing eight bars, dance a time step, and wiggle my ears—no problem. I wouldn't even blink. Spelling bees, track meets, speeches—I was great in front of an audience, always willing to bare my soul for the chance to get some attention. Just don't stick me in a small dark room alone; that's when my imagination runs in the wrong direction. And don't put me next to a gorgeous guy with sultry eyes and a knack for ignoring me. Then I'm done.

Joey Vickery in the third grade was the first. He was dirty blond and rakish for an eight-year-old. I used to skate down to his block and hang around while he played with the other boys. I'd sit on his front stoop while they threw a ball or chased each other around on their bikes. He never even acknowledged my existence. One fall day I rolled up just as they were splitting into two teams to play touch football in the street. They were one person short to make it even.

"I'll play." The audacity—I knew nothing about football. As much of a sports fan as my mother was, football was the one sport she never watched. She found it unnecessarily violent.

"Do you know how to play football?" Joey asked.

"Of course," I scoffed, my heart racing.

"Okay, then, what's a first down?"

I took the briefest of pauses as I heard myself start to sweat. "Well, it's when the ball hits the ground the first time, of course." My heart paused waiting for his answer.

"Okay, you can play."

I couldn't believe it. Boy, could I think on my feet! At that moment I felt I could probably guess my way through anything—a skill I was to rely on most of my school years and beyond, come to think of it. Guessing/lying/pretending is acting.

Joey moved away after sixth grade, and I never saw him again. But every time I pictured that crooked smile and that straight dirty-blond hair falling over his green eyes, I still went weak in the knees. Come to think of it, that's who Detective Lopez's smile reminded me of. Detective Lopez had dark eyes instead of green, but they had something in common. Something in the smile. Something behind the eyes. It was poison elixir deluxe. I should keep away from Detective Lopez if I knew what was good for me. But I wouldn't have to worry about that. Detectives Lopez and Barry had certainly forgotten all about me.

I turned the channel on the radio and caught a Blondie song in process, Debbie Harry bemoaning her bad luck with romance.

I finished putting on some plum-colored lipstick and gave my cheeks another swipe of powdered blush. *Yeah, that's me,*

"Heart of Glass." Things had only gotten worse in high school. Every time I looked for love, it didn't end well. My experiences had taught me only one thing: Nothing worked, so why try? I was on a break for now. Like Blondie, I would find my life pleasing in between relationships.

I took a final look in the mirror at the results of my efforts. I was no makeup artist. It would have to do. I skipped the skates, since I was in a dress, and got myself out the door.

By ten AM, I was hurrying down the last block. The line wasn't too bad. I scanned the crowd as I looked for Marissa. The casting call had been for ethnic-looking females in their twenties. There were probably three hundred people already waiting, all similar to me. All had dark hair, some long and wavy like mine, some short and curly, and everything in between. How would I distinguish myself in this homogenous group? My arrival went unnoticed by my near twin sisters in front of me.

I didn't see Marissa, so I got on the end of the line and opened *The New York Times* to the international news. According to them, Iran seemed about to explode. Ayatollah Khomeini and his Islamic Revolutionaries (sounded like the name of a punk rock band) had announced that if any newspaper articles were written against the Islamic Revolution or the government, the journalists would be prosecuted. (Beheaded?) I looked up from the bad news to see that the line was growing quickly behind me. I estimated that there would be over a thousand hopeful dark-haired actresses before noon.

"Hey, Esposito, did you save me a spot?" Marissa came sidling up to me. The dozen women who had gotten on the line behind me gave us half-hearted glares at Marissa cutting in, but no one spoke up.

"Hey, you look fresh and ready for anything." I already felt wilted from the heat.

"Thanks." Marissa looked around. "What a crowd. We're going to be here for a while. Can I have a section of the paper?"

I gave her half, and she buried her head in it. Marissa had chosen a miniskirt and peasant blouse, and with her shoulder-length curls parted in the middle, she looked like Jennifer Jones from some fifties western. She was smart, talented, and hardworking, plus she was three inches taller than I was. She was going to get somewhere in spite of the odds.

The line started to move a little. It was too early to think they were letting us in. They were probably just consolidating us so we took up less space. The art of corralling. I turned to the Metro section and folded my newspaper the long way like a pro. And then, there it was: not in the gossipy *Post* or the gritty *Daily News*, but apparently it was included in "All the news that's fit to print," right there in the *Times* on page three.

Murdered Twenty-Year-Old Actress Attended
The Studio in Greenwich Village

CHAPTER 8

"Marissa."

"Hmm?" She was deep into the Arts section. I put the page in front of her eyes. She read the headline.

"Why do they mention The Studio?" She lowered her paper.

"You tell me." I scanned the article. Marissa poked her head closer to the paper to read along with me.

"Do they mean someone at The Studio had something to do with her death?"

The Studio. Where we had class in a few hours. Where Ron Meyers had been Jessica's teacher and was still ours. My mind spun.

"Last night you said maybe Ron could be the murderer."

Marissa took the paper from me. "Come on. I wasn't serious. They don't mention a suspect. And didn't you say there was another murder the week before?"

"Two weeks, but—"

"There's nothing about that here." Marissa handed me the paper. "If *The New York Times* isn't linking the two murders, they must not be connected. It's not a serial killer, Nina."

But that familiar description was right there in black and white: approximately five foot tall, dark hair, aspiring actress. Just like the other one. I lowered the paper and looked at the hundreds of other dark-haired, ethnic New York actresses. Some had hair down to their waist, some had a short bob; some were voluptuous, while others looked like they weren't getting enough to eat, as my grandmother would say. But we could all easily have been sisters. We were as distinct from each other as a litter of white rabbits.

The similarities between the two murdered women, out of the hundreds of murders so far this year, was probably a coincidence rather than a pattern. I was just one of seven million people minding my own business, right?

I wasn't doing a very good job of convincing myself. I turned back to the article. It was a little more specific on the cause of death.

"Broken neck, it says." I pointed to the paper. "This guy Charlie at the bar said the cops told him Jessica had a twisted neck. Is that the same thing? I thought that meant strangled. That first girl, Teresa, they did say broken neck. Maybe they aren't connected, but maybe they are. Is that the same MO?"

"Same MO. Who are you now, Columbo?" Marissa went back to reading the Arts section. She wasn't worried. Cold sweat trickled between my shoulder blades. How could she just shrug it off?

"Marissa."

"What?"

"Doesn't it bother you?"

"What?"

"That The Studio might be connected to the murders." I elbowed her. She wasn't even looking up from the paper.

"Stop freaking out already. Why is it your business? You're making a big deal out of nothing."

Was I? Probably none of these other girls waiting to be discovered had even heard about Teresa or Jessica. They were all just going about their business. I should do the same, blend in with the crowd, embrace anonymity, invisibility. It was good advice. I just had to take it.

Eventually we all paraded by the panel of experts and flashed our pearly whites. I didn't know how they decided who to choose for callbacks. We were all so similar. When you advertised for young ethnic women, that's what you got. Okay, some were taller than I was, big deal. Anyway, they didn't tap me, or Marissa. Just as well. I had laundry to do.

That night at The Studio everyone was buzzing about Jessica. I tried to ignore it, but I heard the whispers. No matter how I tried to distract myself, I couldn't shake that creepy feeling crawling up the back of my neck. My thoughts drifted to the two detectives. I hadn't liked the way Tom the Cop looked at me, like a dog eyeing a bone. I was used to that from men, but with this cop it was different. It was like there was no meat left and he just wanted to bury me. I preferred to think about Detective Lopez, who was more like a sweet puppy you wanted to scoop up into your arms.

The thoughts of murders and cops distracted me enough during class that it showed in my work. Ron had us do some more improvisations that were less intense than the night before. He paired me with Skinny Larry, who kept giving me this weird evil smile, and I couldn't concentrate. Everything I tried fell flat. Ron was impatient with me, and I couldn't help thinking of him as a suspect now that Marissa had suggested it. *How do I go about this?* I wondered. *Just come out and ask him? "So, Ron, what were you doing last Saturday night?"* Right. At the end of class, I walked out with Janette while Marissa chatted with some of the others.

"You weren't friends with that girl Jessica, were you?" Janette leaned close.

"No. Were you?" I couldn't help looking over my shoulder.

"Me? Hell no, sister, she couldn't be bothered to give me the time of day." She fluffed her Afro.

"She wasn't the friendliest person I ever met," I agreed.

"I never could understand why Ron gave her so much attention. She wasn't that good. Not to speak ill of the dearly departed or anything." Janette paused as if she was going to continue.

"And?"

"And he'll have to pick another victim, now that she's gone," she said.

"Victim?" My voice squeaked.

"Did I say victim?" She gave me a wink. "I meant teacher's pet." Then she moved toward the ladies' room. Ron came out of the classroom, spotted me by the coatrack, and made a beeline in my direction. I froze.

"What was your problem today, Nina?" He pulled on his chin with one elegant hand. "Big difference from yesterday."

"I'm really sorry. I guess I was kind of preoccupied." *Damn, I've blown it.* He could help me with my acting career if he thought I was good enough, but he would ignore me if he thought I was a slacker.

"I see. Well, concentration is something you really need to work on." He looked at me seriously. "You can't be a believable character if you aren't in *that life*. You have to be able to let go of *your life*."

"I'm working on it." *Let go of my life?*

"I'm around if you ever want to talk about it." He casually pulled a card from his wallet and handed it to me. "Call me sometime."

I watched his strong, slim body walk away before I could get any words out of my mouth. Ron Meyers, gorgeous award-winning Broadway actor, had just given me his card. Ron, my hunky acting teacher, gave me his card with his unlisted/personal/private/home-phone number? *Call me sometime*? Did he care about me as an actor? Was he just after a piece of ass? Or was he looking for his next "victim," like Janette said? I stood there like a dope with my mouth open. I didn't even hear Marissa come up behind me.

"Sorry I took so long. I was seeing if anyone had heard anything else about Jessica. Nothing juicy." She searched in her bag, pulled out her lipstick, and applied it to her lips perfectly without a mirror. A rare skill.

"You're positively morbid." I lowered my voice.

"Oh please." She finished her lips and dropped the tube back into her bag. "Aren't you interested?"

"Yes, it's just—" I felt my stomach turn. "If the murderer is connected to this place, I want to know who or what or how, and I want it to stop."

"Okay, Wonder Woman. Let me know if you come up with a plan for that." Marissa was still looking around, distracted, not taking me seriously. "Did I see Ron talking to you?"

"Well, yes." I tried to sound nonchalant. "He did stop to talk with me for a moment. And then he, uh, well, he gave me his phone number."

"Get out of here!" Marissa's eyes popped open.

"Truth." I lifted my right hand in a Girl Scout salute.

"Under what pretense did you ask for it?"

"I didn't ask for it." I was indignant. "He said if I had a concentration problem with my acting, and I needed to talk, I could call him."

"Well, you better watch it, girl." She took my arm and moved us toward the exit. "He chews 'em up and spits 'em out faster than a vendor sells hot dogs at a ball game."

"Thank you for that colorful analogy."

I'd never told Marissa about the teachers I had in high school who'd tried to get a little too close. One got closer than the others.

I was a sophomore, fifteen, in the high school band led by Martin Rudy. He was cool, a talented musician who sported a beatnik goatee and drove a red Alfa Romeo. He was friendly with the students, and we all called him Rudy. He even had parties at his house for us. It wasn't exactly cool to be in the band, but we enjoyed our clique, and for me, hanging out with Rudy was the best part. He treated me like an adult. We had conversations, he actually listened to me, he opened my eyes to new kinds of music, and he took some of us out to try sushi for the first time. Maybe he made me feel like a grown-up, or maybe I just liked being treated like one.

One day I was in one of the small soundproof practice rooms we had near the band room, trying to make a musical sound come out of my clarinet. My mom had played it in school, and when it was time for me to learn an instrument in middle school, my grandmother had given it to me and said it shouldn't go to waste.

I'm not being modest when I say I was not very good. When I practiced at home, my grandfather would complain that I sounded like a dying cow. But I didn't want to give up, so I tried to practice at school as much as possible.

There I was, struggling with the latest piece of music Rudy had given us to learn, when he came into the practice room. I was happy to see him, although I really didn't want him to hear me play without the rest of the band there to drown me out. We talked for a while, I don't remember what about, the bell rang, and I told him I had to get to my next class.

"Don't worry, I'll give you a late pass." He stepped closer to me, and suddenly the room felt airless. He put his arms around me and planted a rough kiss on my mouth. I was too surprised to do anything. Here I was, fifteen and a virgin, being kissed by my thirty-five-year-old favorite teacher. His body was pressed against mine and I felt all of his embrace, if you know what I mean.

"See what you did to me?" He smiled as he looked down at his crotch. I was shocked and horrified, and my fifteen-year-old hormones were confused. I was speechless. The room seemed overly warm and I could barely breathe. He stepped in to kiss me again, and I squeaked out a protest. "I've got to get to class."

He tried to hug me, but I pushed past him toward the door.

"I'll write you that note."

I seemed to be having trouble walking. I couldn't get the door open right away, and I banged my knee on the way out. I wasn't really sure what had just happened. I'd had a schoolgirl crush on him, but I never thought of him sexually. It just hadn't occurred to me. I had looked up to him. I had trusted him. What was I supposed to do now? How did I say no and still go to band practice? I certainly didn't want to say yes. My head was spinning and I couldn't stop shaking. It was novel to me, any attention coming from an adult male; I didn't know how to reject it. Was there a right way?

He wouldn't be the last older man to make moves on me. My high school English and French teachers shot me more than a few leading comments and suggestive looks that I pretended I didn't comprehend. I felt like I was a magnet for that scenario and thought it was my fault somehow. The more it happened, the more ashamed I felt. It always took me by surprise, and each time it broke me apart a little more.

I couldn't stop wondering if it was it me, if I had done something to bring it on. When it came back to me, it was always a double attack, the shame and humiliation of what had happened and my mind telling me I was a bad person.

I began to wonder if all men were like that. I hated to think that my absent father was out there making passes at each young woman he met. When it came to grown men, I couldn't shake the feeling that I was always prey and they were predators.

High school was in my past, but I'd pushed away more than processed those experiences. Ron was talented and attractive, but his attention didn't feel like a good thing. A teacher was a teacher. They should do better.

"What are you going to do?" Marissa took my arm as we walked down Bank Street. "Are you going to call Ron?"

I tossed my hair. I'd play it cool, but I knew I didn't have the guts to call him, and I didn't want to. Why was he interested in me? Was it just that Jessica was no longer around and he needed another doll to play with? Was that how he occupied his time in between Broadway shows?

"Let's go get a drink or something." Marissa gave my arm a hug as we walked. "I don't want to go home just yet."

"Is Dave working?" I slowed as we reach the corner. "We can go to his bar."

"No, he's off tonight, probably at the gym or out with the other kung fu fans. Let's go somewhere else." She turned her face away from me, sounding annoyed. "How about that place you go to around here—what's it called?"

"The Saz? That's not very exciting." I shrugged. "It's just a restaurant with an old man's bar."

"That's okay, it's close, come on."

I'd never brought Marissa to the Sazerac House because it didn't seem to fit—my friendship with her and my time at the Saz. But what was the big deal? If my worlds collided, that would fit right in with all the other insanity whirling around me.

We took our time walking there, going over the lines for our scene for next Monday's class.

Benny was on duty and greeted us with a surprised smile. Cheerful Buckwheat Zydeco music floated softly through the speakers.

"Hey, Benny, this is my friend Marissa Gold." I felt a little hesitant as we settled on barstools.

"Nice to meetcha, Marissa Gold." Benny grabbed the tips of her fingers in a floppy handshake. "What can I get you?"

"I'll have a white wine spritzer, please." She beamed him a bright smile. A little too bright.

"Club soda and bitters for me." I dropped some cash on the bar.

"Per usual." Benny whisked our drinks together in front of us. "What's new?"

"Oh, almost nothing." I reached for my drink. I was suddenly not altogether calm. "But that girl from the alley went to The Studio; she was in my class. And that other girl who was killed a few weeks ago, the paper said she was an actor too."

"That doesn't mean they were killed by the same person." Benny polished the bar in front of us, even though it was already clean.

I jiggled the sip stick in my drink. "One of those detectives I met here the day she was murdered seems to think differently, and he knows more than you."

"Nina." Marissa plunked her drink down on the bar. "You didn't tell me you were here the same day they found Jessica's body."

"Yeah, lucky me." I couldn't bear to tell her I was the one who'd found her.

"What did he say?" Benny stopped polishing.

"Who?" I was confused.

"That cop." Benny leaned toward me, his face serious. "What does that mean, he knows more than me?"

"He's a detective, isn't he?" My face felt hot. "He's on the case, right? He should know more than you do because it's his job. And he said he wouldn't rule out a connection." I couldn't help rolling my eyes in frustration. "The other one asked me questions about The Studio, but I told him I didn't know anything."

"Oh, I thought you meant they had some kind of evidence they were connected." Benny made me another drink, squirting in the soda water from the gun, shaking in the Angostura bitters, the blood-red liquid trickling down until it all turned pink. "Stop getting yourself all excited about it."

"Oh, yeah." I shook my head. "I'm the one getting excited."

Marissa laughed and put her empty glass on the bar.

"So, what are you girls up to tonight, besides causing trouble around here?" Benny refilled Marissa's glass.

I was suddenly out of the mood for small talk, so I leaned back, sipped my drink, and listened to Marissa and Benny chat. Something about how quickly they got along bothered me. Why was I so irked? These were my two best friends and here they were, meeting for the first time. It was a momentous occasion. My emotions didn't make sense to me. Was I afraid Benny and Marissa were going to run off together? *Great, I'll take Dave.* I laughed to myself and Benny looked at me.

"What's so funny?" Benny dropped a couple of cherries into my glass.

"Nothing." I smiled at him and he winked. I just had my crazy moments sometimes. It didn't bother Benny. He was the kind of friend who accepted you for who you were. In spite of my multiple neuroses, it was good to see my two friends hit it off. It was looking like I'd have to work hard to get a word in edgewise.

Just then, Gorgeous Charlie walked in. I saw Marissa's eyes take him in, his soft blond curls, his strong physique. She almost started drooling. *Okay, time to go.* I'd fill Marissa in on Charlie later.

"Hey, Benny, beer please." Charlie turned to us. "Hi, Nina, who's your pretty friend?" He smiled that million-dollar smile.

"Charlie, this is Marissa." I picked up my money off the bar, leaving a generous tip. "Too bad you got here just as we were leaving." I drained my glass and got to my feet.

"What?" Marissa looked at me. I turned my body so Charlie couldn't see my face and raised my eyebrows at Marissa with significance. She didn't pick up on the hint fast enough.

Gorgeous Charlie took her hand and held it firmly in both of his. He looked deep into her eyes and smiled his devilish angel-smile. Marissa was hooked.

"You must be an actress too, am I right?" Charlie practically purred. "So beautiful and talented, I can tell. Do you sing and dance also?"

"Yeah, and she can juggle and do backflips too." I tried to change the tone. Did Charlie like petite dark-haired actresses in particular or just all pretty women? "Marissa, won't Dave worry if you aren't home soon? It's getting late."

I poked my knee into her thigh, and she was finally able to speak.

"Oh, look at the time!" She played along. "It was nice to meet you, Charlie, but if I don't get home to my boyfriend soon, he'll send out a posse for me."

"What a shame." Charlie dropped her hand, but his eyes were still locked on hers. "A beautiful girl like you, already taken. I hope we meet again under better circumstances."

Marissa was still trying to unhook her eyes from his. I was reminded of Kaa the cartoon snake in the Disney animated movie *The Jungle Book*. He would hypnotize his prey by staring at them right in the eyes, and their eyeballs would turn into whirling spirals of red and white. Marissa's eyeballs were still spinning.

"Well, Charlie"—I smacked Marissa on the back to break the spell—"anything is possible." I felt a cold chill. Charlie sure hung around this neighborhood all the time, and he was making eyes at Marissa, a dark-haired actress. I shook my head. Crazy thoughts. It was late. I was just tired.

We escaped to the streetlights and cobblestones of Hudson Street.

"Well, he's a charmer." Marissa gave me a mischievous smile as we walked north.

"If you like snakes." I frowned at her. "Pun intended."

"You'll have to tell me about him sometime." She stepped toward the curb. "Let me get a cab. I'm too tired to walk." The nearby subway didn't go to the East Village, where she lived, and the crosstown busses were too few and far between at night. I was tired myself from standing all day waiting to be discovered and fumbling distractedly in my acting class. Ah, the thrilling life of an aspiring actress. I gave Marissa a hug just before she popped into her taxi.

I didn't have far to go. I'd be home in ten minutes if I walked fast. That is, if I didn't run into any bloody-nosed businessmen or serial killers. What a week. It was enough to make a girl a nervous wreck. I turned on the radio of my portable cassette player to calm my mind. The Crusaders were singing about "Street Life" and how there was nowhere else to go. Yup. As I walked home, my stomach started to growl.

I hadn't been to Maria's in a while. It was a little Mexican place on West Thirteen Street, right on my way home. The idea of soft tacos sounded good to my stomach. The spices might add to my dreams, but a full tummy would put me to sleep faster.

As I entered the restaurant, I stowed my cassette player in my shoulder bag and scanned the bar for a single seat. It was pretty crowded, more than a few people standing around the bar laughing and talking, mostly men. Then I saw that flashing white smile. Tall, dark, and handsome Detective Lopez was standing in the crowd.

Chapter 9

Was Maria's a cop hangout? I'd never noticed that. I looked at all the men standing around the bar—the tall ones, the not-so-tall ones, some plump, some lean, the brown and tan and pink complexioned. Short hair topped them all, and they had the same something in their eyes too. Something hard, yet also vacant in a way. Yeah, that was it for sure: They were all cops. They must've come in together after their shift.

A seat opened up at the bar, and I took it. I ordered two soft tacos with shredded pork and extra pico de gallo. I sipped my club soda, no bitters this time, just plenty of lime to pair with my tacos. I snuck a look at Detective Lopez, wondering if he'd remember me. He caught me looking, and I tried to hide my smile by turning back to my drink. Next thing I knew he was standing close, looking right at me.

"I knew it was you. Find any other bodies lately?"

I felt the heat of his body close to mine, contrasting with the chill of the overly conditioned air. "That is a *really* bad pickup line." I turned to look at him. "Use it often?"

"First time." Even his sheepish smile was sexy.

"I'll let it go." I allowed myself to smile back.

"Seriously." He leaned on the bar next to me. "How are you? It's not something that's easy to put behind you."

"Yeah, I noticed. I guess I'm still a little . . ." I paused.

"Unsettled?"

"Something like that."

"It's Nina, right?" That smile again.

"That's right." I noticed how well his blue NYPD T-shirt fit his body. "I never got your first name, though, Detective Lopez."

"Good memory." He put his beer bottle down next to my club soda.

"Everything about that day is kind of burned into my brain, if you know what I mean." I tried to smile, but the image of that naked leg floated into my brain.

"Sure." His voice was gentle. "Call me Frankie. It's really Francisco, but everyone's called me Frankie since I was a kid."

He had the slightest whisper of an accent that was almost undetectable. There was just something around the *r*'s and the cadence of his speech. I guessed his family had moved here when he was pretty young, maybe six or seven.

"So, is this a cop hangout?"

"When we're hungry for Mexican food, it is." He lifted his bottle of Tecate to his mouth and tipped it back. I swallowed with him. He seemed nice so far, but there had to be a catch—he was a cop. And a guy, for that matter. My tacos arrived and the seat next to mine opened up.

"Mind if I sit down?" He pulled at the barstool.

"Be my guest." I shifted my seat a little. "Do you want a taco?"

"Oh, no thanks. You should've seen the plateful I already put away." His bicep flexed as he rubbed his flat stomach.

I almost lost my appetite—for tacos, that is. But I leaned in and took a bite. The warm spiciness filled my mouth, and my eyes watered with pleasure. My brain responded, *Oh yes, this was a good idea.*

I looked at Frankie while I chewed. Frankie looked back at me.

"You'll have to do the talking until my food gets into my belly." I tried to speak politely around my bite of taco.

He laughed.

That smile, it's going to kill me.

"Well, let's see, I'll tell you a little about myself. I'm twenty-seven, single, and I have my own apartment and a good job with a pension." His eyes twinkled as I laughed around my taco. "I like sports, movies, and good music. Oh, and I'm an excellent dancer."

"And a good salesman."

"Well, you tell me." He leaned on the bar, closer to me. Normally, a man leaning that close to me in a bar would ring alarm bells in my head, but somehow my nervousness melted away.

"Hey, I just came in for the tacos." I wiped my fingers on my napkin. "I wasn't prepared for a pitch."

"No pitch." He put his hand on his heart. "Just telling you a little about myself. Your turn."

I pushed my empty taco plate away and dabbed at my lips with the paper napkin. "Well, I'm younger than twenty-seven, single, and I have my own apartment and a crappy bartending job with no pension." I raised one eyebrow at him. "I like sports, movies, and good music. Oh, and I'm an excellent dancer."

"What a coincidence." He tried to contain his enthusiasm. He was unsuccessful. I'd beat him easy at a hand of poker. "I don't suppose you were born in Puerto Rico and have four brothers and sisters?"

"You got me there." I swirled the last of the soda in my glass. "I was born in Brooklyn, and I have no brothers or sisters. In fact, at this point, I have no family whatsoever." I stopped short in surprise. Why had I blurted that out? I usually didn't offer that information, especially to someone I hardly knew. I let the last of my soda slide down my throat.

"Let me buy you a drink." Frankie moved both our empty glasses to the edge of the bar to signal the bartender.

"I should probably get home." My flirting bravado had evaporated into thin air.

"Wait, don't go. I haven't told you my life story yet." He touched my arm to stop me. His hand felt warm, his skin rough.

"I'll have to hear all about it on another night." I spoke softly. He took his hand off my arm, but I still felt the warmth of his fingers. His face was understanding. How could I talk to this guy without thinking about dead bodies?

"So maybe I can call you sometime?" His tone was puppy-dog purity.

I thought for a second or two. "Why don't you give me your phone number?"

He looked surprised, but quickly recovered and asked the bartender for a pen. He wrote the number on a bar napkin and folded it before he handed it to me. I took it from him and slipped it into my purse, pulled some cash out of my wallet, counted it out, and piled it on my bar tab.

"Before you go, do you mind if I ask you a question?" he asked. "About the other day?" I waited. "In the Sazerac House, you mentioned the earlier murder, Teresa Torres, and you asked if they were connected."

"Yes, I remember."

"What made you think that?" He looked seriously interested in my opinion. This was no pickup plan.

"Well, they were both actors, both dark haired, neither were tall. Maybe I wouldn't have noticed if all three of those details weren't a bit too familiar to me personally, if you know what I mean."

"Yeah, I know what you mean." He looked at me with those eyes.

"I don't know if you have any evidence that points to them being connected, like if they were killed exactly the same way—"

"I can't discuss those kinds of details."

"I get it." I looked at him. Was he more interested in trying to solve these two murders than his partner?

"My partner doesn't think the two deaths are related. Or he doesn't want to. But I think they're too similar to be a coincidence."

"It's not a coincidence, it's a pattern. Someone has killed two short dark-haired actresses that hang around the West Village." My face showed how I felt about that. "And what's next?"

"Don't let it worry you." Frankie shifted closer. "Statistically—"

"Don't give me statistics. If I believed in statistics, I wouldn't have gone into acting."

His face changed from serious to amused. "An optimist, huh?"

"Not really. I'm more of a . . . truculent contrarian."

His laugh was full, and it vibrated deep. A man who got my sense of humor—now that was sexy. But I wasn't completely joking. My mother had believed in statistics, and that didn't stop her from being the one in seven million to die in a freak accident that day. I pulled my purse toward me and stood.

"It was nice running into you." I felt my Sunday school manners surface.

"I hope I'll see you soon." He touched my arm again.

"Well, I've got that life story to look forward to." I hoped there was no sarcasm inferred. It would be easy to listen to him talk all night long. He walked me to the door, some of his cop friends yelling after him.

"Hey, Frankie, where're you goin'?"

"Yo, Frankie, it's early!"

He laughed them off. I wanted him to give me a big hug before I left, let him knock the breath out of me, give me a reason to feel the dizziness I already felt around him. But I knew the trouble I'd be in if that happened. One hug would lead to more than I could handle at the moment. I'd have no defenses. I was better off keeping my distance from any man for the time being. Especially Detective Frankie Lopez.

I waved as I slipped out the door. He raised his hand and stood watching me through the glass as I walked down the street. It'd been a while since I'd had a date, but I wasn't looking for one anytime soon.

The thing is, I'd never found any evidence that romantic relationships were a good thing. My grandmother had tried to teach me that any marriage was better than being alone, but I knew she was wrong. She fought night and day with my grandfather. I was always trying to stay out of the fray. I figured that was why my mom had me on her own. *Fighting is a waste of time,* she used to tell me. *There's no point in expelling all that energy; there's too much to do as it is.* My grandmother seemed to thrive on arguments. Maybe it was the only exercise she got. She taught me a lot, both in what she told me and what she showed me.

When I moved in with my grandparents, I was left with a strange feeling of impermanence. I'd spent many weekends with them before my mother died, and after I moved there, I would wake up each morning and think, *This is the day I go home.* Then the sleepy fog in my head would clear and I would cry a bit before getting out of bed.

Nights in that bed were a mix of sleeplessness and surreal nightmares. It had been years since I believed in monsters, but I had other fears to keep me awake: the pictures in my head of my mother lying in that hospital bed and then in her coffin, the silence of my grandparents' house at night broken by their sudden fights, the thoughts of what terrible things might happen to my grandparents and the question of who would take care of me then. I had already learned that fears came true.

My grandmother took care of me after my mother died, until I had to take care of her at the end of her cancer. It was a horrible thing to go through at thirteen, but I didn't have a choice. I sat with her every moment I could. At the very end, my grandmother died alone in the hospital while I was at school. My grandfather was useless during that time. He didn't know what to do with Grandma while she was sick, and after she was gone, he didn't know what to do with me. Nothing could have prepared me for his decline or the travesty called high school.

That night after Maria's, lying in bed, I kept seeing Frankie's face. What a sweet one it was, not to mention the rest of him. Sleep wasn't coming, and my thoughts couldn't help drifting to my own personal romantic history.

School fell apart for me after Rudy started on me. Nothing about it was good anymore, and my previously good grades were in the toilet. Rudy's passes became more and more frequent and serious in my senior year. I was becoming more disgusted. Every time he approached me, I felt sick, but somehow I couldn't tell him to go jump in a lake; I just squirmed out of his grasp. I tried to avoid him, but sometimes he would get me before I could escape. He probably told himself I was playing hard to get.

I tried to keep out of situations where he could get me alone, but one day he caught me at my locker after school. I was getting my gym things to go to track practice. My locker was at the end of a hallway, and the corridor was deserted. He seemed to pop up out of nowhere.

"Hi, Nina, where have you been lately?" Rudy said.

"Just busy with schoolwork and stuff." Before his advances, I had been in the band room every free second. "I gotta get to track practice."

"Wait, I'll walk you." What could I say? It was a free country. "Nina, I miss seeing you outside of band practice."

"I—" Suddenly he pulled me into an empty classroom. I was up against the wall and he was pressing his mouth against mine, and his body had me pinned to the wall so I couldn't take a breath. My hands were full with my book bag and gym stuff, and I didn't want to drop them because I wanted to get out of there without having to stop and pick them up. But that made it harder to fight back. I don't know why I was so hyperlogical in that situation. I should've just dropped everything, pushed him off, and run, but I was paralyzed.

I finally squirmed, rolled, wiggled, and got away from him. Bright red and breathless, I scuttled out of the classroom and ran down the hall. He called out my name and laughed, like I was being silly and he hadn't done anything wrong. I got myself to track practice, but I have no idea what I did or how. I just wanted to run and sweat and then take a good hot shower.

Now I tossed and turned in my bed until the sheet tangled itself around my legs. Thinking about Frankie had started out sweet, but it made my mind drift to the wrong things. How could I go out with Frankie when all my experiences had been so messed up? What was the point? Who needed romance? Or sleep, for that matter. I gave up on both for the night, turned on my reading lamp, and reached for my book, *The World According to Garp* by John Irving. It was the second time I was reading it, because I could count on it to quickly take me out of my world when I needed it.

The alarm woke me on Wednesday, and in a hazy consciousness I imagined what it might be like to live somewhere else. Part of my acting training, I told myself, but who was I trying to fool? I'd done it since I was a kid. I pretended I lived with the imagined version of my father, in California or Kansas or Paris, France. Of course, anything I knew about these places I learned from books or movies. California was Disney's version, the one in *The Absent-Minded Professor* or *The Love Bug*. Kansas was pure *Wizard of Oz*, complete with dust-bowl tornados. Paris was more *Madeline* than anything else.

That particular morning, I was in a small Southern town, waking to the smell of pancakes. My dad was cooking for me. I could hear him call out *Time to get up, sleepyhead!* It was Saturday, and we were going fishing together (*To Kill a Mockingbird* meets *Tom Sawyer*). My nose took in the fragrance of the pancakes, which was real but coming from the greasy spoon on the corner.

Oddly, I could conjure my father at any place and any time, and I'd never even met him. Yet my mother, whom I'd known for eight formative years, eluded me. I could recall memories, of course, but any imagined fantasy seemed blocked from my grasp. She could not exist outside of what was so concretely real. It made my heart ache.

But it was late. I had to get to work.

Skates strapped on, I sped across town. At one point I rolled across Eighth Avenue and made a quick swerve to avoid getting hit by a taxi taking a turn. Skates weren't more dangerous than walking, despite popular opinion; I could get out of the way faster on wheels. Both my mother and my grandmother used to say, *Don't take any chances. It's not worth it. Be careful and don't get in any risky situations.* It was some kind of family mantra. Every time I left the house, it was the same thing: *Be careful, don't take any risks.*

It didn't do my mother any good. Had she taken a risk by walking down the street? Apparently, but how could she have known? What risk had Jessica taken before she met her killer? Or Teresa? What precautions did I have to take so I didn't end up like them? Today I would just assume the killer wouldn't wander above Fourteenth Street. If only I could prove that the two murders were connected. That might spark some fire in Tom the Cop.

On Wednesdays my shift at work was ten AM to eight PM, the mid shift. I caught the lunch, happy hour, and early dinner tips at The Realm. Weekdays were different than Saturdays. I had my regular salesmen in for lunch and happy hour, nice middle-aged family men with wives and kids in the suburbs. Quite a change from the people who frequented my grandfather's place in Brooklyn. My salesmen wore suits every day and overcoats in the winter. In the summer, they didn't take off their jackets or roll up their sleeves. Their ties came in beautiful colors and patterns and they mainly talked business, although, like my Brooklyn customers, they liked to talk sports. I kept up with them there. They appreciated it when I updated them on the play-by-play from the night before.

I got to work a bit early, dressed in navy capri pants and a blousy paisley top, and started setting up. Cart the ice, cut the fruit, polish the bar. My lunch crowd treated me well. Only rarely did we get the lowbrow in The Realm. Maybe it was the name that kept them out.

Working for a living could be worse. Four shifts a week was enough to pay the rent, keep my refrigerator from getting empty, and let me put a little money in the bank.

Two waiters worked my shift, and they couldn't have been more different. Sam was almost sixty, grandfatherly in the classic sense, nothing like my own grandfather. He was a good person, always helpful but a little slow on the uptake. Matt was as quick as lightning and always working some angle. He was in his mid-twenties and thought the world owed him a living.

After the lunch rush, Sam and Matt sat at the bar, eating sandwiches and counting their tips. They traded in all their singles and coins to me for the bar register and gave me my percentage for making their drinks at the service bar. I got myself a plate of salad topped with a warm piece of breaded chicken cutlet and sat at the bar with them, close to the service opening. I didn't really get a formal lunch break, but I had no customers at the moment. I'd just have to jump up if someone walked in.

"When my wife makes a sandwich like this, she toasts the roll evenly, and she makes this pesto mayo that goes perfect with the arugula." Sam took another bite. "And her chicken cutlet is never dry. When we open our restaurant, that's going to be the best-selling sandwich for sure."

I pictured that for a moment, Sam and his wife running a restaurant. They'd have to call it the Molasses Café. Sam was slow enough, but I'd met his wife and she made him look like the Road Runner.

Now Matt, he was always thinking, usually out loud. But today he was quiet as he ate his lunch. He was busy filling out American Express applications, occasionally pausing to scratch his head with the end of his pen.

"Hey, Matty." I looked over at him. "What're you doing?"

"Applying for credit cards." He kept his eyes on the paperwork.

"How many do you need?" He had at least six applications in front of him.

"Well, if you keep filling them out, they eventually approve you, and sometimes you get more than one." He flipped over an application to fill out the second side.

"You using your real name on all of those?" I bit down on the last perfect forkful of cutlet and arugula laced with balsamic vinegar.

"Don't ask stupid questions." He shot me a dark look.

"Gee, someone once told me there were no stupid questions, only stupid answers." I got up, clearing my empty plate and his. He mumbled something rude. Some people just didn't get my sense of humor.

Nick came to the bar and sat in the first barstool by the service area that I had just vacated.

"Nina, honey, can I get a club soda?"

"Sure, Nick, honey." I wasn't so much sarcastic as teasing. He could walk behind the bar himself; he knew his way around a soda gun. But some men just loved to be waited on, especially by women. Well, that's what I was there for, to wait. I poured him his "two-cent plain," as my grandfather used to call it, and put it in front of him on the bar. Nick opened his *New York Post* flat on the bar, turned a page, and then paused, his hand in midair, his eyes wide open.

"Holy shit, Nina, what's your picture doing in the *Post*!"

Chapter 10

"What?" I almost lost my grip on the glass I was filling, soda water squirting across the dark-wood bar.

Nick put his hand on the newspaper page and leaned closer in the dim light.

"Oh, that's not you. It's that girl that got murdered in the Village the other day." He gave a weasel-like laugh and pointed at the black-and-white picture. "I sure thought it was you for a minute. You two could be twins."

"Hilarious." Cleaning up the soda with a bar rag, I felt my hands go cold. I wanted to read the article to see if there was anything new, but I couldn't see it without getting closer to him, and that was hardly worth it.

Matty leaned closer to Nick to see the paper.

"Shit, Nina, Nick is right. That dead chick is a dead ringer for you." He smiled maliciously. "Get it? Dead ringer." His guffaw was obnoxious. My return smile was one of indifferent condescension, but my hands were clutched together just under the bar top. Nick and Matty were still peering over the paper when Amir, the bus boy, slipped over to the service bar with a rack of freshly washed glasses from the kitchen. He set it gently on the bar, glancing at the paper.

"Hey, Amir, doesn't this picture look just like Nina?" Matty pointed at the paper.

"What, that picture?" Amir shook his head. "Just because they both have long brown hair and brown eyes? Look at the eyebrows, too thin, and that nose is wider than Nina's, and her lips are too skinny."

I smiled appreciatively at Amir, reached for some of the clean glasses, and put them carefully on the side bar. Amir worked quickly with me to empty the rack.

"Wait, don't you take classes at The Studio?" Nick turned to me. I knew where he was leading. Amir put the last glasses on the bar and escaped with the empty rack.

"Yeah, I take classes at The Studio."

"It says this girl went there. Before she died, anyway." He slurped his soda loudly. "Did you know her?"

"A little bit."

"The paper said she studied with that Broadway actor Ron Meyers," Nick continued. "Did you have a class with him?"

"Yeah, I'm in his class." I stopped sorting highball glasses. "Why did they mention his name?" Apparently, the newspapers weren't letting go of the story. In fact, now they were adding Ron and The Studio into the drama.

"I don't know," Nick said. "Sells more newspapers, I guess. Famous actor knew dead actress."

"Yeah, I guess."

"Pretty gruesome murder, huh?" Matt sure was cheerful about it.

"Yeah, gruesome is a good word for it," I said.

Nicky pulled Matt to one side. "Matty," Nick said, lowering his voice. "You going to the union meeting later?"

"Yeah, boss, I told you I would." Matt looked uncomfortable for a moment but then found his swagger. "I been spreading the word about the vote. I got a lot of guys on our side. They get what the benefits are if our guy wins."

Nick gave him a literal pat on the back. "Good boy, Matty, your help won't go unnoticed."

Matt disappeared into the dining room. I knew better than to ask what they were talking about. I had never been encouraged to join the restaurant workers union. They only seemed to recruit the male bartenders and waiters. The Realm paid me under the table, and that was okay with me; I wasn't planning on being there forever, and with the politics involved, it wasn't worth it. The union leadership names I'd heard mentioned were associated with the Tommy Ryans of New York. Since they'd succeeded in taking over the gambling, prostitution, and drugs, they moved on to labor unions and construction businesses. I just hoped they wouldn't take over the Broadway theater trade by the time I got my foot in the door.

Nick closed his newspaper, moving some air in my direction, and I caught a rank smell of garbage from his soul. "Well, I hope you're being careful down there in the Village." Nick got up and stowed his newspaper under his arm. "It's a crazy neighborhood."

"Yeah, cra-a-azy." I waggled my open palms up in the air like a dancer right out of vaudeville. I was curious to know if there was any new information about the murders in the article, but I stopped short of asking Nick for his paper.

The front door pushed open with a little burst of noise from the street, giving me a start. Enter Bill and Robert.

Robert was a veteran designer of necktie fabric. He always wore the most beautiful ties, gorgeous colors with intricate patterns. Lingerie salesman Bill put his folded copy of the *Post* on the bar.

"Good afternoon, gentlemen." I pasted on a smile. "Beefeater martini on the rocks, Robert? Bill, Dewar's and soda?" They nodded. "Late for lunch, isn't it?" It was almost three thirty.

"I ate already," Robert said, "but I'm starting happy hour early."

"I skipped lunch today," Bill said, "and I'm starting my weekend very early. Taking the rest of the week off. I'm going to jump on the train home to Connecticut in about an hour."

I put the drinks down in front of them.

Robert pulled out some cash. "I got it. Cheers." They tipped their drinks back, and I rang up the sale.

"Oh, Nina." Bill called me back. "I almost forgot—I have a sample for you. Size four, right?"

He stood and, not unlike a professional magician, pulled a long stream of pale-peach silk out of his jacket pocket. It was a negligee, spaghetti straps, lace details. I'd never seen anything so elegant.

"Wow, Bill, it's gorgeous." I held it high with one hand, feeling the silky fabric with the other. "Thank you."

"Oh, it's nothing." He picked up his drink. "You're the only size four I know. If my wife was smaller, she'd get a lot more samples. Enjoy it."

He went back to discussing the garment business with Robert. The salesmen often gave me samples as extra tips.

They knew all my sizes—bra, panty, and negligee. None of them were shy about it; it was their business. I was the only female employee at The Realm, so I reaped the benefits.

I folded the negligee neatly and put it in my bag down by my skates. It was normal to give out samples, but I still felt embarrassed when my customers gave them to me. At first, I thought it was kind of creepy. Undergarments were personal, even if it was everyday business for them. And these were all men; not a single saleswoman in the garment industry had come into the bar, if they existed. I was still trying to brush away the feeling that they had an ulterior motive or that I owed them something when they gave me a gift.

My world had been full of men who believed in that kind of quid pro quo, and it was an adjustment to experience people just being nice. The lingerie samples were my customers' way of tipping, and so far, the gifts seemed free from strings, spaghetti straps excluded. They didn't seem to want anything except the service-with-a-smile I always give them. I didn't know if I'd ever be able to trust it. I appreciated the samples, but taking them raised my anxiety in a physical way, like wearing a scratchy wool sweater in the heat of the summer.

I noticed Bill's newspaper on the bar. It was double folded to the page he'd been reading, and when I moved it to place bowls of peanuts and pretzels near the salesmen, the newspaper flopped open flat.

ASPIRING ACTRESS GRUESOMELY
MURDERED IN GREENWICH VILLAGE

My breath froze in my lungs. The half-page picture of Jessica's face was indeed chillingly similar to my own, even more so than in person, something about the angle of the camera. Her long dark hair was parted in the middle, like mine always was, and she had wide dark eyes like mine. Bill reached for his paper.

"Oh, wait, did you see this, Nina? This girl reminded me of you." He turned it so Robert could see it.

"Yeah, I see what you mean," Robert mused. "But our Nina's prettier." He winked at me. It was an innocent gesture, but I flinched inwardly.

"Prettier than a dead girl? Thanks, Robert. I'll put that on my résumé." They chuckled and returned to their conversation. My words were false nonchalance, my hands less than steady as I casually lifted the newspaper and leaned against the back bar to scan the article. Jessica Roman . . . broken neck . . . Greenwich Village . . . The Studio . . . Ron Meyers . . . no suspects. They rehashed the details I already knew, but as usual for the *Post*, they made it more sensational.

Robert and Bill finished their early happy hour. Mike, the night bartender, joined me, and the dinner rush pushed through. I barely had time to gulp down some dinner for myself. Busy was good. Busy stopped me from thinking bad thoughts. My mind was full of drink orders, the latest sports, and ringing up the right amount of cash. That was the way I liked it.

Near the end of my shift, Mike served the customers so I could finish closing out the register and focus on stocking the bar. I was leaning under the bar, pushing a few extra bottles of beer into the ice sink. I heard him before I saw him.

"Hey, gorgeous."

It wasn't my favorite line. Beauty is only skin deep and all that. I stood up. Cousin Bobby sat at the bar right in front of me.

"Hey, gorgeous yourself." I put a cocktail napkin in front of him. Of course, in my case, I meant it as an insult to his intelligence. But he wouldn't get that. "Cutty Sark?"

"Sure, if I have time for one before you get off."

I knew he was implying he wanted to leave with me, but I didn't acknowledge it. Was Cousin Bobby too far from Greenwich Village to make my suspects list? The first time I met him, he said he had dated actresses who went to The Studio. I just poured his drink and placed it in front of him. Nick appeared at that moment.

"Hey, Bobby, I didn't know you were coming in after the union meeting. How did the vote go?"

"It was a lock. Everything went as planned. I just stopped in for one celebration drink." Bobby broke his eye contact with me to give Nick a cousin-hug. "How's business?"

"Typical Wednesday, right, Nina?" Nicky took the tab I'd started for Bobby and put it in his pocket.

"Right, Nicky." I turned to get my split of the dinner tips from Mike.

"Nina."

I turned back to face Bobby as he lit a Marlboro Red with his gold lighter and blew smoke to one side.

"Are you doing anything tonight?" Bobby had decided to be more direct. I already had my answer. The last thing I was going to do was let this guy get me alone. Killer or not, he was deadly.

"I'm seeing *Apocalypse Now* at nine. It just opened today. I already have my ticket."

"What's that, a movie?" If Bobby did not know that Francis Ford Coppola had a new movie out, he would never be the guy for me. Not like I thought there was a chance.

"Yeah, it's a new movie." I tried not to sound patronizing. "Maybe you've heard of the director, Francis Ford Coppola? He directed *The Godfather.*"

"Oh, yeah, I saw that movie." Bobby looked peeved for a moment. "It was interesting. Too bad you're busy; I thought you might be free for dinner." Bobby's sexy smile came back. "I guess I need to make an appointment. How about this Saturday?"

"Well, Bobby, actually." I planted my feet in a wide stance as I crossed my arms. "I have a rule that I don't date customers. So, if I went out with you, then you wouldn't be able to come in here anymore, which would be tough on Nicky. I know he likes seeing you."

I dropped into a squat under the bar to get my purse and to stash my tips in my wallet.

"It would be tough on me too." His voice hardened. "Since I'm one of the owners."

I almost raked my forehead on the edge of the bar as I popped up from my crouched position. Bobby lifted his chin as he drained his glass. I knew that The Realm was owned by several partners, but Nicky hadn't mentioned that Bobby was one of them. It would've been nice if he had slipped me that information.

"Well, that's worse." I let my frozen smile melt to a pout. "I could never date a boss; that would just be too complicated."

"Or it could be smart." Bobby smiled that dangerous smile. I wasn't sure if he meant that as a tip or a threat. I reached under the bar for my skates and swung them over my shoulder by the laces.

"Well, I better get skating, or I'm going to miss the beginning of the movie." I made my way out from behind the bar. He touched my shoulder.

"I guess I'll see you around."

"I guess so, boss." I produced my employee-of-the-month smile. "Have a good night." I escaped into the warm night.

I rolled to the Ziegfeld Theater with my thoughts of the day, the newspaper story of those murders and the picture of Jessica still swimming in and out of my consciousness. Bobby, Nicky's cousin, my boss, still giving me the creeps—it made me tired in body and mind. I was relieved I'd escaped Cousin Bobby, but why was he so focused on me? There were plenty of girls around. Nicky had said that Bobby "really liked actresses." Should Bobby really be on my list of suspects, or was I being paranoid? All these months I'd been working at The Realm, and Bobby hadn't shown up once. Why was he hanging around now? The timing was disturbing.

The crowd outside the Ziegfeld Theater surprised me. I knew it was opening day and Francis Ford Coppola was a big deal, but I'd never witnessed this kind of frenzy. There were masses of people waiting to go in, but also fans and press and the usual New York extras that took advantage of such a situation. Musicians playing, beggars asking for spare change, people selling flashlights, key chains, and of course pot and other illegal substances. It was a veritable carnival. Federico Fellini would've appreciated it. I leaned against a building to take my skates off and put on my sandals before I got too far into the fray.

I had to push my way through the throng on the sidewalk to get to the line. The crowd was thick, and I was too short to see above anyone. My lungs felt tight as I got bumped around. It was as if no one could see I was there at all. The faces were dark and strange, and maybe it was my imagination, but they seemed to turn mean and threatening. Then I thought I saw Black Net Shirt Guy, his curly hair framing that round face, slipping through the crowd. Was he following me again? I forged ahead and wove quickly between a group of taller guys near the line. I looked back—had I lost him?

The crowd was pushing, and suddenly I was being thrown off balance. I felt myself falling, my feet slipping out from under me. Everything spun around; I was being pulled under by a human wave. I surprised a stranger by grabbing his arm. He looked annoyed, but it saved me from getting trampled. I finally got myself into the line, which was a bit more civilized. I was too small to contend with a strong current. This was the last time I'd go to a movie on opening night by myself. I should've invited Benny. I didn't like thinking I needed a big strong guy around to protect me, but five foot is as five foot does.

The line moved quickly, and I knew the good seats would go fast. But it wasn't too hard to grab a single seat in a good spot. I was just a few rows in front of where I'd sat for *Dracula* and right smack in the middle. It was a little close, even for me, but I'd rather be too close than too far back. It was all about immersion.

The mood started right away. I was in it, on the edge of my seat and my sanity. I was glad I hadn't had the chance to buy popcorn, because my stomach was in a twist the whole time. The movie was both fascinating and horrifying. The director's point was clear, but in my case, he was preaching to the choir. You didn't have to convince me that war—violence, power, paranoia, death, destruction, danger—made people insane. But it all came down to one thing: fear. That's why we went into war in the first place. Fear of people who weren't like us, fear of losing something like land or resources or control. War might cause the most intense fear of death while being the biggest cause of death itself at the same time.

But it wasn't the only place death waited. Death was always around as far as I was concerned: violence, freak accidents, and lately, lurking in the guise of a serial killer in Greenwich Village. My own list of potential suspects was growing, and Detective Frankie Lopez had agreed that the two murders could be linked.

After the movie I followed the crowd outside. Everyone was much quieter than they had been on the way in. Zombie-like, even. I swung my skates over my shoulder and headed for the subway. A lot of people avoid the subway late at night, but a midnight ride for a few stops was no big deal to me compared to the hell I'd just witnessed on the screen. Having seen *Apocalypse Now* in the Ziegfeld Theater, I felt like I'd just survived a war.

The graffiti-covered train arrived, and I sat across from a big burly guy with puffs of chest hair peeking around the edges of his tank top. He had his boom box with him, not blasting too loud, but we could all hear his choice of music. That was the point, wasn't it? The boom box gave the voiceless a voice.

I watched the cassette tape rolling as "Psycho Killer" by the Talking Heads played and David Byrne sang about being tense and nervous and a live wire. The lyrics hit too close to home at the moment. Was there a psycho killer on the loose in Greenwich Village? Black Net Shirt Guy? Cousin Bobby? My teacher Ron? Marissa's Dave? Skinny Larry? Gorgeous Charlie? How could I find something that would be useful to the detectives? Ask anyone on my list of suspects what they were doing last Saturday night? Follow them all next Saturday night? I sat with my elbows on my knees, chin in my hands, looking down at my skates as I rolled them between my sandaled feet. I was wired for sure. How was I going to get to sleep?

I realized what really pissed me off was dealing with Bobby. In the movie, when Captain Williard left Kurtz's hut, all the villagers knelt down as he came out. It reminded me of *The Wizard of Oz*. When Dorothy melted the witch, she assumed the guards would kill her, but they honored her instead. So why were they working for the witch? Did they bow down to the people they feared just so they wouldn't be targets themselves, then, when the danger was gone, admit they'd been against it all along? Was that cowardice or intelligence? Bobby was a bully and I hated bullies, but should I play along? It was the smart move. But not if he tried to take it too far.

My grandfather was the last person I ever obeyed out of fear. I sure wasn't going to let Cousin Bobby bully me. I wasn't going to let anyone bully me again, ever. I refused to live on my knees. At my grandfather's funeral, no one cried. People said things like they were sorry for my loss or he was a good man. I couldn't respond. Nothing seemed appropriate.

My most trusted bartender-friend, Donna, was the only one who didn't lie. She hugged me and said matter-of-factly, *Now you are on your own.* In the eyes of the world, I was an orphan. But she and I both knew my life would only get better. Too bad she moved to California after I closed The Corner. She took the opportunity to make a big leap. Moving to Manhattan was the biggest leap I could handle.

I stood up and hung on to the center pole of the rushing subway car as it rocked to the rhythm of "Psycho Killer." I was anxious to get home to my safe quiet loft. A half-drunk guy in a suit, who'd gotten on at the last stop, stood up and took an unsteady step toward Big Burly with the boom box. I was right between them.

"Hey, I said turn that down, will ya?" Half Drunk's voice was louder than the music.

Big Burly looked at Half Drunk calmly as if he'd just said pass the salt. Then he reached down to his boom box, his eyes still locked with Half Drunk's, and tweaked the volume knob. The Talking Heads blared even louder. I cringed. Half Drunk covered his ears, his face bright red as he walked toward Big Burly and screamed.

"I SAID SHUT THAT FUCKING SHIT OFF!"

I tried to flatten myself against the pole.

Big Burly stood up, his boom box rising with him. Half Drunk hadn't noticed that Big Burly was a good six inches taller and fifty muscle-pounds heavier. One on each side of me, they blocked my way so I couldn't escape in either direction. If Big Burly decided to throw that boom box, I was in for some shrapnel. The train barreled through the tunnel, the lights blinking, the floor vibrating; the music was deafening. Suddenly the train hit a curve too fast, and we all lurched to one side. I clutched the pole. Half Drunk fell over on the floor. Big Burly plopped back down in his seat. His tape ended and he roared with laughter. Half Drunk crawled back to his seat, and the train pulled into the station.

I jumped out as soon as the doors opened and ran all the way up the stairs out of the station and the two blocks to my loft. Apocalypses, serial killers, New York City subway riders—who knew how much time I had left?

Chapter 11

I locked all three locks on my door: the knob lock, the dead bolt with the chain, and the top lock. I knew people who had even more locks than that. I undressed slowly and emptied my wallet. At least it had been a good tip day, over two hundred dollars. I put the cash in the top drawer of my dresser, my sock drawer. I kept my money in the bank, but my bank was out of the way, so I let the cash accumulate before I got around to depositing it. I kept the bills neat, an old holdover from how my grandfather taught me to keep it at the restaurant, ready for the cash deposit. Small bills in front, corners smoothed, faces forward, all right side up. When it hit a hundred, I folded it over so I could quickly assess how much I had. It was up to seven hundred and fifty. It would be time to go to the bank soon.

It was past two AM, and as usual, sleep didn't come easy. I had to trick myself into it. If I thought about my day or anything in the past tense, it would lead to insomnia. Too much bad would creep its way in. I tried to shut out the pictures of war in my head, from both the movie and my life. My usual technique was to think up stuff that hadn't happened yet; then I could make sure it was only good. My mind drifted. I had two phone numbers to think about, Ron's and Frankie's. Would I call either of them? Should I? *Girls don't call boys,* I heard my grandmother say. *Boys call girls.*

Maybe I'd run into Frankie again. Or maybe I *would* call him. I was attracted to him, but I didn't want my hormones telling me what to do. And what about Ron? What did he really want from me, and should I take the chance to find out? And Cousin Bobby? Would he leave me alone, or was I going to have to do some kind of dance to keep him away without pissing him off in order to keep my job?

I was done for the night. Like Scarlett O'Hara, *I'll think about that tomorrow.* I flipped over to my other side and faced the window.

I let my thoughts wander to fantasy. Maybe Frankie was honest and sweet and would be the love of my life. We'd marry, have seven or eight beautiful kids, and live happily ever after. Or maybe Ron wanted to date me because I was the most gorgeous, talented thing he'd ever seen and he'd bring me stardom and fame, riches beyond belief. Maybe he'd adore me till the day I died.

Right. And maybe I'd wake up on the French Riviera.

I love a diner breakfast. It gets me every time. I cook a mean breakfast myself: omelets, home fries, and of course, Italian frittatas. But nothing beats sitting in a diner booth, plates laden with eggs over easy cooked by someone else—golden yolks spilling onto the home-fried potatoes, bacon so crispy it melts in your mouth, whole wheat toast with pools of salty butter, and that never-empty teacup. I could start every morning that way, but I'd have to skate eight hours a day to work it off. And who has that kind of time?

I didn't have to be at work until ten AM on Thursday, but bad dreams woke me at six. I got myself showered and dressed in a simple seafoam-green dress and out of the house quickly. Sometimes I thought a roommate might help dilute my lack of ease with late nights and early mornings, but I just couldn't make the move. I guess I just didn't like to share—a side effect of being an only child, maybe. If my apartment felt too solitary in the early morning, I just headed out to the diner on Ninth Avenue and Twenty-Third Street. It usually worked, even when war was raging inside my head. Between *Apocalypse Now*, my bad dreams, and *The New York Times*, there was plenty of war to go around. The paper, spread in front of me at the diner as usual, proved my thesis.

It was quiet in Iran, too quiet. Journalists, out of fear, were merely copying what they were told to report. Guards lined the streets, guns ready. Men and women still sat segregated, even in protest, but there would be less reporting of the protests because of the threat of death to journalists.

I turned the page. That was enough about the imminence of war. After that movie last night, I didn't want to hear about war for a while.

The waiter poured more hot water on my soggy tea bag, and I paused to press it with my spoon to make another cup of murky brown tea, sipping it as I caught up on baseball. I'd missed last night's Mets game for the trip into the war zone. Lee Mazzilli was called out on a little collision at home plate, but the Mets beat Atlanta, six to three. I closed the paper on this positive note, saving the rest for later. I paid my bill and skated to work. The morning was heating up, but I made my own breeze as I wove between pedestrians on the sidewalk.

Thursday was a good quick workday. In for the setup, stock the bar, do a mini inventory to prep for the busy weekend, sling some food and drink for lunch, and then out by five before the night bartenders came in for the happy hour crowd and the pre-theater dinner shift. I was ready for it all, as long as Cousin Bobby didn't stop by to toy with me.

Sometimes bartending was like acting: I lost myself in the performance. But sometimes the opposite happened and I couldn't help but see myself reflected in the mirror behind the back bar every second of the day. And when it was a shift like that, every time I poured booze from a bottle, the ghost of my grandfather slid out.

My first customer walked in wearing an old gray suit and a crumpled black tie. It was going to be one of those days. He wasn't anyone I'd met before, but I knew his whole life story. He started with a martini straight up, made with cheap bar liquor. When I poured it right up to the rim, he asked for the shaker of ice on the side. He probably wanted to suck the cubes from the shaker for any additional alcohol. I asked him if he wanted some lunch, and he looked at me as if I just puked on his shoes. I took his cash and he put the change in his pocket, no tip. I hadn't expected one.

The bar finally got busy with lunch customers around twelve fifteen, just when he was ready for another. His eyes were already watery, but you couldn't make a martini weak; that's why he drank them. He sipped his second one not altogether slowly and crunched the ice cubes for a snack. At twelve forty-five he wanted a third. I waited for him to pay up first. I poured it and reached for his cash. He grabbed my hand.

"Don't the house ever buy?" His grip had the strength of desperation.

I looked at him steadily as my hand shrank under his clammy paw. The rule was that the house bought the third or fourth drink, and the discretion was mine. I pulled my hand away, his cash crumpled in my fingers.

"We buy the fourth." I smiled winningly, and as soon as I said it, I knew it was a mistake. There was no way I wanted to serve a fourth martini to this guy. Maybe he'd forget. *Fat chance.*

He practically chugged the third one, and as he put the glass down, he hit the padded rim of the bar. The glass tipped but it didn't fall. He righted it and caught me looking.

"I'm ready for one on you."

I walked slowly, reaching for a new glass, not wanting to break the grip he still had on his. It might be the only thing holding him upright. I took my time. I was about to make the most flawless ice-cold martini in existence.

I filled the funnel-shaped martini glass with ice and water to chill it. Then I packed the glass shaker with ice, sprinkled in some dry vermouth, and turned it upside down, holding back the ice with the strainer so that any vermouth not clinging to the ice would drip out. I poured what I knew was exactly the right amount of gin, holding the bottle high, arcing the stream of clear liquid. I stirred it and stirred it with the long silver bar spoon until the condensation on the outside of the shaker began to drip down in rivulets. I emptied the ice water out of the martini glass and shook the droplets out. It was perfectly frosted. I picked the best three olives from the bin and dropped them home. Then gently, so as not to bruise it, I poured the martini through the strainer into its waiting funneled glass chamber. I knew the drunk wouldn't appreciate the perfection of this drink, but making it gave me a certain pleasure. The kind of pleasure you get from any perfect act: viewing a painting by da Vinci, eating a piece of homemade lasagna, listening to "Ramble On" by Led Zeppelin, making love while the rain beats a rhythm on the roof—

"Hey, what's taking so goddamned long with my martini?"

Keep your shirt on. I put the drink down in front of him, with some regret, and knocked twice on the bar to indicate it was on the house. "Good luck."

He was going to need it, the way he was going. Busying myself with other customers, I tried to forget he was there, but I felt his presence like a lead weight somewhere near the middle of my liver. That kind of customer always got me. There was no avoiding his type if you worked behind a bar, and some days it was enough to make me feel like quitting the restaurant business. Yet there I was. It was like driving by a car wreck: You were sickened by what you saw, but you just couldn't pull your eyes away. I was stuck behind the bar for the foreseeable future.

My grandfather hadn't abused alcohol until after my grandmother died. He was around booze his whole life, even made wine and other liquors at home. But once she was gone, something changed. I couldn't believe it was because he missed her. Their relationship had been too turbulent. But I think she kept him in check. He had to answer to her values, her rules. Once she was gone, there were no boundaries. When it was just the two of us left, he turned his custom of fighting toward me. There was a good deal of yelling and throwing things, all from his side. I spent a lot of time in my room with my door locked and my head under the pillow—if I could get there fast enough.

By the time I was ready to graduate high school, he was a completely different person from when my grandmother had been alive. Sometimes I'd come home from school and he'd be passed out on the couch. I'd stare at him and think, *Who is this messed-up old man, and why am I living with him?*

We were lucky we didn't lose the business before he died. Employees quit or ripped us off. The clientele went from friendly to fierce. I kept the books to the best of my ability, making the cash deposits, paying the staff in cash, covering the bills. I propped up what I could while he tore it down. In the end it was all too much for his heart.

The one thing I thanked the heavens for was that I turned eighteen before he died so I didn't have to go into foster care. That's all I had been praying for, once I gave up on him. I prayed to a God I wasn't sure existed that nothing really bad would happen to him until after my eighteenth birthday. That may sound harsh, but I knew where he was headed. I just wanted him to be out of pain and for me to be free.

The morning I turned eighteen, I woke up full of pure relief, and it poured out of me in tears. *Now I'm my own responsibility. Now, no matter what, no one can claim me.* I had no idea that my grandfather would last only a few more months. I wasn't thinking about life without him, only a life for myself.

Bartending served me. I made a living, even if I had to deal with all the exposure to drunks. Some ex-drinkers had trouble being around alcohol. Just seeing a bottle made them thirsty. It was the opposite with me. Watching other people drink reminded me every day why I'd quit. And besides, what else could I do to support myself until Broadway discovered what a great actress I was?

Mr. Martini Breath rolled out on his own, but I never really got him off my mind. Every time I had a customer like him, it all came back to me. They say time heals all wounds. The clock was still ticking for me.

It wasn't my fault that my grandfather had drunk himself to death, I kept telling myself. He was lost even before he started drinking. He was from another generation, another country, another century. Life for him was all about making a living and putting food on the table for his family. For a while he did that well—he brought home the food, that is, and I cooked it. I was the only family he had left. He didn't know how to show affection, not in the normal way. But when I cooked a meal for him, his empty plate was evidence. That was my one fond memory of him. Did I miss him? Hard to, when his ghost kept popping up in front of me drinking martinis.

The little knife squirming below my left ribs reminded me it would get worse if my stomach stayed empty. I forced some pasta down as I stood at the service bar, even though I didn't feel hungry.

Just when I thought the day couldn't get any worse, Cousin Bobby walked in. My brain ran through all the Italian swear words I'd inherited from my grandfather as I walked toward him with a smile. I placed a bar napkin in front of him as I considered his smirking face. He hadn't appeared once at The Realm for the first four months of my employment, and now he couldn't seem to stay away. I blamed Nicky.

"Hey, boss-man. The Realm seems to be your favorite hangout lately."

"Someone's got to keep an eye on Nicky." He tapped the bar napkin. "The usual for me."

As I poured his Scotch, I wondered if Nicky was in trouble, in which case Cousin Bobby's visits had nothing to do with me. That would be a relief. I gave Bobby his drink and moved toward the front of the bar to fill empty beer mugs for some regulars. The front door opened, and I looked up, expecting Mike, since my shift was ending soon. Instead, I watched Marissa walk in the door and sit on a stool two seats away from Cousin Bobby.

"Hey, Nina." Marissa's smile was mischievous.

"Hey, what're you doing in the fashion ghetto?" I tossed a little white napkin in front of her.

"I'm temping just a few blocks away."

"Convenient. Do you want to come home with me before class?"

"If only I'd planned better. No, I have to go home and change."

"Me too." I leaned one elbow on the bar.

"What a god-awful gig that office was. They were all either leering or sneering."

"Sounds like you need a drink."

"I'd be happy to buy your friend a drink," Bobby broke in. Apparently, he'd been eavesdropping. What a snoop.

"Marissa, this is Bobby. He's one of the owners." I felt that formal introductions were in order. "Bobby, this is Marissa. We study together at The Studio. We have class tonight."

"Hi." Marissa shook Bobby's hand. He seemed to release it rather slowly. "I'll just have a stiff diet soda, thanks. I don't want to get sleepy before class."

I moved down the bar to pour her a glass. Out of the corner of my eye, I watched Bobby move a seat closer to Marissa. I didn't have to hear him to know what he was saying. Surely they were the same lines he'd already given me, or something equivalent. Mike came rushing in the door, and after I gave Marissa her soda, I made haste finishing the chores to end my shift.

"What can I say to talk you girls into staying for a drink?" Cousin Bobby didn't give up easily, I had to give him that. I stood next to Marissa with my shoulder bag and skates, thankful she was there as an excuse to get me out quick.

"We've got to get to class." I was convincingly disappointed.

"We'll take a rain check." Marissa jumped off her stool.

"I'll hold you to that." Bobby rattled the lonely ice in his glass at Mike. I hustled Marissa out the door.

"He's intense," she said with a laugh.

"Exactly." I walked Marissa to the corner, and we split with a quick hug.

Back home, I put on some worn summer khakis and a coral T-shirt I'd bought because it reminded me of the color of lipstick my mother used to wear. It brought out the pink in her cheeks. I left my half-read newspapers on the kitchen table and my skates by the door, deciding to walk flat-footed to The Studio in the early-evening humidity.

I was early, so I sat in the playground a couple of blocks from The Studio. I watched the kids on the swings, thinking about a million different things, as usual. Mostly trying to focus on the future and figure out what to do with my life. I wasn't coming up with anything useful, so I put the radio in my ears. Prince was singing "I Wanna Be Your Lover," claiming he wasn't like other guys, and it was easy to believe him.

I guess I was lost in my own world, because I didn't even hear Ron walk up and sit next to me until he spoke.

"What's doing, Nina?"

"Huh?" I jumped about a foot. "Jeez, you scared me!"

"Sorry." Ron leaned back on the bench. "Just thought I'd say hi."

"I'm sorry." *Regain composure, girl.* "I'm just killing time until class. What's up with you?"

"Well, you're up right now." He slid closer to me with that look on his face, that tomcat smile he seemed to be using on me since that improv. "That color looks so pretty on you, or maybe it's you that makes that color look so pretty."

I really hate it when a man I respect goes creep on me. Why did he have to start off with a line like that? It was fairly original, but it came out sleazy nonetheless.

"It's so amazing that you should show up just now," I pivoted. "Here I am, sitting here, wondering about my future as an actor, and suddenly there you are. It's as if you heard me call."

"Well, I am a bit psychic, you know."

"You are?" *Psychic, or psycho?*

"Yes." His smile was hours-past-dinner hungry. "You were thinking of calling me, but something held you back. Am I right?"

Okay, he had me. But it was a pretty easy guess.

"I have to admit I was a bit shy to call you. I mean, I figured you were just trying to be nice." I hated playing the innocent young thing, but it seemed to be my current role.

"Why don't you and I get together one night this week? We can meet anywhere you like, have a drink, talk, get to know each other better."

A little necking (pun intended), a little rape? I couldn't help reaching for my throat. What game was he playing? It was hard to say no; what if there were repercussions in class? And he had a lot of influence in the Broadway scene. Besides, it could be my chance to grill him about Jessica.

"Sure, Ron." My voice sounded higher than usual to me. "I'd love to. What night?"

"How about Saturday?"

"Saturday?" I almost squeaked. Weren't both girls killed on Saturdays? "This Saturday?"

"Do you already have plans?"

"No, no, Saturday is fine." *But it'll have to be on my turf,* I thought. "Do you know Texarkana, on Tenth Street near Sixth Avenue? How about eight o'clock?"

"Sure, I know the place. Eight is fine." He stood. "Now we better get to class."

"Right." So much for my concentration.

We walked into the building together. I looked around to see if Marissa or Janette was there to witness my escort. They weren't, but I did see Tom the Cop talking with the receptionist. Great. He saw me, too, and he nodded as I walked by. I gritted my teeth, hoping it would pass for a smile. I was almost impressed that he was finally getting around to doing some investigating.

Acting class was kind of low energy for me. Marissa got paired with Janette for the improvisation exercise, and I was able to muster up a brilliant moment or two in an improvisation with a new tall, hunky guy from Oklahoma, Andrew Lee. No chance for a romance with him—he already had a boyfriend—but we got along great. I walked out of class with him.

"Andrew Lee, huh? Are you related to the general?" I joked.

"Well, not to my knowledge, ma'am," he replied in his best John Wayne imitation.

We almost bumped into Tom the Cop.

"This your boyfriend?" Tom stuck his chest out when he spoke, like a cartoon gorilla. Some people really know how to get on my nerves.

"Not at the moment. What's it to you?" I tried to keep a civil tongue in my head, but it was an effort.

"Perhaps he can excuse us so we could talk." Tom the Cop glowered at both of us.

I shrugged, and Andrew Lee gave me a wink as he left.

"You really have a way of making people feel comfortable." I was seething. Marissa and Janette came up behind me, laughing and chatting loudly.

"Nina, you and Andrew rocked that last one." Janette gave me a one-armed hug and turned into the ladies' room. Marissa leaned into me, shoulder to shoulder. I froze and glanced at Tom the Cop. Then Marissa saw him.

"Who's this?" She smiled her actor's smile. She probably thought he was a teacher or an agent. No one would expect a cop at The Studio.

"Marissa, this is Tom. He's investigating Jessica's murder." I tried to act casual. "You know, Kojak."

"You want to talk here, or should we go have a cup of coffee?" Suddenly he was all business.

"They're closing up here. It's the last class of the night."

"Coffee it is, then." He gestured toward the exit.

"I'll call you." Marissa waggled her fingers at me. I mouthed *Goodbye* and rolled my eyes.

Tom the Cop took my elbow and guided me out the door. I hated it when people I didn't know touched me. Why was he here and not Frankie? Talk about losing the lottery. I wiggled out of his grasp and tried to walk just ahead of him till we got to The Bus Stop.

He ordered two cups of coffee while I sat in silence, storm clouds gathering over my head.

"I get the feeling you don't trust me," he said. I almost laughed out loud. He dumped four heaping teaspoons of sugar into his cup.

"You're very perceptive, Detective."

His neck turned red. I guess he heard some sarcasm in my response. He put his spoon down on the table a bit too hard. I flinched.

"Let's see if we can just have a little conversation. Okay?"

"I don't understand why you want to talk to me again. I barely knew Jessica. Is it because I found her body?"

"I didn't show up at The Studio looking for you." He made an effort to calm himself. "But I saw you walk in with that actor, Ron Meyers. What are you doing with him?"

"What do you mean? We were just talking before class. He's my teacher." I suddenly started to sweat. "Why?"

"Because," said Detective Barry, "we're questioning him for the Jessica Roman murder."

"Does that mean he's a suspect?" My stomach twisted.

"We're keeping an eye on him."

I kept my mouth shut. I didn't know if this cop was baiting me or trying to scare me into telling him something. But I had nothing to tell.

"How well do you know this guy?" Tom slurped his coffee, indicating his level of class, or lack thereof.

"He's my teacher." A chill suddenly crept up my spine. How well did I know Ron? Hardly at all, yet I had a pending date with him.

"And?"

"And what? Everything I know about him comes from what I've read in the tabloids, but I'm sure you've read all that."

Tom the Cop leaned back in his chair, his gut hanging over his pleather belt. He didn't look like a healthy man. Too much coffee and doughnuts, or burgers and beer.

"Why don't you just tell me anything you know about this guy, and the victim, and I'll decide what I need to know for my investigation."

I blinked and kept my face expressionless. In my head, I recited the Mets starting lineup before I answered him, just for dramatic pause. *Mazzilli, Henderson, Youngblood, Taveras, Hebner, Stearns, Flynn, Montañez.* Then I took in a slow, deep breath.

"Ron is my acting teacher. I've been in his class for less than a year. I do not have a personal relationship with the guy, but as far as I can see, he likes the ladies. As far as I know, this is not illegal." My tone fell just under the line of snotty.

"Unless he decides to break necks in the heat of passion."

"I'm guessing you'll need more motive than being a ladies' man to put Ron in jail." My fingers busied themselves scrunching up the little napkin next to my coffee cup. "If you really want to keep the streets safe from whoever killed Jessica, you should keep looking. You're wasting your time with Ron. It's obvious that Jessica's murder is connected to Teresa's. The fact that Ron knew Jessica practically proves he *didn't* do it."

I didn't know what made me act like such a brat with this cop, but I couldn't help myself. Tom looked at me with an expression that was half impatience, half contempt, all cop.

"That's your opinion. I'm doing my job the way I know how to do it. The way I've been doing it, successfully, for almost twenty years. Tell me what you know about Jessica Roman."

"There's not much to that either. I hardly knew her." I tried to be less annoyed, but it wasn't easy. He got under my skin, itchy as poison ivy. "Just, well, sometimes people used to confuse us. We're both sort of short on stature, long on dark hair. Not that there's a shortage of us at The Studio."

He raised his bushy eyebrows. "How do you mean, confuse you two?"

"It was just a couple of times."

"Give me an example."

"Well, one time I was in a showcase at school and a few people who didn't know either of us went up to her the next day and told her how good she was." I slid my spoon back and forth on the table. "It really pissed her off."

"What's your point?" Tom didn't seem to be able to grasp the concept.

"It's just ironic. I didn't know her at all, I had her in one class, we never spoke. But people would get us mixed up. Someone would come up to me and say, 'Aren't you in my scene study class?' and I knew they were talking about her. It was annoying." I frowned. "I heard once she tried to take advantage of the similarity. Another teacher saw me do a scene and thought she was me and asked her to audition for something. She knew he meant to ask me, but she went along with it. But once he saw her audition, he realized his mistake."

"That doesn't seem relevant." Tom's sneer gave me that creepy feeling again. Then he suddenly looked inspired, if it was possible for *suddenly* to happen in slow motion. "Unless, of course, her murder was another case of mistaken identity."

Heat flushed my face and a cold shudder crept up my spine simultaneously.

"Look, that kind of stuff happens to me all the time. Every week someone tells me I look just like their cousin or their neighbor or the waitress they had the night before. Brown eyes, brown hair, that's all anyone sees."

"This sounds a bit more specific, though." He leaned forward on his elbows, cradling his coffee cup in his palms. "The same studio, the same hair and height. The killer might've been looking for you, but he missed." He tried to look concerned. It didn't convince me.

"Thanks for the coffee." I hadn't even taken a sip, since I didn't drink coffee, not that he'd bothered to ask. I didn't even fake a smile. I was too tired. I just got up and headed toward the door. Tom was too surprised to say anything at first, but he couldn't let me have the last word.

"Better watch your back," he called out as I opened the door.

It's hard to watch your back when you're walking home alone at night. But I was almost too angry to be scared, angry that he'd made me scared. I'd spent too much of my life being scared—scared of being alone, scared of men, scared of risks, scared of being scared. I'd been trying to get over being scared my whole young life. I tried a lot of techniques to overcome it. I asked myself, *What's the worst that can happen?* Picturing it in vivid detail sometimes made it go away, although sometimes it just freaked me out even more. But I had other ways, like turning it inside out. I worked through missing my family by becoming a loner. I worked through failure at school by setting my goals on acting instead of college. I worked through my fear of poverty by working for cash and squirreling it away.

But this time, this time the worst-case scenario was death. How could I work through that? Religion? Faith in the afterlife? I hadn't been able to make that work for me. Since my mother died and I wasn't able to talk to her or get her to hear me or feel like she could hear me, I lost my belief in life after death. How could I turn that inside out? What was the opposite of being scared of dying? Becoming a daredevil? That would be a hell of a turnaround for me.

I had been so focused on my thoughts, I was surprised to find myself on my street. I ran up the stairs and burst into my apartment, my heart banging with fear and frustration. I stood just inside my doorway, breathing hard, looking at my kitchen table, at the pile of unread newspapers waiting for me there. Safe, black-and-white text. Other people's stories, other people's problems, triumphs, failures, decisions. Other people's, not mine. I made a pot of chamomile tea and sat down to read them all.

Chapter 12

On Friday morning it was clear that this summer was doing its best to be hotter than any other summer in history. I threw on some gym shorts and a T-shirt after my shower and ran down to the corner to buy the paper. Back home I put Spyro Gyra on the turntable. *Morning Dance* with its happy Caribbean sound was a good way to start the day. In this heat, with that music, I could imagine myself on vacation on a tropical island. Too bad I hadn't picked up a mango for breakfast at the bodega down the block. I made myself an iced tea to go with my cold cereal; it was too sultry to drink my morning leaf hot. You know what they say: It's not the heat, it's the humidity. I didn't need any more steam in my face.

The news was as hot as the weather. The Kurdish Rebels were making themselves heard in Iran, although the Islamic Revolutionaries were still very much in control. Hey, it's the battle of the bands. The ayatollah had announced solidarity with Palestine and branded Israel and the USA as "enemies of Islam."

I dressed gingerly after my shower, trying not to sweat too much before I got to the cool, conditioned air of The Realm.

I twisted my long hair into a knot on top of my head and put on a violet T-shirt dress.

I thought it might feel cooler outside, but it was worse. Over ninety degrees already without a hint of a breeze. The stink of the garbage on the sidewalks was impossible to avoid. Even on my skates, there was no cool wind, just hot air hitting me harder.

I skated slowly and got to work by ten. Everyone seemed worn out by the heat. There was just the slightest murmur of *Good mornings* while we prepared for the lunch rush. In this heat, we'd be packed with customers. No one would want to leave the cool climate of The Realm and go back out in the heat to get to their office. There'd be more than a few three-martini lunches.

It started out as one of those hectic days when everything was aggravating. Maybe it was just because I'd wanted it to be over since the moment I got up, or maybe the heat just did funny things to people. Every customer had a special request, and the kitchen was putting out the pasta too slow.

Finally, it got so busy that I forgot the time. Lunch blended right into happy hour. I didn't even get a break. Some Fridays were like that: My customers just clean forgot about going back to the office. The bar was three deep at happy hour, and Mike and I poured as fast as we could. I lined up six highball glasses at once, filled them with ice, poured in the booze, and mixed in the soda or juice requested. Mike took four mugs in each fist and filled them at the beer tap. I rang up cash as fast as I could count it. Then there was a moment when I looked in the mirror and saw someone pushing their way through the crowd. Cousin Bobby.

"Hey, bartender, too busy for me?" Even his flirting sounded bossy. I already had a glass of ice and was pouring the Cutty Sark into it as I turned to greet him.

"Hey there, boss-man. The usual?" I put his drink down in front of him, not bothering to ring up a tab. In the same motion I scooped up three empty glasses from the customers next to him and started making their refills. I could tell Bobby wanted to chat me up, but I was moving too fast, and how could he complain? He was the boss and here I was, working hard and doing my best to fill his coffers. I kept moving so he couldn't catch me in conversation, and even if I had a moment between making drinks, there was plenty of setup work to do. At one point I saw him talking with Nicky. It was getting close to my exit time.

I had to plan my escape.

I cashed in my tips and counted out my register a bit early and asked Mike to ring up all the drinks for the last twenty minutes of my shift on his bank. He didn't mind; it meant he'd get the edge on the tips. Nick didn't question that I counted my register early; it was still busy, and I kept on the move. I flew from one end of the bar to the other until the crowd finally started to calm down. I made sure Mike had everything he needed, and then I waited for a moment when Bobby was in conversation with Nicky away from the service bar. I said a quick goodbye to Mike and slipped out the door. I'd hear about it tomorrow, but it was worth it.

I skated down Fifth Avenue real slow. It was six thirty and Benny didn't get off till eight, so I had time before I met him. There was no breeze except when a big city bus went by, and that was full of exhaust, but the warm, fading sun still felt good to me.

At home I brushed out my hair, extra wavy from the twist it had been up in all day. I removed my damp T-shirt dress and pulled on cutoff denim shorts, a gray T-shirt, and my Pro-Keds high-top sneakers without socks. My skates stayed parked in the kitchen; no use dragging them around with me all night.

When I got to the Saz, it was pretty crowded, but there was an empty stool waiting for me. I climbed up on it and flipped some money on the bar. Never the type to run a tab, I told every bartender to take it out as I went. It was this claustrophobic thing I had. I'd be in a place, having a perfectly good time, and all of a sudden I'd just have to leave. Maybe the joint would get too crowded; maybe I'd just get terminally bored. Whatever it was, it would come on me like a panic, and I'd have to get out. I didn't want to have to wait for the check.

Benny appeared with my drink: club soda with bitters. *How did he guess?*

"Hey, Nina, what's new?"

"I haven't seen anything new in the papers for a couple of days about those two girls."

"That's all you ever talk about. It's so boring."

"Every time I'm on the street, that's all I'm thinking about."

Benny leaned his grizzly-bear-sized body over the bar until his face was close to mine. A whiff of Old Spice mixed with beer and cognac floated my way.

"Don't let it worry you, kid." He tapped on the bar with his sausage-sized forefinger. "There's stuff going on in this city all the time, right next door even, that would shock you, but you don't normally hear about it. You just happened to hear about this thing."

"These things." I picked up my drink and slumped on my padded barstool. "I know they're connected, even if no one believes me." I took a sip of my soda. "And don't call me *kid*."

"C'mon." Benny leaned against the back bar. "One of them probably just had some whacko for a boyfriend, and the other was your typical mugging out of control. I'll bet you a movie they are two separate things."

"That's a bet I hope I lose."

"You will. Come on now, cheer up. I'll be off soon, and then I'm going to whip your butt at pinball for the next couple of hours."

"Oh yeah, right." I smiled at his optimism. He hadn't once beaten me at pinball in all the times we'd played. "You've got to stop living in a dreamworld, Benny. It just ain't healthy."

He moved down the bar, scooping up tips and wiping the dark-wood surface. He cut up pieces of fruit to fill the bins and added little napkins to the piles along the bar. I twirled the little straw in my drink. Club soda and bitters with a piece of lime, my daily sipping drink. I'd spent years surrounded by alcoholic beverages, but I chose club soda. I had that power of will. At least now I did.

The summer after high school had been a weird one for me. I didn't know what the future held, and I didn't care. School was over, I had no plans, and I felt free to do anything, so I did, in an impulsive kind of way. I had the bar to open and close up, my grandfather to avoid, and I worked as the second bartender on Friday and Saturday nights. Other than that, I played. I played the way I thought adults played, but my role models hadn't been the best.

On the evening of my eighteenth birthday, August 8, I ended up at a fancy Italian restaurant in the Brooklyn neighborhood south of mine, whose owners frequented The Corner. I usually didn't celebrate my birthday, but since I was turning legal drinking age, everyone wanted to buy me a drink. A lot of my bar friends were there, meaning people I partied with but who would leave me hanging in an instant if I actually needed anything.

The owners of the restaurant bought me a bottle of Dom Pérignon champagne. I was finally able to drink alcohol in public as an adult for the first time—as if I hadn't been drinking in bars already. No place I frequented cared about checking IDs. That night of my birthday, everyone was drinking and having a good old time. I nibbled on some appetizers at the bar, but I really didn't have any dinner. Several friends kept handing me their coke stashes and sending me to the ladies' room. I'd tried it a few times in the past, but I hadn't done it that much. That night I just kept saying yes. It made me hyper and thirsty, so I kept draining my champagne glass. Everyone was being especially nice to me, like I was the guest star of the night. The place was hopping. I felt like I was an adult having an adult celebration.

Suddenly, everything changed. The music felt too loud. There was no air in the room. I could hear my heart beating too fast. I got up, then sat down and wiped the sweat from my forehead. My substitute big sister/bartender Donna looked at me funny, her dark-brown eyes concerned.

"Nina? Nina, what's wrong?" She touched my hand.

"Nothing, nothing, I just need some air." But I couldn't move and I couldn't breathe. Donna grabbed my arm and steered me out the front door.

The evening air wasn't cool, but it was fresher, no cigarette smoke, no smell of booze, and it was quiet. I leaned on Donna and she hugged me. Then she walked me up and down the block a few times until I was feeling better. We went back inside.

I was able to slip away soon afterward. So much had been building up inside me; there had to be some release. When school was finally over, instead of feeling free, I'd felt trapped. I didn't know how to escape my life, so instead I kept up a pace that was headed nowhere fast—lots of meaningless dates that filled up my empty time with more emptiness, but faster, to make the rest of the summer speed by.

In the fall, when my grandfather died, I hit a brick wall.

In my new life, club soda with lime worked for me. It looked enough like a cocktail to pass, and choosing it kept me from finding out if I actually had a drinking problem. I didn't really want to know. The bitters were another story. It was Benny who'd suggested I add that to my seltzer. I had been going to the Saz for a couple of weeks when I mentioned my stomach pangs. I took it for granted that it was a by-product of my life. Things bothered me; my stomach let me know about it. Just the occasional stab to say *Don't forget, I'm still here, your colorful past.* Benny loaded my soda up with bitters, telling me it was good for my digestion. I liked the taste and I figured it couldn't hurt.

Benny finished his shift, and we took off for Jimmy Day's, our favorite hangout: U-shaped old-wood bar, baseball on TV, great jukebox, and one of the last pinball machines in the Village. Most places had switched to those new video games, but I was old-school. Benny hit the jukebox while I grabbed a couple of seats at the bar and ordered drinks from Hector, who was tending the bar. He was almost seven feet tall and, if I went by the ink on the bathroom walls, very popular with the ladies.

"Hey, Hector, what's on?" Perfect seats, right in front of the screen.

"Mets in Cincinnati, but there's a rain delay." Hector chewed a toothpick and gestured to the commercial on the TV screen.

Benny sat down next to me just as Van Morrison's "Brown-Eyed Girl" came on the jukebox. He always played that one for me.

"Thanks, Benny. Got you a beer."

He drank half of it in one gulp and put the mug down with a sigh.

"The first beer right after you get off work is the best-tasting beer ever," he declared.

"No." I shook my head. "An ice-cold beer at a ninety-five-degree baseball game, that's the best-tasting beer."

"You're both wrong." Hector took the toothpick out of the corner of his mouth in order to speak, signifying the importance of his pending announcement. "Picture this. It's a summer night and it's so hot that you can't sleep." He paused for effect. "You roll over and make wild passionate love with your girl. When you're done, she gets up and grabs you an ice-cold beer from the fridge and brings it to you in bed. That's the best-tasting beer ever."

Benny and I looked at each other and then back at Hector before we burst out laughing.

"No wonder you get all that PR on the ladies' room wall." I shook my head.

"Jesus, Hector, you better get me another beer." Benny surrendered his empty mug. "It's hotter than hell in here now."

Hector pulled Benny another beer from the tap with a self-satisfied smirk.

"Speaking of hot, Hector," Benny said, "could you turn up the volume on the tube? They're doing the weather."

Hector reached up to the TV above the bar. The weatherman showed us a map of the tristate area and proceeded to tell us of our hot and humid fate for the next few days.

"I sure wish it would rain." Benny sipped the foam off the top of his beer. "This heat is getting to me."

"I love it." I swirled the ice in my drink. "Can't get enough of it. The nights are so nice you can walk around with shorts and a T-shirt, no jacket."

"And all day?"

"All day I'm behind an overly air-conditioned bar. And when I'm not and it's too hot, I go to the movies until sunset. That's what I love about this city. There are plenty of double features going on at all times for four dollars and fifty cents."

Benny shook his head and took another long hit from his beer.

"I don't know, Nina, sometimes I just can't believe how different we are." He looked sad as he said it. Van Morrison finished singing about his brown-eyed girl, and at that moment the whole mood of the evening changed.

The weather report was over and the news came on.

"There's new information on the recent murders in Greenwich Village." The anchorman on the news used his serious reporter voice. "Last week a young woman, Jessica Roman, was found dead in an alley in the West Village. Her neck was broken, and she had apparently been raped. The alley in which her body was found was only three blocks from The Studio, the well-known acting school where she studied.

The police are not admitting to any connection between the Jessica Roman murder and the murder of Teresa Torres, who was found two weeks earlier in a stairwell of her apartment building in the same neighborhood. Our reporters have recently discovered that Teresa Torres, also known as Terry Trenton, attended The Studio as well. Both victims had head injuries, broken necks, and were sexually molested. The police have no suspects."

I almost fell off my barstool.

CHAPTER 13

"Thanks, Hector. You can turn it down." Benny avoided looking at me. "Well, looks like a scorcher, no end in sight."

"Benny—"

"Hey, Hector, we're both empty here, what gives?"

"Benny!"

"Two more coming up." Hector turned to pour our drinks. I almost asked for something stronger, but I took it out on Benny instead.

"You owe me a movie, Benny Banlon. Now it makes sense: She went by Terry Trenton at The Studio. I knew her too. I thought she dropped out. I didn't know she died!"

"What do reporters know? They're grasping at straws. Trying to be sensational." Benny finally looked at me.

"Bullshit. You know it and I know it." He made no response. "I think I'll make you take me to one of those art cinemas way uptown." I tried to joke, but I almost couldn't swallow; things felt like they were closing in on me. I looked at my club soda, wishing it was vodka, something that would light a narrow stream of fire down my throat and make my brain fuzzy. Things were too clear in my head.

"Aw, come on, Nina, there's plenty of movie theaters here in the Village." He groaned. "You don't want to have to be taking the subway all the way uptown just to see a movie."

"That's the only reason I can see for taking the subway." I shot him a defiant look. "I skate or walk to work. I walk home. I walk to The Studio." Walk, walk, walk.

"Hector, gimme some quarters for the pinball machine, will ya?"

"Forget it, Benny, I don't feel like playing."

"Don't give me that shit, Esposito." Now he was annoyed. "I came here to play pinball."

"I'm not in the mood, Benny. Go play with yourself." Now we were both annoyed. Or were we both afraid?

He picked up his beer and stalked across the room.

"Damn it." I couldn't help it. Who could play pinball when people you knew and who looked like you were being murdered? Jessica and Terry were too alike. Was that why the killer had chosen them? The Studio was going to freak at this publicity. What if Ron was involved? What about my date with him tomorrow night? *He can't be a serial killer. He can't be. Can he?*

I turned to look at Benny. He wasn't playing pinball. He was at the table next to the machine. He was just sitting there, facing the wall. I slid off my barstool and made my way over to him.

"I'm sorry, Benny, I didn't mean to start a fight with you." I sat down next to him. "The whole thing just gets me nervous."

He turned to me. I'd never seen him so upset. "How do you think I feel? I'm thinking about you. Maybe there is some danger. I'm scared for you too."

This complete change in his line of thought threw me. My stomach did a somersault. My lungs forgot how to expand. *This isn't happening. This isn't happening to me.* And then I remembered what my grandfather used to say to me almost daily: *What makes you so special? The whole world doesn't revolve around you.*

"Wait a minute." I needed to soothe Benny's fears and my own. "It's pretty egotistical to think that I could be in danger of getting murdered. Me? Out of all seven million people in this city? I'm not that special. Who the hell do I think I am?"

Benny laughed, a little choked, and took my hand. "Well, *I* think you're special. If *I* was a murderer, *I'd* pick you out of all seven million."

I gently pulled my hand away. Benny sure had a twisted sense of humor.

"That is not even close to being funny."

"You're right." He stood up. "Look, are you going to play pinball or what?"

"Boy, you are a glutton for punishment. Benny, if you want to get beaten at pinball so badly, I will oblige you. Let's just stay off the murder subject."

"Deal." Benny Banlon dropped two quarters into the machine. Silverball Mania, my favorite game. He stepped aside and bowed. "Ladies first."

"No, please, age before beauty." I saluted him.

"Wiseass kid." Benny started to play.

"How old are you anyway, Benny?"

"I never told you how old I am?"

"No, you never told me."

"Well, actually, my birthday's next week."

"It is? When?"

"Tuesday the twenty-first."

"So, you were born August twenty-first. Eighteen sixty . . . ?" I prodded.

"Stuff it, brat." He bumped the machine with his hip; too late, the ball was lost. I stepped up to the plate, pulled the plunger, and let it go. Pow. I hit the ball with the left flipper, right through the circle loop, double bonus points.

"I hate beating you so easily, Benny. Makes me feel real bad." I bumped the machine with my pelvis.

"Watch it, you'll tilt 'er."

"You wish." I concentrated on the game, and Benny was silent for a moment. A few months ago, he said something that made me realize he thought I was near the end of my twenties. I let it go. A lot of people thought I was older; since I used to run a bar and I'd been working in the restaurant business for years, they figured I'd started when I was eighteen. It always made me laugh when people said I looked young for my age. Benny didn't know I had just turned nineteen a couple of weeks ago.

Since I was born on August 8 at eight in the morning, my mother used to say eight was her lucky number, and then she'd hug me and call me her lucky charm. Birthdays used to be fun. She always baked me a cake from scratch, chocolate of course, and let me invite as many friends as I wanted to my birthday party. We played pin-the-tail-on-the-donkey and musical chairs, and there would be prizes for everyone. Now I told myself I was lucky; some kids never had a birthday party or a homemade cake. I'd already had more than my share. I didn't need any more birthday parties.

"Nina?" Benny was right behind me as I flipped the flippers, a little too close.

"What?" I focused on the ball.

"Do me a favor." He got closer to my ear and spoke low. It made the hair on the back of my neck prickle. "Don't walk home tonight. Take a cab."

"Don't start, Benny. Don't you get paranoid." I lost my ball, and he stepped in front of the machine.

"Well, I'll walk you, then." He flipped both flippers.

"Forget it."

"Nina—"

"Don't piss me off. I'm sick of talking about it, between you and those cops—"

"What cops?"

"Those detectives. The ones who interviewed me at the Saz on Sunday. I ran into the cute one at Maria's the other night—"

"Which one was the cute one?"

"Hilarious. And last night the other one shows up at the studio after my class, asking me some stupid questions, almost like he cared about the case. What the hell do I know about it? Nothing, that's what."

"Did he say they have any suspects?" Benny flipped the flippers too fast.

I crunched some ice. "If you ask me, they barely know anything, and I get the impression they're not even trying."

"Shit, game over." Benny stepped back from the pinball machine and sat down in a chair near the wall. He was past the pool of dim light from the ceiling, almost disappearing into the shadows.

"Let me just see if I get high score of the night." I'd already beat him, but I still had my bonus ball to play. I waited before I shot it out of its resting place. "Don't you get tired of me beating you all the time, Benny?"

He took a second to light a cigarette, the match illuminating his face in a flash of warm orange glow, his eyes on me.

"Nope." His voice was soft. "Never." I concentrated on the game, but I knew he was still looking at me. From little slips he'd made, I figured Benny was around thirty-eight. I believed that age didn't make a difference if you were in love with somebody. But I wasn't in love with Benny Banlon.

I walked home alone that night. I didn't want Benny walking me home and finding out where I lived. It kept things simpler. And I had to prove to myself that I wasn't afraid. Or convince myself. I took my usual route from the West Village, through the meat-packing district and past the gay and transgender sex workers who hung out near the loading docks of the warehouses; they were used to seeing me, and some of them nodded and smiled or called out "Night, girl!" or "Where's your wheels?" and I waved. I walked north on Tenth Avenue to my block. I was used to being alone, and most of the time I liked it that way. The night was quiet and I had my eyes open for any trouble. I wasn't going to let these murders change my life. All the same, my heart thumped louder than a bass drum in a marching band.

Safe at home, I stripped off most of my clothes and flipped the TV to channel nine. I watched the Reds beat my Mets in Cincinnati, 4–3. Heartbreaker. Especially after the game the night before and the sweep of the Braves. *Chin up, boys. Joe Torre may lead you to the playoffs yet.*

I tried to finish reading the paper, but my eyelids wouldn't cooperate. I let the newspapers slide to the floor. I was pretty comfortable in my T-shirt and undies with the windows open and the ceiling fan on. Who needed air conditioning? I could just dream I was on a tropical island, drinking rum punch from a coconut. What could be better? Except for no dreams at all. I'd take that too.

CHAPTER 14

BAM!

I woke and sat up in my bed. What was that noise? A gunshot? Or was someone trying to break into my apartment?

All my lights were out except my reading lamp. I reached out and clicked it off. I was lying flat on my bed and tried to be as still as I could to listen for any strange noises in my apartment but my heart was beating so loudly, it was all I could hear. I held my breath.

My eyes slowly adjusted to the dark. All the windows were open and the shades up to let the breeze in. Streetlights gave the room a dim eerie glow. My door was closed and locked, I was sure of it. The window screens were still in place. It didn't seem that anyone was in my apartment except me. But there were too many shadows to be sure. The only sound was the distant traffic noise from the avenue. I got up in slow motion, tiptoed softly to the door, and flicked on all the lights from the wall switches. Nothing to see. My apartment was normal. I went to the bathroom and turned on that light too. Nothing.

What was going on? *Did I dream that sound?* Maybe it was a backfire from a passing truck. But it was so close. I begged my brain to calm down. *It's okay; nothing funny is going on around here. Just a normal night at home. Go back to sleep.* I left the bathroom light on, turned off all the others, and flopped on my bed, pulling my sheet over me and crumpling the edge in my fists at my throat. My breath still shallow.

Maybe some more TV until I was sleepy? No, the radio would be better; music would help calm my savage breast, as it were. I clicked on my little clock radio to WNEW. Michael McDonald's mellow voice cut through the silence, singing about fools and wise men. *Come back to me, sleep,* I prayed, *sleep with no dreams.* But anxiety wouldn't leave, and my prayers weren't answered for hours.

Around eight in the morning I woke from a dream. It was one I had often. I was reaching, stretching long, trying to grab for something. It was dark in my dream, what I imagined it would be like to be blind. I knew there were things around me, but I couldn't see them. I was turning, twisting, trying to figure out where I was. Flailing in the dark. I woke frustrated, my legs twitching, yearning to be up and moving, needing light and air. I didn't know how long I'd had that dream or what it meant, but it sure got me going some mornings. Got me out of bed, anyway.

As I got ready for my Saturday shift, Marissa called. I hadn't told her about my date with Ron yet. I couldn't think of a legitimate reason to cancel. Oh, I could've given him a million excuses in order to back out of the date, but I couldn't find one for myself. Not one single thing that didn't make me seem paranoid. I was just being silly. Ron a murderer, a serial killer? Targeting me as his next victim? It just wasn't real.

"Want to go to a movie tonight?" Marissa's voice sounded strained on the phone.

"Aren't you and Dave doing anything?"

"No, he's got to work. Are you free?"

"Well, actually—"

She wouldn't believe me at first. I told her she could stop by Texarkana and see for herself.

"I'll do better than that: I'll bring my camera. No, wait, I got it, I'll call all the gossip columns and they'll come take your picture. Ron's a hot item; he's going to be in a new show this fall. That ought to get you an agent."

"Don't even joke. I'll probably just be fighting him off all night."

"Why fight? Enjoy yourself."

"Enjoy? That's not my idea of a good time."

"What?"

"Oh, I don't know, Marissa, I guess I like to have a little relationship first."

"Bullshit, Nina, you just like to be the one to start it."

Was that what I was like? Did Marissa see so easily what I couldn't see at all? Or maybe she didn't know me as well as I thought she did.

"Maybe you're right." I fidgeted with the phone cord. "But that's only because that's the only control you can get with his type."

"So jump his bones first."

That wasn't what I meant. Marissa didn't get it.

"Marissa"—I paused, not sure if I should ask—"do you think he could have had anything to do with Jessica Roman's death?"

"Is that what you're afraid of?" She was quiet for a few seconds. "It's pretty unlikely, Nina."

"But he had something going with Jessica; you said you saw them." I shifted the heavy phone receiver on my shoulder. I told her what I'd heard on the news about Terry Trenton being the other murder victim and that I didn't know if she had been in one of Ron's classes. "But Ron never paid any attention to me until after Jessica was killed."

"That's just a coincidence, Nina." Marissa sounded exasperated. "Don't mess up this chance."

"You sound like you wouldn't mind taking my place."

"Hmm, let's see, break up with my starving-actor broke bartender boyfriend to date gorgeous, talented Ron Meyers?" Marissa let out a bark of laughter. "Ha. I'm not crazy."

"No, not much you ain't." I was more than a little surprised that Marissa would even kid around about giving up Dave. I'd take him over Ron any day. But maybe I was the crazy one.

Either way, she'd calmed me down a bit. Marissa was one of my few friends. I had some good friends in high school, but after graduation they scattered all over the country, that go-off-to-college thing. They came home on vacations, but we lost what we had in common. All they talked about was keg parties, term papers, and frat boys.

It was different, making friends after high school, harder. My life was full of work-to-survive jobs, acting classes, auditions, and men, not boys. Marissa didn't know my history and I was too tired to tell it, but she had more in common with me than anyone I knew. That made her feel like my best friend. It felt good to have someone you could count on, someone you knew counted on you. Benny was different. We had fun, but there was always that underlying tension, the feeling that he wanted more than I could give.

After I dressed in tan linen pants and a pale-pink top, I picked up my handbag and began cleaning out all the flotsam and jetsam that seemed to collect there. Receipts, tissues, gum wrappers, bar napkins. I came across Frankie's number and stared at it for a minute. Should I call him? What would I say? *Hey, big boy, why don't you come up and see me sometime?* Hardly. Well, not now, anyway, not tonight, maybe tomorrow. I tucked his number in my wallet. It was time to go. Another day behind another bar. And if I was lucky, no Cousin Bobby.

Saturday, another long, slow Saturday. I blocked Ron and the murders from my mind by becoming someone else. My magic trick. I pretended I was someone who hadn't heard of dead girls or acting classes, someone with no cares or woes. She was fast and free and came from the heart of the Bronx. She was working class, had no fancy dreams, and had a solid family at home. She had a safe, typical life to look forward to. Marry the high school sweetheart, pop out a couple of kids, volunteer at the school library. I loved being someone else. When I got it right, it was like a vacation. I rode the day and the worries fell away . . . although every time the door opened, I held my breath and said a little prayer until I saw it wasn't Cousin Bobby. That worked until the last hour of my shift.

Nick stood behind the bar with me. He liked to do that sometimes. He fiddled with items on the back bar, straightened a few bottles of top-shelf booze, poured a few free drinks for some flashy regulars like a big shot. He mostly stayed out of my way.

The pre-theater dinner buzz was just beginning. I didn't have many customers, but I was pouring cocktails for the waiters to bring to their early tables when the phone rang.

Before I could turn toward it, Nick picked it up. I busied myself opening some house wine: a few bottles of Valpolicella and some pinot grigio.

Nick turned to me. "Nina, phone for you."

Who'd call me at work? That just didn't happen. Besides, Nick already had half a conversation with whoever it is. *Oh. Who else?*

"Hi, Nina. It's Bobby."

"Hi, Bobby. What's doin'?" The phone receiver was warm and sticky from Nick's hands.

"I didn't get to talk to you last night. You took off pretty quick after your shift."

"Yeah, I had to get to rehearsal." Okay, it was a lie, but I was winging it.

"For acting school, right? See, I listen."

Boy, if he wanted points for that, he had the wrong game.

"Yup, I have acting class three nights a week and a lot of rehearsals. You, know, it's homework." He'd have to agree that my life was too full to fit him in. "And then there are all the auditions. It keeps me pretty busy."

"Right, well, I'm on my way downtown, and I thought I'd check and see if you're still going to be there in the next hour."

"Oh, no, I'm just heading out. I have plans." For once it was true, and I wasn't going to apologize.

"I thought I might be too late. You're a tricky one to catch."

What am I, a trout? "I'm kind of a planner, not really a last-minute kind of person." I turned away from Nicky. Bobby seemed more like the *I just thought of it* kind of person.

"Yeah, well, I was just on my way down, so I thought I'd check." Exactly.

"Sure. Well, have a good night, Bobby."

"Yeah, catch you later in the week."

Catch me later. Great. Nick was still standing right next to me, hanging on every word, apparently. I handed him the receiver since I couldn't get past him to hang up the phone.

"Bobby's a nice guy, you know." He looked at me with what I figured he thought was a winsome face, but to me he just looked vulturous. I backed up.

"I'm going to count out my register now, Nick." I felt no need to engage in a conversation about his cousin. At least Bobby was easier to deal with on the phone than in person.

When I got outside The Realm, I didn't feel my usual relief at finishing my week of servitude. My date with Ron and what I knew about the murders pressed on me from all sides. It was like the air was suddenly empty of oxygen and my lungs were vacuum packed. I put on my skates and rolled home slower than the rush-hour traffic.

I had to meet Ron in a couple of hours. I knew the normal thing was to have the guy pick you up, but I didn't like anyone knowing where I lived. When you had no family, no one to watch over you, you had to take precautions, however paranoid. There was time for a shower and a little baseball on TV. Maybe the Mets would rebound from yesterday's loss and kick it to the Reds.

I turned up my stereo while I showered and let the guitar strings of Jimmy Page vibrate through me while Robert Plant finished singing about what a long, lonely time it had been since he rock-and-rolled.

Oh yes it has, I agreed as I dried off to the sound of the Mets pregame chat. I looked in my closet as I combed out my hair. Dressing for dates was problematic. I wanted to look great, but if you looked too good, they didn't talk to you; they just tried to get you out of those clothes. And that wasn't paranoia; that was personal experience.

You tried to hold them off, because if you didn't, they treated you like garbage. But it wasn't that easy; I had hormones too. Ron was one of the sexiest guys around, and I was weak. I'd be like a starving child at a gourmet buffet. How much willpower could a girl have?

So, for my date with Ron, I put on a lavender dress with French capped sleeves. It was a good color for me and fit me well without being snug. Not too revealing, not too low cut or too short. *Led Zeppelin IV* rolled on my turntable, finishing with "When the Levee Breaks."

I looked at myself in my dusty full-length mirror, my hands on my hips. Time to make a move, but was this the right one? Jump back into the dating pool with a cannonball? Robert Plant was right: Praying never seemed to do any good, and neither did crying. I would just have to go with my instincts in hopes they were right. Maybe I knew a little more than the last time I dated, when the levee broke, so to speak. And if I could rally some courage, if I was smart, I might find out some things about Ron. If I could find out anything useful, I'd call that number Frankie Lopez gave me. I slipped on a pair of low summer heels with rubber soles. They were cool and comfortable, even if I had to do a lot of walking. Or running. Okay, deep breath; ready, steady, go. I pushed myself out the door.

Ron wasn't at the bar when I walked into Texarkana a few minutes early. I chose a barstool at the end of the room near the door. My stomach fluttered, and I reminded myself to breathe. Gordon, the barkeep, made his way over to me, wiping the bar and picking up stray sip sticks as he ambled along. He was one of the best bartenders I knew and a real sweetheart. I always stopped to visit when I happen to be in the neighborhood. He was the reason I'd chosen Texarkana to meet Ron. He was someone I could go to if I needed help.

"Hey, Nina, don't you look nice."

"Thanks, Gordo, nice to see you."

"Nice to be seen. What can I get you?"

I asked for a seltzer with lime, and I stirred it as I watched the door. I let Gordon start me a tab so Ron could pay for it—not that I was old-fashioned, but he did make about a million times more money than I did and besides, he'd asked *me* out. It wasn't the two-fifty for the drink. It was the principle.

Ron finally walked in about ten minutes late. He was going for upper status all the way. I was prepared.

"Evenin', lady." He slid onto the barstool next to me and brushed his lips against my cheek. "Bartender, I'll have a Black Label on the rocks."

Gordon shot me a fatherly look. He knew who Ron was, but he wasn't impressed.

"I'm hoping you'll let me take you to dinner. I know this great French place on the Upper East Side. Normally you need a reservation weeks in advance, but the maître d' is a big fan of mine."

Gordon put Ron's drink down in front of him. Ron almost drained it in one sip.

"Dinner sounds great, but we don't have to go anywhere that fancy. We can just sit and talk for a while, and then Gordon can get us a table right here." I felt safe in

Texarkana. People knew me. I didn't need any long taxi rides uptown.

"Whatever you say, Nina, but I hope I can talk you into going to my place for dessert." Ron took a good look at my dress. Or what was in it.

I laughed politely, as if he'd just told a joke. This was crazy. Was I going to be able to enjoy any date if the police didn't find this killer?

"Bartender, give us two more drinks here."

"Sure, I'm ready for another." I drained my glass and handed it to Gordon. "And make mine a little stronger this time, Gordo. I can take it."

I winked and he nodded. A little game I played sometimes—let 'em think your guard is down. Club soda with lime looks just like vodka and tonic.

Ron looked at me. He took my hand and stroked it. It was almost romantic.

"You look amazing. I've never seen you in a dress."

"Thanks." Legs will get 'em every time.

"It fits you very well." His eyes traveled up from my legs and hovered on my breasts. I thought he might actually lick his lips.

"And my mind?"

He laughed. Gordon placed our drinks in front of us.

"But why are we here, really?" I took a sip. "I mean, what made you ask me out?"

"That's something we have to figure out together."

He looked at me so seriously, so right in my eyes, that I couldn't respond. I tried to focus on his bad traits—there were plenty to choose from—but his eyes, the warmth of his body close to mine, his smile, his *charisma* all took over. It was hard to breathe normally. I felt like someone had punched me in the stomach and knocked the wind out of me. His charms were powerful and intoxicating. Suddenly, the air conditioning didn't seem to be working so well. I palmed my cold glass. Ron finished his second drink and motioned to Gordon.

"Could we get a nice quiet table in the back?"

Gordon did Ron's bidding. I was still trying to get my bearings. I had to dehypnotize myself from this guy or I was going to be in trouble. Good thing I wasn't drinking. That would have left me way too open to suggestion.

As we stood to move to our table, Ron gripped my arm and pulled me toward him, kissing me hard on the mouth. It seemed Scotch gave him a boost in physical strength. I let him kiss me, as if I had a choice. It happened too fast for me to react. He tasted like good Scotch with the promise of sex. I felt in danger of being swept off my feet. As we turned to walk to the back of the restaurant, I caught Gordon watching us, his arms crossed. I avoided his eye.

What if Ron was the killer and his plan was to make me his next victim? Had Terry Trenton been in one of Ron's classes? What the hell was I doing there? I was walking a thin line and putting myself in danger.

I toyed with a plan to excuse myself to go to the ladies' room and slip out the back door. But then I remembered Tex didn't have a back door. Maybe I should just run right out the front door. No, running was the coward's way out, and how would I ever face him in class if I snuck out on him? I'd have to buck up and handle it.

"What'll you have?" Ron perused the menu.

"The blackened redfish and a salad first." As if I could eat.

"How about some wine?" Ron lifted his eyebrows. "Or champagne? We could have some champagne, that would be nice."

"No, no really, I have a kind of allergy to white wine. I can only drink red." The truth was, champagne got me drunk faster than anything. Red wine was like part of my blood; I barely felt it. A few sips wouldn't affect me.

We ordered our dinner. Ron talked about the current Broadway season and the play he had coming up. I tried to relax. *Ron's no killer,* I told myself. He was just a regular guy, I was just a regular girl, and we were on a regular date. I almost started to enjoy myself. Our mutual love for the theater made for great conversation. But my brain wouldn't stop working. What had gone on between him and Jessica? Why was he so unconcerned about her death? My brain got my mouth involved.

"Did you know Jessica well?" Nothing but innocence in my tone.

"Jessica?" His fork froze halfway to his mouth.

"Jessica Roman. From our class?" I tried to sound nonchalant. "The one who was just found murdered?"

"Jessica Roman? Yes, yes, I know who you mean, long dark hair, about your height." He paused and looked straight into my soul. "Not very talented." He speared a chunk of rare steak with his fork, delivered it to his mouth, and chewed distractedly. "She had something, though, very attractive. Do you like the wine?"

"Oh yes, it's delicious." It had barely touched my lips.

"Drink up. The night is young." He picked up his wineglass. His smile was hungry, or thirsty, or both. My stomach lost the ability to accept food.

"Did you hear where she was found?" I moved the food around on my plate so it looked like I had eaten some of it.

He settled his wineglass to the right of his plate carefully and looked at me. "Were you two friends?" His eyes took on a serious and sympathetic quality.

"No, I hardly knew her."

"I hardly knew her myself." Ron finished off the wine in his glass. "She didn't work very hard. I don't pay much attention to students that won't put in the work."

I swirled the ruby liquid in my glass. I knew I had seen the two of them be more than friendly at The Studio, and Marissa had sworn they were cooing in the hallway. Why was he lying?

"What about Terry Trenton? Was she ever in one of your classes?"

"Trenton? Yes, I think I remember her. Why?"

"She was found murdered two weeks before Jessica."

"It's a shame about them both," he answered without any pause. "They were so young." He poured more wine for both of us. It seemed nothing I could say fazed him.

"Not to mention *the way* they died." I kept my voice low.

Ron picked up his newly filled wineglass and stared off into the distance. He turned his eyes on me, that ravenous smile on his face. He leaned closer to me, and I felt his warm breath on my cheek. "You know, all my favorite plays have death scenes."

All breath left my body, and my hands flew to my throat.

"Have you ever played Juliet? You would kill in that role." He downed half the glass of wine in one gulp.

I consciously tried to take in air and regain my composure. Was he really that unfeeling? Did he even know the difference between reality and acting? Maybe that was it: He was always playing a part and didn't even know what was real. Classic psychotic stuff.

As the dinner went on, Ron got more demonstratively affectionate, and that was putting it politely. Just after I picked up my fork and knife, he slid his hand up my thigh under the tablecloth. I almost stabbed him with my fork but brushed him off instead. I had my answer about whether he thought I was a good actor or a piece of ass. Or maybe he really was the killer and I was next in line for a death scene with him. Well, this piece of ass was getting tired of fighting off Ron Meyers. But somehow I felt paralyzed. I couldn't finish my dinner. I couldn't leave. I felt sick to my stomach. Ron was initiating a visceral reaction that was all too familiar.

One evening in the last days of summer after high school was over, I had a dinner date with a man I'd met at The Corner. His name was Jimmy and he was in his late twenties, although he looked younger. He had curly reddish-brown hair and a close-cropped beard and mustache. He was into bodybuilding and worked for some big firm on Wall Street. He picked me up at The Corner in his BMW. The car didn't impress me. I'll take an American car any day—a Camaro, a Corvette, even a Mustang.

He took me to dinner at an upscale pub, his choice. I guess he thought it was classy, but to me it was still a pub. He had a pint of ale. I stuck to my club soda. The food wasn't bad, but it was heavy. The conversation was the opposite. I couldn't really connect with him about anything. He was all football and stocks. He'd never been to a Broadway play and didn't like movies much. *Well, at least he's cute,* I thought. *That'll get me through dinner.*

Barely. I was so bored I couldn't wait to get home. Afterward, he drove slowly, which was a good idea, since he'd had three pints and two well-spiked Irish coffees. I was trying to come up with something else to talk about when he turned the car down a street that had more warehouses than apartment buildings.

"Is this a shortcut?" I knew my way around Brooklyn, and we were no longer moving in the direction of The Corner. He laughed and pulled the car over.

"No. I thought we could just sit and talk a little more before I take you back."

Talking was something we could do in a bar or restaurant. Making out was what you did in a car parked in a back alley, especially if you still lived with your parents, which I was just realizing must be the case. No wonder he could afford a BMW; it was his only expense. Below impressive. But he was sexy and had a twinkle in his eye that drew me in. He kissed me, and it was sweet. But he was trying to take it too far. I wasn't going to go all the way in a car with an almost-thirty-year-old—or anyone, for that matter. But he didn't much like me putting on the brakes.

"Hey, what's wrong?" He tried to pull me closer.

"It's late." I slid back to the middle of my seat. "I really have to get back."

"But we're having such a good time."

"Jimmy, please take me back to The Corner."

"Come on, how can you leave me like this?" He leaned his car seat back and pulled me on top of him. He was too strong and somewhat drunk. If I didn't play this right, I'd be in trouble.

"Come on." I tried to sound playful as I slid back to my own seat. "If you get me back before closing time, I'll buy you a nightcap."

"But I just bought you dinner." He laughed, but I didn't see what was funny. He reached past me, hit a button, and suddenly my seat back was flat and I was prone. He rolled over with his full weight on me and kissed me again. He was on top of me and he had the advantage. I tried to butter him up so I could talk him out of it. Then I out-and-out just told him to stop. But I couldn't get him to change directions, and he just kept going. The more I struggled, the rougher he got.

When I was young, my grandmother used to tell me that I had to let the boys win or they wouldn't let me play with them anymore. I found the dating world was full of winning and losing too, and as strong as I thought I was, I wasn't always strong enough, physically or emotionally. There were nights when *no* went unheard and I couldn't escape. Sometimes it seemed smarter to just get it over with fast. Fighting was tiring and dangerous. Giving in saved time and risk; so what if it stripped my soul? Ron was just another example. *If you want to play, you have to let the boys win.* It was true whether I wanted it to be or not.

Sitting in that restaurant with Ron, I tried to push away those memories, but they wouldn't leave. I became more repulsed and nauseated as the date went on. If only I knew how to defend myself better, or if someone had taught me I deserved better. Or, for that matter, if the world taught men they couldn't just do whatever they wanted to women and girls.

What was I doing here having dinner with Ron? I hadn't succeeded in getting any information about the murders, and his reactions to any mention of Jessica or Terry turned my stomach.

Ron ordered brandy, and I looked toward the bar for a glimpse of Gordon. I needed a friendly face. Sitting at the end of the bar not ten yards away from our table was Marissa, drinking a glass of white wine and waving to me. I couldn't believe she actually came to witness this.

"Are you wearing a bra?" Ron leered at my chest.

"What?" Oh, for Pete's sake. "Ron."

"Yes?" He looked up to my face.

"Would you excuse me for a minute?"

"Don't be long." There were plans in his eyes.

I wound my way between tables toward the bar, gave Marissa a scowl, and turned toward the stairs and the ladies' room. She followed me.

Inside I leaned against the sink and raised one eyebrow.

"What is this, junior high?"

"I was on my way home from visiting Dave at work, and I couldn't resist stopping in."

"I'm here all right. A little bruised but none the worse for wear." I took my brush out of my purse and used it vigorously. "I'll tell you one thing, I'm ditching him soon. The whole setup gives me the creeps."

"Oh, come on. Ron is no serial killer." Marissa fluffed her long dark curls in the mirror and smoothed her flowered skirt, which went perfectly with her pink scoop-neck blouse. The outfit looked great on her, but then, Marissa could make a burlap sack look classy.

"I don't know if he is or not. I'm just not enjoying myself."

"Then you're a fool."

I stopped the primping ritual and looked at her. "You don't know what you're talking about."

"No, but I'd like to."

"Look, Marissa, I'm no prude, but he's a pig!"

She just laughed. Hadn't she, like me, spent her life fighting off the likes of Ron Meyers and worse? She was pretty and sexy; had her life been so different from mine? Maybe it was just my bad attitude. I put my brush away and stared at my face in the mirror. I felt like I was going to cry. Marissa was the closest thing I had to a best friend, and she didn't know me at all.

What difference did it make? I pushed into a stall to grab a wad of toilet paper. I blew my nose and wiped my eyes. Suddenly, my fear and loneliness turned to anger. That was it. I was getting out of there. Why did I subject myself to so much shit?

"Come on, I want to get this evening over with."

Back downstairs, Marissa sat herself at the bar. I sat back down with Porky.

Ron tried to talk me into going to a different place for dessert, like his place, but I told him the bourbon pecan pie at Tex was the main reason I ate there. It wasn't a lie. By the time the waitress brought it to our table, I had my plan.

"It's been a wonderful evening, Ron." I took the last bite of sweet bourbon nuttiness.

"The night is young." He gave my earlobe a nibble.

"Actually, it's late for me. I have to get up tomorrow morning to go to church." He almost choked on his Rémy Martin.

"Can't you go to an evening service or something?" he almost squeaked.

"No, I have to read the gospel according to Matthew at the eight-thirty Mass. I read every Sunday at the Holy Name church." I could play the hell out of The Good Catholic Girl. I smiled and dabbed my lips with my napkin. "I want to thank you so very much for everything. I had a lovely time."

"Wait, I'll take you home."

I stood and walked behind him. He tried to get up, but I was too fast for him. I put my heavy hands down on his shoulders from behind and gave him a peck on the cheek.

"Good night, Ron."

"Wait—"

"See you in class." I prayed he wouldn't rush out after me. After all, he hadn't paid the check.

Sometimes my prayers get answered. Maybe I really should go to church.

As I passed the bar, I didn't see Marissa, just her empty glass of wine with some money next to it. I wasn't sure if it was a tip and she'd left or if she was in the ladies' room. I didn't have much time. I paused at the bar and glanced back to see Ron trying to flag down the waiter for the check. Gordon approached me.

"Gordo, did Marissa leave?"

"She just left a few minutes ago."

I smiled gratefully and slid out the front door to freedom. I thought I might be able to catch up to Marissa, but which way did she go? If she was walking home, she'd go west. I got to the end of Tenth Street and looked both ways. She'd keep going straight, unless she wasn't going home. I couldn't see her up ahead, but I crossed Fifth Avenue anyway; there was little traffic. When I got to the other side, I thought I saw her heading uptown. I hurried north for two blocks, and as I got closer, I realized it wasn't her. It was some other woman with a pink top and a skirt, and she was with another woman, laughing and smoking. Marissa must've gone south.

I turned and went down Fifth Avenue, passing where I had turned off Tenth Street. Was that her, walking down Fifth? It was dark, and there were other people on the sidewalk partly blocking my view, but I could see someone with dark curls, a pink top, and a patterned skirt. That must be her. She must be on her way home to Seventh Street and Avenue A.

I hurried down Fifth Avenue, weaving around the night revelers crowding the sidewalk, hoping I'd catch her so we could go grab a cup of tea or an ice cream cone or something to get the taste of the evening out of my mouth and brain. I almost called out her name, but she was more than a block ahead—it would've been embarrassing to shout, and she probably wouldn't have heard me anyway. I almost ran to the corner, the other pedestrians giving me funny looks as I passed. I crossed Ninth Street. I could see her cross the next corner, Eighth Street, still going down Fifth Avenue, and I almost missed the light. There was plenty of traffic moving across Eighth Street, including a crosstown bus that blocked my view; I crossed behind it, and when I landed on the south corner of Eighth Street and Fifth Avenue, she was gone. I kept walking down Fifth Avenue. Had she suddenly sped up and crossed into Washington Square Park? I didn't think she'd walk into the park at this late hour, and that park wasn't the safest in broad daylight, never mind after midnight.

Had I been imagining things? No, I was sure I'd seen her, but where had she gone? I called out, "Marissa! Hey, Marissa, where did you go?" There was enough partying activity around me, so I didn't feel as shy to call out. People who were walking home from clubs or just hanging out at the edge of the park. As I kept walking down Fifth Avenue toward the park, I looked left down a cobblestoned alley lined with old buildings. There was a kind of iron gate at the entrance, but it was open. The buildings on that alley looked like they came right out of a 1900 French musical. Maybe she had turned that way.

"Marissa! Are you down there?" I entered the dimly lit alley. I could see almost to the end of it where it came out on University Place, and I recognized it as part of New York University. "Marissa!" At first, I thought it was deserted. It was darker than Fifth Avenue, no streetlights, but then I saw a dark form running away, close to the buildings, in the deeper shadows. Whoever it was ran toward the other end of the alley.

And then I saw the crumpled heap on the ground—that pink top catching the dim light and standing out from the shadows.

Chapter 15

I ran toward her.

"Marissa, Marissa!" She was unconscious, lying on the cobblestones, blood on her pink blouse and one leg twisted underneath her body. "Marissa, it's me, Nina. Can you hear me?" I saw that blood was coming from the back of her head, her dark curls turning darker near the wound. "Marissa." I leaned closer; I fumbled with touching her wrist, then her neck. I didn't know how to feel for a pulse. Then she groaned, and I tried to straighten her leg and make her more comfortable. She was alive, she was okay, she was going to be okay.

I looked up. I wanted to go for help, but I didn't want to leave her alone. Whoever had done this had just run away, and he might come back to finish the job. But she needed a doctor, a hospital.

"Hello, help! Hello!" I yelled. "Is anybody there?" I didn't know if anyone lived in these little French houses or if it was some kind of office complex, but if I kept yelling, maybe someone would hear me. "Hello, please, someone help me! Help, I need help!"

I started to think of Kitty Genovese, that woman in the 1960s who had been savagely attacked outside her apartment building. How neighbors had heard her, heard her screams and cries, but no one had come to her rescue. Some people said they'd called the police, but by the time anyone actually came to the location of her rape and murder, it was too late.

"Please, can someone please help us!" I yelled as loud as I could. Then I saw some people standing at the end of the alley, by that iron gate. "Hello, please, we need help, an ambulance, the police—my friend has been attacked!" The three people seemed to confer, and then one of them came toward me.

"Hello, hi, what's happening?" He was a young man, looked like a tourist, neat khakis and a pale-blue golf shirt. He had probably been out on the town and was on his way home. "My friend went to call the police. Are you all right?"

"Oh, thank you, thank you. I'm okay, but my friend, she was attacked. She's unconscious." I sat on the rough cobblestones, lifting Marissa's head into my lap. I could see that I had her blood all over my hands and my lavender dress. I didn't care. She hadn't made another sound, but the blood seemed to have stopped flowing, and I hoped that meant the wound wasn't serious. But I didn't know anything about head wounds, or any wounds really. Now that I knew help was on the way, I tried to calm myself, tried to breathe evenly, which just made tears start to flow. Another young man came and joined the tourist next to me. I tried to stop sniveling.

"Our friend is calling the police and an ambulance."

I nodded, but I couldn't talk. I felt so tired. More tired than I'd ever felt in my entire life.

At Saint Vincent's hospital, I waited until they told me she was stable. She hadn't regained consciousness, but the doctor told me she was out of danger. I tried to call Dave at their apartment, but there was no answer. I considered calling Detective Frankie Lopez, but it was almost dawn by then. A uniformed cop had taken my statement, and I figured I'd be talking to Frankie and Tom the Cop soon enough.

I was a mess. I had washed as much of the blood as I could off my hands and arms, but so much of it had dried on my dress that I looked like an extra from a horror movie. Luckily, the uniform got me a ride home, and I just had enough life left in me to peel off my clothes and draw myself a bath. I didn't think I could stand up long enough to take a shower.

I turned on the hot water and was liberal with the lavender bath oil. I needed to erase all smells and feels from the evening. I flipped on the radio before I climbed into the tub. The latest from Bob Dylan was playing: "Gotta Serve Somebody."

I soaked in the fragrant warmth and let everything from the day and night steam out of me: the cursed dinner with Ron, finding Marissa attacked, the blood, the hospital.

All the while Bob Dylan kept singing about the devil and the lord and how we all have to serve somebody.

Serving alcoholics my whole life felt like serving the devil. But I'd had my fill of trying to serve the Lord too. I had escaped from Ron by telling him I had to get up for eight-thirty Mass. Sunday was a new day, a new week, but church was the last place I'd be on a Sunday morning. I'd gone to a Catholic church every Sunday when I was a kid. I loved the music and the community; there was even something about reciting the prayers in unison that felt comforting. But real church was different than the movies. It wasn't *Going My Way* or *The Bells of St. Mary's*. Few priests and nuns I met ever treated me with respect or kindness. Catechism class and Sunday sermons seemed mostly about making sure we were obedient and that we knew what horrible sinners we were. The Lord would forgive us, whether we deserved it or not, as long as we had enough fear and awe in our souls and went to confession.

My grandmother had bought into all the drama, but my mother hadn't. She told me that God was about loving and giving, not about sins and fear. Sometimes church was like that and it sounded right to me, but it was harder to imagine after she was gone. I stopped going to Mass after my grandmother died. My grandfather's funeral was the last time I'd stepped foot in a church.

I got out of the tub, wrinkled and warm, just as dawn was breaking, and dried myself off. I slipped into bed wearing an old T-shirt. Sometimes a bath would put me right to sleep. Cleansed of my sins, I could occasionally slumber undisturbed by dreams. I put my head on the pillow and let sleep take me.

I didn't make it to any eight-thirty Mass, but eleven o'clock was too early for someone who had crashed at first light. I had been startled awake by a disturbing dream. I was running in the dark and it was hot as hell. In fact, that's where I was, in hell. I ran this way and that, trying to get away from something or someone (the devil?). I was yelling something as I ran, my bare feet pounding on hot cobblestones. I woke up, the dream still buzzing in my head. What was I yelling? Oh, right, prayers. The Hail Mary over and over again as I searched for a way out of hell. *Holy Mary, mother of God, pray for us sinners, now and at the hour of our death. Amen.*

I called the hospital, and they told me there was no change. Marissa was stable, but she hadn't regained consciousness. I tried Dave again; still no answer. I didn't have a phone number for her family, but I had given the police all the information I knew about Marissa, and they'd said they would get in touch with her parents in Chicago.

It was Sunday. I was still booked for brunch at the Saz with Benny, but I had to find Dave and go back to the hospital. Exhaustion made me feel like a ninety-year-old woman. My muscles were sore, my bones ached, my brain hurt. I dragged myself out of bed and pulled on cutoff shorts and my softest T-shirt. I'd have to stop and tell Benny what was what first.

He was waiting for me at the Saz. He looked like something was up.

"Are you okay? Did you read the paper? Your friend Marissa—"

"I know, I was there."

"What?!"

I told him the short version of the night before. How Marissa had left Texarkana before me and how, in trying to catch up to her, I'd followed her and apparently interrupted her attacker.

"You saved her life," Benny said, his eyes wide.

"I don't know if that's true yet; she's still unconscious." I rubbed my eyes to stop them from tearing up. "I have to go back to the hospital."

He grabbed me by the wrist and pulled me to his chest. He hugged me so tightly I couldn't breathe.

"Benny, Benny, let go, you're crushing me." I struggled, and he released me. The look on his face was pure torture. I couldn't stand it.

"You're right, there's something terrible going on." His eyes had a blank look to them. Blind panic.

"Stop it." My hysteria was one thing; if Benny started to lose it, I'd go off the deep end. I walked behind the bar and made him a drink. Not much to making it; I poured him a snifter of cognac and sat down next to him.

He took a healthy sip and looked at me through his thick glasses. His eyes were wet and shiny. He'd done a lousy job shaving that morning. His face had patches of a day's growth with a few spots of dried blood, like he had nicked himself on his left cheek. He had gray puffy bags under his eyes, and for the first time it sank in that he really was a lot older than I was. I'd never seen him like this. I'd never seen anything faze him. He was a tough guy from the Village. A sweetheart, but a tough guy nonetheless.

"Look, I have to go. I have to talk to the cops, and I have to go back to the hospital." I fidgeted in my seat. "And I don't know where Dave is. I don't know if he's heard what's happened."

"Listen, I've been thinking. I think we should go away; we've got to get away. I'll get George to fill in for me, and we'll go somewhere for a while."

"Where're we going to go, Benny Banlon? You've never been out of this neighborhood, never mind New York City."

"We could take a plane to Miami, Florida."

"Miami in the summer?"

"Okay, Alaska, then. I don't care. But it's not safe here. We should get out of town until the whole thing blows over."

"Forget it."

"Just you and me. I have some money saved. We'll take off and have a vacation. Or we'll start over somewhere else and never come back."

That was never going to happen.

"It won't go away, just like that, and I'm not hiding. I was there, I was right there, and I was almost too late."

"Did you see who did it?"

"No. A dark form running away—tall, I guess. He was too far away; it could've been anyone." I shook my head. "If only I had seen who it was."

"If you'd seen who it was, he would have killed you too." Benny's voice got louder as he finished his sentence, and he stood up. I stared at him. He was trembling. In that moment I saw that he was even more scared than I was.

I looked at his desperate gray eyes through their thick glass windows and gave his shoulder what I hoped was a comforting squeeze. I couldn't muster up any more physical contact than that.

"I have to go." I reached for my shoulder bag. He barely moved.

It made my heart ache, but I left him sitting there. I had to deal with it my own way. I had to go to the precinct. I didn't know if the officer I spoke to last night had gotten my story straight. I had to talk to Detective Frankie Lopez.

I turned onto West Tenth. Why Marissa? Was it a throw of the dice? If I had walked out of the restaurant first, would it have been me? If Marissa hadn't come to watch us, me and Ron, she wouldn't have been attacked. Did that make it my fault? I'd known Marissa for only a few months, but I was closer to her than anyone else in my life. We worked our scenes together, we talked about everything. *Talked. Past tense.*

No, she was going to be okay. Who could have done this to her? Why couldn't I find Dave? Could he be the one who'd attacked her? Could Ron have left the restaurant and gotten ahead of me? I had gone the wrong way for a block or two before I turned around and kept walking until I saw Marissa and tried to catch up to her. No, it wasn't possible. Had Cousin Bobby or Black Net Shirt Guy or someone else been trailing me and caught Marissa coming out of Texarkana before me and followed her? Instead of me? Every scenario I could imagine convinced me it was my fault. My eyes blurred with tears. I could barely see my way down the street.

The sidewalk changed into a double-wide driveway, and I stopped. I was in front of the Sixth Precinct. I walked in and approached a giant uniformed officer behind a tall desk.

"Can I speak with Detective Lopez?"

"Name?"

"Nina Esposito."

"Sit over there."

He waved me over to a wooden bench against the wall. Hardly a concierge vibe. They didn't train them on customer service at the police academy. Ceiling fans were going full speed and there were a couple of window AC units, but the room was too big and crowded for them to make a dent in the heat. I tried to sit so the backs of my thighs didn't stick to the bench. How many perpetrators had occupied this spot, or victims of crimes, or innocent bystanders waiting to tell their side of the story? I rummaged in my bag for a tissue and blew my nose.

"Nina." Frankie was in front of me.

"Can we go somewhere to talk?"

"Sure. Come on." He turned and led me through the room. We passed a dozen dented metal desks; the men at each of them looked equally worn, like they'd been rubbed with an eraser. The sound of droning voices on telephones filled the stale air, punctuated by two-fingered typing on antiquated typewriters. The uneven *tik-tik-tok-tok* sounded like inebriated clocks. The walls were lined with metal file cabinets, mismatched sizes and colors. We walked all the way to the back corner and stopped at a desk that was slightly neater than most. Frankie gestured to a chair, and he waited while I sat down. Then he sat, pulling his chair closer to me. It wasn't private, but it was far enough away from most of the activity.

"I heard about it." Frankie's voice was gentle.

"Yes." I didn't know how to start.

"Tom called the hospital, but she's not awake yet," Frankie said. "He told me you know her from The Studio. He met her with you that night."

"Marissa. Her name is Marissa."

"Yes. Marissa."

"I don't just know her. She's my best friend." I reached for a tissue in my bag. I was not going to cry.

"I'm sorry." Frankie leaned closer. "But I don't have anything to tell you. I don't know anything new—"

"I didn't come here to get information," I interrupted. "I came here to give you information. I don't know if the uniform I talked to last night told you anything or even got it right. I was hardly together after what happened. I wanted to make sure you knew everything that happened."

"Okay, good, great, tell me everything." Frankie pulled his eyes away from mine, opened a notebook, and clicked open a pen.

"I was at Texarkana on Tenth Street, having dinner, and she was at the bar. We talked for a bit, and then later, when I was leaving, I noticed she was gone. She had just left, and I tried to catch up to her."

"What time was this?"

"When I left? After eleven thirty, I guess, closer to midnight." I stopped while he wrote. He finished and looked at me. "I was trying to hurry out the door, but I saw her wineglass at the bar. It was mostly empty, with some change next to it. I wasn't sure if she'd left or was just in the ladies' room, but the bartender, Gordon, said she had just left just a few minutes before. I almost didn't stop to ask him. I was in a hurry. I almost just went home." I couldn't believe how close Marissa had come to being the next victim. There was no doubt in my mind that if I had gone straight home after running out on Ron, she would've been found with a broken neck and—

"Why were you in a hurry to leave?"

I searched Frankie's face. Would he understand what it was like to be afraid of a man on a date even in a public place? Would he understand that even though you had agreed to meet the person and you wanted to meet the person, there was always the possibility that it could go wrong and you could be in danger? It had nothing to do with a serial killer being on the loose; that was just everyday life.

"I . . . I was on a bad date, and—" I didn't know how to explain. "I wanted to get out of there and get home. I practically ran out the door."

Frankie didn't speak right away. Then he seemed to make a decision. "Listen, the blow to the back of her head, it's consistent with Terry and Jessica. If you hadn't been there—" He put down his pen and notebook. "But then again, you could've been attacked yourself."

It was too real for me. I covered my mouth and tried not to make any sound. My lungs seized up and my head reeled. Frankie put his hand on my arm.

"Can I get you a glass of water or a Coke?" There was real sympathy in his eyes. I couldn't imagine Tom the Cop ever treating me like this.

"No, no, I'm okay." I wiped my eyes. "Marissa came to the bar at Texarkana because I told her I would be there. She came to watch me, and now—"

"Why would she come to watch you on a date? I don't understand."

"I was having dinner with Ron Meyers." I looked straight at Frankie. Whatever he was going to think of me for going out with Ron, I wanted to see it in his eyes. But I didn't see any judgment. "He asked me to meet him. He said he wanted to talk about my acting career." I sniffled, embarrassed. "But it was horrible. He was a pig, he drank too much, he put his hands on me right in the restaurant." I squirmed at the memory. "I know I should've known better."

"But why was Marissa there?"

"I told her we were going there for dinner. I didn't know she'd turn it into her evening's entertainment." I stopped. I was angry, angry at the world right now.

Frankie picked up his pen, made a few more notes.

"We have more to go on for this one. We'll interview the people at Texarkana. We can try and trace her last few hours before, see if anyone saw someone following her or with her . . ." He stopped himself.

"So do you think Marissa's attack is connected to Jessica and Teresa's murders?"

"Don't you?" His voice was soft but his meaning clear. He agreed with me.

"Yes, but it doesn't matter what I think. What is the NYPD going to do?"

"I've been trying to convince the bosses, even just Tom, that we have a serial killer here. I haven't made much progress. They don't want it to be true. But this? Marissa's attack? It might make a difference." Frankie leaned toward me, his eyes deep brown and sincere. "I can't catch a serial killer on my own. I need the whole city to be part of this."

"If there's anything I can do."

"This is helpful, really helpful. Thank you for telling me everything."

I knew he was trying to sound encouraging. He stood. My time was up.

"I'm glad you were here." I stood up too. I couldn't imagine having to bare my soul to Detective Tom Barry. "I mean, I'd rather talk to you than . . ." My voice trailed off.

"Who? Tom Barry?" Frankie's smile returned. "He's a teddy bear once you get to know him."

"Right." Some kind of bear, I was sure. I just hoped he could be convinced of the danger. I turned, and Frankie walked me back through the maze of desks to the front door.

"You have my number. If you need me for anything." Frankie touched my elbow so briefly I might've imagined it.

"Thanks." I paused.

"Thanks for coming in, Nina."

"Detective—"

"You don't have to call me *Detective* just because we're in the precinct." He gave me that goofy one-eyebrow-raised look.

"Right." But it suddenly felt weird to call him Frankie. I almost smiled. "I just want to say, thanks for believing me, and if there's anything I can do—"

"Just keep yourself safe, okay?" He tried a lighthearted smile, orchestrated to make me feel better. I lifted the corners of my mouth so he'd think it worked. "Don't—" He paused.

Was he going to say *Don't go on any more dates with suspects*? *Don't be a bumbling detective*?

"I get it." I looked at his handsome face. "Let you do your job."

"We're going to do our best. Leave it to us."

When I walked out the door, I couldn't help thinking about the night at Maria's and how I felt when we parted. This encounter couldn't have been more different. I thought we had some chemistry. I mean, he did ask for my phone number. Now he was all business. Now that he knew I had a date with Ron, he had probably filed me in the shallow category, an enterprising, ambitious, conceited actor. And why shouldn't he?

I stood in front of the precinct with my two best friends, chagrin and sorrow. I didn't know what to do next.

And then Dave walked out of the precinct door behind me and blinked in the bright sunlight.

"Dave."

He couldn't speak at first, just hugged me. I felt both of us trying not to collapse into tears. We held each other up with our collective grief and fear. It occurred to me that this would either pull us apart or bring us closer together.

After a moment, Dave finally let me loose.

"What are you doing here? Did the police want to talk to you too?" He kept one hand on my arm.

"I came in to talk to them." I watched him straighten himself, trying to stay in control. "Didn't they tell you I found her?"

"What?" He pushed his wavy bangs away from his red eyes. "What happened?"

"Let's go somewhere we can sit down."

"I got to get back to the hospital. I have to be there, even if she's not awake. And Marissa's parents are flying into town soon."

"Oh, thank god, you got in touch with them. I didn't know how to find them, or you. I tried to call you. I told the police everything I knew about you and Marissa."

"They found me all right." He rubbed his head. "I rushed to the hospital, and then they took me here. I barely got to see Marissa for twenty minutes."

"Let's just go sit on a bench by the hospital for a little while."

I walked and he followed. We sat on a bench in the shade. I didn't know how to start. My brain was buzzing from exhaustion as I stared at the sun-drenched cement sidewalk in front of us. Then I was startled out of my numbness by seeing a thumbprint-sized bruise on my wrist. Where had that come from? Ron? No, it must've been when Benny grabbed me in the Saz. That guy didn't know his own strength.

I told Dave everything that had happened, from when I'd told Marissa I was going to meet Ron at Texarkana to when I left her at the hospital.

"It's all so horrible." Dave pushed his fingers through his dark curls and lowered his head. "I can't stop seeing her face. She's as white as a sheet. How could this be happening?" His tears wet his cheeks.

"She's going to be okay, I know she will."

"The doctor said they can't know when she'll wake up, or how she'll be when or if she does."

"She's going to be okay." I refused to believe otherwise.

"I feel so guilty." He held his head in his hands, as if it couldn't possibly stay up without the support.

"Why do *you* feel guilty? She followed *me* for fun, and now—" I took a shaky breath. "Say something." I felt my throat closing up. "Tell me what you're thinking. Blame me. Yell at me. It's my fault she was in Texarkana."

"I'm not mad at you." His voice was calm. "You saved her life."

"But if she hadn't come to Tex to see me, it never would've happened."

"Who could've done this?" He looked at me, his eyes so pitiful. In my head, I started listing the suspects, and suddenly felt shitty that Dave had been on that list, however fleetingly. I didn't know what to say. His eyes were blank.

"Are you okay?" I leaned closer.

"Am I okay?" Dave looked away from me. "I just spent hours being questioned by a fucking police detective—who couldn't care less about Marissa, by the way." He rubbed his face with both palms. "I haven't slept in twenty-four hours or eaten in sixteen. And Marissa is lying upstairs in that hospital." He gestured toward Saint Vincent's. "Who knows when she'll come out of her coma, or if she will. When I saw her lying there in that hospital bed, I thought she looked dead. I felt like she was dead. Do you know what that's like? To see someone you care about and think they're dead?"

I knew exactly what it was like to see a loved one dead, stripped of life, lying right in front of you. It's not something you forget. I watched both my mother and grandmother approach their deaths, even though I missed their final moments. But it was even worse when you actually watched someone close to you die right in front of you.

One Sunday morning, my grandfather sat at the bar at The Corner, his pale hands fidgeting and restless on the dark-wood top. I was behind the bar, setting up, substituting for the latest fly-by-night bartender that had quit on us. My grandfather looked like hell. He hadn't had a drink yet that day that I knew of, but I wasn't sure when he'd last eaten. It was October 30, and I had flung all the front windows open wide to let the cool fall air do its best to blow away the residual aroma of booze and cigarette smoke from the night before. I'd worked until two AM and then hit a disco in Manhattan with a last-minute date, so I was running on only a few hours of sleep. But I had quit all alcoholic beverages and any inebriating substances since my birthday three months earlier. Someone at The Corner had dubbed me the Club Soda Kid, and it stuck. I accepted it as my new persona.

After graduation, it had been a summer of experimentation. I said yes to every proposed date, just to see if it upped my chances of meeting someone who would treat me right. Or maybe I was hell-bent on destruction, I didn't know, but I couldn't stop. I let the hurricane wind take me. At least it kept moving me forward. It felt better than the other choice: stagnation. That morning I was tired but invigorated by the cool fall weather and the memory of the music and dancing of the night before.

My grandfather sat at the bar in front of me with his head in his hands. I didn't dare ask him if he was all right for fear that he'd take my head off. I moved back and forth, quickly and quietly, cutting fruit, placing ashtrays and napkins in strategic positions, stacking beer mugs. Normally I'd throw some red quarters in the jukebox and play a few of my favorite classics, like "I Wanna Be Around" and "Fly Me to the Moon," sung by Tony Bennett, but I didn't want to set my grandfather off. When I landed right in front of him, behind the bar, to load extra beer into the ice sink, he suddenly spoke.

"Nina."

He startled me. I lifted my chin. We were face-to-face, and he looked at me tenderly. Then there was a moment I regret. I gave him a puzzled and probably scornful look, as if to say, *What the fuck?* It had been so long since I had seen one from him—a tender look, that is. Then he grimaced and said my name again louder.

"Nina!"

He hugged himself and fell off the barstool. I dropped the two bottles of beer I was holding. They exploded at my feet.

"Grandpa!" I hadn't called him that since childhood, but it flew out of my mouth.

I ran around to the other side of the bar, yelling for Danny, the weekend cook. I had no idea what to do. I hyperventilated as I loosened my grandfather's shirt, and he groaned for a moment with his eyes closed while Danny called an ambulance. I held his hand and stroked his head, but he grew still right away. I felt like I was growing roots and sprouting leaves waiting for that ambulance.

They gave him oxygen and hit him with those electrified paddles that made his emaciated body bounce with the shock. It's an image I can't forget. But his heart was finished. His thin, alcohol-ridden body couldn't be revived. In the emergency room I silently thanked him for going quickly. Sitting for days at another deathbed would have finished me too.

It was the first time I had to make funeral arrangements by myself, but I was not unfamiliar with the local funeral director. Simple and tasteful was the way to go. Hide the relief with a face of grief. Now I could sell the bar, move to Manhattan, concentrate on growing up instead of growing old. I told myself I was ready for the change, however it had to happen.

Yes, Dave, I'd had more than my share of experience with death up close.

"Am I okay?" Dave repeated, and hung his head. "I don't know how to answer that."

"I'm sorry. Stupid question." I felt like there was a piece of jagged glass in my belly. It was all feeling real to me.

"There's something I've got to tell you, Nina." Dave looked at me with his red-edged eyes. "I haven't been completely truthful with you lately."

"What do you mean?" Just what I needed, more truth.

"Marissa and I weren't doing so well. As a couple, I mean. I know she didn't say anything to you, but we were ready to call it quits. I've been seeing other people, and I think maybe Marissa was too."

"What?"

"That's why I feel so guilty." He shook his head. "I feel sick about what happened. It's all so horrible. I was out with someone else last night. If we hadn't been breaking up, Marissa wouldn't have gotten attacked. But we didn't love each other anymore, not like that. There's nothing I can do about that."

No. And there was nothing we could do about Marissa being in a coma. Dave's confession was a surprise, but at the same time it helped the pieces fall into place. I hadn't seen the two of them together in weeks. Marissa always had an excuse; so had he. Now I understood. But something Dave said didn't make sense.

"Marissa told me she was at your bar visiting you just before she came to Texarkana last night."

"I wasn't working last night."

"Why would she tell me she was visiting you if she hadn't been?"

"Maybe she didn't want you to know we were breaking up."

"Why not, if she was seeing other people?" I looked into his eyes. He turned his gaze away from mine.

"I said I think she was seeing other people. I'm not sure she was." Dave shifted in his seat. "She wasn't telling me much lately."

"But you're seeing someone else." I was starting to get the whole picture.

"Yes." Dave looked right at me. But something behind his eyes had slammed shut.

I sat there for a minute. Maybe Marissa hadn't told me they were finished because she hoped they would patch things up. She hadn't been seeing anyone else that I knew about. The real truth was Dave had been cheating on her but was trying to convince me it was a mutual breakup. He'd been trying to dump her, or worse. The little sharp pain in my gut expanded.

We didn't say much more to each other. It seemed he wasn't the dream boyfriend I had envied. Maybe I'd seen him as the greener grass just because he was on the other side of the fence. Maybe Marissa was more like me than I knew, always dating guys who treated her badly.

But maybe I was being too hard on him.

"I'll come up with you," I said.

We went up to Marissa's hospital room. She was lying there like an angel against the white sheets, her pale face surrounded by dark curls pushed forward by the bandage on the back of her head. Dave sat next to the bed and held her hand. Somehow I didn't really want to meet her parents.

After a while, I left him. He promised to call me when she woke up. I hugged Dave goodbye.

I left the hospital and floated through the streets in my own fog. My feet walked of their own accord, pointing south. The Sunday city was slowly coming awake. I was faintly aware of tourists finding their way, workers opening their shops, and families coming out of churches. I walked until I hit the bottom edge of the island of Manhattan. I looked through the summer haze at the Statue of Liberty and thought about Marissa and acting class and wondered what it was that made people want to perform. What was it in Marissa's life that put acting in her body and mind? Was being seen from the stage or screen somehow better than just being seen? There were certainly more important things in the world. Would Marissa question what she was doing with her life when she had so nearly lost it? It certainly made me think: What the hell was I doing with mine?

I watched the water lap against the dock; the rhythm hypnotized me. When I finally looked up, the ferryboat to the

Statue of Liberty was pulling away full of happy tourists. The sun had broken through the fog and was already sinking. My nose felt burnt, and my clothes were damp with sweat. I had no idea how long I'd been standing here.

I felt like I'd just come out of my own coma, and I thought of my mother and grandmother. I had no feeling that they were still with me somewhere in my heart or soul. There was only emptiness.

"Are you all right?" A motherly-looking woman stopped next to me and touched my arm. The skin of her warm brown hand was soft and her voice was gentle. I realized my face was wet. She handed me a tissue.

"I'm okay." I wiped my cheeks. "Thank you." I tried to smile at her as I walked away. There were always nice people in New York City, just when you least expected it.

I walked back uptown. I was tired enough to go straight back to bed, even though the sun hadn't yet set. But the Saz was on my way. Brunch was long over, but I had to go back and talk to Benny. I'd left him hanging and that wasn't right.

When I got there, George was behind the bar.

"Hey, George, where's Benny?"

"He left already. Called me up and asked if I could come in a couple of hours early. So here I am." He paused with an empty glass in his hand. "You want a drink?"

"No thanks."

Back out on the street, the brick buildings began to take on that rosy glow they got when the sun was low. I looked at my watch. Six thirty. How had that happened? I hadn't eaten, and I hadn't even gotten the paper.

Newspapers. What good were they, anyway? Nothing but bad news.

I stood on Hudson Street. Maybe I should just get some sleep. The clock said it was too early, but time didn't seem to have much relevance at the moment.

"Nina."

I jumped. Gorgeous Charlie stood in front of me.

"Don't sneak up on me like that, Charlie."

"Didn't mean to." He smiled his brilliant smile, the sun behind him turning his curls into a halo. "What are you doing? Just going in or just going out?"

I realized I was still standing in front of the Saz. Where else would I run into Gorgeous Charlie?

"Out."

"You don't look so good. Why don't you let me buy you a drink?"

"I think what I need is some dinner and a hot shower." I started to walk away.

"Wait." Charlie walked along with me. "I know you won't let me help with the shower part, but let me buy you dinner."

I was not in the mood for Charlie's humor, but his offer was tempting. A sharp gnawing in my stomach reminded me that I hadn't eaten all day. There was no food in my apartment, and I didn't have the strength to cook or even decide on a takeout place. I needed someone to take over for me, and there was Gorgeous Charlie, the path of least resistance.

"Okay."

He whisked me two blocks away to a tiny French place where they waited on us hand and foot. Charlie played the benevolent host, ordered for both of us, and made sure the waiter brought us the best of everything. The food was so delicious I had no choice but to eat.

"I'm beginning to think you have a heart." I dabbed my mouth with the fine linen napkin.

"Nina." He placed his hand on his chest as if I had physically wounded him. "Haven't I always been nice to you?"

The waiter came over to pour more wine, confident of a good tip. Charlie must be a regular. Nice to have money.

"How is everything, sir?" The waiter directed all communication toward Charlie. To him I barely existed.

"Superb. Delicious." Charlie looked at the waiter with a natural and empathetic smile, different from the way he looked at me. When we talked, it was like a volley back and forth, never a real conversation. In front of the waiter, I seemed to be part of the expensive food and wine, more like a prize than a person. Then again, he hadn't tried to put his hands on me, unlike Ron. Had that date really happened only last night?

"Not only do I have a heart, I'm a gentleman." Gorgeous Charlie continued his sales pitch about himself, leaning back in his chair with pride. "I treat you like a lady."

Yes, that was it, Charlie treated me like a lady instead of a person. Ron treated me like a piece of meat. Bobby treated me like a conquest. The distinction was clear, but none of them saw me as a person. Charlie smiled a benevolent smile, making sure the waiter observed. I smoothed the linen napkin in my lap. When the waiter disappeared, Charlie leaned closer.

"I heard the news this morning. That girl who was attacked, Marissa, that was your friend you brought to the Saz, am I right?"

Acid tears sprang to my eyes. I had pushed reality out of my mind for a few minutes, but it all came rushing back. I nodded in response, not trusting myself to speak. The last thing I wanted was to start weeping in front of Charlie.

"I'm sorry. Is she going to be okay?" Charlie picked up his wineglass. I shrugged.

I looked at the remains of my dinner and my almost-empty wineglass. I shouldn't be so hard on Charlie, I decided. He'd taken me to dinner and tried to be kind. He hadn't tried to molest me. He'd treated me with his version of respect. It wasn't fair to expect more than that. I took the last sip of wine from my glass. It was time to go home.

"Thank you for everything, Charlie."

"That sounds like an exit line."

"Charlie, today has been the longest day of my life. If I don't get home soon, I'm going to crash right here."

"Okay, let me put you in a cab." He shot the waiter a look and signaled for the check.

I almost couldn't take Charlie being this nice. I was able to hold it in until I got in the taxi; then the floodgates opened. The cab driver probably thought I was crazy, but I was sure he'd seen worse.

I stepped out of the taxi in front of my building, wiping my eyes with the back of my hand. The cab pulled away as I reached into my bag for my keys.

Then I saw Detective Tom Barry step out of the shadows and come straight at me, fast and hard.

Chapter 16

"I've been looking for you all day," he growled. "You can come down to the station, or we can talk in your apartment."

I almost sat down right there by the garbage-strewn gutter, I was so tired.

"Look, Detective, can't I come see you in the morning? I'm beyond exhausted. I already told Detective Lopez everything I know."

"I appreciate that you came in to the precinct. But I'm the lead detective on this case, and I need to interview you. Detective Lopez shouldn't have let you go until I talked to you." He looked at me without any pity in his eyes. "Now, upstairs or the station?"

The last thing I wanted was this gorilla in my apartment. But the precinct felt miles away, and I barely had enough strength to climb my own stairs. He knew he had me beat. He smiled that gray crowded-tooth smile, but his eyes were mean. We climbed the long flight to my converted loft apartment. I unlocked the door and led him to my kitchen table.

"Make yourself at home." I gestured. For a moment I wondered how he knew where I lived, but then I remembered he'd copied down my address when I showed him my driver's license at the Saz. Did that mean Frankie knew where I lived? I turned away to put the kettle on for tea. I knew I wouldn't be rid of Tom the Cop anytime soon.

He sat at my kitchen table. I stood by my bookshelves. The smooth honey-blond wood was cool to the touch. The shelves were solid, like the trees they came from. I leaned up against them, trying to absorb their strength.

"I want you to tell me everything you can about your friend Marissa."

His casual reference made me wince. I didn't trust myself to speak, but I managed to nod my head. I had so many pictures of her in my head: Marissa performing in class, Marissa sitting at the bar, Marissa bleeding on the ground, Marissa in the hospital, dressed in white. "I especially want you to tell me what you know about her last twenty-four hours."

The whistle blew on my teakettle, giving me some stalling time.

"Tea, Detective?"

"Got any coffee?"

"Just instant Sanka."

"Skip it. Just start talking." He reached in his shirt pocket. "Mind if I smoke?" He was so polite.

"If you must." His request irked me, but I gave him an ashtray. I sat across the table from him as I arranged my teapot, cup, and saucer, my irritation building. "I'll tell you everything I know, but don't give me a hard time, don't interrupt me, and save all your questions for when I'm done."

"Fine." He took out a small tape recorder. I gave him a dirty look, but I didn't protest. Maybe it would save me from having to repeat myself.

I started with my phone call with Marissa on Saturday morning. I told him every fact with as little emotion as possible. I ended at my talk with Dave.

"And where were you all afternoon?"

"Walking, thinking, then I had dinner with a friend."

"And how long did you have that date planned with Ron Meyers?"

"He asked me Thursday afternoon."

"You already knew you were going to see him that night when we spoke over coffee?" His face turned red.

"Yes." He made his last interrogation of me sound like a social occasion.

"What else aren't you telling me?"

"Nothing." I sipped my tea. His anger made me feel in control of mine.

"Why didn't you tell me you had a date with him coming up?" He started to steam.

"You didn't ask."

"Do. You. Have. Another. Date. Planned. With. Meyers?" He spoke slowly and deliberately through gritted teeth.

"No."

"Do you realize how close you came to getting killed yourself?" He was ready to spit nails.

If he was trying to unnerve me, it was working. I put my cup in its saucer before I spilled any tea. My hands had lost their steadiness.

"So you think it was Ron? Marissa could've run into anyone after she left Texarkana. How could he possibly have left the restaurant that fast and gotten ahead of me?"

"He slipped out right after you did and followed her. You said you went north on Fifth Avenue for a block or two before you turned around and caught sight of her. He must've come straight out Tenth and gone south immediately. He was probably following you but found her instead."

"No, no, that can't be what happened." Was it true? Had he run out to follow me but ended up with Marissa?

"Why do you find it so hard to believe that Ron Meyers is a killer?" Tom the Cop spat the words at me. "Because he's your lover?"

He made me so angry I almost couldn't speak. "He's not my lover," I sputtered. "That was my first date with him, and I walked out of that restaurant because he wouldn't keep his hands off me. If I wanted to be lovers with Ron Meyers, I would've been his alibi last night."

"What makes you so sure he wouldn't have killed you instead?"

Why is he trying so hard to make Ron the murderer? Something didn't fit.

Tom the Cop continued, "Ron Meyers doesn't have an alibi for last night. He claims to have gone straight home after he left Texarkana, but he doesn't have any witnesses. And he has no alibi for the other two murders either."

"So now you think they're all connected?"

He looked at me sharply. "I didn't say that."

"But you can't deny all three have things in common."

"Two slightly similar murders don't make enough of a pattern to launch the city into a panic. We've been through that. It doesn't help us solve the case."

"Three cases."

"Last night's attack does not make a third."

I held my anger in. It wouldn't help me convince him. "But the first two aren't just slightly similar, are they? Isn't it true that the killer killed them first and then"—I almost couldn't say it—"r-raped them?"

"Yes."

"How do you know it wasn't the other way around?"

"It's called forensics." His sneer was both condescending and amused. So glad I could entertain him. "Death occurred before penetration."

"Okay, okay, I believe you." I didn't want any details.

"Why does it matter?" He lit another cigarette. The ashtray was already overflowing, the smell making me sick.

"What do they say about necrophiliacs—that's what they're called, right?" I poured the last of the tea from the pot into my cup. "People that get their kicks out of sex with dead bodies, they can only get turned on that way. I read somewhere that they can't do it with a live person. That doesn't fit Ron Meyers."

"What do you mean?"

"The way he was going after me, he would've done it right there in the restaurant if I'd let him. He's not a necrophiliac kind of guy. He's a pig, yes, but a necrophiliac? I don't think so."

Tom the Cop smoked. I swirled the tea in my cup. For a moment I felt like we were in it together. Like he'd actually heard me and he was really trying to solve the crime. Maybe Frankie was right: Tom wasn't like the corrupt and useless cops I'd grown up with. Maybe I'd misjudged him.

Then he started to laugh. It was a cold, mean laugh that came from deep inside his black heart. It gave me the heebie-jeebies.

"You think you could look at a man and tell what he's capable of?" His laugh got deeper and ended with a hacking cough. He cleared his throat and then took another drag of his cigarette with a squint and a grimace.

I drained my teacup and put it down quietly. He didn't get it. I wasn't going to get in an argument with him, but I knew what I was talking about. When it came to men and their sexual urges, I practically had a PhD in behavioral science. I sighed and stood up.

"I'm done. Now please get out of my apartment." I spoke without energy or malice.

As he gathered his tape recorder, I walked across the room and opened the door.

"Be smart and watch out for yourself. And make sure you tell me everything from now on." He stood in the doorway, his face too close to my nose. I held my breath to avoid his cigarette stink. "If you're going to see Mr. Ron Meyers again, I want to know about it in advance."

"You're barking up the wrong tree." I started to swing the door closed.

"I'm serious. If you go out with him again, which I advise you not to, you better let me know." He put his meaty hand on the door to stop it.

"I'm not planning on going out with him again, although I don't see why I have to keep you informed about my private life." I kept up the pressure on the door.

"I'm glad to hear it." Detective Dim Twit was so attractive when he smirked. "But don't think you have a choice about disclosing information to me. You're in this now, whether you like it or not. Anything less is obstruction."

"I'm just an innocent bystander. This has nothing to do with me." I tried to convince myself as I edged him out the door.

"You are under an obligation to cooperate," he hissed, not unlike a snake. "How can you not want to? Don't you want to help catch the guy who attacked your best friend? The guy who bashed in her head and was about to wring her neck and rape her—"

I tried to close the door on him, but he blocked it with his out-of-shape body. He was trying to scare me out of seeing Ron again, but I didn't need his help. I was holding up pretty well, but I had to get him out of there before I broke. He stopped the door from closing the last few inches with his scuffed-up shoe and looked at me with his square pasty face.

"If Meyers calls you or asks you out, I expect you to call me or come by the precinct." He removed his foot.

I shut the door in his face and locked the top lock. My eyes closed, and I tried to erase the picture of what had almost happened to Marissa that he put into my head. My body gave in to violent shuddering, and I shuffled over to my bed, shedding my clothes as I went, and crawled under the covers. *This isn't really happening,* I mumbled through my tears. *This isn't really happening. Tomorrow I'll wake up and it'll all be just a dream. Just a long, bad dream.*

Thinking about bad dreams wasn't the best way to fall asleep. In my experience it tended to bring them on. I woke about three o'clock gasping for breath. No chance of going back to sleep after that. I slipped a videotape into my VCR. Movies, my usual way to avoid reality.

It wasn't an original mode of escape, but it always worked for me. It wasn't so long ago that I would go to the movies five or six times a week, some of them double features. The structure of opening and closing the restaurant every day had been my last tether to reality. After my grandfather died, I sold the restaurant and paid off the bills. Then I was rudderless. All I could do was obsess about the abuses of my past and sink deeper into murkiness. I had never applied for a job in my life, never rented an apartment. I didn't know where to begin. All I wanted to do was escape into movies, and after I found the loft, I let myself do just that.

I told myself that watching movies was research for my acting career, which wasn't exactly a lie. Bonus: While I was doing this important research, I could forget who I was, forget I even existed. The problem was, as soon as the credits rolled, I was ejected from the fantasy right back into real life. It was painful, like scuba divers who get the bends when they come up to the surface too fast. Reality didn't make sense anymore. It took me months to crawl out of that hole.

As dawn broke, I popped another VHS cassette into my VCR and watched more of the black-and-white murder mysteries, noir thrillers, and spy stories from the forties and fifties that I had in my videotape collection. Murder, mayhem, handsome villains, secret spies, good cops, bad cops—it was all somewhat like my real life at the moment. Yet while I watched the movies, I could avoid thinking about what had happened to Jessica, Teresa, and Marissa. I convinced myself I was a moviegoer just a bit too close to the screen but not part of the plot. On the edge of danger but still safe. I was suspended, floating on the borderline. I finally drifted off to sleep for a few hours.

I woke at ten o'clock and called the hospital. I spoke with Marissa's parents, who told me that she had regained consciousness and was going to be all right but also that she was asleep and needed her rest, so they didn't want me to visit. Marissa had spoken to the police, but she hadn't seen anything that could help them. The attacker had approached her from behind and knocked her out. They thanked me for getting her to the hospital, but I got the feeling they also blamed me. They were cold and dismissive. Or maybe they just thought I was too far below their North Chicago suburban class.

There was no reason to go to Ron's scene study class that night: no scene partner, no scene. And I was hardly enthusiastic to see him. There was really no reason to leave my apartment. If I needed food, I could order it. I slid in another videotape, then ordered in Chinese. My phone was off the hook, my door triple-locked. I felt safe. As safe as a monkey behind bars in the zoo.

I felt more human after I had some food and a shower. Then I got hit with claustrophobia. As much as I felt safe locked in my apartment, I also felt trapped. I paced back and forth from my kitchen area to the front windows, back and forth, back and forth, overthinking. This murderer had been in my sights. I had seen his dark form, a shadow, however briefly. He had attacked Marissa, and if I had been a moment later, she would be dead. A moment earlier and I might be. Did he know who I was? Either before or since I'd interrupted him? I shivered. I had to get out and do something. I wasn't going to let fear keep me in a cage. No one was going to have that dominance over me. I had made that promise to myself after my grandfather died.

Marissa's parents didn't want me to bother her at the hospital. I didn't want to talk to Tom the Cop. And Frankie? He seemed to have made it clear that I should let the police do the policing. But I had to have some forward motion.

I couldn't walk around looking for a murderer on the streets; that would be useless, and even if I waited till Saturday, the killer's apparent choice of deadly date nights, what would I do, haunt all the alleys in the West Village and try to spoil his fun again?

Then it hit me. Tom the Cop refused to believe it was a serial killer because he wouldn't count Marissa and claimed two didn't make a pattern, but had Teresa and Jessica been the only victims? The killer had targeted each girl on a Saturday night, not quite consecutively. There was a Saturday between Teresa and Jessica when nothing had happened. Or was that true? Maybe he had attacked someone outside the Sixth Precinct on another Saturday night and the cops hadn't connected the dots. What had Tom the Cop said? He had a dozen murder files on his desk? How many other detectives could say the same? Dozens, at least. The newspapers reported there had been over a thousand murders in NYC since January 1979, and the NYPD didn't sound too organized to me. There might be another petite dark-haired dead actress's file sitting on the desk of a cop in another precinct. Or even more than one.

Chapter 17

I pulled out my map of Manhattan and spread it out on my long kitchen table. It showed subway stops, libraries, government buildings, and the outlines of police precincts. What was closest to the Sixth Precinct? The Ninth was the mirror of the Sixth, and the two precincts split the Village down the middle at Broadway. The Ninth was the east side. That had to be a worse place to work, I thought. The East Village and Alphabet City were rough streets: a lot of burned-out buildings, squatters and drug gangs, punk rock runaways. Maybe they had found a dead girl from another Saturday night and no one had made the connection.

Would they tell me if I asked? I could try. Maybe I could say I was a reporter. Would that be better or worse than a plain old citizen?

I walked down to Houston Street and straight across town and into the Ninth Precinct. What a circus! While the Sixth had been busy, the Ninth was complete chaos. There were more waiting perpetrators and complainants than cops in the dimly lit room. And a lot of yelling. I stood to one side of the crowded entrance waiting for my chance to talk to the cop at the front desk. He looked mean, and I wasn't sure there was anything I could say that would result in him giving me information. Even if he believed I was a reporter, would he talk to me? Maybe that was the wrong plan. Then a tough-looking woman in uniform took his place. Tall, powerfully built, in her thirties, she looked like she could pick up any of the unruly perps and throw them across the room if they got too far out of line. I wasn't sure she would be any easier to talk to, but I went for it, changing my plan.

"Hi, hello, um, sorry to bother you, but I have a missing friend, and I was told that someone at the precinct could tell me if, god forbid, she was found, um, dead." The desk sergeant looked at me with annoyed pity and glanced at the ringing phone.

"How long has she been missing, and what did she look like?"

I gave her the date of the Saturday between the weeks Teresa and Jessica were attacked, and I described her as petite, with brown hair and eyes. The sergeant took a few notes, then put the pen down and stared at me.

"Do you have any idea how many murder cases have come into this precinct since that day?" I shook my head. "Dozens, and I don't have them all memorized. It would take me hours to get that information for you, and I'm pretty busy, as you can see."

"I can see." I stood there, my brilliant plan collapsing, my brain scrambling for the next one. I must've looked pretty pitiful.

"Look." She leaned on the stack of files in front of her. "You're better off calling all the hospitals or going to the morgue. They'll have all the possibilities from all the precincts." She looked at me with what probably passed for kindness in her world, her foot tapping with impatience.

I thanked her, and as I turned to walk away, she got swallowed back up by her job at hand, as if I had never been there.

The New York City morgue was in the bowels of Belleview Hospital up on First Avenue in the section of Manhattan called Kips Bay. As I searched for the right entrance, I couldn't help thinking about all the stories I'd heard about people being detained at Belleview for mental health issues. It's a full-fledged hospital in every regard, but there had been too many jokes referring to "ending up at Bellevue" when I was growing up that put that part of it first in mind. Besides, since it had been built in the 1700s, the design of the main entrance was Gothically dark and creepy. I felt like I was in the opening of a horror movie.

I found the main office, and while it was about as busy as the Ninth Precinct, the vibe was completely different. People moved quietly in the harsh fluorescent lighting, shuffling files and boxes from one desk to another. It wasn't noisy, but the clacking sound of typing was relentless.

I walked up to what seemed to be a reception desk, but no one was covering it. I stood there, waiting, trying to catch someone's eye, but I was invisible. After at least five minutes, an older man entered the room from a door toward the back and approached the desk. He sat without looking at me as the smell of cigarettes floated in my direction. Smoke break. I waited till he settled himself, and then he looked at me with eyes that said, *If you're here, it can't be for a happy reason.* His vague empathy put a lump in my throat.

"Hi, I'm looking for . . . that is, um, I have a friend who's been missing the last few weeks, and the police suggested I come here? Maybe something happened to her and she had no ID on her?"

He nodded, his white shaggy eyebrows framing his clear brown eyes.

"Description?"

I gave it, and the date of that first Saturday in August, and he walked over to another desk, grabbed a file box, and brought it to his desk. He took out a handful of files and started leafing through them. Was this his main job, I wondered, looking up reports of unidentified bodies? He looked up at me as I stood over him and stopped.

"This is going to take a while. I got a few boxes of these files to look through."

"All of those are unidentified?"

"No, but all of these bodies are unclaimed, which includes the John and Jane Does."

"I see." I was going to offer to help, but I didn't think he'd be open to me looking through his files. I took a half step back and tried to look more patient than I felt.

As he went through the stack, he would occasionally pull out a file and put it aside. When he got to the end of the first box, he moved on to the next one. Eventually, he had a shorter stack that he scrutinized more closely. I was impressed at his resolute approach to the task. He knew his job and went at it with commitment if not enthusiasm.

Finally, he held up three files and asked me if I'd like to look at them and see if I recognized my friend. I felt a little guilty at my ruse, but I nodded and took the files from him. I avoided looking at the small black-and-white photo of each woman's face clipped to the top corner of each report and instead looked for the date the body was brought in. I put the first one aside; that poor Jane Doe died on a Thursday. But the next one had been brought in on the morning after the Saturday between Teresa and Jessica, and the third was found the Sunday morning of the weekend before Teresa was found. Could these two girls be part of the pattern? They'd both been found in the East Village, in a different precinct than where Frankie worked. I couldn't tell how they died or if they even had autopsies. The language in the reports was indecipherable.

I transcribed the file numbers into the pocket notebook I kept in my shoulder bag. My hands were shaking as I handed the files back to him.

"One of these top two might be her. I'll report it to the police detective I've been talking to."

He took the files, put them aside, and gave me a nod. He wasn't cold, exactly, but I read something in his eyes. Something like *Hey, it's just a job.*

Walking with purpose toward the Sixth Precinct, I considered calling Frankie, but I figured he wouldn't be home. It made more sense he'd be at the precinct. At least that was my hope, because the last thing I wanted to do was talk to Tom Barry again. But if I wanted them to do something about this case and Frankie wasn't there, I'd have no choice. Maybe these two additional victims would convince him.

When I got to the precinct, it was the dreaded worst-case scenario. No Frankie, but Tom the Cop was available. He led me to his desk at the back of the squad room, and we both sat on banged-up metal chairs.

"Come to your senses, have you?" he said with a smirk. "Came to tell me something you didn't tell me last night?"

I tried to tell myself that this was a good exercise in control. Not losing my temper would be a big success, proof that I was more together than this mook of a detective.

"No, I didn't forget anything, but I thought of something. I was thinking that if this serial killer—"

"If he's a serial killer," Tom the Cop interrupted.

"—if this killer was in the habit of murdering on Saturday nights, he skipped one. Or there was a victim out there that you guys didn't know about." His face started to turn red. "So I went to the morgue, and they found two other similar Saturday night victims that were unidentified. Both in the Ninth Precinct." I handed him the slip of paper with the two file numbers.

Tom grabbed the piece of paper from me and practically crumpled it in his fist. "If you think this proves it's a serial killer instead of separate murders, you're the worst kind of sensationalist fanatic—"

"I'm not a fanatic!' I stood. "I just want it to stop. If you don't want to listen to what I have to say, I'll take it to your boss, or no, better yet, I'll go to the papers. They'll have a blast with this information." I started to walk away.

"Hey." He stood and grabbed my arm. I shook his hand off. "I didn't say I wasn't going to look into what you found. I'll call the morgue. If you found something that can help, great, we'll take it. But you've got to stop interfering."

"Yeah, right, interfering," I said. "You're welcome." And I walked away, hoping I would never have to talk to him again.

After the rush of adrenaline that the last few hours had given me, my brain and my body started to shut down. I hadn't had nearly enough sleep in days. I felt like the walking dead. I stopped at a deli, picked up some food, and made it to my loft. I pulled all the shades down, wolfed down a sandwich, and crashed.

A dozen hours later I woke, starving and foggy headed. I lay in bed staring at the ceiling, my brain ticking off the events of the last few days. Now what? I had to feed myself and move on with my life. Whatever that meant. I poured a big pot of tea and managed to eat some toast. Tuesday morning was launched.

I still didn't want to leave the sanctuary of my loft. I put on Tom Waits's latest album, *Blue Valentine*. Blues, jazz, tragedy, comedy—it told stories I could relate to. Before I realized it, I had a rag in my hand and I was cleaning my bookcase, jostling each book to get at the dust as Tom sang "Somewhere" from *West Side Story*. A new way of living? Yeah, right. The album continued with "Whistling Past the Graveyard." Admittedly more appropriate.

The phone rang a couple of times, but I let my answering machine pick up and listened to the callers as they recorded their messages. Dave called to tell me Marissa's parents were flying her home and that she'd call me next week. Benny called to ask if I was still going to meet him at Jimmy Day's for his birthday after class. I had almost forgotten it was his birthday. I couldn't ditch that.

I had no motivation or reason to leave my apartment till class. The thought of going to The Studio made my breath shallow, but I had decided to return. I had missed one class, but I didn't want to miss another. Not because of the money I'd paid for it or for the career skills; I wanted to see Ron, look him in the face, let him know that even though he'd behaved like a pig, he hadn't beaten me. I wasn't going to run. I didn't think he had attacked Marissa—that was a long shot—and I wasn't going to drop out of classes just because Tom the Cop suspected him. I had made my choice. Cleaning my loft from top to bottom made me feel I had some kind of control, even if I was probably just fooling myself. But it gave me some of my spirit back.

At the end of my cleaning frenzy, I was ready for a shower. Afterward, I put on a soft black cotton tank top, my worn denim not-too-mini skirt, and those rubber-heeled sandals. Pulling my wet hair into a knot on top of my head, I felt almost human. I made myself a tuna sandwich and ate it with some potato chips and, for dessert, a banana that I kept dipping in a bowl of mini chocolate chips. Chocolate always helped.

The humidity had dropped, and a fresh breeze wafted across the Village from the Hudson River. I walked down Tenth Avenue, then cut across at Thirteenth Street to Ninth Avenue and followed it downtown. I cruised my usual route without thinking. My sphere of home, work, and school hadn't changed in months, and it had felt like a safe zone until now. The route was ingrained in my feet, my eyes barely noticing Ninth Avenue change into Hudson as I approached Bank Street, The Studio just a couple of blocks west.

And then I just kept walking south down Hudson, right past where I should have turned toward The Studio. I couldn't go to class. My plan, to look Ron in the face to show he hadn't beaten me, felt like it could wait. My feet just wanted to keep walking. I turned east on Tenth Street.

At Sixth Avenue I automatically stopped at a newspaper stand. Just as I started to look at the papers on display, I froze.

The piles of newsprint, the headlines blaring their bad news, the humid smell of paper and ink.

"You wanna paper, miss?" The old man with a scraggly beard was slouched on the stool. He gave me a strange look. My face must've shown the panic I was fighting.

"Um. No. No. No, no, no. Thanks." I backed away. *What is wrong with me?* It was only paper. Newsprint couldn't hurt me. But I wanted none of it. It made me feel sick to my stomach. I walked the last block to Washington Square Park and sat on a bench near the chess tables. I felt a crushing pressure in my chest; my face was hot, my mouth dry.

I focused on trying to breathe and watching the people playing speed chess. One muscled Black man in a tank top moved a piece, slapped the clock timer. Then his opponent, an older Latino man with long sideburns and a narrow-brimmed straw fedora, moved his piece quickly and, same thing, *bang!* Move. Smack the clock. Move. *Bang!* That's how I always felt, like I was trying to beat the clock. *Quick, make the next move before it's Too Late.* Suddenly, everything I saw felt like a metaphor. I rubbed my face. I watched too many art films. At least I saw the world in living color.

And where did I think my life was heading? Was my brilliant future going to lead me to Broadway? Hollywood? Assuming I made it past the summer, that is. I got up from the park bench and walked away from that thought.

I exited the park at seven o'clock and killed time sitting at the counter of the Washington Square Diner. My class wasn't supposed to get out until eight, and Benny knew that. But I could barely sit still long enough to finish a cup of tea. After I paid my check, I hoofed a zigzag pattern on the crooked West Village streets to fill up the time, and when I rounded the corner by Sheridan Square and stopped in front of Jimmy Day's, it was 8:10. Benny walked up right behind me.

"Have a nice walk?" Benny put his hands on his hips.

"What?" I was confused.

"Did you have a nice walk around the Village?" Benny started to laugh.

"What are you talking about?" I didn't see the humor.

Benny looked at me with a smile that could've been described as mischievous or creepy, depending on the context. "I saw you come out of the Washington Square Diner, and I followed you." He laughed again, and I felt the hairs on the back of my neck start to prickle.

"What's the joke?" Why was he following me around? "Why didn't you say something? I was just killing time till I had to meet you, you big dope."

"Didn't you have class tonight?"

"What are you, my grandfather?" I felt my face get hot. "I didn't feel like going; is that okay with you?"

"Sure, shortcake, don't be so sensitive." His arms dropped to his sides. "It was just for a laugh."

"Well, I'm not laughing." I had no control of the words flying out of my mouth.

"I can see that." He suddenly seemed physically smaller.

"And don't call me shortcake." I couldn't make myself stop.

"Okay." His voice was quiet as a mouse.

Then I felt bad. Nothing was going right lately. It was his birthday, for Pete's sake. Benny couldn't look me in the eye.

"I'm sorry, Nina—"

"No, no, I'm sorry." My anger turned to guilt and something else. I fought back tears. "What I meant to say was happy birthday. Happy birthday, Benny. Happy birthday. Come on. I'll buy you a drink."

"No, I'll buy you a drink." Benny smiled shyly.

"No, no, it's your birthday, I'll buy *you* a drink." I started to smile a little.

"Okay, you buy me one, I'll buy you one. Even trade." He winked.

He opened the door for me, and we entered Jimmy Day's. The room was more crowded than a normal Tuesday night, but Hector had saved us seats at the bar. I did my best to make the mood celebratory. I even let Benny beat me at a game of pinball. I was good. He thought I was really having some bad luck.

We avoided mentioning Marissa or the murders. I pretended we'd traveled back in time, before I'd ever brought Marissa to the Saz or found that red shoe. Before any girls who looked like me had been found dead. I didn't want to ruin his birthday. Birthdays were supposed to be special.

After his success at pinball, Benny wanted to go to the movies, and how could I say no? He picked *The In-Laws* at the Thirteenth Street Quad, showtime nine thirty. We would just make it.

"Let's stop at my place for a sec. We're supposed to have a thundershower, so I want to pick up my umbrella. The best way to make sure it doesn't rain is to carry an umbrella." He was such a cornball.

I'd never been to Benny's apartment. Oh, I knew where he lived—I'd met him at his corner many times—but I'd never gone up.

"I want to show you the plants I bought." Benny got ahead of me on the sidewalk and turned around and walked backward as he spoke. "I've really been getting into them. I just keep buying more and putting hooks on the ceiling to hang them up."

Benny didn't know about my own penchant for plants, although I tended to visit the captives in the botanic gardens more than grow my own. I had a few succulents in my loft, nothing finicky. Too many times a plant in my care either slowly rotted to death from too much water or died from thirst. I couldn't seem to get the balance right. I couldn't even think about getting a pet.

We walked over to Perry Street, where Benny lived on the second floor of a three-story building. On the ground floor there was a bar called McGowan's Off-Broadway. It wasn't our type of place—too many preppy college kids.

We walked up the narrow flight of stairs to Benny's apartment. It was so dark I could barely see where I was going. Sheesh, I'd complain to the landlord if I were Benny. Benny unlocked the door and walked in ahead of me. I stood in the doorway.

The apartment was a studio of about three hundred square feet with brown walls, a brown carpet, and, in the middle, a small brown table with one chair. There was a tiny kitchenette that opened up like a closet to the left, with a bathroom next to it and a captain's bed built into the far wall covered with a brown blanket. I felt like if I walked all the way in, it would be too crowded for the two of us. This was how much space you got when you lived in the Village on a bartender's tips. My loft in Chelsea was the hinterlands to some people, but at least I had some elbow room.

"See my plants? What do you think?"

I took a few steps into the room and looked up where he was pointing. In evenly spaced rows across the ceiling near the only window were a couple dozen medium-sized plants. They were still in the white plastic hanging pots they'd come in, and they were hung on hooks. It struck me that they were so evenly placed and so close to the ceiling that they couldn't be getting much light. They were those common houseplants, philo-something, sort of a vine with heart-shaped leaves, that you could buy at any five-and-dime store. I didn't think they needed much light anyway. They were the kind of plants that were hard to kill.

"Nice," I said. Kind of weird, I thought. It seemed obsessive, the way he was collecting them. His whole place was extremely neat and organized, in an impersonal way. It looked like a furnished room at a boardinghouse just before someone moves in. And so brown, except for the plants. It was the brownest room I'd ever seen. It made me think of overturned earth in an empty garden or a freshly dug grave.

"Let's go." I found myself at the window, unconsciously drawn to the glow of the streetlight. I turned back toward the door, and I realized Benny was blocking the way out, smiling at me, holding his umbrella like a sword. I felt my breath go weak.

Benny didn't move; he just stood there looking at me, and I started to sweat. Had I just walked into a setup? I actually hadn't heard any forecast for rain. Was this trip to get his umbrella just a ruse to get me into his apartment?

Benny had never tried to jump me, but that didn't mean he wouldn't, given the perfect circumstances. And here they were, the perfect circumstances. The brown room seemed to be shrinking, the walls closing in on me. Benny stood at the door, feet wide, blocking the entrance like a hockey goalie in the crease. If I ran at him and shoved him hard, could I get out the door? He might be caught off guard just enough for me to escape.

"C'mon." He took a step toward me. I took a step back. "Let's go or we'll miss the beginning of the movie." Benny turned and walked out into the hallway. "Pull the door closed; it's already locked."

He walked out of my view. I followed him. Adrenaline seeped out of my body, leaving a residue of guilt.

CHAPTER 18

We got inside the Thirteenth Street Quad Theater just before a thunderstorm exploded, the timing certainly due to umbrella magic. *The In-Laws*, with Alan Arkin and Peter Falk, was hilarious. It was about allowing yourself to take chances, enjoy adventures. For a few moments I released myself from the guilt of being afraid of Benny, the guilt of Marissa's death, the guilt of being alive. The comedy was like a healing balm. The second it ended, I felt like I had been dropped into the dark, quiet theater with a thud. The escape hadn't lasted long.

After the movie, I walked Benny to Sixth Avenue. I didn't know if he had been expecting anything special for his birthday; I just tried to be his friend and make him feel like it was a fun night. No problems, no disagreements, no serious talk. Every once in a while he looked at me with those big bleary marbles of his in a funny way, but I kept the conversation lively. It might have been my greatest acting challenge to date.

I left him at the corner after he gave me a goodbye hug that almost knocked the breath out me. Walking home, I realized I was hungry, and it was easy to turn one extra corner to get to Maria's Mexican place. The fact that it was a

Tuesday night and that I had run into Frankie there the previous Tuesday was not lost on me. I didn't know if he wanted to see me at all now that he knew I'd had that date with Ron. Plus he had seemed so different at the precinct. Either way, if it was a chance to see Frankie's smile and eat some soft tacos, I'd take it. Those were two things I needed.

I pushed through the door and, after noting that the tables were packed, headed straight for the half-empty bar. I sat down without looking around and ordered a club soda and my food. Then I twisted my stool to the left until I saw a table full of off-duty cops. I looked at each face. No Frankie. My stomach fell. I hadn't realized how much I was hoping to see him.

But then Frankie Lopez walked out of the back hallway by the bathrooms, and he saw me straightaway. He walked right past his table, scooping up his beer without stopping, and sat next to me at the bar.

"I wanted to call you, but I didn't want to be pushy. I hear Marissa is better." He tried to look serious, but his smile wouldn't let the corners of his mouth point downward. "How are you?"

"Not really sure." I stirred my club soda absently. I couldn't stop thinking about how impersonal he'd been at the precinct. Was that just because he was at work? What did he really think of me? Or had our budding something died before it bloomed? "Did your partner tell you I stopped by yesterday?"

"What? No. Were you looking for me?"

"I hoped you'd be there, but I talked with your partner instead. He didn't tell you?"

"No." Frankie's eyebrows curled upward with his question. Why did it figure that his partner hadn't told him my information?

"I went to the morgue yesterday. I asked if they had any similar women. I kind of suggested that I was looking for a missing friend." I don't know why I was suddenly embarrassed about that. My strategy had worked. "And I found two other women, murdered on Saturday nights, in the Ninth Precinct. I told your partner about them. That they might be connected. Did he tell you?"

"He had me at the morgue first thing this morning."

"But he didn't tell you I was the one who figured that out?"

"No. That was you?" I could see Frankie's brain working. Tom the Cop hadn't told him I was the one who'd found the other girls. Why had he cut me out of the story? "Tom didn't tell me you came to see him, but it was an important lead. This is the kind of thing that can put the whole city on alert. All the precincts need to be working together to catch a killer like this." He looked at me seriously, right in the eyes. In that moment I thought, *He's even more beautiful without his smile.*

"So we're not the only ones who think they're all connected now?"

"This is huge." He took both my hands and smiled that Frankie smile. "I didn't have enough evidence before. When you have over a thousand murders since January and not enough manpower . . ." I saw the frustration in his face, then the smile broke out again. "Now this has to convince the PC."

"PC?"

"Police chief."

I nodded.

"What made you think of it?"

"I just thought that if he was doing this on Saturday nights, I wondered about the Saturday between Teresa and Jessica."

"It was a brilliant thought."

I suddenly felt embarrassed. I wasn't used to praise. I looked down at our hands. He cleared his throat and gently released me.

"I've been thinking about it," I said. "There're lots of people that knew all three girls, besides Ron."

"You don't think it was Ron."

"No. I mean, I don't know for sure that he didn't do it, but listen, your partner said . . . that the . . . the rape part happened after the killing part."

"That's how it appears."

"And I was thinking. I've read about those kinds of people, people that do it with dead bodies; I read that's the only way they can do it." I was almost stuttering. In my head it made sense; saying it out loud to Frankie made me turn red.

"You've done your research." Frankie picked up his beer and leaned closer.

"It's just that, on that date, with Ron . . ." I pushed ahead. "You know, I told you it was a bad date."

"Yes. I think I know what you meant." Frankie was trying to make it easier for me, but I needed him to just be quiet and listen.

"He's a great actor, and a great acting teacher. But—" Too much about that night started to come back to me physically. "He's a pig. He drank too much, and he couldn't keep his hands off me. In public." *Shake it off, Esposito.* I took a sip of my club soda. The fizz cleared my throat.

"And you think a necrophiliac would act differently."

"Exactly." Thankfully, he'd connected the dots.

"It's logical. Definitely something to put in the mix." Frankie took a swig of his beer. "On the other hand, if he's a brilliant actor, changing how he acts and reacts just might be part of the game."

"You could be right." There was more than logic to figuring this out. My taco plate arrived, and I stared at it.

Frankie looked at me. "That doesn't mean you're wrong. We need to consider any and every part of this case. You never know what will lead us in the right direction."

"I just want to do something."

"I know it's frustrating." His eyes were comforting. "But you have to trust me. We'll do everything we can. And it's going to be at a whole different level now."

"I do trust you." I turned to my tacos, but I couldn't think about eating at the moment. "I can't say the same about Tom Barry."

"Look, Tom's old-school. He works hard, like a mule." He smiled. "He's not Einstein and he's not Ghandi, that's for sure." He laughed at his own joke. "But he does his best to get the job done."

I felt a little better talking about it with someone who listened. I sighed, gathered a taco in my hands, and took a bite. Spicy pleasure cleared my mind.

"Sorry to make you work when you're off duty."

"With a case like this, I'm never really off duty. I'm just taking a meal break. I'm going back to the precinct. But I still have some time. What did you mean when you said there were other people that knew all three women?"

I hesitated. Was I just being paranoid? Why did everyone I know feel like a possible suspect? If I mentioned someone like Dave, could he get in trouble for nothing? Did I tell Frankie about Cousin Bobby, Black Net Shirt Guy? I suddenly felt stupid.

"Just . . . other people at The Studio or even around the Village, I don't know."

"Well, if you have any specific names of people we should look into, you can tell me. We can do it down at the station anytime."

I nodded and chewed.

"Look, let's change the subject for now. Okay?" He relaxed his posture and gave me one of his smiles. I wondered if he knew the impact it had on people. Or was it just me? I swallowed my taco gratefully.

"What about that life story you promised me?" I tried to sound lighthearted.

"I'm all ready for you." His body relaxed. "Shall I start with the day I was born and tell the whole story chronologically? Or do you want me to start from today and work my way backwards?"

I couldn't help myself: He made me laugh. Not the way I usually did, that pretend-happy way I had with Benny or the stressed cheerfulness I had with Ron, but comfortable and real and like everything was going to be okay. How did he do it? Separate real life from his job so easily? While I ate my tacos, he shared some memories of his early childhood life in Puerto Rico. He described growing up in Spanish Harlem, and he mixed in some funny stories about his brothers and sisters. He had two of each. He told me how he'd gone to City College right after high school and then straight into the police academy. He'd been a cop for six years and he liked it, especially working in the Village. He'd only recently gotten promoted to detective, one of the youngest on the team.

"Being a cop is always interesting."

"It must be especially interesting these last few weeks." My mind drifted back to the murders.

"This is certainly a different kind of case than what I'm used to." He finished the last of his beer and dabbed his mouth with the back of his hand to catch a stray drip. "Most homicides are related to other crimes like robbery or drugs, or they're domestic issues."

"Just my cursed luck that I get to be part of this interesting case." I tried not to sound whiny about it.

"Your luck is about to change, Nina Esposito." Frankie stood up.

"Oh, really, Frankie Lopez?" I must've looked surprised, because he laughed and squeezed both my hands for a split second.

"Yes, I'm going to give you a good-luck charm." He put his bottle on the bar next to my club soda. "I'll be right back. Don't go anywhere."

He walked back to his table where his cop friends were paying the check. He added some money to the pile, pulled something else out of his wallet, borrowed a pen from a friend, and wrote on it. He came back to the bar and presented it to me with a little flourish. It was a Police Benevolent Association card, and on the back was his name and phone number.

"This is lucky?" I looked up at him. His face was as open and earnest as a kindergartener waiting for a cookie. Maybe I could put aside my worry about the disappointing interaction at the precinct.

"Yes." Frankie sat close to me. "If you get in any trouble with the police, like if you get stopped for speeding, just show them this and they'll give you a break."

"I don't have a car." I turned the card over in my hand.

"Well, the other lucky part is my phone number on the back." Frankie pointed to the card in my hand. "Just in case you lost that bar napkin or it went through the wash. This card you could put in your wallet so you'll have it next time you want to call me. For any reason; it doesn't have to be about the case. Like if you just want to take a night off and relax."

He looked me right in the eyes, like he was really seeing me. It was a nice look, but how could I think about dating with everything that was going on?

"I'll keep it in my wallet for when I'm ready." I could only tell him the truth.

"That sounds good to me."

"I should be getting home now." I took my change off the bar, minus a tip.

"Let me walk you." Frankie stood.

"To a cab?" I raised one eyebrow. I figured he already knew my address, but my guard wouldn't drop.

"To a cab." We left, and I carefully kept a few feet away from him while he hailed me a taxi. Even at a distance I felt his significance, like I was metal and he was a magnet pulling me closer. I barely had enough will to get into the cab. What I wanted was to jump into his strong arms and let him carry me away. In the corniest way possible. But I knew going home was the smart thing to do.

Back at my apartment, the red light on my phone machine was blinking. I hit the button.

"Nina? It's Ron, just wondering why you haven't been in class. I hope everything is all right. Would you please call me back? 555–9230. I'd like to talk to you before class on Thursday. Okay, good night."

It was more than too late to call Ron back. I could call him from work tomorrow. If I decided to call him at all. I had to go back to class eventually; I wasn't going to drop out of school, whatever Ron's deal was. And what if I didn't call him? Would that make things worse for me in class? Was I still programmed to do whatever Teacher said? I pushed the whole mess out of my mind.

In bed I was able to float a picture of Frankie's smile in my head without any murders accompanying it. It made for sweet sleep, until six o'clock Wednesday morning when darkness entered my dreams. I was walking alone down that alley. It seemed like a longer and darker alley than it actually was in real life. A long, narrow, brick-lined tunnel. I approached the dumpster, and it suddenly came alive. The top popped open like a jack-in-the-box, and it spilled over with naked legs. I sat up in bed, wide awake, my heart hurtling. Just another thrilling morning.

After my shower I dressed in a wine-colored cotton dress, its scoop neck only as low as my collarbones, its hem just at my knees. I walked to work for my Wednesday shift, feeling a nervous twinge about Cousin Bobby. What did he think, that I was just playing hard to get? I'd run out of excuses and I was a little afraid to be rude, since he owned the place, not to mention that I didn't know what else he was into besides owning bars. His union talk, that bulge at his waist shaped like a handgun, his penchant for actresses and his connections with "movie people" . . . yes, I was more than a little afraid.

Speaking of people who knew Marissa, I'd introduced the two of them. And he'd told me he knew The Studio. He could've easily met Teresa and Jessica at some point. I wasn't going to count anyone out.

I walked into The Realm right on time, the end of my shift feeling days away. Lunch was busy, and instead of my usual quick and efficient self, I felt like I was swimming through Jell-O, behind on every order, playing catch-up all day.

At three thirty, I took a quick break to call Ron. It had been on my mind all day, and I decided I needed to call and make nice for the sake of class and whatever might happen outside of class. Slinging booze always made me have hopes toward my alternate career. Something had to get me out from behind the bar. I slipped into the kitchen to wolf down some rigatoni and use the house phone. Between clanking dishes and the cooks chattering in Italian, I heard the phone ring three times. Then the machine picked up.

"You've reached the residence of Ron Meyers. Please leave a message after the beep." And then it did—beep, that is. I took a deep breath.

"Hi, Ron, it's Nina. I'm sorry I've been missing class. Things have been . . . crazy the last few days." I wondered if he'd even heard about Marissa. "I'll be at work until eight tonight, and then I'll be at the Sazerak House on Hudson for a couple of hours if you're in the neighborhood. I guess you can try me at home after that. Otherwise, I'll see you in class."

I didn't like leaving phone messages; I sound so stilted and unnatural. Some actress. I didn't know why it was so important for Ron to talk to me before class, but I tried. I called

Dave, too, just to check in, and left a message on his machine before I trotted back to the bar. Nick looked from me to a few customers with empty drinks and back to me with raised eyebrows.

"What? I don't even get a bathroom break?"

Mike came in at five, and we didn't stop for a minute. We worked the bar together for happy hour, but for the life of me I couldn't figure out what was so happy about it. I poured all the drinks for the waiters to keep their customers lubricated while I kept the customers on my end of the bar happy, but I was in no mood to be there. In the back of my mind, I said my usual prayer that my shift would end without a visit from Cousin Bobby.

My thoughts kept drifting to Marissa, and that made me dwell on the *What the hell am I doing with my life?* question. I was almost ready to quit acting school and join the Peace Corps. For most of the day, I was too tired to think anything that made sense, but by the end of happy hour I started to feel like I was getting my second wind.

Usually there was something about bartending that brought me out of myself, especially when it was busy. It was one place where I could dazzle them with my fancy footwork. I flipped those glasses and bottles so fast and so on target that back at The Corner people used to come in just to watch me work, like a trained seal. I guess when you do something from a young age, all that practice pays off. Too bad it wasn't tennis instead of bartending. I could've made a lot more money.

The dinner rush was large, and so were the tips. Mike took a quick dinner break at seven thirty, and by then business was beginning to lull. The theater crowd left for their curtain time and the late diners hadn't yet arrived. I started to think about how great it would be to take a vacation, maybe a Mediterranean cruise or a slow boat to China. Then at seven forty-five, Tom the Cop walked in and sat at my bar.

"What can I get you, sir?" I looked him in the eye without smiling and dropped a little square napkin in front of him.

"Bottle of beer."

"Would you like me to start you a tab, or will you be paying as you go?" I stood right in front of him, making no move to get his beer until I saw the color of his money. He reached in his pocket and put a five on the bar. I grabbed him the warmest imported beer I could find, popped the top, and put it in front of him, no glass. Then I took his cash, rang up three dollars, and made sure he saw me put the other two in my tip cup. I gave him a smile of superiority and thanked him. Behind the bar I had the advantage.

Tom the Cop took a long drink of his beer and looked at me. Was he stalking me? I'd given him good information, maybe turned the whole case around, and what did I get from him? Persecution.

"Let me ask you something. Why didn't you tell Detective Lopez I gave you the tip about the other two victims from the Ninth Precinct?"

"What does that matter? You wanted credit?"

"I don't care about credit, but it just seems odd."

"That's not why I'm here."

"Why are you here?" Why did he always make me so angry?

"I wanted to be the one to tell you that Detective Lopez is off the case."

"What? Why?"

"Conflict of interest. He's been seen out with you twice."

"We've never been out together. That was coincidence." It was true, but I felt myself blush. "We ran into each other. And besides, what does that matter?"

"It matters."

"But why—"

"It's none of your business. I also wanted to know if you'd had any other contact with Meyers."

I thought for a moment, glanced at the busboys and waiters resetting the dining room, and then figured I better play along.

"He called me last night."

"What did he say?'

"I wasn't home." I leaned against the back bar. "He left a message on my machine. He wanted to know why I missed his class twice this week."

"Why did you?"

"I didn't feel like going. What do you care?"

"Did he say anything else?" His voice edged toward a growl.

It was hard not to enjoy having the upper hand over Tom the Cop. I took my time.

"He asked me to call him back because he wanted to talk before class on Thursday." I felt like I was under a hot light being interrogated. Or maybe I was just hot under my collar.

"And?" I could tell he was about to lose his patience.

"I left a message on his machine that I would be at the Sazerak House tonight after work, if he wanted to stop by." I saw exasperation on Tom's face. I turned away. "I don't know if he'll show up or if he'll even get the message."

I moved down the stretch of empty bar, polishing it with a cloth as I went. I didn't look back. I heard his stool scrape against the floor. *Good, he's leaving.* I listened for the door. Instead, I felt Detective Tom Barry's grubby paw grab my wrist. Pain shot up my arm.

"Hey!" Adrenaline pulsed through my body.

"Listen to me." His whisper was rough. "You're not being very smart, meeting him. But I'm going to do you a favor. I'm going to be at that bar, and if you go anywhere with him, I'm going to stick with you, in case he tries anything."

I ripped my wrist out of his grasp and stepped back, glad of the bar separating us. "You really don't have to do me any favors." I sounded hard, but my heart was in my mouth.

"It's no trouble at all." He flashed his crooked teeth at me.

"It's Wednesday. The killer only works Saturdays," I said with mild petulance.

"If these cases are all connected and it is a serial killer, then Ron Meyers makes the most sense out of any suspect."

I couldn't believe this guy. His thinking was off. He just wanted to railroad the easiest choice through. That was probably how he closed all his cases. He took the last gulp of his beer. "See you downtown." Then he left.

Matty the waiter turned from setting up a two-top and squinted at me. I turned away and cleared Tom's beer bottle, dropping it in the bus tray gingerly, as if it were contaminated. New customers sat down, and Mike came back from his break. I counted my tips, gripping the bills tight to keep my hands from shaking.

After I counted my register and closed out, I sat at a back table near the kitchen and picked at a plate of pasta tossed with pesto and fresh mozzarella. The pesto was extra garlicky, and the cubes of mozzarella melted in the hot pasta like heaven. It helped a little. Tom's stunt at my bar notwithstanding, I was pretty sure I didn't want Ron to show up at the Saz tonight. What was I thinking? Though maybe clearing the air before class would be worth it. I finished eating, gathered my strength, and left. The only upside to the day was that Cousin Bobby hadn't stopped in to pay me a visit.

I got to the Saz just before nine. Tom the Cop was already at the curve of the bar near the door. I walked right by him to my usual seat near the service station at the other end.

"Hey, Nina, how are you?" Benny was surprised to see me. "I had a great time last night. Thanks for the movie."

"Sure, anytime. Can I have a Stoli rocks?"

"Sure." He paused, then packed a glass full of ice and poured a shot of the vodka on top. Russian snow cone. He put it down in front of me. It was the first time I'd ever asked Benny to pour me a real drink in all the months I'd known him.

"What's up, Nina?"

"Nothing much. What's up with you?" I took a quick sip. The icy promise of oblivion tickled my throat. I knew Benny meant the question more directly and not just as the usual conversation starter, but I had nothing to say. Tom the Cop was ten barstools away, and I didn't want to get Benny involved. I wondered if Benny recognized Tom from that Sunday morning. He didn't say anything.

"Anyone come in here looking for me?"

"No. Why, expecting somebody?"

"No. Maybe. Not definitely."

Perfect timing, Gorgeous Charlie walked in and sat next to me. I'd never been in the Saz when Charlie didn't show up.

"Hey, Benny, hey, Nina." He touched my arm gently in greeting.

"What's up?"

"You are." He smiled that angelic smile.

"What a sweet talker you are. Benny, let me buy Charlie a drink." I had a pocketful of tips. Maybe I'd buy the whole place a round.

"Absolut martini, rocks, lemon twist."

Benny moved to make the drink. Charlie turned to me. "Feeling better?"

"Sure, now that you're here." I couldn't help teasing him. It might be my only entertainment for the night. Benny returned with Charlie's drink.

"I'm ready for another, Benny. Put it right on top." I drained my glass and pushed it toward him. Benny didn't look very happy with me. Too bad; it was going to be a long night. Benny seemed to pour my drink as slowly as possible.

Charlie clinked my glass with his, and we drank. *Charlie, Charlie, why aren't you as perfect inside as you are outside?*

"Penny for your thoughts."

"Aren't you Mr. Cornball?"

"I am, if it will get you to go out with me again."

I sipped my drink with a half roll of my eyes.

"Oh, come on, didn't we have a nice time at dinner the other night?"

"It was nice."

"Then why not try it again?"

How could I explain to him that he was exactly the kind of guy I didn't want? We had nothing to talk about, nothing in common. But right now, anything that would keep my mind off Tom the Cop and Ron Meyers would do.

"Well, here we are, aren't we?"

That seemed to make him happy, for a while. It wasn't easy, but we found some neutral ground. Rock and roll.

"Come on, Charlie, how can you say that? You can't compare the Rolling Stones to Led Zeppelin. Zeppelin will win every time."

"In potential, maybe, but not longevity!"

"Well, the candle that burns brightest . . ."

"Benny, two more!"

The vodka was burning bright somewhere just below my collarbone, and I couldn't help noticing that Gorgeous Charlie had a tight, slim stomach and biceps that could easily lift me out of my chair.

"Don't you think so, Nina?"

"Oh, yeah, whatever you say." I heard myself laugh, almost a giggle. Who cared about a stupid serial killer, haunting the streets, looking for my sisters? Not me. "You must be strong, arncha, Charlie? You must be real strong with those big ole arms of yours, arncha?"

He put one of those big ole arms around the back of my chair and smiled. "I got a little gym set up in my office. Lift every chance I get."

I drained my drink and put the glass down on the bar a little too hard. It brought Benny over. I didn't think he liked what he saw.

"Nina wants another."

"I don't think so." Benny stood right in front of Charlie.

"Yes, you do, don't you, Nina?"

I nodded. My head felt wobbly.

"I don't think she needs another one." Benny crossed his arms.

"Maybe you're right. Maybe I better take her home. Want to go home, Nina?" Charlie leaned closer to me.

"No." I shook my head. I was having fun here. There was no fun at home.

"Well, I'm not pouring her another." Benny didn't move. He put a glass of water in front of me.

"Want to come see my office? It's just around the corner." Charlie wouldn't quit. "I'll show you my weights."

For some reason I found this hilarious and broke out into a peal of laughter. I stood up. Charlie dropped his arm lightly to my waist. It felt familiar. I smiled at Benny.

"Where you going?" Benny was not amused.

That confused me.

"Oh. The bathroom." I unwound myself from Charlie's arm and lurched toward the back of the restaurant. I rounded the corner and started down the hallway. I had completely forgotten about Tom the Cop. He followed me, and just before I entered the ladies' room, he grabbed my arm and spun me around to face him.

"I don't know what kind of game you're playing, but I don't like wasting my time. Did you really leave Meyers a message to meet you here, or were you just screwing me around?"

"I told you the truth. It's not my fault he didn't show up." I tried to wiggle my arm loose.

"It's almost midnight, so it's pretty safe to say your boyfriend's not coming. Since you've already found a new one, I guess you don't care. Try and get yourself home before you become the next victim. I'm done."

He let go of my arm with a push, and I bumped against the wall. I watched him stalk away. Nothing seemed particularly funny anymore. In fact, I felt like crying. Just when I thought I had escaped reality through the warm and fuzzy state of inebriation, I'd wound up back in the thick of it. It was like going round and round in a maze. No matter how many times I thought I'd found a way out, I ended up right back in the middle. Getting drunk felt like a good idea after the first drink, right up until you got sober.

I used the bathroom, then looked at myself in the mirror. I wasn't really feeling all that intoxicated anymore; that nice, relaxed feeling had flown out the window. I splashed cold water on my face and took a deep breath. Back to the world.

There was cash piled on top of Charlie's tab, and he looked like he was itching to go. Benny had come out from behind the bar and was standing with his hands on his hips, looking right at me as I came around the corner.

"I'll put you in a cab." Benny wasn't asking, he was telling.

I sulked. Charlie was harmless, just a big ole teddy bear, a puff of cotton candy. He wouldn't jump me. I'd probably have to be the one to make the first move. He'd be too busy looking at himself in the mirror while he lifted his weights. That made me laugh. And then I hiccupped.

"Excuse me." I pushed past them both and stood next to the bar.

"I'll walk you out." Benny just wouldn't quit.

"I'll hail her a cab, Benny." Charlie stepped up to him and looked Benny in the eye. Great, so now they were going to fight over me. They were a match, both over six feet, thick with muscles in the same places, including their brains. Suddenly, I felt tired. I climbed up on my barstool. Maybe I'd just spend the night here.

"Gimme a cup of tea, please, Benny." I rubbed my arms. "I'm cold. Why you gotta run the air conditioner so high?" Benny broke his locked stare with Charlie to do my bidding. Charlie sat back down next to me.

"I'll take you home if you want." He sounded contrite.

"Thanks just the same, but I can get myself home."

"Fine. Thanks for the swell time." He stood. He wasn't so steady himself, and now it looked like I'd pissed him off.

"Aw, don't go away angry, Charlie." I didn't want any bad feelings between us.

"Yeah, I know, just go away." He stomped out like a little kid. That wasn't what I'd meant at all. Benny came back from the kitchen, the teacup and honey pot balanced in just one of his big hands, and he lifted the hatch door to get back behind the bar with the other hand.

"Where's Charlie?"

"He left."

"Good."

"You didn't have to piss him off, Benny."

"Good if I did. He pisses me off, falling all over you, getting you drunk."

"Charlie didn't get me drunk, Benny, you did."

"What?" His face turned so dark red it was almost purple.

"You did the pouring."

"Why, you—"

"Relax, Benny. Ain't nobody's business but my own." I smiled weakly. "I'm responsible for my own lack of sobriety." As the words came out, my tongue still felt a bit thick.

"Responsible, huh? That's a word you're pretty unfamiliar with."

"You . . . have no idea . . . what you're talking about." I felt heat start at my collarbones and seep up, coloring my face.

"I think I know a bit more about being responsible than you do." Benny leaned closer. "Sometimes you act even younger than you look. You're not in high school anymore. This is the grown-up world."

I no longer needed the tea to warm me up. I was red hot. Benny knew nothing about my history. How I sat by my mother's hospital bed when I was eight years old for days. How she disappeared from my life one night while I slept at my grandparents'. How I'd taken care of my grandmother while she wasted away to nothing when I was thirteen. How I'd kept a drunk old man from making us destitute by running a bar since I was fifteen. How I watched him die in my arms, his body wasted away to nothing. How I sold everything I owned to start a new life.

How could he know? I'd never told him. Because he'd never asked. He just saw tits and ass with a pretty smile like everybody else did. I wouldn't ever tell him my personal history, never. He didn't deserve it.

I stood up and straightened my dress.

"Fuck you, Benny Banlon." I gave him my best audition smile. Then I turned on my heel and walked out. *Nobody knows the trouble I've seen.* Somehow, whenever I drank, life was a vaudeville musical. Except the only songs I could think of were the blues.

I'm no fool. I treated myself to a taxi. I even asked the cabby to watch me until I got in the door. The nice ones would do that. By the time I got inside, I'd talked myself into believing I was completely separate from the whole serial killer threat. I was watching from the outside of the story, and there was no way this guy could hurt me. He wasn't after me, I told myself. He couldn't be. I'd just make myself invisible. I fell into bed and oblivion.

Chapter 19

Waking up on Thursday was no labor of love. I wasn't so much hungover as sore, as if I had been a Louisville Slugger in the 1978 World Series. It must've been from that long shift and then staying out so late, not to mention not getting enough sleep the night before and the vodka involved. How long could my poor young body keep this up?

I blasted the radio and dragged myself into the shower with a giant mug of tea. Blondie was singing about how she would give someone the slip, one way or another. Yeah, she was singing for me. I just had to convince myself I was trickier than the killer. Or luckier. After all, I had that lucky card Frankie had given me. Why couldn't he be following me around instead of Tom the Cop?

I dressed for work in gray capri pants and a pale-blue half-sleeve blouse with three buttons open at my collarbone. I looked at my worried face in the mirror. There was no way I could relax or expect life to get back to normal unless the killer was caught. Was Tom the Cop right? Could Ron be the killer? What could I do to find out?

What was that saying? *Fools rush in where angels fear to tread.* Well, I was no angel, but my patience, if I ever had any, had just run out, and if that made me a fool, so be it.

Normally, in the daytime, everything appeared harmless to me, all sunlight and kittens. It was nighttime that raised my anxiety, manifesting in my nightly 'mares. But now even the daylight hours felt threatening. I tried to talk myself down from that ledge. Murder? Mayhem? Brush it off. That was someone else's life, not mine.

But this hot and sunny morning, I wasn't believing my own bologna. Every shadow made by the harsh daylight looked like a demon. Maybe it was the aftereffects of the vodka, maybe it was every shitty situation from my life filling my brain, but the day felt like night. It was like I was in a bad French New Wave film. I made it to work with thirty seconds to spare, refusing to admit to myself that I was wobbly on my wheels. My brain decided to protect itself by retreating into a haze.

Work spun dizzyingly by. It was a blur that didn't register. Everything I did was automatic. Once I put the wrong checks down in front of two different customers, switching them with each other. But what did it matter? They didn't notice and they paid anyway. The math all worked out in the end. I knew if I tried to concentrate on what I was doing, a lot of other useless stuff would come up, like reality. So I drifted. I just wanted to go home and go back to bed. But I couldn't miss another one of Ron's classes. I didn't want to go back to sleepwalking my way through my days the way I had done a year ago. And besides, if Ron was the killer, I had to know.

After my grandfather died and I moved to Manhattan, I spent all my time in my apartment or at the movies. Eventually

I widened the circle when I started bartending again. Then I signed up for classes at The Studio and found the Sazerac House. I'd slowly clawed my way out of that hole, one inch at a time. Going to class, hanging out at the Saz, spending time with Marissa and Dave, skating in the park—it was a circle I could handle while I watched the outside world through newspapers and television. I had been making progress, slowly widening my world each day.

But ever since I picked up that red shoe and walked into that alley, I was backsliding. My anxiety built every time I walked out of my apartment. How Benny acted last night, dealing with Ron in class, and stressing out about Cousin Bobby pressuring me, my circle was closing in on me. Everything around me in the outside world felt wrong. I wanted nothing but to bury my head in my pillows. At The Realm the customers at the bar now seemed demanding and rude. Suddenly they were treating me like I was a servant. Which I was, but hey, they didn't have to throw it in my face.

After the lunch rush I sat at the bar with Sam and Matty as I tried to cut through my brain fog with a strong cup of tea, but it didn't lift. Matty entertained us with a story from his escapades. I barely listened, but it had something to do with how he talked his way into Studio 54 and met Liza Minnelli. I was sure that when he said he "met" Liza Minnelli, it meant he stood next to her in a crowd for a minute. A few weeks ago, I might've been impressed. Meeting someone famous felt that much closer to *being* famous. But the last thing I wanted now was to see my own name in the paper. Girls I knew who had chased fame now had it in the most twisted way. Their pictures were in the paper for the wrong reasons. Anxiety began to break through the haze in my head. That was one way to wake myself up. I knew I should try to call Ron again, before I saw him in class tonight. But I just couldn't make the move, so I sat until I couldn't sit anymore.

It wasn't much of a happy hour, and I had no energy for making scintillating conversation with my few customers. I put some effort into polishing the bar as an excuse to keep my distance. I hypnotized myself with the rhythm, the cloth sliding on smooth wood, my dark reflection in the shine, my brain trying to find a place to escape in the back-and-forth tempo.

I began to feel a strange vertigo. All the times I had polished the bar at The Corner, the same deep reddish-brown wood, the same reach and slide with the same sort of cloth—suddenly the past and present mixed and shifted. Where was I? The Corner or The Realm? Brooklyn or Manhattan? I felt dizzy, and a wave of nausea washed over me. I stood back against the register and dropped the cloth as I gripped the back bar. *This is crazy. I am here at The Realm. Those other days are over.* I forced my brain to stay in focus. My shift finally ended.

I rolled slowly to class on my skates, still feeling a little spacey. I passed through Abingdon Square and bought some tea in a cardboard cup at The Bus Stop. They never asked me to take my skates off at The Bus Stop like some other joints. I loved that about them. I stood by the counter stools where Marissa and I often sat after class, planning our futures. The speckled Formica countertop was worn and cracked but so clean it shone. I thought of Marissa's happy face and I tried on a smile. It felt forced. I ripped a little triangle in the thin plastic lid of my tea to make a space where I could sip the hot brew, and I floated down Bank Street.

I untied my skates outside The Studio, and time seemed to slow down. Inertia hit me as I climbed the stairs. Whenever I take off my skates, walking feels like I'm pushing through Jell-O. Tonight I felt especially lead-footed. Maybe this was a mistake, going to class. I was a few minutes late, with everyone else already settled in their seats in the drab classroom. I almost looked for Marissa, and that gave my heart a squeeze. Andrew Lee waved and pointed to an empty seat between him and Janette. Maybe they were saving it for me. Maybe they were going to be my new best friends. The thought choked me up.

Ron had his back to us as I slid into the empty chair. He turned and looked at the class slowly. When his eyes rested on me, he smiled that hungry smile of his. My stomach flipped.

"Nina, why don't you come up here and do an improvisation with me. I'd like to show the class something about the importance of physical awareness."

There was no way I could get out of it. And what could possibly happen in front of the whole class? I walked to the front and waited for instructions. He took two chairs and put them facing the class. Then he took my arm and walked me around to one chair, miming opening a door and holding it for me. *Ah, we're going for a little drive.* I sat and tried to breathe air in and out in a normal way. He slammed my "door" and came around to sit next to me. I had no idea what relationship I was supposed to have with him. Was he my friend, my husband, my father? I waited for him to give me a clue. He seemed to be driving along, relaxed, unconcerned. I hoped he would speak soon, but my heart was beating so loudly I wasn't sure I'd hear him when he did.

"Beautiful night out, isn't it?" He smiled at me sweetly. It must be a date.

"Yes, as long as the rain holds off." I couldn't hide my nervousness. *Use it,* I told myself. *It's our first date.*

"Shall we drive out by the old mill?" He turned the wheel.

"That would be lovely." Our first date and my first date ever. I pictured a yellow cotton dress and white gloves, early 1950s, East Texas.

"Here we are." He turned to the right and stopped the car. Then he leaned back and put his arm around me. I clenched my teeth to keep them from chattering.

"Look at the ring around that moon! Sure will rain soon enough." I applied a subtle Texas accent, a la Sissy Spacek. Ron's face was only inches from mine.

Ron's improvisations were always based on a certain structure: two characters, each wanting something that conflicts with what the other wants. What will they do to get it? The tension drove the drama for the audience. How far will they go? Who will win? I could play this game.

"Did you enjoy the dinner?" He touched my hand, lifted it to his lips, and looked into my eyes. Aha, so this improvisation was going to be reality based. He wanted to seduce me. What did I want?

"The dinner was fine, but it was the company that I really enjoyed." I gave him a wide-eyed innocent look. This wasn't going to be interesting if both our characters wanted the same thing, but I was stuck.

"It doesn't have to end so soon. We could go to my place for coffee." He put my hand over his heart. I felt weak.

"I—I don't know if I should; I have to get up so early tomorrow." I couldn't think.

"To go to eight o'clock Mass?" He smirked.

"Well, yes, but—" My blush was real.

"Don't leave me yet. On nights like this when the moon is so round and the air is so clear, after I bring you home, the loneliness just engulfs me. You can't leave me alone, not tonight." He buried his head in my bosom and hugged me tight. With acting like that, I could almost feel sorry for him. But that was what he wanted me to do. I stroked his head, motherly.

"I'll never leave you, not really. But you've always been like a brother to me, and I know you feel close to me too, maybe in another way. But I've known you all my life and never thought of you like that. I'd do almost anything for you, but not that. It would be like . . . incest." There were a few snickers from the class. Ron slowly lifted his head and sat up straight next to me. There were tears in his eyes.

"*Incest* is a dirty, disgusting word." His expression took an ugly turn.

"I'm sorry." I reached out with my left hand to touch his face. He grabbed it and twisted it behind my back, turning me away from him.

"Sorry?" His voice was a coarse whisper, his lips at my ear. "Nobody feels sorry for me."

"I didn't say I felt sorry for you. I'm just sorry things can't work out—between us." I tried to keep my voice from wavering.

"Why can't they?" His voice was petulant.

"Because we don't want the same thing."

"What you want is unimportant." He twisted harder.

"You're hurting me." He was playing the part a bit too on the nose.

He laughed.

"I'll scream."

"No one will hear you."

"I'll tell the whole town." I choked back real tears.

"They won't believe you." He put his left arm around my waist, pulling me closer, his cheek on my cheek, my back touching his chest. The class was holding its breath; they loved it. "They had us married off years ago. They all know we were meant for each other."

I was breaking. Lack of sleep, vodka still in my veins, fear of Ron, Cousin Bobby, Tom the Cop, the Psycho Killer still at large, all the violent men in my past. The struggle was a little too real. Tears trickled down my cheeks. No one had ever said life was going to be fair. I heard my grandmother's voice in my head: *If you want to play, you have to let the boys win . . .*

"Whatever you say." My voice was a hoarse whisper.

He turned me around and wiped the tears from my cheeks. Then he put his arms around me tenderly and kissed me on each cheek. I didn't know if he was still acting. He reached in his jacket pocket and pretended to pull something out. He mimed opening a ring box and took something out of it.

"For you." He put a ring on my finger. I almost felt it. Then he kissed my hand. "Let's go home now, together."

I leaned back, limp. He "started" the car, drove for a few seconds, then stood. I followed suit. The class clapped. He gave me a hug and looked into my face.

"You okay?" He was sincere. All traces of the scene were gone.

"Yeah, I'm fine." I rubbed my face.

"Okay, everybody, let's take five, and then we'll talk about the scene." My classmates talked among themselves or exited the room for a quick smoke or a stop in the restroom. Ron held me back.

"By the time I got your message, it was too late to call you or meet you. What are you doing after class?"

"Tonight?" My voice almost squeaked. I wouldn't be able to get a message to Tom the Cop on such short notice. "Oh, no, tonight is bad."

"Friday's no good. How about Saturday?"

"Saturday?"

"I want to take you out again. We have so much to talk about." He gave me a sweet smile. "We hardly had a chance to get to know each other."

I opened my mouth, but no words came out. Maybe this was my chance to find out if he had anything to do with Marissa's attack.

"Are you free on Saturday? Nine o'clock?" His face was so open, hopeful. *Think fast, Esposito.*

"Do you know the White Horse Tavern around the corner?"

"Of course."

"I'll meet you there at nine."

"Perfect." He squeezed my arm gently. "And hey, great scene. I hope I didn't scare you."

"You really had my adrenaline pumping." *And my stomach twisting.* The class started to trickle back in. I kept up the convincing smile as I went back to my chair. Janette sat down next to me and leaned close to my ear.

"You were great in that scene, but he was bullshit." Her voice was low and harsh. "Next time he pulls that domination crap, you kick him in the balls and I'll throw him out the window."

I gave her a nod and a wink, but inwardly chastised myself for not being able to muster that kind of nerve when it came to Ron. All I could think about was going home and crawling into my own soft bed. It seemed like days since I'd been there. Andrew Lee slid into the seat on the other side of me. He took my hand, squeezed it, dropped it back in my lap and gave me a supportive smile. Maybe there were still some nice people in the world.

The rest of the class was uneventful. I dashed out as soon as it was over.

I was surprised and grateful that Tom the Cop wasn't waiting for me outside The Studio or by my apartment. Or anyone else. I hit the pillow hard, but sleep took its time coming. Too tired to think up any pleasant thoughts, I finally let the tears come around one o'clock, and then I floated off. At first, I found a beautiful dream that took me to the forest. Everything was cool and green, and I heard a stream gurgling somewhere out of sight. I walked through the trees, looking for the water, damp leaves brushing against my face. The woods got thicker and it started to get dark. Soon I could barely see my hand in front of my face, and a familiar panic set in. I crashed through trees and smaller brush, the sound of water getting louder. I felt something move next to me and I screamed, tripping at the same time, and then I was falling down a bottomless pit. Endlessly falling. I woke with a start, still screaming. When I realized where I was, I choked back my cries and jumped out of bed.

I stood by the window, my eyes reaching for the light of the streetlamps. Thunder boomed and lightning flashed so bright that the streetlights turned off for a moment, plunging the street into darkness. When they flicked back on, I could see that my windows were streaming with rain and water was leaking into my apartment. I moved across the front of the room, closing all the windows, wiping the puddles with a towel. I was grateful to have something physical to do to put me in reality. Nights like this made me wish I had someone I could call. Somebody who'd just tell me I was being silly and then fill my head with jokes so there was no room for anything else. I wondered if Frankie was at the precinct. Now that he was off the case, was he still working all hours? Maybe he was safe at home in his bed. What if I called him right now? What would he think? I looked at the clock: three in the morning.

He'd think I was nuts, that's what. I went into the bathroom and washed my face with cool water. Red eyes looked back at me from the mirror, and I tried to laugh at myself. It came out choked. If I didn't find the end of this puzzle, I might never sleep again.

Saturday I'd find out.

I went back to bed and stared at the ceiling for a while, making a conscious effort to breathe deeply. Next thing I knew the sun was streaming through the windows and the alarm clock was going off.

Friday was a fog. There had been times in my life when I'd found myself somewhere, at work or school, and I'd think, *How did I get here today? Did I walk the same city blocks, as I always do?* I'd remember doing it in a vague sort of way, but I couldn't recall the details. *I remember brushing my teeth, but was that yesterday or this morning?* Whether it was too much routine or paddling through exhaustion, sometimes it frightened me. Where was my mind?

Questions like those flitted through my head at work. Thursday tried to fade off into the distance while Friday seemed real enough, yet so similar to so many other days. Days that before everything started had seemed so boring. Now I wished for boring old Friday to last forever. Tomorrow I'd have to deal with another date with Ron. *What was I thinking?* I shook my head and poured another bottle of Michelob for a nice young businessman. He seemed happy. Maybe his life was boring, maybe he had a wife and family to go home to, maybe he was from out of town. *Take me with you,* my eyes tried to tell him. He didn't. But at least he left me a nice tip.

It was slow for a Friday. Most people had taken the day off and headed to their beach weekend. Due to my ban on newspapers, I was a little lost at the slow part of the day, so I cleaned. I was glad I'd chosen my one-piece zebra-striped linen jumpsuit to wear. It was conservative enough for The Realm and comfortable enough to do all the bending and stretching required. When business was slow, I couldn't help seeing all the dirt that had accumulated, metaphorically and in reality. The dusty liquor bottles and the grimy shelves they rested on called out to me. My fingers itched to make them shine.

I moved every bottle onto the back bar until the long shelves were empty. I sprayed and wiped the dark wood until they shone like mirrors, then I switched to the bottles. I rubbed each one with a soapy wet cloth, removing the dust and any dry dribble of liquor, then polished them with a dry cloth till they looked brand new. I placed each one back on the shelf, in their own special spot, one by one: Stolichnaya,

Smirnoff, Gordon's, Tanqueray, Beefeater, Johnnie Walker Black, Johnnie Walker Red, Cutty Sark, Dewar's, Seagram's 7, Canadian Club, Crown Royal, etc. They were all old friends. I'd been looking at them, reading their names, polishing their glass bodies since I was a kid. They were familiar and I was comfortable with them. They were the only family I had. I suppose some people remember their stuffed toys or the building blocks from their childhood. That's their nostalgia. I had liquor bottles. Pathetic? Maybe. But it was my history and there was nothing I could do about it.

After my cleaning foray, I sat at the first chair near the service bar and lingered over a plate of veal piccata with capellini.

"Nina, honey?" Nick came out from the back of the house and stood close. Too close.

"Yes, Nick, honey, you want a soda?" I got up automatically and moved to get a glass.

"Hold on a sec."

I stopped next to him. He looked like he was deciding if he should peel a Band-Aid slowly or pull it off in one quick rip. His face hardened. A quick rip, apparently.

"Listen, Bobby really likes you, you know." His eyes were dark. "You should give him a chance. He's a lot of fun."

"Fun, huh?" I knew his kind of fun. I relied on my old excuse. "Look, I don't like the idea of dating the owner of a place I'm working. It makes things too complicated."

Nick put his cold, clammy hand on my wrist, pinning it to the bar. For the first time I saw something nasty behind his eyes. Something I'd never seen in him before, way past his milquetoast, snake-oil-salesman personality.

"Too complicated?" His grip tightened. "Maybe it would be simpler if you didn't work at The Realm."

I felt a wave of nausea roll through me.

Nick looked straight at me, almost through me, unblinking, like he was saying, *Do you get it now?* And I got it, all right. I got it good. Go out with Cousin Bobby or lose my job. He let my wrist go and continued. "Now, I think that Saturday, tomorrow when you get off at five o'clock, it would be real nice if you were free and available to go out with Bobby." Nick set his mouth in a line. "What do you say?"

What could I say? I already had the date with Ron at nine o'clock, but it didn't sound like I had a choice, and I'd juggled two dates in one night before. It was either go out with Cousin Bobby or join the unemployment line. What could I do, call the cops? Yeah, the date police. That almost made me laugh. I smiled at Nick with my best Broadway baby smile.

"Sure, Nick. I'll be ready after my shift. Why not?" I gave a flirty little shrug as my stomach quivered. I backed a few steps away from him, filled a glass with ice and soda, and slid it down the dark-wood bar. It stopped right in front of him. *Yeah, I'll be ready.*

Nick's mouth formed a gloating shape, more snarl than smile. I watched him take his soda to the back of the restaurant. And then Dave Kapour walked in the front door.

"Hi."

I gave him a big hug. Tears sprang to my eyes, and my throat swelled so I couldn't even respond. He hugged me back, but I felt him try to find the end of the embrace, so I released him and went quickly behind the bar. I hadn't seen him since the day after Marissa's attack.

"Can I get you something? On the house?"

"Just a Coke, thanks."

I filled a highball glass with ice and squirted it full of Coca-Cola from the soda gun. Dave's eyes still had circles under them, but he looked like he'd gotten a haircut and his short-sleeved shirt was neatly pressed. He was functioning. I went back around to his side of the bar, took a seat next to him.

"How is Marissa?"

"She's going to be fine. She flew home already, back in Chicago, being pampered by her parents."

"Oh. That's good." I felt a sting in my chest as I toyed with my half-empty seltzer glass. She hadn't even said goodbye.

"She'll call you for sure."

I didn't respond. I hoped she would; I cherished our friendship. But maybe to Marissa, I had just been convenient. She might be planning on living a different life now, one that didn't have room for me.

"You think she'll stay in Chicago?" I asked. He shrugged. He looked like he had something to get off his chest.

"So . . ." He looked away from me.

"What is it?" Whatever he had to say, it was not good news.

"I came to tell you, um . . ." He looked at his hands as they clutched his glass of Coke. I felt my nerves shred. What was so bad? Had they taken Ron away for the murders? Did Dave himself have a confession for me?

"Speak, Dave. I can't take any more anticipation."

"I'm moving to California."

"What?" Not what I expected. "When?"

"I'm flying there tomorrow." Dave looked pained.

"Tomorrow?" I was confused. This didn't seem right. Did he have something to hide?

"I have some friends out there; they've been asking me to go for a long time. They're getting some work in TV and movies. Marissa never wanted to go—she was all about the theater, you know—but now . . ." His words evaporated into the tense air between us.

"But now it's over between you two, and she's back in Chicago, so . . ." I finished for him. I started to get up and clear my plate. He touched my arm. I stood still, my plate in my hand, his hand heavy on my forearm. I couldn't blame him. He was just going off to live his life. I gently slipped away from him, placed my plate in the bus tray, and walked behind the bar. I poured two fancy fluted shot glasses of Kahlúa liqueur, Marissa's favorite. I put one in front of Dave and raised my glass to him.

"To California," I said.

"To California," Dave said, and drank. I drained my glass.

There wasn't much more to talk about. We said our goodbyes and swore to keep in touch, but I knew how quickly those kinds of promises faded. Just like with my high school friends who went away to college, I'd be out of sight, out of mind in no time. It seemed that, for him, Marissa already was.

Dave left, and happy hour was waiting to get happy. I leaned on the bar, suspended in my own world, until the customers started shuffling in. Suddenly, work couldn't last long enough. I was feeling oddly safe at The Realm at the moment. Bobby wouldn't be in; his messenger had done the job, and he'd make his appearance tomorrow. And where was I going to go after this Friday shift? I didn't want to go home. What was there for me, more movies? I didn't want to go hang out with Benny. Marissa was gone. Dave was moving. I should've gotten Andrew Lee's or Janette's phone number, but it was too late for that tonight. I could call Frankie. But being with him would just make me think about the murders, and I wanted to forget all of that for now.

I had thousands of choices of things to do in New York City, but I was stuck, overwhelmed. Choosing was suddenly too much for me. *I could just stay here all night,* I thought to myself. Mike came in to relieve me, and he practically had to push me out the door.

"Can I get you one more bucket of ice, Mike? One more case of beer?"

"Get a life, Esposito."

If he only knew.

I had to tell Tom the Cop that I had a date with Ron on Saturday at nine o'clock. I'd rather talk to Frankie, but now that he was off the case, what did that mean? I went to the kitchen, picked up the phone, and dialed Frankie's number. I let it ring ten times. No answer. He was probably working. I had to go to the precinct. If I was lucky, Frankie would be there.

I rolled down Eighth Avenue on my skates. The rain hadn't cooled anything off. The air was as heavy as a five-ton water balloon. So was my mood. Was I crazy to make that date with Ron? And now Bobby would be waiting for me when I got off my shift at five o'clock tomorrow. More crazy. Flashes of my last summer at The Corner jolted through me.

"Looks like I'm back in the game," I muttered to myself.

I sailed across Thirty-Second Street and then down Seventh Avenue, through the fashion district, past the wholesale flower district until I got to Saint Vincent's hospital at Fourteenth Street, where Marissa had been. People were hanging around the emergency room door. Some of them looked distraught, some just impatient. I turned down Greenwich Avenue and stopped to look in the window of a restaurant that I passed often. They had the most beautiful lace curtains hiding the interior from view. I'd never eaten there, but I'd always wondered what it was like inside. Why hadn't I ever gone in there? It was as if I thought the place was too good for me. Like my clothes weren't fancy enough or I'd speak the wrong language and everyone would laugh at me or, worse, ignore me like I didn't exist.

My head down, my skates rolled, I let gravity take me where it chose, the path of least resistance, hopefully toward the precinct. Luckily, someone was just leaving when I got there; I wasn't sure I would've opened the door for myself.

"I need to speak to Detective Barry, please, or Detective Lopez." I had rolled the few feet to the front desk to speak to the bulky man in uniform behind the tall desk.

"No skating in here." He barely looked at me.

I'm not skating, you twit. I'm just standing here. Why was it that whenever I went into a place wearing skates, they busted my chops? Did I look like I was going to skate through the place and knock everyone over? I was five foot nothing and 115 pounds; so threatening. I sat on the bench, took off my skates, and slipped on my sandals.

"Okay? So, I'm here to see Detective Barry or Detective Lopez."

"Neither of them are in. Do you want to wait?" said the empathetic human in uniform. His smile was one of petty victory.

This was my experience with authority: They played any little power move they could, just because they could. I tried not to fume. I looked around. The walls of the precinct were cement block, painted gray. There were a few cops milling around, one practically dragging a young Black man across the room. I could think of less depressing places to be.

"I'll just leave a message."

He pushed a pen and a piece of paper toward me. I decided to leave it for Tom the Cop. It was his case and he was the one so interested in my dealings with Ron. It would feel too weird to leave a message for Frankie that I had another date with Ron. I wrote:

Det. Barry,

I am meeting your favorite suspect on Saturday night for a date. We're meeting at the White Horse Tavern at 9 PM.

Nina Esposito

I gave the message to the desk sergeant and walked out.

It was Friday night; normally I'd meet Benny and play some pinball. The Saz was only around the corner. He was probably mad at me for Wednesday night, but I wasn't holding a grudge. It was just one of those stupid nights that happened sometimes. And where else was there to go? I didn't want to go home. Not yet. I wasn't even in the mood for a movie. I didn't bother to lace up. I walked the few blocks toward the Saz flat-footed.

I paused in the playground and watched the kids play in the fading sunlight. Some were with a parent or two, some with a nanny. I couldn't conjure a memory of my mother taking me to a playground, although she must have. When I was in middle school, before my grandmother got sick, I would go to the park after supper and swing on the swings. I'd swing so high and feel so free it felt like flying. After my grandmother died, I would sometimes run off and escape there again. I must have been a strange sight, a teenage girl in raggedy bell-bottom jeans swinging away, pumping so hard it probably looked like I was trying to take off for the moon.

The kids in this playground were so small they needed their parents to push them on the swings. That wasn't such a bad feeling if you had parents around to do it. Sometimes I wondered if my father had a whole new family. A wife he loved, kids he played with. If I ever met him, I was going to ask him to push me on the swings. I didn't care how old I was—he owed me.

I made my way to the Saz. Benny was sitting at the bar drinking Hennessy's, done with his shift and waiting for me. He turned around when I opened the door, anticipation in his eyes.

"Hey, I wasn't sure you were coming."

"I wasn't sure either." I sat at the bar next to him. "Sorry about the other night."

"Oh, forget it."

I nodded. I felt tension lift my shoulders almost to my ears. I told him Marissa was okay and back home in Chicago.

"Feel like playing some pinball?" He looked half hopeful, half pleading, all puppy dog. I shook my head.

"Not really, Benny. I just came by to say that I really don't feel like doing anything tonight."

"Hey, why don't we catch a flick?" Benny turned his body in his chair so his gaze could sharpen on me. "There's a Bogart double feature at Saint Mark's."

"No thanks."

"Don't be that way."

"Come on, Benny. I could've just not shown up."

I was too antsy to be here and talk for two minutes, never mind sit for a double feature. I realized that something in my mind had changed the other night. What was I to him, anyway? All we did was talk about movies and baseball. I hung out with him so much because he always prompted, *Are you coming by Sunday for brunch?* or *Will I see you Friday night for some pinball?* I just went along. Well, I was more than movies and baseball and hanging out in bars. Why did he even think he liked me when he knew nothing about me?

"Come on, you made it here, let's go out and do something fun."

"No. I—"

"Look." Benny stood up in front of me, almost blocking my exit. "I know you're still upset about Marissa, but she's okay, and she'd want you to be out having a good time, not moping around."

"You think you know what Marissa would want me to do after meeting her once?"

"What do you mean, once?" Benny said. "She came in here a few times without you after that first night. She could really down those white wine spritzers, and she sure liked to talk when she'd had a few."

"What? How come you never told me this before?" I felt sweat break out on my upper lip.

"I thought you knew." He was nonchalant. "That last night she told me she was going to go meet you at Texarkana when she left."

I gaped at him, my mouth wide open like a codfish at the fish market.

"What night? You mean Saturday night? Last Saturday night? The night she was attacked?" It was hard not to sound hysterical when it was how I felt.

"Yeah, Saturday night." He sat down and drained his glass of cognac. "I was hanging out after work and she came in. I bought her a drink, she bought me a drink, you know. She was telling me about her boyfriend."

"Dave? What did she say about him?"

"That he was a no-good lying cheater. Stuff like that."

Marissa had told me nothing like that about Dave, and yet she'd told Benny. I thought we were the kind of friends who told each other everything. Why would she keep that from me?

"But she didn't seem to care that much about him." Benny smiled. "She was talking about how great it was to be free and how she was ready to party. She was all about having a good time."

I pictured Marissa that night, sitting at the bar next to Benny, enjoying herself, laughing, talking, drinking. Then she went to Texarkana. Had someone followed her from the Saz? Those were my routes, my paths, all places that I had been, and I could've easily met with the same fate. I felt hysteria rise in my throat like a stifled scream.

"Marissa would want you to be out having a good time too. So how about a movie? *Rocky II* is playing if you're not in the mood for Bogie. Or we could just go to Jimmy Day's, play some pinball." He was looking at me kind of funny. I was having trouble taking in air; the mud-brown walls of the Saz seemed to be closing in on me. The air conditioning felt like it had shut down.

"Is something wrong?"

"Wrong? Why should anything be wrong?" I stood up too fast and almost knocked over my barstool.

"I mean, you look kinda funny—"

"I really gotta go."

"Wait—" Benny stood, his bulky body hovering over me.

"No!" It came out too loud. I saw the hurt on his face. I took a deep breath. "I just have to go."

I turned and lit out of there before Benny could take in what was happening. The warm summer night air hit me as I reached the sidewalk. I forced myself to breathe in and out as I put one foot in front of the other, fighting back the panic. I was losing it. I had to go somewhere with lots of people, but people I didn't know. I didn't want to talk to anybody.

Tomorrow was going to be a big night, and I couldn't just wait out the time; I had to race it down. Fill it with something so I wouldn't think, or the anticipation would kill me. Why die of anticipation when you could be murdered and make the headlines? I certainly didn't want to miss my fifteen minutes of fame. My thoughts were spinning. My sanity was running amok.

I stepped down off the curb to cross the street, and a taxi spun by, just missing me. I jumped back up on the sidewalk, and my skates, slung over my shoulder, hit me sharply on my back.

I felt the pain and it almost felt good, like something real in a mess of surreal. I had to go somewhere that would get my mind off all this. Someplace real, where I wouldn't have to think. I didn't want to think. I just needed motion.

The rink. The Roxy disco skating rink. I'd blend in with the crowd and drown in the music. I didn't even have to go home and change. My zebra-striped jumpsuit was perfect for skating at a disco. I could skate till two in the morning, exhaust myself, and then maybe I'd get some sleep.

The Roxy was on the west edge of Chelsea. It would be bursting with sound and lights and people. It felt good just approaching it. Perfect. Anonymity. No one would look for me here. No one would see me. No one could hurt me. I dove inside.

The Roxy wasn't the biggest roller rink, but it was the only real roller disco in Manhattan. Flashing, swirling, pink and blue lights, the best dance music, an oval bar that sold juices and mineral water. And the people, they were all there—the glitziest disco queen, the Upper East Side wealthy types, the ragtag street skater. I laced up my skates and rolled onto the dance floor. Earth, Wind & Fire was playing "Boogie Wonderland," and to me it was like angels singing. I picked up speed, swaying to the music as I tried to lose myself.

Goodbye, newspapers, I won't miss you. So long, movies, I don't need your twisted fantasies. Tonight, Earth, Wind & Fire was all I needed and they were telling me to dance.

I was always a little awestruck at the people I saw at the Roxy. Most of them looked so rich and happy. Some of the faces were familiar to me although I didn't know them personally. When I saw them in newspapers or on TV, I always thought of them as special people, nothing like me. I was nobody. But at the Roxy I felt like their equal. As I skated, I knew that not a single one of them was better on wheels than I was. And the music backed me up.

I rolled into the middle of the rink and spun, just hugged myself and went faster and faster until I let go, spreading out my arms and pulling out of it till I stopped. I loved doing that. Some nights I'd spin myself dizzy. I sat on one of the little benches they had in the center of the rink. It cut down on solo space, but sometimes it was fun to sit in the middle and watch the river of people flow by. By then Donna Summer was singing her lungs out in "Hot Stuff."

A man of about thirty-five skidded to a stop in front of me and just stood there, smiling. Maybe I was supposed to know him, so I smiled back.

"Sugar, you are hot stuff, do you know that?"

Now, what was I supposed to say to that? *Yes, I know I am* or *Aw, pshaw, go on*? What I wanted to say was *Go skate into a wall, bub.* But I held my tongue and smiled sweetly. I looked at the empty seat next to me, then back to him, and batted my eyelashes. When he sat down, I got up and skated away backward, waving bye-bye. *Sorry, pal, I just wasn't in the mood.* Donna Summer was wrong tonight. If only it was always that easy.

I alternated between skating as fast as I could in the widest circle around the whole rink and doing a meandering snake, weaving around every person I passed. The music faded into the back of my brain. What was I doing with all these days of my life? Each night of my young adult life—sitting in bars, hanging out with friends, going out on a date, even just walking from work to a café—there was a feeling of anticipation that something might happen, should happen, could happen. Something that was going to make it worthwhile getting up each morning. But each night I went to bed without finding it.

Teresa, Jessica, the other two Jane Does—they had all had hopes and dreams, and they'd run out of time. Tonight, whirling with the crowd, ogling the rich and beautiful, wandering in and out of other people's paths on my skates, I was forced to look at my own path more clearly. My world was so small I was stuck spinning inside a tight circle. But I was the one who'd put myself there. I could try to blame my mother's and grandmother's deaths, or my grandfather, or all the shitty men who'd abused me. Those who made me a prisoner of fear. But maybe I could choose to look beyond the corners of my mind where I'd been hiding. Past the fear that held me down. How would I do that? Not by hiding in newspapers or movies or drink, that was for sure.

All those stupid nights I'd been waiting for some kind of savior, Prince Charming, famous Hollywood agent, or million-dollar lottery ticket. Maybe I actually had the power to choose how to live the rest of my life instead of being afraid to live it and waiting for someone or something to save me from it.

Skating around the Roxy, I suddenly felt grateful. Grateful to have that night, grateful to be alive and skating among a crowd of strangers. Living the way I had been, mired in my past, was a waste of life, an insult to the lost lives of Teresa and Jessica. And to the lost life of my mother. I was sick and tired of feeling sorry for myself.

I took a break and sat in the bleachers to watch the skaters make their rounds. Suddenly, the irony hit me. I'd been skating around in circles my whole life, never getting anywhere. Physically going from home to work or to a couple of bars, to movie theaters or out skating and back home again, physically and metaphorically going nowhere in the process. I'd been plodding along in a circle so long that the path had become a rut, making it harder and harder to get out of it. I started unlacing my skates. A new song began.

It was Cheryl Lynn, singing one of my favorite songs of the summer, "To Be Real." It was a love song, but it made me think: What did it mean to be real? All my paranoia, all my fear, brought on by my past and the recent threat of a killer at large, what was it? It wasn't real. I had the power inside me to think and feel and know what was real. Inside me. I had to trust myself to separate reality from fantasy. To believe in what was real, not fall into fear and worry that was just taking me down.

I had the strength to get through this and then figure out what to do with my life. It was my choice to listen to myself. I was capable, dammit, and I could play the hell out of this game. No more letting them beat me. *I choose to win. What I think and feel and know is what is real.* I finished putting on my sandals and flung my skates over my shoulder.

I stepped out into the cool night air. Either I had just missed a thundershower or an army of elves had polished the street shiny since I'd been outside. The potholes full of rain-water shimmered with the reflection of the streetlights. There was a line of taxicabs and limos picking up the rich. I started hoofing it. It was after one AM, but I was only six blocks from my apartment and I felt full of energy, like I just woke up from a good night's sleep. Or a coma.

On Tenth Avenue I passed the sex workers I knew by sight. One of them called out, "Hey, roller girl!" I waved. Soon I turned onto my street, and before I reached my door, I noticed two cops in a car at the curb. As I got closer, they lit up the spinning reds, and the two uniformed cops I'd never seen jumped out.

"Nina Esposito?" one of them asked.

"Yeah, that's me."

"Somebody wants to talk to you." He came toward me fast.

"What? I—"

But it didn't matter what I wanted to say; he grabbed me and pushed me into the back seat and ignored my indignant rage. I knew who wanted to talk to me. I guessed this time he was too lazy to come out to find me himself.

The uniformed cops walked me into the precinct and to an empty room occupied by a table and two chairs. They locked me in. I held in my fury. It felt like I was hugging a wild dog to my chest. What rights did you have if you could just get grabbed up and shoved into a cop car for no reason? All the power was with whoever was in authority, no matter what the situation was. I had no influence and nobody to stand up for me. I was all on my own, and at the moment that meant being locked in an interrogation room.

The ancient air conditioner wedged into the window put out more vibrating noise than cool air. I counted the dead flies trapped in the dim ceiling fixture shaped like a bowl as tightness built in my chest. I tried to add some variety by switching from sitting on the worn metal chair to pacing the six strides across the room and back again. Fifteen minutes later, my buddy Tom the Cop arrived. His wrinkled gray suit matched his complexion. By that time, I was standing in the corner, one leg bent with my foot up against the wall. I didn't look at him.

"Why don't you come over and sit down so we can talk?" His condescending tone turned my stomach. I had to hold on tight to keep my cool. I strolled over to the chair, pulled it a few feet away from the table, and sat. But I barely felt the seat under me.

"That's a good girl. Now maybe we can have some cooperation."

It took everything I had left not to tell him to go fuck himself.

"When she was good, she was very, very good." I recited instead.

"I got your note." He spoke the words as if they were sweet, the same way strychnine is like sugar. It made my flesh crawl. "I told you to stay away from Ron Meyers."

"It's not so easy. He's . . . my teacher," I muttered around the lump in my throat, my bravado-rage starting to crumble. Obedience had been beaten into me for so long, I suddenly realized, that even though I had decided to change my life, it didn't mean it was going to be easy. I couldn't say no to Ron, and now this cop had me locked up until I did whatever he wanted me to do. Life was like an acting exercise, I reminded myself. I could let my anger spin me off course, or I could use it to help me focus. I had to try to wiggle out from under Tom's control. "Maybe I'll end up getting some evidence on him."

"I thought you were under the impression that he's innocent?" His face was a sneer of contempt.

"I don't trust any of you pimps at this point." My shoulders were frozen halfway up my neck. "What are you charging me for? Walking down my own street?"

"No charges." He opened his empty hands, palms up, as if I thought there was an arrest warrant in them. "We just wanted to have a talk with you and make sure you understand how dangerous this situation is."

"Is that the royal we, or do you have an accomplice?" My inner brat gave me some of my strength back. "Is Detective Lopez involved in this harassment?"

"I told you he's off the case."

"There's nothing between me and Detective Lopez." My neck throbbed.

"That's your interpretation." He adjusted his wilted suit jacket. "Let's get back to the subject at hand."

"Which is?"

"That you're not going on a date with Ron Meyers."

The way he ordered me around was too familiar. Familiar, like every man in my life who believed he had authority over me. And made me believe it too. But I was not playing that role anymore.

"By going on a date with Ron, maybe I'll help prove he didn't kill anyone at all."

His face started to turn red.

"You have no idea what you're talking about." The volume rose with each word. "Are you trying to get yourself killed?"

He knew the right buttons to push. I bit back tears that would only give him more power. My eyes focused on the multiple sticky coffee rings on the surface of the gray table between us. The oldest ones were furry with dust. I cleared my throat and swallowed hard.

"What about those new cases? Aren't you going to alert the city that there's a serial killer on the loose?"

"A task force takes time to put together."

"Time? You're going to let bureaucracy put women at risk? It's almost Saturday night. There's going to be another death." I couldn't believe his bullshit.

"Putting together a serial killer case with the evidence we have . . . it's still weak." Tom the Cop leaned back in his chair, his bloated belly straining at the buttons on his shirt. I suddenly realized what was happening.

"You still don't think it's a serial killer, do you? I can't believe it. This is why you had Detective Lopez taken off the case. It had nothing to do with me. He's trying to make the case for a serial killer, and you're trying to stop him. Why? What do you have to gain from that?" I pushed my chair back, the screeching-scraping noise echoing in the empty room.

"You're way off base. It's more complicated than that. Putting the whole city on alert for the wrong reasons can be catastrophic. It's not something we take lightly."

It was useless. I shook my head and turned away. I just wanted out. "Just tell me what you want." My voice was barely above a whisper, but I managed to fill it with contempt. "And let me out of this rat cage."

"We want you to cancel the date." I watched him calm himself down. He could afford to be calm.

"I'm not going to do that." He was talented at bringing out the stubborn in me. It was the only power I had over him.

Tom the Cop banged his fist on the desk, and I flinched.

"Damn it, Esposito." He raised his voice as he stood. "You're not listening to me."

"What do you care if I go out with him or not?"

"I don't want any more corpses piling up. Not even yours." His pasty face loomed closer to me.

"We'll be out in public." I turned away from his bad breath. "Surrounded by a Saturday night crowd."

"You think there's no danger in that?" Anger seemed to emanate from his pores. It stank like week-old sweat.

"Nothing I can't handle." I mustered up a smidgen of nonchalance.

"You are even stupider than I thought." He spit out the words.

Now I had no choice.

"I'm going on that date." I jabbed my finger on the tabletop. "And by the end of the night, we'll know if he's the killer or not, one way or another." When the words were finished coming out, I realized what I had said. I just might prove that Ron was the killer. At the risk of my own life. But I wasn't backing down.

Tom the Cop leaned away from me, slouching over his potbelly, making the wrinkles in his shirt even more pronounced. What could he do, keep me locked up? I couldn't read his face. He was angry but certainly not beaten. In his eyes I saw him flip through his choices.

"Then we'll follow you."

It wouldn't be the worst thing. I still didn't believe Ron was the killer, but I could be wrong. Either way, I'd need witnesses.

I shrugged. "It's your overtime."

"Go home." He stood. "And don't screw with me on this. Tomorrow, nine o'clock at the White Horse."

He walked out the door, leaving it open behind him. I felt my heart twitch as I waited a moment before I left the room. What the hell was I doing? Someone else could've talked me out of meeting with Ron, helped me get out of it, but Tom the Cop had just pushed me farther into it. And I'd let him. Maybe that was what he really wanted: a decoy to help him close the case. So much for control.

I made my way through the precinct, passing the gray metal desks with the men in cheap suits talking on the phone or interviewing flustered civilians. Part of me wanted to knock the piles of papers off each desk, push over every chair. But I floated past it all in my zebra jumpsuit, my skates slung over my shoulder as if nothing mattered. When I got to the lobby, the door opened and Frankie Lopez rushed in. He was wearing worn jeans and a blue soccer shirt. He stopped when he saw me, his usual smile absent.

"Nina." He looked toward the desk sergeant, who turned discreetly to straighten some papers on the other side. Frankie came closer to me. "Someone called me and told me you were here. What happened?"

"What happened?" My anger was still boiling. "Tom Barry had me picked up so we could have a little talk."

"Had you picked up?" Frankie looked puzzled.

"Yeah." I tried not to let my rage pour out at him. "I got stopped by a couple of uniforms and shoved into a cherry-top."

Frankie looked at me blankly.

"I really need to get out of here."

"Wait." Frankie turned with me. I didn't want to start blubbering in the police station, or screaming. I walked out the door before I could melt down. Frankie followed me.

"Nina, wait." He put himself right in front of me and looked at me like he does, like he sees only me. There was no precinct, no uniformed cops coming in and out, no city street. Just me and Frankie. "I had nothing to do with this, you know that, right?"

I stood still and tried to calm myself down. I believed him, but that didn't make me less mad. My anger could only turn to tears, and I didn't want that to happen. He took both my hands in his.

"You know you can trust me." His eyes begged me. "You know that, don't you?"

"I've never had anyone in my life give me a reason to trust them, Frankie. I don't know what that means."

"But I've never given you a reason not to trust me, have I?"

"Not yet." I squeezed his hands, then dropped them. I almost flinched at the disappointment in his eyes, but I didn't know how I could trust anyone right then. "Frankie, I'm mad right now, and I don't know if I should talk to you about it."

"What happened? What did he want?"

"Shouldn't you ask him that?"

Frankie looked back in the station.

"Come on, let's talk over here." I followed him half a block down the road, just out of sight of the precinct entrance. "Look, someone told him we talked at Maria's, and he took me off the case. He won't tell me anything."

"I know. He told me he took you of the case. It's such bullshit." I couldn't keep the petulance out of my voice. My skates felt like an anchor around my neck. I set them down on the ground in front of me.

Frankie paused. "Someone's in his ear about me." He put his hands in his pockets and leaned against the building. "He says I'm not objective about anything to do with you. And since you found those other cases, it's like he's fighting even harder against the serial killer theory."

"It wasn't his idea, so he's against it. So typical."

"I still believe he's a good cop. He wants to solve these cases."

"Or just close the cases. He's trying to railroad Ron Meyers. Is he even looking at other suspects?" Was Frankie with me on this or not? My arms hung from my shoulders like dead weights.

"What did he want from you? Why did he haul you in?"

"The other day he came into the restaurant where I work. He told me to contact him if Ron Meyers got in touch with me, and he did. Ron did."

"Outside of class?"

"Yes, he called me, but I wasn't home; he left a message. So I told Detective Barry. But then after class last night, Thursday night, Ron asked me out to dinner for tomorrow night. Well, tonight. Saturday night."

"And what did you say?"

"I said I'd meet him."

Frankie didn't speak for a minute. I wondered what was going through his head. He was probably thinking I was a bimbo or complicit in the murders or an opportunist. Something awful for sure. But he surprised me.

"Good. You're being smart. If he is involved, you can't avoid him. You have to go along or he'll try to get to you in a more covert way. This way you're out in the open."

"Detective Barry wouldn't agree with you. I left a message at the precinct to let him know the time and place, and then when I got home tonight, that cop car was waiting in front of my place and they brought me here."

"He sent a car to pick you up? Why?"

"He wants me to cancel the date with Ron."

"What did you say?"

"I said no. Several times, in fact. So now he says he'll follow me. Watch us on the date."

"It's the only thing to do."

"I know. I don't care about that. It's fine, it's good. But to have me shoved into a car by a couple of uniforms and dragged here—"

"That was wrong, Nina. Tom was wrong to do that." Frankie reached for my hands. I let him take them for a moment, but I was too angry to hang on. Cops were cops.

"What the hell is his problem?" I asked.

"He's under a lot of pressure. He's working the only way he knows how—by the seat of his pants."

"I just can't stand it anymore. I have to find out the truth. If Ron is the only person he's looking at and it's not him, he'll never find the real killer. I had to do something. It has to stop. It has to stop." I was babbling and I knew it. I finally just made myself shut up.

"I know. I know. It's okay. I understand." He was quiet for a minute. I looked back toward the station. The chance that Tom the Cop might come out made my head buzz with anxiety. The sky was already turning lighter at the horizon. In the dim light everything looked gray: the streets, the sidewalks, the buildings. There was no contrast, no black or white, no color.

"I gotta go." I swung my skates up onto my shoulder. The laces cut into my flesh.

"Wait. Where are you meeting Ron Meyers?" Frankie took a step closer to me.

"At the White Horse at nine."

"Wait. Let me get a uniform with a car to drive you home."

"No, it's okay, Frankie."

"Please, let me do this for you. It'll just take a minute."

"I'll just take a taxi."

"You'll never find one—" Just as the words come out of his mouth, a checkered cab cruised by, its white vacancy light lit. I flagged it down and opened the door. "G'night, Frankie." I tossed my skates in ahead of me.

He watched me get in the cab, his mouth set. I cranked down the window and raised my hand to him as the cab began to move. He lifted his hand in return. The taxi picked up speed and just made it through a yellow light. We were at my place in three minutes.

I ran up the stairs, dropped my skates on the floor, peeled off my clothes, and threw myself into bed. But my mind was still full of fury. Bastards! If cops could just drag you in for no reason, how could I ever be safe on my own? What if Tom the Cop had trumped up some charge against me? What kind of defense would I have? I was alone in the world, no family to protect me, no money to buy my way out. I felt like I was in some third-world country or behind the Iron Curtain, not in a democracy.

I thought I was doing okay, taking care of myself. Being alone had its advantages. But maybe I was wrong. Maybe I should be spending my time looking for a sugar daddy instead of working on a career. I never understood those women before, gold diggers; I thought they were despicable. How could you marry a man for money? But I was seeing things differently. Maybe that's why they did it—for protection. When you're a target, it's important to have a shield, some kind of defense. A defenseless target, that's what I was.

I got out of bed and paced. I was scared but also enraged. It wasn't fair. We were vulnerable alone because of the way the power structure was set up. We almost had to be with a man just for protection. They were in control. It was a losing game. I felt like breaking something. I felt huge with my anger, like the Incredible Hulk.

Tom Barry was my worst nightmare. And wouldn't Frankie eventually be corrupted by the authority he had?

Would I ever be able to trust him? I was crazy to even think about being with him.

My mind wouldn't stop spiraling. It was hours before work, then a date with Cousin Bobby, then I had to meet Ron. I just couldn't wait for it all to be over. I was brimming with panic. I didn't know who scared me more at this point: Ron or Bobby. I tried to push it out of my mind. It used to feel normal, this inertia. Letting life happen around me, *to* me, waiting for it to mean something. But now it was just pissing me off. I was pacing so hard I was stomping. I stopped and looked at my apartment, resisting the urge to start cleaning. My loft was already spotless. The only control I had was over dirt. Pathetic.

I sat on my bed. I was sick of the fear. Cops, killers, relationships. I was through with it all. Where was that resolve I'd felt at the Roxy? I wasn't going to let Tom the Cop squeeze it out of me. For once I would remember that it was my life and I got to choose.

I wasn't going to take any bullshit from Cousin Bobby, that's for sure. He didn't know what I had in store for him. And whatever was going to happen with Ron, I could handle it. He was no killer. Tom the Cop could watch all he wanted, but nothing was going to happen. It was just another date with just another octopus. And I could handle an octopus. I've handled them before. Maybe I'd even loan Ron a piece of my mind. Why should I take any more shit than I already had? It was my life, dammit. Even if I didn't know what to do with it yet.

I got back into bed. My sheets were soft and cool, and my new angry confidence followed me into my dreams. Dreams that started out light and gentle but quickly turned. I was caught in a sticky web that wouldn't let me go no matter how much I struggled. I turned around and found myself upside down, like there was no gravity. I felt panic rise in my throat. In my dream I held the panic back with all my strength, and that made me feel like I had some power over my fear. Then I remembered something my mother said to me once after a nightmare, something I had forgotten until that moment: *Fear can only take you if you let it.* I held the sound of her voice in my head, the first time I'd heard it since she died. I fought for my balance. *Fear can only take you if you let it.* Soon the gravity returned and I felt righted. The darkness started to fade, and so did the fear. I half woke and turned over. *It's only a dream,* my mother's voice whispered. I drifted back into a peaceful sleep.

I had trouble waking. I felt drugged and was so deeply lost in my sleep that I pressed the snooze button four times before my mind realized what my fingers were doing. It was Saturday. *Gotta get up and go to work,* I reminded my brain. I got in the shower, scrubbed myself nearly raw, pulled on a charcoal-gray cotton dress, and rolled to work as fast as I could in the midmorning sun.

The morning was already warm. I skated alongside the Manhattan traffic, which flowed smoothly for a change. No traffic jams, no honking horns, just people going where they were going. Some of them even knew where that was supposed to be.

All the colors—the red brick, the blue sky, the white clouds—looked brighter. The humidity had lifted, the air was clear. I felt like my anger had cleansed me, washed away the fear and obedience that I had let control me for so long. I did that, no one else. I began to believe I had power over it after all.

I'm going to get through this, I told myself. As I rolled east, my thoughts drifted back to *What am I going to do with the rest of my life?* but I pushed those words out of my way. I'd think about that when the summer was over. I had time. I had plenty of time.

I arrived at work a little early. The air conditioning had already been pumping, but the lights were still off, and I walked into the dark, cool darkness of The Realm. It greeted me like an empty grave.

Work was dead, even for a Saturday. Each minute fell on the last until they built up like so many fifty-pound sacks of flour. It was one of those rare shifts that hadn't been worth showing up for. But as boring as it was, as slow as the day went, as little money as I made, I didn't care. It was a day in a life that finally felt like it belonged to me. It was a slow, boring, wonderfully normal day. Every minute of it was mine. I could only hope for a million more.

When five PM came, I totaled my tips. Twenty-five dollars. What a living. Nick stood at the service bar as I counted out my register. He was fidgeting so much I kept losing count.

"Nick." I glared at him. "Do you have to stand over my shoulder while I count? It's distracting."

He smiled at me. It wasn't a nice smile. It was almost intentionally nasty but in a blurry sort of way. Nick didn't have that much focus in him. "Just making sure you don't run off before Bobby gets here."

I smiled back. My smile felt mean inside, but I frosted it with sweetness.

"Wouldn't think of it," I cooed. "I can't wait till he gets here." That was an understatement. My adrenaline was flowing like lava. I finished counting and closed out my bank. Nick paid me my week's wages in cash. Mike was already behind the bar, checking that he had everything he needed, serving some newly arrived customers. I hoped his night was going to be better than my day. I poured myself a tall, icy glass of club soda with a lot of lemon and sat at the first stool next to the service opening. I was ready.

Bobby didn't keep me waiting long. Nick was still hovering, but I ignored him. When Bobby came in and stood next to me, I had my purse on my lap, my club soda was empty, and my skates were under my stool. I turned to greet him.

"Hi there." My smile was candy-apple red. But with candy apples, you never know if the fruit underneath the red sugar crust is sweet and crisp or mealy and full of worms.

"Hi, Nina. Shall we have a drink before we go?"

"Sure, I'd love one." Mike turned to take our order.

"Cutty on the rocks for me, Mike. Nina?"

I was ready to top off the day. "I'll have a shooter of ice-cold Stoli, please."

Bobby smiled in anticipation. Mike gave us our glasses: Bobby's old-fashioned glass full of ice swimming in caramel liquid, mine a tall frosted skinny glass on a stem, clear vodka to the top. We clinked in a toast. He was drinking to a wild and fast night. I was drinking to my independence. I drained my glass and stood. My hands smoothed the front of my gunpowder-gray dress, erasing wrinkles that didn't exist. I looked straight at Bobby.

"Time to go already?" Bobby's smile was unsure.

"Actually, yes." I picked up my skates. "*I* am going."

"Wait a minute." Bobby put his glass down firmly on the bar. "Didn't you get the message?"

"Oh, I got it all right. Nicky made it very clear. Either we go out together or I'm out one bartending job, right?" I hung my skates on my shoulder by the laces. "Fine. I quit. Have a nice life."

This rendered Bobby speechless. The look on his face was as brilliant as the *Mona Lisa*'s, and I felt just like Leonardo da Vinci. I turned to go, and I saw that Nick was standing right behind me. I paused for a moment to appreciate his expression. He was going to take some shit for this. Good, he deserved it.

"Thanks for nothing, Nicky." His mouth opened, but nothing came out. I walked out the door.

I stood in front of The Realm for a brief moment, blinking in the late-afternoon sunlight. Time to find a new job. Come to think of it, pretty much everything in my life could use a change. I walked around the corner before I put on my skates, just in case Nick decided to run out of The Realm after me. Then I rolled west on Thirty-Second Street toward home.

I skated past Penn Station, where thousands of people boarded trains every day, going places I'd never been. *No risk, no gain,* I wanted to tell my mother and grandmother. *Are you listening wherever you are?* I remembered reading Emerson when I was in high school. *Lift is a journey, not a destination.* I'd never really understood what he meant until just now. I could take off in one direction and then turn off the road anytime. I could double back and start over again; what did it matter? I'd get somewhere eventually. What was more important was how you enjoyed the time you spent on the way. I didn't have to have all the answers yet, but the journey belonged to me, and I'd choose the way. No more following the path of least resistance. Or the ones I got forced into.

First, I had to get rid of all the debris in my life. Ditching Bobby and Nicky was a good start. Next, Ron Meyers and The Studio. Benny, Gorgeous Charlie, and the Saz. What good was any of that? None. I'd find a new direction. I knew how to work hard. I just had to pick something else besides bartending and acting. Pick a point on the horizon and move straight toward it instead of going in circles. I didn't know if Frankie might still fit into the picture, but he was the one loose thread I didn't want to trim off. I did trust him.

The sun was sinking low, glowing orange in a brilliant blue sky. I felt like a fog had lifted. A fog that had been there so long I didn't even know how clear the world could be without it.

CHAPTER 20

Back in my apartment, I stood in the middle of the room. The setting sun slanted through the window blinds and made a striped pattern on the floor. I stepped into the middle of it like I was trapped in a noir film. To break out of this prison, I was going to have to fight my way out. Walking out on Bobby and quitting The Realm was the easy part, but it made me feel like I was ready for more. I was ready for Next.

I remembered all the times I'd let my grandfather and his anger push me into a huddled mass in the corner, sometimes literally. The way he fought with my grandmother—all of that noise was stuck in my head. I never wanted to be like them, so I retreated from any conflict. That led to all the times I let someone else win, just because I didn't want to fight or was too afraid to fight, and all the men who took advantage of that. I was an easy victim.

I pulled the strings on the blinds, moving from window to window, until they were all wide open and I'd erased the shadows. I was done hiding behind fictional characters, characters in movies, or even the ones in newspaper stories. Tonight, on my date with Ron, I was going to be Nina Esposito, no one else. I turned to see my flushed face in the full-length mirror.

"A nice hot shower and I'm ready for anything," I said out loud.

I combed out my hair while it dried and scrunched it in my fingers to bolster its waves. When I was young, I'd wished for a big mass of curls. A lot of people with curly hair wished their locks were straight. The grass was always greener. Tonight, I liked my hair just the way it was.

I chose clothes for my date. *They can all go to hell.* I wasn't letting anyone intimidate me tonight. I put on a slinky sleeveless silver dress with a racer back and black platform sandals. I didn't have much in the way of jewelry, but I dug up a thin sliver chain with a heart-shaped locket that belonged to my mother. On the outside, the Virgin Mary was carved in silver on a mother-of-pearl background. The inside still had a tiny photograph of Joey Vickery, my first crush from elementary school, that I'd cut out of the class picture that year, just before my mother died. I guess I left it in the locket because it was the last time I remember being happy.

I took a taxi to the White Horse Tavern. I was fifteen minutes late. Joke 'em if they can't take a fuck. Ron was there, sitting at the bar. He had his back turned to me, but I couldn't mistake his slim, muscular build.

"Hey there." I sat in the empty seat next to him.

"Well, stranger, I almost thought you were going to stand me up." He kissed my cheek.

"Oh, am I late?" I wasn't apologizing to anyone tonight. "Would you order me a drink?"

"Of course. What's your pleasure?"

I looked up to the ceiling in a pose of deep thought. How close to the vest was I going to play these cards? "Campari and soda with a wedge of lime."

He ordered for me, then turned and looked in my eyes. "You are gorgeous tonight."

"Tonight?" I challenged him.

"Especially tonight."

"Well, let's stick with tonight. What do you have in mind, Ron? What do you have planned?"

"Nothing up my sleeve." He pushed up the unbuttoned cuffs of his whisper-thin linen shirt. "Dinner and conversation. And I promise not to drink too much."

Imagine the look of surprise on my face.

"I want to apologize for last time." His face was contrite. "I came on a little strong, and I want you to know that's not who I am."

"Really?" I wasn't buying any day-old bread, as my grandmother used to say. But I wasn't bitter about it. *Ron is who he is. And I yam what I yam, as Popeye used to say.*

"Well, Ron, this drink is delicious, but it's almost done. Where are we going for dinner?"

"I thought we'd—hey watch it, will ya, buddy?" A large, hairy man in jeans and a polo shirt sat next to Ron at the bar and jostled his elbow.

"Sorry, I'm a klutz." The man winked at me. Some guys are pigs even when you've got an escort. I held myself back from flipping him my middle finger, still simmering with the anger born from the night before. It fed every cell in my body. My eyes went to the door. Detective Tom Barry stood there with a tall mug of beer in his hand. He nodded a quarter of an inch. *Oh, I get it, Godzilla and King Kong.* I had nurtured a tiny hope Frankie would be part of the surveillance team. Maybe this was better. Letting Frankie watch me on a date with someone else might feel weird. Still, he was the only one I actually trusted.

I turned back to Ron. Oh, yeah, what was I doing?

"I thought we'd go to J. S. Vandam's." Ron was focused on his plan for the evening. "It's a quick taxi ride, and the food is excellent. So is the ambience."

"Well, any place would have a better ambience than this place right now." I set my empty glass on the bar. "Let's go."

As soon as we reached the curb, a taxi pulled up in front of us as if part of the script. I half wished Tom the Cop and his gorilla wouldn't get a cab. But I figured Kong had heard Ron mention J. S. Vandam's at the bar, so it didn't matter how closely they followed us.

On the taxi's radio, Donna Summer sang about bad girls. I closed my eyes, and it felt like we were flying downtown.

I wasn't going to be a bad or a sad girl tonight, no matter how loud Donna Summer sang about it. Ron's attention was with the driver, making sure he knew where to go. Seventh Avenue South hit Houston Street and magically turned into Varick Street. The restaurant was just a few blocks farther south.

We walked into the crowded room, walnut wood paneling everywhere. Waiters spun by in black vests and long white aprons like a 1930s Fred Astaire movie. Bundles of greenery and candles were tucked into all the right spots. The staff treated us with the utmost respect and courtesy, and I felt like a queen. Ron was a Broadway star, after all, even if he was between shows. Celebrity brought such a lack of privacy; the least you could ask for was a little special treatment once in a while. New York City was the best place to be famous. Most locals wouldn't be caught dead fawning over someone famous or asking them for their autograph. It just ain't cool.

Godzilla and King Kong walked in right after us and sat at the long, sleek bar. It was a convenient setup with the wall-to-wall mirror on the back wall. They could watch us without straining their thick necks.

The cuisine was gourmet but not exotic. Ron ordered chicken breast coated with crushed hazelnuts, roasted potatoes, blossom of broccoli. I chose pan-roasted salmon with capers and olives, rice pilaf, bouquet of asparagus. Ron kept to his word and was a perfect gentleman. We discussed theater and movies, not the business but the stories, the depth of the art we both appreciated. It was a rare hour of intellectual pleasure, and I realized that was it. That was what I was looking for. Real conversation. Why was this the exception instead of the rule? After our meal, we sipped coffee and tea.

I glanced toward the bar and saw the wide backsides of my guardian angels. Seeing them reminded me of my last dinner with Ron and how Marissa had been parked at the bar that night.

"I've been meaning to ask you something." I interrupted our nirvana.

Ron's eyes reflected my change in tone, and his posture stiffened.

"That night at Texarkana." I paused. *How do I put this?* "Did you notice Marissa at the bar? Maybe after I left?"

"No. I had no idea she was there until the cops questioned me the next day." He frowned. "What was that all about, anyway? Did you two have something planned?"

"I just happened to mention to her that I was having dinner with you. I didn't know she was going to hang out at the bar and watch." If he was trying to deflect my suspicions, it wasn't going to work. I hadn't forgotten why I was there. "I thought maybe you saw her after I left."

"I didn't see her that night. Do you think I followed her after you walked out on me?" He tried for humor, but I could see he was irked.

"It was late and you were less than a gentleman. We already agreed on that."

"I hate to dwell on my shortcomings." He fiddled with his coffee spoon. "But along with apologizing for my behavior last time, I also want to explain."

I poured more Earl Grey from the porcelain pot into my cup. *Here we go. Goodbye, intellectual stimulation.* He took my hand and traced each finger gently. I was acutely aware that I was being watched from the bar, and I was suddenly relieved that Frankie wasn't there. This was an acting job for me, nothing more, but I wouldn't want Frankie in the audience.

"I was nervous that night at Texarkana. That's why I drank too much."

"Why were you nervous, Ron?" Confession was good for the soul.

"Just being with you." His somber brown eyes tilted up to mine. "Just that there was the chance of screwing it up. The chance that I might turn you off and you wouldn't want to get to know me better."

Boy, this sounded good. For bullshit.

"Well, Ron, by drinking too much and acting the way you did, you did screw it up. But you are certainly making up for it tonight." I slid my hand gently away from his touch. "Would you excuse me while I go powder my nose?"

I'd always wanted to say that. I actually did have to use the facilities, and this would give him a chance to pay the bill without exposing me to the sordid details of the evening's finances. I was so freakin' couth.

I purposely walked by the bar and cleared my throat as I passed Tom the Cop before I disappeared around the corner into the ladies' room. I didn't think he'd follow me inside, but I figured he'd be waiting for me when I came out. I took my time.

I washed my hands, using a generous amount of soap from the porcelain dispenser on the black marble counter. The lavender fragrance transported me to thoughts of my mother, who spiked every drawer with packets of the dried flowers. I looked at myself in the mirror—my bronze summer tan, my pointy nose and strong chin, so similar to my mother's face. My generous eyebrows were probably the influence of the father I'd never known.

What would my mother say to me right now? She would tell me to think carefully about this date with Ron. She wouldn't tell me what to do or how to do it, but she'd say, *Be smart, Nina, always be smart.* I didn't always know what that meant, and maybe she didn't either, but it made me stop and think. Maybe that was the lesson. All I knew was that she loved me. And all I could hope for was to learn from my mistakes and be grateful for what I had.

I rinsed my hands and imagined that Ron was sincere. He really might think I was gorgeous and talented and interesting. *Mm-hmm.* I might let my ego fall for that. But Ron Meyers nervous about having a date with me? No, that was too much. He was a damned good actor, but he'd never make it writing his own scripts.

What did he really have in mind? I dried my hands carefully on one of the individual cotton towels that I plucked from a pyramid stack. Whatever it was, I was ready. I tossed the towel into the wicker hamper placed perfectly for my convenience and walked out the door.

"Hello, Tom." I stood next to him in the hallway outside the ladies' room. My smile was as natural as gefilte fish. Everything was swell. "How's tricks?"

"What's going on over there?" Impatience emanated from Tom's hulk with his standard-issue body odor. He must be miffed I was making him late for his date with a stripper.

"Just your usual wining and dining." My calm outranked him.

"Where are you going next?" Tom's beetle eyes squinted.

"Oh, I don't know." I strung him along with pleasure. "Perhaps I'll suggest a stroll in the moonlight, see if he drags me down any back alleys. Would that suit you?"

"Just fine," he growled, dinosaur-like. "We'll be right behind you."

"By the way, nice partner you got there." I started to turn away. "I feel so safe with two big strong men like yourselves right behind me. And I do mean big." I batted my eyelashes. "I just hope you're both not as slow as you look. Just in case you have to give pursuit."

I sauntered back to my table, and Ron smiled when he saw me like he was ready for more dessert. *Okay, buddy, let's see what else you got.* As I sat down, he slid closer to me on the padded banquet seat, crowding me to the edge. Just like a man—take up all the room, steal all the covers. An old children's song ran through my head: *And they all rolled over and one fell out.*

"Would you like to take a walk in the moonlight?" I went for the corny approach, pulling him in with melodrama straight from a soap opera script. "Take a little stroll back toward my place and have a nightcap on the way?"

He almost beamed. I knew this safari game and I had this tiger by the tail—the one in front, that is. He'd already paid the check, so we left immediately, King Kong and Godzilla in tow.

Ron put out his elbow, and I held his arm as we walked. He almost felt good to hold on to, warm and strong, the solid-man persona. In spite of everything, I allowed myself to enjoy the moment. We strolled north through the West Village, past sidewalk cafés full of good-looking men smoking and drinking together, late-night head shops selling glass bongs and rolling papers, string-tied stacks of Sunday newspapers next to newsstands waiting to be unpacked. The night air felt cool and comfortable for a change, full of oxygen that filled my lungs with purpose. If Ron was the killer, I'd know soon enough. For some reason I didn't feel any fear. For once I knew who I was and where I was going.

I peeked behind us to look for my escort. Tom seemed far away, so I tried to slow our pace. His surveillance should've made me feel safer, but it just gave me a lump in my belly. We passed Christopher Street and Sheridan Square up the west side of Seventh Avenue South. I was about to suggest we stop for a drink at the Riviera, but as we walked, my feet felt heavier with each step. My amusement at having one up on Ron was wearing off. Here I was, strolling up the avenue with a beautiful, famous, talented man, and all he really wanted out of me was a good lay. My crest began to feel fallen.

All my energy drained out of my body, and I could barely drag myself forward. The fatigue from the years of fighting off dates, bosses, teachers—it all caught up with me. I was just playing a game to get through it, and I was sick of games. Sick and tired.

Disco music that I didn't recognize poured out of a club as we passed an unmarked door. It opened to let out two men dressed fabulously in colorful disco wear. They were holding hands. I was momentarily jealous. They knew how to be happy, even if it might be just for the night. The pounding disco beat brought me back to the Roxy, and I remembered my earlier resolution. I was heating up. My head felt like a silver Jiffy Pop balloon ready to burst. *If this is a game, the next move is mine.* Time to call Ron's bluff.

"Let's be honest, I'm too young to get serious." I slowed my step. "I'm not looking for any kind of relationship. I just want to have a good time. You know what I mean?" I closed with a wink.

We stopped in front of a darkened five-and-dime store. The window was plastered with signs advertising the latest sales. *Buy one get one FREE!*

Ron took both my hands in his and faced me. "Not only are you smart and beautiful, but you're much more mature than I thought." I could almost see the wolf ears peek out from his wavy hair, his canine fangs slip out between his lips. "What's the point of life if we can't have a good time? That's always been my philosophy."

He pulled me closer and kissed me passionately on the mouth. He acted so fast that I just let him kiss me. His Ralph Lauren Polo cologne mixed with his sweat and turned my stomach. How many times had I let men kiss me thinking it was easier than putting up a fight? If I only had a nickel. I was so disgusted at the speed with which he dropped his facade, I didn't even kiss him back. He stopped kissing me and looked at me, surprised and a little insulted, as if I had just scuffed his newly polished shoes.

"Is something wrong?" Ron's eyebrows punctuated his puzzled thoughts.

"Yes, actually." I peeled his hands off my body. "You're wrong."

"What?"

"Look, you were right about one thing." I stepped back and looked at him head to toe. "I'm smart, or at least I'm no fool. The truth is you're a great acting teacher and a very sexy man, but this—this just isn't right. I've been through enough crappy times in my life, and now I'm looking for something else."

"But I'll make you feel like a princess." His lack of empathy astounded me. He couldn't even fake it anymore.

"Look, I'm sure going to bed with you would be something I'd never forget." I almost laughed at the magnitude of his self-importance. "But I seriously doubt that sleeping with you would do anything but make me feel used. And for once, I don't believe I deserve that."

Looking past Ron a half a block away, I saw Tom the Cop lurking in the doorway of a punk rock jewelry store. The sign hanging just above him proclaimed *Ears Pierced Your Way! With or Without Pain!*

"I don't want to use you." Ron wouldn't give up. It was annoying, to say the least, like a mosquito you just can't swat. "I just think we could have a lot of fun together."

"Fun's just not all it's cracked up to be." I looked at him curiously. How many other girls had put up with his shit? It was like he'd never taken a no from anyone his whole life. Well, there's a first time for everything. "Why don't we just keep it professional? No hard feelings. Thanks for the lovely evening."

I reached for his hand and shook it firmly. He was too surprised to speak. I started to walk away, westbound on West Eleventh Street.

"Let me take you home at least," Ron called out after me with a last dash of hope.

I raised my hand and waved without turning around. He was surely standing there dumbfounded. I didn't need to see it. I was tired of dumb. I kept walking. Tom the Cop would be livid. But what did he want me to do, stay with Ron till dawn just to see if he was going to attack me? In my experience, more than half the men I'd ever dated would try that on some level. Maybe closer to three-fourths. Let King Kong and Godzilla split up. I wanted to go to the Saz and see if I could have a few laughs and then just go home, like the good old days, only better. Because tonight I was celebrating a new start.

I turned south on Hudson toward the Saz, feeling pretty good about how things were turning out. Screw the Ron Meyerses of this world and the Cousin Bobbys. They thought they could just go from girl to girl, from fuck to fuck, and it didn't matter. Didn't they know we were human beings and we deserved simple human kindness and respect? Was that too much to ask? Maybe they thought it was. But from now on, I was asking. Maybe that had been the hardest thing in the world for me to learn, but it was inside me now, and I wasn't letting go of it.

The Saz was packed with the usual New Orleans loving customers. Through the plate glass front of the restaurant, I could see their food-laden plates and the beer, wine, and cocktails on the tables. The revelers were happily talking with each other or holding hands and mooning into each other's eyes. The music was loud, and the waiters rushed between the crowded tables. Just another Saturday night in the Village. I opened the door, and Gorgeous Charlie almost fell out on top of me.

"Hey, Nina, what are you doin'?" He was glowing. "I was just thinkin' about you. Lemme buy you a drink."

"Is Benny in there?" I stepped aside cautiously.

"Benny got off hours ago. Come on, lemme buy you a drink." Charlie moved a little too close, his golden curls damp with perspiration at the temples, his eyes the darkest of blues.

"No thanks, I'm just heading home." I turned away and headed uptown.

"Wait, I've been dying to show you my office. Why don't you come with me now?" He fell into step with me. "You going uptown? I'll walk you. It's on the way, just a few blocks up the street."

I didn't answer, and he kept pace with me. I'd have to ditch him when I could. We passed the White Horse Tavern where my night had started. I had a sudden feeling of circular vertigo, like I was in a déjà vu nightmare.

"I've got some excellent tequila that I got in Mexico last year." Charlie wouldn't give up. "We'll break the seal. What do you say?"

"No thanks, Charlie. It's late—"

"How could you say no? I've been such a friend to you these last couple of weeks, haven't I?" His gorgeous smile was almost shy. "Come and have one drink with me."

I kept walking, trying to keep a few steps ahead of Charlie. Wherever his office was, I'd just keep walking past when we got there; I wasn't going out of my way. We walked north on Hudson and passed Bank Street, home of The Studio that had been my life's center for the last few months. We went by The Bus Stop coffee shop where Marissa and I had planned our futures. Soon we passed the alley where I'd found the red shoes and Jessica's body. I felt like I was walking through flashbacks. Charlie kept right next to me and gave me one of his beautiful smiles every time I glanced at him. He was not getting the hint.

Maybe I was selling him short. Just because he was a good-looking man didn't mean he was automatically a jerk, in spite of what I'd experienced in my past. He'd never even laid a hand on me. He's been nothing but nice to me, a true gentleman who only treated me like a lady. But wasn't that part of the problem? I was no lady and I didn't aspire to be one. Besides, it was late and I was tired. Bone tired from the last ten years of my life. The question was, how to get rid of him?

"It's pretty late." I stepped up my pace, putting a little distance between us, but his long legs strode forward and easily overtook me. We passed all the restaurants and stores of the neighborhood and were on a lonely block of brick apartment buildings and garbage alleys. The street curved a bit to the west.

"Come on." Charlie moved forward excitedly, and this time I let him get ahead of me. I looked back down Hudson Street behind us. Hey, what happened to my double escort? Had they both gone off and followed Ron? I couldn't see past the curve in the road we just passed.

"It's this way." Suddenly he grabbed my wrist and pulled me around the corner to the left onto Gansevoort Street.

"Charlie—" I tried to pull away, but his grasp was too tight. Panic started to rise in my throat like bile.

"Come on, the door is down this alley. We're almost there." He pulled me around another corner to the right into a narrow alley.

"I don't really want a drink, Charlie, I just want to go home. Can you let go of me, please?"

"It's not even late. Since when are you such a pansy?" Charlie wouldn't look at me. Every time I tried to pull away, he held on tighter. It was like trying to pull my fingers out of woven bamboo finger cuffs.

"Where are we going?" I felt tension rising in my chest. "Ow, you're hurting me!"

He yanked me hard, and I realized just how strong he was. Those rippling biceps I had admired were no joke. There was no door in this alley. He was taking me down a dead end to the darkest and emptiest place he could find. I tried to dig in the heels of my platform sandals, but they just slid on the dirt and asphalt. He dragged me past the stinking garbage bins and stacks of broken wood pallets. I turned and twisted and tried to pull away. I went limp, thinking my dead weight would at least slow him down. Nothing worked. It was as if I weighed nothing. I wanted to yell, but I couldn't find my voice. My breath was frozen in my lungs.

He stopped at the end of the alley, grabbed my other wrist, and contorted my arms behind me. Pain shot up to my shoulders as he pushed me up against the rough brick wall with the whole weight of his body.

He had my arms pinned behind my back as he held both wrists in one of his viselike hands. My shoulders scraped against the rough brick, pushed back by his weight. Leaning into me, he tried to kiss me, thrusting his mouth at my face. I turned my head back and forth to avoid him. This was all happening too fast. I thought I could just say no and that would be it. I thought I would be able to just walk away from him. I thought Charlie was a normal guy with normal compulsions. In other words, I wasn't thinking. Why had I expected him to show me any respect? He was just like all the other guys I'd ever met or even worse.

"Stop! Stop it!" Somehow I still thought I could talk him out of it. My voice was weak. The pressure of his body crushed me against the brick, compressing my lungs. His free hand pulled up my dress. I was struck and panicked by how skillfully he manipulated his strength over me. I didn't have the practice for escape that he obviously had for attack. I was pinned like a wrestler in the wrong weight class. My mind raced to figure a way out. If I could just move out from under him, roll him off me, push him away . . . But his weight was overwhelming, my twisted arms pinning me in place. I couldn't take in a full breath.

"This feels so good, doesn't it? Doesn't it feel good?" He pushed his face into mine, smearing me with saliva slime. He jerked my arms to the right, twisting one elbow painfully. I was losing it, my eyes full of tears, my throat too swollen with fear to do anything but cry. It suddenly occurred to me that I might be about to die. My new resolutions wasted, my resolve to take control and do something with my life all too late.

This week was the first time since my mother died that I had started to believe in myself. Believe that I was not a loser, that I was worth something, that I didn't have to let the boys win. Here I was, finally fighting back, but I was still losing.

Was this what the other women felt at the end? Was this how it happened? Had Charlie used his charm to lure Jessica and the other girls to places where no one could see them or hear them? Did they think they could just say no and walk away? But then he turned rough and he was too strong, and it was too late for them to do anything to help themselves and they lost.

But I wasn't going to give up, not now. I wouldn't give up, no matter what anyone did to me. I was not a piece-of-shit loser. I didn't care who tried to make me feel that way—not my grandfather, not Tom the Cop, not some guy on a date, not Bobby, not Ron, not Charlie. *Not Charlie!*

"No!" I mustered up the last ounce of strength I had. I wrenched my shoulders to one side and roared, "No!"

With my eyes closed and what remained of my *self*, I struggled, I fought, I yelled. I tried to pull my arms free, I twisted and turned. This wasn't it. This wouldn't be it. It couldn't be. I screamed out. "No!"

Suddenly, Charlie was ripped away from me. My body was free of the weight that had me pinned me to the wall. I fell to my knees. My arms were throbbing, my throat raw. I opened my eyes and looked up. Standing in front of me stood Benny with Charlie in his grasp. Benny shook him like a rag doll, then grabbed his throat. I heard a crack and saw Charlie's head flop to one side. Benny had snapped his neck easier than a toothpick. He threw him on the ground like an empty gum wrapper. Charlie's body fell in front of me with a dull thud. I put my hands to my own throat and tried to swallow, but my throat was too dry.

It was suddenly as quiet in that alley as an empty cave. Quieter. It was a vacuum. Sound didn't exist. I felt like I was moving in slow motion, like I was in one of my own twisted dreams. I looked up at Benny. His hands hung down at his sides as if they didn't belong to the rest of his body. The smell of garbage and anticipation were electric in the air. Benny looked at me, his gray eyes foggy through those thick glasses. His hulking frame, normally so familiar, looked like it belonged to a ghost or a monster. Charlie's broken body lay like a shadow at his feet.

Still on my knees, I leaned closer to Charlie. He could've been mistaken for passed-out drunk if you didn't look too closely. My eyes wouldn't let him go—his strong shoulders, his soft blond curls. He hadn't seemed like such a bad guy till tonight. Had he really killed those other girls? He wasn't too smart and he couldn't control himself when he drank, but could he break a girl's neck as easily as Benny had just broken his?

I tried to take a deep breath to slow my heart rate. I put my hands to my throat, sore from fear and crying. Charlie had lifted my skirt, pulled at my underwear. He had pawed at my body, pushed my legs open, grabbed me in private places. He might have raped me if Benny hadn't come along. But Charlie hadn't touched my neck. My throat was sore only on the inside from trying to scream. It didn't make sense. The killer always broke their necks first, before he raped them. I looked up at Benny.

Where had he come from? Had he been following me again, or was it a coincidence? How had he found us down this dark alley? I got up off my knees, feeling less than steady, and stood in front of Benny.

"How could you let him do that to you?" Benny's voice sounded like he'd swallowed glass.

"Let him? I wasn't *letting* him do anything." Nothing made sense. I rubbed at my cheeks with scraped palms.

"Well, what the hell, Nina? I find you and Charlie like this, what am I supposed to think?"

"What are you supposed to think? How about that he was trying to rape me!" I wanted to ask him how he just happened to be there at the right moment, but something stopped me.

Benny looked at me funny. Then he looked down at Charlie's dead body. "I had to stop him." Now there was fear in his eyes.

"Thank god." Where were Tom the Cop and his sidekick?

"I had to do it." Something was wrong. His eyes filled with tears. "Don't tell them, Nina."

"What are you talking about? You maybe just saved my life." The look on Benny's face was not the tough Benny I knew but the face of a person about to lose control. I took a few steps sideways, away from Charlie's body, away from Benny.

"Don't tell them it was me, Nina," he said. "You're right, I just saved you. I did you a favor; now you do me one. Even trade." He tried to untwist his lips into a smile, but they didn't seem to be working right.

"But why shouldn't I—" My mind couldn't untangle this. He wasn't making sense.

"Don't tell them it was me, Nina." He moved toward me, and I backed up automatically. My breath I had so recently caught was sucked out of me. My body prickled with a new, deeper fear. A freezing, paralyzing, asphyxiating realization hit me.

"What do you mean, don't tell them it was you? What are you talking about?" It came out in a hoarse whisper that echoed in that brick cave of an alley. Where were Tom the Cop and his partner? How could Benny have found me while those stupid cops were still bumbling along somewhere? If only Tom the Cop had let Frankie work with him tonight. Frankie never would have left me alone on the street. He'd be here by now.

"Those other girls—they looked so much like you." Benny stopped. His eyes begged me to understand so he didn't have to say it. I thought I knew what he was trying to tell me, but I didn't want to know. I looked at his hands. Those strong hands that had broken Charlie's neck in the blink of an eye. His fingers slowly flexed.

"What do you mean?" I took another step back. I was up against the brick wall.

"I didn't want to hurt any of them." He took another step closer. I had no place to go. Benny blocked my path out of the alley.

"What are you talking about?" My fear turned to anger. I wanted to yell at him. *Shut up! Shut up!* What was he saying? That he had chosen them because they looked like me? That he had followed them and hit them on the head and broken their necks so they were quiet and then—? I tried to stop my brain from putting two and two together. I had trusted him, felt protected by him. But now I looked at his face, his emotions unstable. *Be smart, Nina.*

"I'm telling you, I didn't want to hurt anybody." Benny took another step toward me. "Do you understand?"

"Yes, I understand." I had to calm down. I had to think straight. If I was going to get out of here, I had to regain some composure so Benny wouldn't think of me as a threat. But I was shaking like a windup toy gone haywire.

Keep him talking. But too many thoughts were racing through my mind. I had trusted Benny. He was my friend. And now everything I believed to be true was false. I felt like I was on a roller coaster and the world was turned inside out and upside down. I wanted to scream and pound my fists on his chest until he shut up. But I wanted to get out of this alive. Benny was twice my size and blocking my way out of the alley. I couldn't lose it now. I had to get out of this. I would get out of this. *Be smart.*

"Of course you didn't want to hurt anyone." I kept my voice calm and soft, even if inside I felt like screaming. He was once my friend, I told myself, the acting challenge in my head. *He is my friend.*

"I didn't want to hear them talk. I only wanted to look at them." His eyes widened in frustration. "I had no choice."

"You had no choice." I could only echo him.

"Don't tell anyone." His hands lifted slowly from his sides. "They won't understand."

"I won't, Benny, I won't. I won't tell anyone." I was losing my false calm as I watched his hands try to reach me. My hands flew to my throat; tears blurred my eyes, my voice a loud whine. "I promise I won't tell anyone, Benny."

"I don't know if I can trust you." He moved closer.

"How can you say that?" I took control over my voice. "You saved me, Benny." I looked toward the exit and got an idea. "We'll say that we were up those stairs." I pointed to the back entrance of the building. "You saw Charlie attacking me up there and you pulled him off me and he fell." I tried to smile at him, but I'm sure my face was distorted. "It was an accident. I'll tell them. You saved me, I'll save you. Even trade." *Will he buy it?*

"What if they don't believe you?" He moved closer to me.

I suddenly realized there was no point in telling him what he wanted to hear: I was the only thing that stood between him and his freedom. How was agreeing with him going to save me? When had that ever worked in my life?

"Benny, listen to me!" I could hear my voice bouncing off the brick walls, and I noticed the alley was a megaphone throwing my voice out toward the street. As loud as I could, I yelled, "You have to let me go!"

I thrust both my fists toward him with all the force I had. I caught him by surprise, punching him in the stomach, hard enough to knock the wind out of him, my low center of balance giving me an advantage for once. He doubled over, and it gave me the moment I needed. I rushed past him and ran as fast as I could. I thought I heard a voice out in the street. I had to get where someone could hear me.

Behind me I heard Benny pushing past garbage bins and kicking empty packing crates with rage. He sounded like a lumbering bear, crashing through the brush, chasing down his prey. I was done being anyone's prey. Maybe it had taken me a long time to decide that, but I wasn't going back.

"Help!" I yelled while I ran as fast as I could. It was like that day I'd found those red shoes, the day that had started the whole nightmare. I ran, feeling like something was chasing me. Something so close it felt like it was crawling up my back. Running so fast that my feet couldn't keep up with my body. So fast that I almost tripped and fell. But this time the something chasing me was not in my imagination. It was real. Benny was behind me, Benny who I had trusted as a friend.

I had the edge. If I could just keep ahead of him . . . I heard someone out in the street calling out my name.

"Help!" My voice was full as I neared the end of the alley. "Help! Somebody help!"

"Nina!" It was Frankie. He sounded like he was at the end of the street on the avenue. "Where are you?"

"I'm here!" I ran toward him down the street toward the avenue. I could hear Benny behind me. Frankie turned the corner. I could see him. I stumbled the last twenty feet; I reached Frankie and fell into him. He grabbed hold of me just before I hit the ground.

"He killed Charlie right in front of me, he just killed Charlie." My adrenaline turned back to panic. "And he . . . he killed them. He killed all the girls. He killed them."

"Who? Who!?" Frankie held my shoulders and looked me in the eyes. I saw his fear and anger, and then he looked down the alley.

"Benny, my friend Benny from the Sazerac House." I slumped against the building. Frankie pulled his weapon from his waist and moved past me, holding the shiny dark metal firearm straight ahead of him. Benny was out of the alley, standing there fifty feet away, looking toward us.

I leaned up against the side of the apartment building, unable to move, feeling the full impact of the moment, my head in a spiral. How I thought Charlie was the killer as he attacked me and then Benny showed up. Everything I remembered about Benny that made me suspect him but then made me feel guilty that I had. Flashes of his creepy apartment, his bleary eyes as he begged me to fly to Florida with him, his laugh after he followed me around the Village that night I skipped class, his confession that he poured Marissa drinks the night she died. I should have known earlier; maybe I could have stopped him. Stopped him before Marissa was attacked, maybe even before Jessica, before Teresa. I should have seen him for who he was.

"Stop! Stay right where you are or I'll shoot!" I heard Frankie say. I watched Benny ignore the order and move toward him. Frankie sidestepped him. He held the gun with both hands, straight-armed, and tried to whip the weight of the gun at Benny's head. But Benny was too big, and the weight of him, as well as his forward motion, rendered the attack useless. He lunged at Frankie and grabbed for his gun.

"No!" I couldn't help screaming. Where the hell was Tom the Cop? What could I do? I looked around for a brick or something to throw. There was nothing. But I couldn't let Frankie struggle with him alone. I moved toward them. "Stop, Benny, stop!"

But he didn't stop. He was trying to get the gun away from Frankie. He was bigger than Frankie, but not by much. Frankie held on as they struggled.

"Nina, get back!" Frankie didn't take his eyes off Benny. I didn't want to distract him. But maybe I could distract Benny.

"Benny, Frankie can help you. He's my friend."

"Nina, get back!" Frankie yelled to me.

Frankie tried to keep the gun pointed down and away. Both their hands gripped it in the struggle. I took a few steps backward. I couldn't pull my eyes off them.

"Benny, stop, please!"

Benny hadn't loosened his hold on the gun. He was still trying to pull it up into some kind of position. Frankie was still trying to keep it pointed down. In Benny's face there was nothing but persistence to win the gun.

"Benny!"

His eyes found mine, and for a moment there was a softer look, a pause in the struggle. His lips parted and I held my breath. Maybe he was going to tell me it wasn't what I thought; maybe there was an explanation, some rationality that turned all this insanity into sense. Maybe he would say something that spun us all back in time before any of this happened. Before Marissa's attack, before Jessica's and Teresa's and the other murders. Maybe he would even utter some magic spell that would turn the clock all the way back until the day before my mother died. But he didn't speak at all. His eyes hardened, his determination returned, and he looked down at his hands, entwined with Frankie's, wrapped around the gun. With one great effort and using the strength of his whole torso, Benny pointed the gun toward himself, and the explosion blew through my ears.

Benny fell to the ground with a heavy, muffled sound. The weapon dropped from his hands and made a sharp crack as it hit the pavement. Frankie fell to his knees. He leaned over Benny and pressed both hands on his neck as blood gushed. Benny's body shuddered. I slid down to the pavement and hugged my knees. Tom the Cop entered the street running, Kong right behind him. They barely saw me. They ran toward Frankie.

CHAPTER 21

I don't know how many hours I was at the precinct. Eventually, Tom Barry was done with me. They questioned me and took pictures of me and put me through more than was necessary as far as I was concerned. I came out of the interrogation room at the back of the precinct and did my best to walk into the main front room without stumbling. My silver racer-back dress was ripped and dirty, my knees scuffed and bloodied. I passed the same faded brown and gray desks and mismatched file cabinets that had been there for decades. There was nothing different about the conversations of the men in uniform or drab plainclothes detectives working the shift. The smell of cigarettes and city dust was eternal. But I felt like a different person.

Frankie was perched on the edge of his desk, arms crossed over a worn brown T-shirt, his faded khakis uncommonly wrinkled. They were probably clothes he had in the back of his locker for just such an emergency. He'd showered and scrubbed himself of any signs of blood and dirt, his curly hair still damp. He looked up when I approached him, and I saw my own pain reflected in his eyes. He walked toward me, his pace cautious. We moved to a wooden bench against the back wall and sat together, so close that our arms and thighs touched. He smelled like clean clothes and night air.

"Tom wouldn't let me in the room. I guess he thought I'd be too much of a distraction for you." I saw the effort it took for him to smile, pretending humor would fix this broken situation.

I tried to smile back at him, but my face broke into tears instead. Frankie put his arms around me, and I buried my face in his chest. I tried not to make too much noise as I wept a wet spot on his shirt. He rocked me back and forth until my tears slowed down and then finally stopped. If I could ever imagine feeling safe again, this just might be what it would feel like, wrapped in Frankie's arms.

"You're going to be okay." Frankie wiped my cheek with his T-shirt sleeve. "It's all over. You don't have to worry anymore."

I wanted to tell him that the threat of a serial killer was only one sliver of fear in the darkness of my life. I wanted to tell him that worrying was my best skill and to give it up just might leave too big a hole in my world. I wanted to tell him that it was going to take more than Benny being dead to make me feel safe again. But his eyes were so sincere, and as he held me, I felt a sense of security that was so completely unfamiliar it robbed me of speech.

"Come on, I'll take you home." Frankie broke his hold on me and stood. "I'll get one of the guys to drive us."

"Is it okay for you to leave?"

"I'm owed some vacation time. I told them I was taking it starting now." I never heard Frankie sound that way. Less than angry but more than annoyed, definitely impatient. I stood up quickly, and we walked to the exit.

Frankie insisted we pick up some bread and eggs, cheese and milk at the corner bodega. I told him I didn't have any coffee, so he grabbed a can of Café Bustelo as well. As we climbed the stairs to my loft, I was a little disconcerted that this would be Frankie's introduction to my life. Not that my apartment was a mess or that I was ashamed of how I lived, but I would've wanted the first time to be a romantic dinner or even a casual movie night.

I couldn't think of eating. I barely had enough energy to shower, but I had to scrub the night off of me. Then I pulled on my oldest Mets T-shirt and gym shorts, and I crawled onto my bed and rolled up into a ball. Frankie enveloped me in a spoon position, adjusting pillows so that I was more comfortable than I've ever been in my own bed. We were fully clothed, and there was nothing erotic about it. It was pure sanctuary.

In the security and care of his embrace, I fell into a dreamless sleep. I woke only once when Frankie released me to go to the bathroom. I was motionless, still breathing his scent, waiting, but not worried, until he returned.

Chapter 22

In the morning, the heat of the day gave me semi-lucid dreams. I was walking across a desert looking for water. My real thirst woke me to the smell of toast and coffee, and I remembered that I was not alone.

"Hey, sleepyhead, you finally awake?" Frankie called from the kitchen area. He was seated at my long wooden table. Arranged in front of him: an open book, a steaming cup of coffee, and a plate of toast.

My voice was still asleep, so I waved. Stretching, I felt every bruise, sore muscle, and shitty memory of the last few days—hell, the last few weeks—and my heart began to reel in flashback. I sat up and clutched my knees with both hands before they could rattle together. Then I stood, not quite as shaky as I felt, and joined Frankie at the table.

"I called the precinct and told them I was going to be here a few days, or longer. As long as you need me. In case they need to call." Frankie rose and turned on the gas under the teakettle, then poured himself more coffee and sat next to me. "If that's okay."

"It's more than okay." I wasn't used to kindness without quid pro quo, but I knew this was nowhere near a give-and-take situation. I wanted to tell Frankie I was grateful he was there, but the words wouldn't come out. The kettle started to whistle, and he caught it before it went into a full wail. He must've had it warming the whole time he was waiting for me to wake up. I got up and scooped some loose Earl Grey leaves into my teapot, and Frankie poured in the hot water.

"Thanks, Frankie."

He smiled at me, and he knew I meant it for more than just a pot of tea. We sat close together.

"Do you want to talk about it or pretend it never happened?" He lifted one eyebrow.

"I keep replaying it in my mind, the whole night, everything before. It won't stop." I had to be careful or it would all come out in a flood and drown me. "How did you find me?"

"I was following Tom, who was doing a lousy job of following you." Frankie shook his head. "I was too far away, so I lost you. I searched every street. Then I heard you, and I finally went in the right direction."

"It all happened so fast. Charlie was walking with me while I was trying to go home, and then he pulled me down that alley." I couldn't make sense of it in my mind. "I never expected that. And I don't know where Benny came from. Suddenly he was there, pulling Charlie off me—then confessing, telling me everything, that he wanted to look at the other girls but not hear them, something like that. That he didn't really want to hurt them but he didn't have a choice. Begging me not to tell. I think he did it because of me. He picked them because they looked like me. It's my fault, everything that happened."

"That's absolutely not true." Frankie moved closer. "He was sick in the head and used any excuse to kill people. If it wasn't you, it would've been someone else."

"But how did I not know? I thought Benny was my friend." I slid my cup of tea away from me on the table. I wanted to throw it across the room. I couldn't sit still. I got up and walked to the windows. I needed the light. Frankie followed me as I spoke.

"What is wrong with me?"

"Nothing is wrong with you."

"I should've known it was him." I turned my back on the windows and faced Frankie. "I introduced him to Marissa. It's my fault she was attacked."

"That's ridiculous. There's no way you could've known. That's how these killers are, manipulative and cunning." He put his arms around me. "He's dead. It's over. We have to move on."

We. Frankie said *we*. Like, me and him, together. It felt like he meant it. He hugged me and it was good, like coming home to a warm room on a cold winter day. As I relaxed into his embrace, I looked out the window, and my eyes tilted up. The sun was bright and there wasn't a cloud in the true-blue sky.

"Thanks for being here, Frankie."

"I wouldn't be anywhere else." He tightened his arms around me, and I wondered how long it would take me to learn how to hug him back without leaking tears.

One thing about living in a big city like New York, it's pretty easy to disappear. You change your phone number and your job, find a new hangout and take new routes, suddenly you have a whole new life. You never even run into anyone you used to know. It's just that easy. Oh, I'd miss some people, like Janette and Andrew Lee from class, Marissa and Dave, but they were all part of another world, a world I left behind. And there were plenty of people I wouldn't miss—Cousin Bobby, smarmy Nick, and Ron Meyers, to name a few. I didn't know if any of them would ever look for me, but I'd always be looking for them, just in case. Just so I'd see them first.

Frankie was different. He wasn't like anyone else I'd ever known. Meeting him was like opening a new door in my life. A door to a new journey. A journey I could appreciate without worrying about the destination. I couldn't know how long Frankie would be in my world, but did I know that for as long as he was, no matter what else might happen, it was a world I wanted to live in.

Acknowledgments

Thanks to John and Valentino who always embrace me with encouragement; to my brilliant writer friends for their years of help and motivation; to all my students who fill my life with inspiration; to my entire extended family who made reading a big part of my life; to Ronni, Margaret, Cristy and Kris who helped me survive high school; to my NYU community that continues to prove anything is possible; to parents, teachers, and librarians everywhere who help make sure the world is full of readers; to my wonderful agent, Murray Weiss; and my amazing editor, Sara J. Henry.